Fallen Women

Fallen Women

Sandra Dallas

St. Martin's Press
New York

FALLEN WOMEN. Copyright © 2013 by Sandra Dallas. All rights reserved. Printed in the United States of America. For information, address St. Martin's Press, 175 Fifth Avenue, New York, N.Y. 10010.

www.stmartins.com

The Library of Congress Cataloging-in-Publication Data is available upon request.

ISBN 978-1-250-03093-1 (hardcover)
ISBN 978-1-250-03094-8 (e-book)

St. Martin's Press books may be purchased for educational, business, or promotional use. For information on bulk purchases, please contact Macmillan Corporate and Premium Sales Department at 1-800-221-7945, extension 5442, or write specialmarkets@macmillan.com.

First Edition: October 2013

10 9 8 7 6 5 4 3 2 1

For Arnold Grossman

My friend of a lifetime

Fallen Women

Prologue

The smell. *It was always the smell that got to him. No matter how many times he'd been inside one of these wretched places, he was overwhelmed by the smell that hit him like the odor rising from a cesspool. He could smell it even in the better houses, such as this one. Others might not pick up on it, but he had spent too much time in these places not to be aware of the faint smell. It was a mixture of perfume and body powder, of cigar smoke, vomit, and unemptied chamber pots. Sweat, spilled beer and brandy, flat champagne from bottles stuck into buckets of melting ice, basins of dirty water. There was the stench of spittoons filled with chewing tobacco so harsh it gagged a man. And over it hung the woman smell of tired and used bodies, something that lingered even after the house was aired out and scrubbed before the evening clientele arrived. He'd smelled that whorehouse stench a hundred—perhaps hundreds of—times, but there was something more this time, the metallic smell of blood and, worse, the odor he always thought of as flesh beginning to rot, to decay. The smell of death.*

He took out his handkerchief and held it over his nose as he walked down the hallway past the half-opened doors, sad girls peering out. They were dressed in their underwear or kimonos that were carelessly buttoned. "What happened, Mick?" one whispered in a voice that was husky from too many cigarettes, too much beer. Her face had begun to show the ravages of her life, although she was not yet halfway through her twenties.

"Hello, Elsie. You tell me," Mick replied, putting down the handkerchief. It didn't do any good anyway.

"How would I know? I just got back." She sniffed and rubbed at her nose, and Mick wondered if she had a cold or was a snowbird. "I liked her. Did she do it to herself? She was kind of snooty, but she was all right. You want to come in? You're always welcome, you know."

"I'm on duty, honey." Mick smiled to think what his fellow officers would say if he detoured into one of the rooms. It was tempting, just to get their reaction.

"You'll come back and tell me, won't you? Madam says it was suicide, that maybe she swallowed that poison, Rough on Rats, but me and some of the girls, well, we think . . ." Her voice trailed off.

"Think what, honey?"

"We're not so sure."

They never wanted to believe it was suicide, Mick thought. Maybe that was because they didn't like the idea that they, too, might be wretched enough to take their own lives. The life of a prostitute was a short one, maybe seven years. "You got any ideas?"

"Maybe."

"I'll come back when I finish up, then." A patrolman had come out of a room at the end of the hall and was beckoning to him. Mick hurried off and told the cop, "I got sidetracked."

"I'll bet." The officer smirked.

Mick gave him a stern look. "Listen, hamfat, she says she might know what happened. Do you have something to say about that?"

"No, sir."

Mick stared at the man until the cop turned and began studying one of the pictures in heavy gold frames that lined the hall. The paintings were mostly of women lying naked on beds or of satyrs romping with nubile young ladies. This particular painting was of a man with a human torso and the legs and horns and ears of a goat, chasing two naked girls whose breasts and pubic areas were hidden by tree branches. "They're waiting for you," *the cop told Mick, without taking his eyes from the painting.*

"His name is Pan."

"Who?"

"The man in the painting."

"I never saw anybody who looked like that. You suppose he's real?" *The patrolman hooked his thumbs over his belt.*

Mick frowned, wondering if the officer were really that dumb. He was young—and hadn't been in the force long. Mick could tell by the new coat with its gleaming brass buttons. But then all the buttons gleamed. No policeman would go on duty with tarnished buttons. He wondered how long the patrolman had worked the beat on Holladay Street, the center of Denver's tenderloin. Maybe not long. The young officer would find out soon enough about the goats in the whorehouses.

"Mick." *An older police officer had come out of the door at the end of the hall and was gesturing to him.*

Detective Sergeant McCauley put his handkerchief into his pocket, and without a glance at the rest of the pictures in the whorehouse art gallery, he entered the room.

"Cronin." *Mick acknowledged the officer who had gestured to him. Then he turned to a second man and said,* "Doctor." *The coroner was tall, ascetic, his face and hands with their long fingers an unnatural white. He dressed in a long black coat, and he himself looked like death. In fact, that was what he was called, Dr. Death. The man gave a single dip of his chin to acknowledge Mick, then turned his glance to the woman lying on the bed.*

Mick had seen dead whores before, seen the lifeless faces ravaged by drugs and liquor and disease, faces (and bodies) that no longer attracted men, and so the girls had ended their lives with laudanum or arsenic.

Those were usually the crib girls, the lowest rank of prostitute, however, girls who might have started out in a parlor house like this one, then gone downhill. It wasn't often that an inmate of one of the better brothels took her life, although it sometimes happened at Christmas, when she started thinking about home, a home she couldn't go back to or maybe a home she'd never known. He'd seen the bodies of prostitutes bruised from beatings, too, scratched or sliced with knives.

But he'd never seen anything like this. When he'd been sent to investigate the death of a prostitute, he'd assumed she'd taken her own life. But this was no suicide. The woman lay on her back on an iron bed, her arms folded across her chest. She was covered with blood. Blood was everywhere—on the floor, the bed, splattered on the walls. Drops of blood were scattered across the picture of a bowl of fruit, making it appear as if one of the plums had burst and was dripping its juice. But mostly the blood was on the body of the dead whore and on the sheet beneath her. The woman was dressed in only a torn wrapper, which would have been sliced by a knife as the killer attacked her. The garment had been pulled across the woman to cover her body, although it hadn't covered much. She was small, maybe five feet two inches, and trim, her skin firm. "Doesn't look like a suicide," Mick said.

"Murder, plain and simple. Eight stab wounds, not counting the ones on her hands and arms where she tried to defend herself. She got two in her neck," Dr. Death said. "Most vicious killing of a woman I ever seen. She looks like a pound or two of dog's dinner."

"She died like that on the bed?" Mick asked. He frowned. The body's position was unnatural.

"Not like that. My guess: she fell on top of the bed and whoever done it to her put her legs up like that and crossed her arms over her. I never saw arms folded that way on a dead woman outside of a coffin. And her robe, it's been pulled across her."

Mick looked into the face of the woman. He'd worked Denver's ten-

derloin for ten years and thought the girl looked familiar, although he couldn't place her. That wasn't surprising, however, since the girls came and went. She must be new, he thought, not just because he didn't know her but because she looked fresh. Under the smear of blood, her face was soft, unlined. Her hair was a pale yellow, untouched by chemicals, and there was no trace of rouge or powder. She didn't look like a whore, so she might have turned out recently. Mick stared into a face that was covered in blood. "Who was she?" *he asked.*

"Lillie."

Mick turned to find a woman sitting behind the door. He hadn't seen her when he came in, and he touched his hat. "Miss Hettie."

"She said her last name was Brown." *The woman gave a soft snort.* "With all the names in the world to choose from, why's so many of them pick Brown? She's been with me only a couple of months, maybe a little more."

"Where is she from?"

"New York, so she said, but how would I know? She didn't have references, but she wasn't no innocent, I can tell you. I don't break in young ladies. I've got my standards." *She raised her chin, waiting for Mick to agree, and when he didn't, she continued.* "But Lillie didn't need no breaking in. She fell off the primrose path before she ever come here. She was real mink, as high class a girl as you'd ever find. Her death is a real loss to me." *Miss Hettie paused, as if in a moment of sorrow.* "You might find something in her trunk. She kept it locked." *The woman rose and walked to a steamer trunk against the wall of the small room. Miss Hettie was short and plump, wearing black satin, her hands covered with gold rings, a diamond cross at her neck, her hair an unnatural color of red. Mick thought she might be in her sixties.*

"The other girls like her?"

The madam shrugged. "She was standoffish, didn't mix much with the others. They thought she was stuck-up. Some of 'em at any rate."

"Enough to kill her?"

"No, my ladies aren't nothing like that. My guess is it was a burglar. She was alone. The rest of the girls went off this morning. Lillie said she was feeling punk. I checked in on her before I left, but she was sleeping."

"One of the others could have come back and stabbed her," Mick mused.

"They didn't none of them come back until later. Like I say, it was a burglar. Her diamond earbobs are gone. I saw them myself on the dresser when I left. They weren't there when I came back. Valuable, they was, shaped like stars."

"You checked when you found her, did you?" Mick stared at the woman, who didn't blush but was defiant. She met his gaze.

"'Course I did. They was valuable, shaped like stars, like I say. They was unusual. I ain't got nothing like them myself."

"Do you now?"

"You asking if I stole from one of my own ladies?" She tried to look injured but failed.

Mick shrugged. "She didn't have any use for them." He pointed with his chin at the woman on the bed.

"I might have my faults, but I wouldn't steal from a dead whore."

"How about one of the other girls?"

"None of them's been in here except to look through the door. I found her myself. I sent Elsie to get a copper, and I ain't left the room since."

Mick went over to the trunk and tried it, but the lid wouldn't budge.

"I told you it was locked. The key ain't around nowhere, either."

"You looked, then. Was that before or after you sent Elsie for a copper?"

"You got no right to accuse me, Mick. You know I run an honest house, and I pay my protection money regular." She stiffened her back. "Now can't you get rid of her? I got a business to run, and no john's going to want his ashes hauled in a house where there's a stiff." Miss

Hettie turned and left the room, calling down the hallway, "Shut your doors, ladies. This ain't your business. You got to get ready for the customers, and I'll skin any one of you that tells what went on here. Poor Lillie died a natural death. Suicide."

"Natural death," Mick muttered.

The patrolman returned to the room and asked, "Was it suicide . . . sir?" He'd started to say "Mick" but changed it to "sir," perhaps in deference to the older officer, who was smarter, more experienced, and had spent more time on Holladay Street.

"You think she stabbed herself eight times?" Mick scoffed, and the young man reddened.

"I didn't count. I just saw the blood and waited for you."

"You think it was a burglar?" Cronin asked.

"If it was, he was a peculiar chap. There's a five-dollar gold piece on the dresser. No burglar I know would leave that behind. And if it was one of the other girls, she'd have snatched it up with the earrings."

"I never saw a robber slice up anybody like that. A robber would stick her once or twice to shut her up, not eight times. And he wouldn't take the trouble to leave her like that, with her arms folded over her. I'd guess it was somebody she knew," the coroner put in.

"Like a mac?" Mick asked.

"Could be. I wonder if she had one."

"Or a customer," Cronin butted in.

"A whore's not likely to admit a customer when there's nobody else around."

"Maybe a special customer."

Mick nodded. "Where's the knife?"

"Wasn't no knife. She was stabbed with a pair of scissors." The coroner picked up a pair of sewing scissors, the tips as sharp as a knife blade. "Hers, most likely, because her sewing box's right there, and I couldn't see any scissors in it."

He handed the weapon to Mick, who tested the tip with his finger. It would pierce skin as if it were butter. "Was she tortured?" *he asked softly.*

Dr. Death shook his head. "Don't look like it."

"Raped?"

"She's a whore."

The patrolman went over to the bed and stared at the body, then looked frantically around the room until Mick pointed to the chamber pot, and the young man retched into it. "Sorry," *he said, wiping his mouth.* "I never saw nothing like this."

"Go outside. Get some air. You'll get used to it. Or maybe you won't. Pray you won't, Officer . . ." *Mick searched for a name, then said,* "Officer Thrasher." *He glanced at the other policeman, who was pasty-faced, and added,* "Cronin, you take him out, then find something to open the trunk. Doc and I'll finish up."

"I'm done. I'll get somebody to haul her off," *the coroner said, and he followed the two officers down the hall, leaving Mick alone with the dead woman.*

The detective listened to their footsteps, then turned back to the bed, ignoring the smell of fresh vomit. He avoided stepping in the blood as he picked up a chair that lay on the floor, pulling it to the bedside and sitting down. The room was small and the furniture filled it up—the chairs and bed and a dresser with a pitcher and washbasin on it, the trunk with a bright shawl spread over it, a wardrobe. Unlike the hallway with its erotic paintings, the pictures in the room were simple—the blood-smeared oil painting of a bowl of fruit, a pastoral scene, the portrait of a young woman with her hand on the collar of a dog. They might all have been done by the same artist, maybe the dead woman. Mick wondered if she'd been a painter. Well, if so, she hadn't been much of one. The paintings were sentimental and poorly executed. Maybe they'd been left by another occupant.

He stood then and examined the room, looking for something that didn't belong—a button or a watch fob that the struggling woman might have snatched. A handkerchief, a hat. A calling card with a name and address would be nice. Mick got down on his knees and peered under the bed, the dresser. Scanning the rug, he looked for something that might have been dropped, but there was nothing. He examined the dresser, hoping for a cigarette butt, a cigar stub, but there was only the usual collection of brush, hairpins, hair receiver, false hair, a pair of gloves, a bottle of perfume. Mick picked it up and sniffed. The scent, lily of the valley, was too delicate for most prostitutes, and expensive.

The crime had been vicious, and the knife wounds on the dead woman's hands showed that she'd fought back. There ought to be some hint to the killer's identity, but if there was, Detective Sergeant McCauley couldn't find it. He looked into the wardrobe where dresses hung on hooks. They were expensive dresses for a whore—a black velvet ball gown, a claret-colored wool suit, and a gray dress of some kind of shiny material. He thought it might be satin. Two or three shifts hung from pegs. That was what the girls wore in the whorehouses in Denver. Elsewhere, in the great brothels of Chicago and New Orleans, they might dress in fancy clothes when they met the customers downstairs in the parlor, but here, they wore shifts that were easy to put on and take off, that wouldn't be costly to replace if they were torn.

He pushed back the curtain and peered at the windowsill, looking for handprints. The killer might have come in this way. But the sill was covered with a coat of dust. He opened the window and peered out at the darkening sky. Snow from a storm the day before had melted early, but it had frozen as the day waned. Black branches obscured a sky as dead as the woman on the bed. A chill wind blew through the window, bringing the smells of smoke and stale air and horse manure, but Mick preferred them to the whorehouse odor that lingered in the room, and he left the window open.

He pulled his coat around himself and sat down on the chair next to the dead woman, studying her face, pulling back a strand of blood-soaked hair that had fallen across her cheek. Her eyes, a blue that was almost turquoise, were open, dull, and Mick stared into them. "You knew your killer, didn't you, honey? You let him in." He stared at the woman's face. She was too young to die. Pretty like that, fresh, she might have found a life outside the whorehouse. She could have married, maybe met a man right there at Miss Hettie's, some railroad executive or perhaps a business-man from Chicago or St. Louis. Mick knew of a few whores who'd gotten out of the life that way, and they'd made good wives.

Miss Hettie had said the dead woman hadn't been a beginner, but that didn't mean anything. She could have turned out after being se-duced, raped maybe, then thrown out by her family, with no place to go. For many women, whoring was a better job than taking in laundry or scrubbing floors. Poor kid with nobody to look out for her.

He'd seen dead whores before, but this one was different. The others were suicides, used-up women with no life ahead of them, many of them glad for a release. But this Lillie hadn't wanted death. She'd fought her killer. She'd fought to live. He picked up her hand and turned the palm up, studying a cut covered by dried blood. "He isn't going to get away with it. I'm going to find out who did this to you, Lillie," he muttered. And then he corrected himself. "Miss Brown."

Chapter 1

The woman stood in the doorway of the police department, looking over the room, her face tight. She was slender, tall, and might have been attractive if her hair under the drab hat had not been pulled back into a tight knot, making her forehead too high. She was dressed in a severe black suit, a traveling costume without a bustle or any of the absurd embellishments that women were affecting in 1885. At first glance, she might have looked a little like one of those dreadful mission solicitors, the sour women who held out their tambourines, demanding donations for the poor. But she was too poised, too neatly groomed, and she did not have the self-righteous look of a salvation peddler.

Most decent women who found themselves alone in the precinct with its tobacco-stained floors, its cigar-fouled air, amid Denver's snouts and boosters and other lowlife, were timid, uneasy. They stood nervously, red-faced, eyes downcast, sometimes shaking, until one of the detectives looked up and asked what they wanted. But Beret held herself erect, businesslike, as she scanned the room, daring anyone to question her presence. The truth was, she was a little unnerved at being in a place that was so distasteful to her, knowing as she did how squalid police stations were, how corrupt the inmates on both sides of the law might be. But it couldn't be helped, Beret told herself.

"Help you, miss?" A policeman spoke up at last.

Beret was startled by the question and almost blanched at the way the man looked her over, but she had had long experience in holding herself together and didn't flinch. "I am looking for Detective Sergeant Michael McCauley." Her voice was low and rather pleasant and had not one hint of her unease.

A man at a desk glanced up as the policeman waved Beret in his direction. Ignoring the stares from the other lawmen in the room as well as the reprobates, Beret walked quickly to the desk and said, "Detective Sergeant McCauley." It was a statement, not a question. She had learned that was the best way to approach a policeman—or almost anybody, for that matter.

She did not appear to be a miscreant or the wife of some poor scapegrace come to beg for leniency for her husband. Perhaps that was why Mick stood up and nodded. "I am. What can I do for you, miss?"

"I've come about the death of Lillie Osmundsen."

"You're her mother?"

"Her sister."

"Oh, sorry, ma'am. The light's poor in here."

Beret did not respond. Ten years older than her sister, Beret was used to being taken for Lillie's mother.

"I wouldn't have guessed you were sisters," Mick said, after an awkward silence.

"You mean I am not a beauty like my sister."

"I wouldn't say that at all." His reply was too hearty.

"Then I hope you are more observant when it comes to searching for my sister's killer. It is obvious by far to anyone with a brain that she is beautiful, and I am unremarkable even on my best day." She should not have been so touchy. Then she added, "*Was* beautiful."

Beret's voice was strident, and Mick frowned. "Yes, ma'am. I'm real sorry she passed over."

"Yes. Thank you. I believe the term is 'murder.'" Beret had repeated the word over and over in her mind, but she found it difficult to say it out loud, and she bit her lip to keep it from quivering. What an awful thing to have to say about one's sister.

"Murder," Mick repeated. "That's what it is, all right."

Beret felt her knees grow weak and asked, "May I sit down?"

"Sure." Mick pulled a chair from a nearby desk and placed it beside his own. Both seated themselves.

They stared at each other until Mick broke the silence. "If you've come for your sister's effects, the judge has them. There wasn't much, a few trinkets. We had to break into her trunk because we couldn't find a key. That's when we learned her identity. I hoped there might be something there that . . . well . . . would have helped us, but there wasn't. Hettie Hamilton, she's the, uh, the . . . owner—"

"The madam, you mean."

"Yeah, sure, that's right, the madam. She said your sister had some diamond earrings that were missing. I guess you'd like to have them if we find them."

Beret did not want the detective sergeant to think she was mercenary. "I've not come here for diamond earrings."

"No." Mick waited her out.

"I came to ask what success you have had in finding the man who killed my . . . my unfortunate sister." Beret took a deep breath and held it.

Mick nodded. "We've sure been working on it. We're doing our best."

"Does that mean there's been no progress?"

"You can rest easy that we'll leave no stone unturned—"

Beret interrupted. "My sister is dead, my only sister. I did not come here for platitudes. Nor do I wish to be coddled. I want to know if you are close to finding Lillie's killer. And if you are not, why not. You may speak plainly." She detested men who treated her like an imbecile. Such straightforwardness in a woman was not a redeeming quality in most men's eyes, but Beret did not care. Lillie had been the carefree one, the flirt, the one who drew men like cats to cream, just as Beret had always been drawn to her.

She wondered if the detective was competent or if he was simply some political appointee. He was nice looking, tall, with reddish-blond hair, not gone to fat from too much free food and drink like so many officers she had encountered. Most detectives were untrained, she knew, and their appointment was political. It was unlikely this man knew much about investigating serious crime. She stared at Mick until he looked away.

"We have some ideas, men she might have known," he said.

"And they are?"

"I can't say just now." Mick looked at two men sitting nearby who were listening in on the conversation. He smirked and pointed with his chin at one of them. "That pickpocket with the copper tried to lift the wallet of the Reverend Tom Uzzell, no less. He must be new in town or else he'd have known that the Reverend Uzzell would have given him the money if he'd asked but would come down hard on any poor thug who tried to steal it."

"I am not here to discuss pickpockets," Beret said, glancing around the room and taking in the stares, the silence as the policemen as well as the malefactors tried to determine her business in the station. "I see that this is not a place conducive to conversation. Well, Detective, I have not had luncheon. Is there somewhere I can get a cup of coffee and a bowl of soup, a place where we can have a private conversation?"

Mick pulled out his pocket watch as if to show he was pressed for time, but he nodded. He stood, and Beret let him take her elbow and propel her back through the room to the door. "There's a restaurant down the street, if you're not too choosy. The food isn't the best, but it's cheap." The two went up the stairs from the basement of City Hall, where the station was located, Beret raising her skirt to keep it away from the vermin and the wads of chewing tobacco that repelled even the rats. Out on the street, Mick pointed to a little café a few doors away.

"I imagine you would rather have a drink, but I am not fond of coffee in saloons," Beret said, and Mick's mouth dropped in surprise. Beret saw that and smiled to herself. She did like shocking people—sometimes, at any rate. She and Lillie had had that in common. She felt a stab of pain at the thought of her sister.

The two walked down Larimer Street, Denver's major thoroughfare, past an undertaker's parlor, a clothing store, a drugstore, without talking, until they reached the Parr Café. Mick opened the door, and Beret preceded him into the restaurant, glancing around the room at the wooden tables bare of any cloths, the mismatched chairs, at the black-and-white marble floor that was chipped and stained. She headed for a table in the back.

"It's not much," apologized Mick.

"I've dined in far worse. Do you eat here often?" she asked.

"I prefer the saloon lunches."

He'd paid her back for her jibe, but Beret liked that. She wouldn't want to work with a policeman who felt he had to sugarcoat everything he said because she was a lady. She hoped they would get along. "Well, have you eaten here often enough to recommend something?"

"Chili. But it will burn your tongue."

"Chili, then," she said. "And coffee. Will you join me, Detective? I am paying, of course." Beret was well aware that the policeman made eighty-five dollars a month, a hundred if he was lucky—plus whatever he got on the take.

"Chili gives me the heartburn."

"What a pity. I'm rather fond of it myself, the hotter the better. Perhaps there is something else you would like."

After Mick ordered for Beret, asking for coffee and a piece of apple pie with a slice of cheese for himself, Beret put her hands on the table and looked directly at the detective. "Now, perhaps you will tell me the circumstances of my sister's murder." Her voice was calm, but inside, her heart was churning.

"It's not a pretty picture."

"No, I don't imagine murder ever is."

"I'm talking about your sister's life. Do you know about it, miss?"

At that, Beret almost lost her composure. Tears came to her eyes, and she turned aside. Mick apparently had no handkerchief to offer, so he patted her hand, but she did not want his patronizing and snatched her hand away. "You must forgive me. I've no experience in this."

"I should hope not."

"I mean in the murder of my sister. I am all too familiar with death itself."

Mick waited for her to explain, but she didn't. She sat, self-absorbed, thinking it was a good thing she knew about the sordid life of the underworld. It would make dealing with Lillie's murder easier. But maybe not. Nothing could ease the tearing of her soul that her sister's death had brought.

The chili came, and she ate it as easily as if it were pudding. "I know, Officer, that Lillie worked in a brothel," she said as she finished the chili and put down her spoon.

"Not for very long, it seems, no more than three months."

"Does it matter how long? She was a prostitute." Beret blanched as she said the words out loud for the first time.

"It's not easy for you—"

"Of course it's not easy for me," she snapped. "How would you like to discover your own sister was a woman of the streets?"

"I only meant—"

Beret dismissed him with a wave of her hand. "I apologize, Officer. My sister's choice of profession is not your fault."

"No, but it was someone's fault, and I'd like to find out who was responsible. In my position, you get used to death, but there was something about Lillie . . . that is, Miss Osmundsen—"

"Yes, she had that effect on men, even in death, it seems." Oh yes, Beret thought. She did.

The sergeant ignored the implication and continued, "Something about her makes me want to find her killer. She was so young." He cleared his throat. "Do you know anything about your sister's murder?"

"I know very little. In fact, my aunt and uncle hoped to keep the circumstances of Lillie's death from me. At first, they told me only that she had died. They didn't want me to come to Denver. They said everything had been taken care of, that I should grieve at home in New York." As she remembered the telegram, Beret sipped from her cup, ignoring the fact the coffee was stale and burned and not very warm. "They were looking out for me, of course." She added to herself, As I did not look out for Lillie.

She had found the telegram mixed in with the mail on the parlor table, had overlooked it until Maggie, the housekeeper, pointed it out, because Beret rarely received telegrams. Then she'd snatched it up with a premonition that it held bad news. But then, telegrams always seemed to bring bad news. The message was brief, cryptic, and told her in as few words as possible that her sister, Lillie, had died suddenly. Her funeral was being held that very day. She would be buried in Riverside Cemetery, in a plot set aside for her aunt and uncle. Everything had been neatly handled, so there was no need for Beret to make the long train trip from New York to Denver. The aunt and uncle sent their condolences. The telegram was signed Judge and Mrs. John Stanton.

Beret's hands shook, and her eyes clouded as she walked to the telegraph office to wire back her response, her condolences, for after all, the Stantons had taken Lillie under their wing when Beret would have nothing to do with her. Lillie had fled to Denver after the sisters had had their falling-out.

As an afterthought, Beret asked the cause of death. Lillie had always been healthy, and Beret wondered if her sister had died in an accident. Her aunt and uncle were right that there was no reason for her to make the trip. The funeral was done with, and Lillie might as well sleep for eternity in the Stanton plot. Beret's traveling to Denver to grieve for her sister would be hypocritical. At least, that was what she told herself. The real reason she hadn't wanted to go was she did not know how to act in front of her aunt and uncle. Did they know about the rift between the sisters? Surely they did. Would they blame Beret? Would she have to reveal the details, to relive that awful time? After she thought it over, Beret realized her reaction was more about herself than about her sister. Lillie was dead, and that changed everything.

The news brought a wave of emotion to the young woman, conflicting emotions that she knew she would have to sort through in the following days in her methodical way. At first, she was overwhelmed by grief. She remembered Lillie as the angel-child she had been as a little girl, her golden curls and curious blue eyes, her sunny temperament, the child's grief when first their mother, Marta, and then their father, Henry, had died, and Beret, young as she was, had taken the responsibility of raising her.

And then Beret was angry, as she remembered Lillie in the last year, her sister's devilish betrayal, the hate that developed between them. Something about the telegram didn't sit right with Beret. It was wrong that Lillie was dead. The thing between them had not been settled. Beret had expected Lillie to repent, to beg forgiveness, and when she did, Beret would hold out her arms, because after all, wasn't the bond between sisters stronger than any other? But Lillie had died, leaving Beret's arms empty, the business between them unfinished.

Beret returned from the telegraph office but could not eat supper and had gone to bed, and to her surprise, she had put her face into her pillow and cried, cried first from loss and then from rage as she realized she would never be able to extract the remorse from Lillie that was due.

She slept poorly, going out at dawn and walking far downtown, along streets enveloped in a gray mist and smelling of animal droppings and cheap kerosene, walking carefully past the human refuse that was huddled against the buildings, ignoring the stench from the bodies and the ragged clothing. She watched a fetid pile of rags move. A woman slowly rose to her feet and took a step or two, then fell to the ground and curled back into a ball. A man in a soiled apron stood in the window of a restaurant, shucking oysters, for at that early hour, men were coming off work for their supper of beer and mollusks. Two newsboys fought over a street corner, the larger boy pushing the smaller one into the thoroughfare and stamping on his hat. She'd gone to the boy who was sitting in the gutter crying out filthy words, and bought a penny paper from him, giving him a dime for it. The lad started to give her change, but Beret shook her head. Then, she went into a restaurant that was all but deserted and ordered coffee and a roll and opened the paper.

The paper was the *World,* one of the cheap sheets that specialized in scandal and murder, bearbaiting and cockfighting, and she did not care to read it. But reading might turn her mind from Lillie, so she broke off a piece of the roll, which was dusted with flour, and ate it as she scanned the headlines, reading of an actress who had overdosed on laudanum, a child who had been trampled under the wheels of a wagon, a sport who had robbed the poor box of a church to pay his gambling debts. As she was closing the paper Beret spotted a small headline near the bottom of a page: DENVER WOMAN MURDERED. She set down the soft roll and unconsciously brushed her hands of the flour as she read the paragraph.

Denver. On Monday last, a Denver nymph of frailty was the victim of foul play, in her room at Hettie Hamilton's House of Dreams, an establishment of ill fame on Holladay Street, in the heart of the Denver tenderloin. Police say that Lillie

Brown, for that was the name by which the frail sister was known, was murdered in a most foul manner, stabbed repeatedly, her blood spraying the room with a fountain of red. Seasoned officers cringed at the viciousness of the crime, which has put the Cyprians of the street on edge. Police are anxious to apprehend the fiend and make sure he is punished. It is hoped the former bride of the multitudes has repented of her wicked ways and that her soul has found peace.

Beret read the story again—and again, four or five times—because she knew, knew as if Lillie's full name had been in the paper, that Lillie Brown was her Lillie. She put her hands to her head and cried, the tears mixing with the flour left on her hands, the hatred she had felt for Lillie replaced by sorrow and guilt. "Oh, Lillie," she muttered. "It's my fault. I should have protected you. I promised, and now you're dead."

She took money from her purse and left it on the table and went out into the drizzle, lifting her face to let the drops of rain wash away her tears. But the tears continued to fall, mixing with the moisture and the smoke of fires from food stands that were being set up along the street, the vendors crying out their offerings of sausages and hash. She had loved Lillie, loved and hated her at the same time, but no matter how she felt, she had been responsible for her. Beret had failed to watch over her, and now Lillie was dead. Lillie was dead because of Beret.

Chapter 2

Beret didn't wait for her aunt and uncle to reply to her telegram. Instead, she wired that she was on her way to Denver, leaving in the morning, and so she never received the message from her aunt begging her not to come.

She had telegraphed her arrival time, and her aunt Varina met her at the depot, arms outstretched, a look of sorrow on her face, explaining the judge would have been there to welcome her, but he was in court and could not get away.

"Oh, Aunt Varina, I should have looked out for her. I should—" were Beret's first words.

Her aunt cut her off. "We all should have looked out for her. It was not your fault." And then Varina stopped a moment, as if realizing that neither she nor her husband had told Beret how Lillie had died. "What do you know about Lillie's death?" Before Beret could answer, Varina added, "You knew it was murder, then?"

"There was an article in the New York papers. I know only what was in that dreadful account."

"You poor dear. We wanted to keep it from you, your uncle

John and I, so you'd remember her as the angel-girl she was once. She left us three months ago. We thought she had run off, and John tried to find her. We didn't know she was in that place until, well, until just before she died. It was embarrassing." She cleared her throat. "Of course, that doesn't matter. What matters is she is dead, the poor, troubled child."

"Why did she leave you?"

Varina paused, thinking, but did not reply because a small man with a long nose like a snout appeared beside them and picked up Beret's trunk. "This is Jonas Silk, our driver. He cares for the horses," Varina explained.

The man snatched off his hat and said, "I'm sorry about Miss Lillie." He glanced at Varina, waiting.

"Thank you, Jonas. You may bring the carriage." The man turned, and moving low to the ground, he hurried off with the trunk. Varina said in a low voice, "I think he had a crush on Lillie. She was horrified, of course, and I had to reprimand him. She attracted so many men, but I suppose it was to be expected, her being such a beauty. Whoever dreamed it would lead to this?" Her aunt shook her head at the distasteful disclosure and changed the subject. "I'll have a bath drawn for you as soon as we get home, and you can rest. It has been a terrible ordeal for you, for all of us."

The offer was tempting. Beret was tired and sooty from the train ride. Still, she said, "I can rest later. I'd like to go to the police station, Aunt."

Varina protested. "Your uncle is being kept informed. There's no need for you to degrade yourself by going down there. It's an unpleasant business, what with all the newspaper accounts making it clear Lillie is the judge's niece. At first, in deference to your uncle, the police let it out that she was Lillie Brown, not

Lillie Osmundsen, but of course, the reporters found out, and it is a scandal. I can hardly hold up my head. I hope it goes away quickly for us—and for yourself, too, Beret. Come home and talk to your uncle before you do anything."

Beret had intended to go directly to the police station, but the trip had been hard, the train cold and dirty, and she was tempted by the offer of a hot bath. Her aunt would have the servants prepare tea and sherry. Lillie was dead. What did it matter if Beret waited a day or two to talk with the police?

"Come, Beret," Varina said again. "Your uncle will want to see you. And you are the only one who can console me. You understand this is not something I can talk about with others."

Her aunt, her mother's sister, had been a comforting presence in Beret's life, kind, generous, and like Beret, she was made of strong stuff. Nonetheless, she looked frail and old, well over fifty. Beret had been selfish, thinking only of herself. This was a family tragedy. "Of course," she said, and Varina led her to the carriage.

They sat in the vehicle, gripping each other's hands. "I asked why—" Beret began.

Varina cut her off. "Not now, dear. We'll talk later." They were silent until they reached the Stanton house. "I hope you will not think me rude, but I must leave you here while I return a call to the wife of one of your uncle's political backers. It is not to be helped. Please understand, my dear. Although it saddens me, life must go on. I won't be long. Your uncle and I will see you at dinner." She told Jonas to stop the carriage in front of the house, and the young man helped Beret out of the conveyance.

As Jonas lifted her trunk from the carriage, Beret walked to the front door, reaching for the brass knocker. Before she could lift it, however, the massive door swung open, and William, the

Stantons' butler, bowed and said in a solemn voice, "Miss Beret, it is a pleasure to welcome you to Denver once again." Beret smiled, not so much at the formality but at the fact the Stantons employed a butler, an extravagance she felt sure was the work of her aunt. Beret's father, Henry Osmundsen, had refused to hire such a servant, remarking that it was a sad day when the host and hostess themselves did not open the door to guests. Beret wondered if her uncle felt the same way and was only indulging his wife in employing a factotum.

"Thank you, William," Beret replied. After the long and tiresome trip, she felt welcome and warm. Stepping into the Stanton house was like going home.

He lowered his voice. "I wish you were here for a more pleasant occasion. This house is a dreary place of late." There was a touch of sadness to his words, making Beret think that Lillie had charmed the servants as she did everyone else. "Mrs. Stanton has readied your room, and Nellie will draw you a bath. Then she will unpack for you." He nodded at the trunk Jonas was carrying upstairs.

"Has Judge Stanton arrived?"

"Not yet. I believe Mrs. Stanton will fetch him on her return."

Beret nodded and started up the staircase, realizing then that she was exhausted, so tired that she had to hold on to the railing to keep herself upright.

She bathed, listening through the door to Nellie hum as the girl unpacked Beret's trunk and put the contents into drawers and the massive wardrobe. When she heard Nellie close the bedroom door, Beret dried herself and put on a nightdress that Nellie had laid across the bed, a huge walnut piece with a carved headboard that reached almost to the ceiling. The bed had been turned down, and Beret decided to nap until her aunt and uncle returned. But her head hurt and she needed one of her powders, so first, she went to the wardrobe for the small case of medicine she had tucked into the trunk.

She searched through the dresses hanging on pegs to find it. Beret stopped when she spotted a blue silk gown. She herself had bought it for Lillie just the year before. Beret remembered that Lillie had worn it with only an ermine jacket and diamond earrings that were shaped like stars, one earring a little different from the other because it had been damaged and a diamond replaced. "I was the princess," Lillie had said when she returned in the early morning from a ball. She'd been too excited to wait until breakfast and had awakened Beret. "Oh, dearest, I wish you could have been there. The evening lacked only your presence. It was such a triumph, and the earrings set off the dress splendidly. Oh, you were right to tell me anything more would be too bold. You should have seen the Hartford girls looking like hoydens with their diamonds—paste, if I'm not mistaken." Beret had taken her sister down to the kitchen, where she built a fire and prepared cocoa, and the two had gossiped and laughed until long after sunup.

Beret lifted the blue dress until it touched her face, and she tried to feel Lillie's warmth, but the dress was cold and stiff. Still holding on to the thin fabric, she stood back and stared at the clothes in the wardrobe. Beret had brought only a few dresses with her, but the wardrobe was full. The clothes were Lillie's. Like the blue dress, many of the gowns had been purchased by Beret. She felt the heavy velvet of a second gown, the fine cashmere of a coat. And she knew that the last person who had used the room, who had sat at the dressing table and stared into the mirror as she arranged her hair, who had slept in the bed, was

Lillie. Beret put her head into the blue dress, which smelled of her sister's lily of the valley perfume, and wept.

Beret had expected to take only a nap, but she slept until the next morning, and when she dressed and went downstairs, she found that her uncle had already left for the courthouse.

"He must consider me terribly rude not to have been awake to greet him," Beret said to her aunt, slipping into a chair and nodding at the butler, who held out a coffee cup for her approval.

"Nonsense. He considers you tired and in great sorrow. Both of us were glad that you slept. I imagine you have had little enough of sleep since you received our telegram. Lord knows, neither have we."

Beret reached out her hand. "You did not deserve this."

"No" was the reply. "Neither did you."

"Or Lillie," Beret said.

"Yes, Lillie most of all." Beret's aunt dabbed at her eyes with her napkin. "I suppose you will want to see her grave."

Beret looked up, startled, then felt ashamed of herself. She had been so anxious to talk to the police that she had not thought of visiting her sister's resting place. She had planned to go to the police station that morning, but now she reproved herself. Her aunt would consider it inexcusable to confer with the police before paying her respects to Lillie. The police visit would wait until the afternoon. "Yes, I should like to do that," she said.

"I thought as much. I have told Jonas to ready the carriage. We shall go after you've breakfasted." She rose. "I have taken the liberty of inviting an old friend to tea. You remember Emily Merritt." Varina paused when William came into the room and set a plate with eggs and toast in front of Beret.

"Of course." Beret remembered her well, a woman shaped like a potato who talked incessantly and was unlikely to leave before the lamps were lit. She wondered if her aunt was purposely delaying Beret's trip to the police station. Still, there was no hurry. The visit could wait until tomorrow—two days after her arrival. After all, Lillie was dead. Nothing could change that.

Jonas was standing at attention beside the carriage when Beret and Varina emerged from the side of the house, and Beret wondered how long the little man had waited. He was an odd fellow, she thought, molelike, sullen, with small, narrow-set eyes. He was twisted, with one shoulder higher than the other, perhaps broken in a fight or accident. He was like many of the men she encountered in the slums of New York, their stories almost too vile to be believed. She wondered how her aunt had acquired such a groom.

As the two women left the house, William handed Beret a bouquet of lilies wrapped in brown paper. As it was too early for such flowers to bloom, he must have purchased them at some expense from a florist. But of course, Varina would have ordered them. Beret raised the bouquet to her nose, but there was little scent. Lillie had loved the flowers she had been named for. Of course she did, Beret thought. Her sister liked anything that called attention to herself. Still, Lillie did favor them, with her white skin, her hair the color of the stamens. And Beret had pampered her sister, ordering the expensive blooms in the winter to please her. Lillie had reciprocated, decorating the house with lilies on Beret's birthday. Beret had thought it odd that Lillie would choose her own favorite blooms instead of Beret's, which were tulips and daisies, but nonetheless, Beret appreciated the gesture. Now she wondered if these would be the last flowers she would give to her sister.

Her aunt made small talk in the carriage, but when Beret didn't reply, Varina stopped, and they rode in silence to the cemetery, which was near the South Platte River. Jonas stopped the conveyance, and the two women got out, walking through dried weeds to a plot of ground that was surrounded by an iron fence. Beret held the gate for her aunt, and the two went inside and stared at the mound of bare earth. Then Beret knelt and laid the creamy white lilies on top of the dirt. They had not brought a jar of water to set them in, and Beret knew the flowers would be scattered by the wind. But they would die anyway from the cold. It mattered only that Beret had brought them.

"When summer comes, we will have grass planted, and flowers. Your uncle has ordered a stone, a simple one. We thought a larger one would be ostentatious," Varina said, adding, "Under the circumstances."

"Yes," Beret muttered.

"I suppose we should have asked you if you wanted her buried here or the body shipped to New York. Perhaps Lillie should have been interred near your parents. But we thought to take care of the burial quickly. We believed it would be easier for us to make the decision, what with the way things stood between the two of you. And of course, we wanted to keep the circumstances of Lillie's death from you."

Without looking at Beret, Varina reached out a hand, and Beret took it. "You acted out of kindness," Beret murmured, and of course Varina had. Beret felt grateful for this strong woman beside her.

As she gripped her aunt's hand, Beret realized Varina had told her little about Lillie's stay in Denver. "You have not told me the reason Lillie left your home," she said.

Varina shivered and dropped Beret's hand. "I can't speak of it, Beret, for the truth is, I don't know. I was as shocked as anyone to learn Lillie had gone to that . . . that place. Perhaps your uncle has better insight. You must ask him."

"I'll ask him tonight."

Varina shook her head. "Not tonight, I'm afraid. Your uncle has one of those dreadful political meetings where they smoke cigars and drink too much. I imagine it will go on until all hours. It is at his club, and most likely he will spend the night there. He sends his regrets. It distresses him that he has not yet welcomed you, but it can't be helped. I told him you'd understand."

"Of course," Beret said, although she was disappointed. It seemed strange to her that she had come all this way to find out about Lillie's murder and would not see her uncle for two days.

Chapter 3

Now, Beret sat in the dingy café with Detective McCauley, thinking about that awful time when she had read in the *World* about the murder of the Denver prostitute and knew the girl was Lillie. She held her coffee cup in both hands, staring into the murky liquid, ignoring Mick.

"Miss Osmundsen," Mick said at last, startling her.

Caught up in thoughts of her sister, Beret didn't answer for a moment. Then she pushed her emotions aside and said abruptly, "There is work to do, Officer. Shall we talk of Lillie's murder?"

Mick nodded and called to the waiter to bring more coffee. He waited until the brew, black as printer's ink, was poured into their cups, leaving an oily residue on top, which he stirred into his coffee with a spoon, then added sugar. "Sugar kills the taste," he explained. Then he asked bluntly, "Do you want *all* the details of the killing?"

"Yes, all of them." Beret didn't, of course. She didn't want to know how Lillie had suffered, but she had no choice.

The detective was silent for a moment as if collecting his thoughts. "Lillie Osmundsen was murdered last week at Miss

Hettie Hamilton's House of Dreams, a whorehouse, er . . . rather . . . a brothel, on Holladay Street. She was stabbed eight times, with a pair of scissors."

"Scissors?"

"Scissors."

"One of the other girls killed her with scissors?" Beret looked at him with black eyes. "Did she leave them behind?"

"We think the pair was your sister's, taken from her sewing basket."

Beret gasped and gripped the edge of the table until her knuckles turned white. She had given Lillie a sewing basket one Christmas and remembered choosing the scissors, a long steel pair with a sharp tip. "I can identify them," she said.

"That's not necessary." Mick took a sip of coffee and grimaced, for even with the sweetening, the coffee was indeed foul. "To answer your question, no, we don't suspect one of the other girls. There are eight of them employed at the House of Dreams, and they were out that day. Miss Osmundsen was alone in the house—except for the killer, of course. Miss Hettie was the last to leave and the first to return. It's possible one of the girls sneaked back, but I think that's unlikely. Whoever killed your sister was strong. The wounds were deep. One of them went halfway through her body." He stopped as if expecting Beret to collapse, which she might have done if she had not held firmly to the seat of her chair. He went on, "It's unlikely a woman had that strength, although who knows, when two whores go at each other as they sometimes do." He started to grin at the picture, then stopped. "Sorry, ma'am. I didn't mean to call your sister—"

"It's what she was," Beret said evenly. She would not let the detective see how much the word hurt her. He would not want to work with her if he thought she was soft.

Mick nodded. "She tried to defend herself but she was over-powered, probably caught by surprise."

"A robber, then?"

Mick blew out his breath as he paused. "The other officers think so. But only her earrings were taken, diamond stars, Miss Hettie said, and there was money left on her dresser. There was no evidence that anyone forced his way into the house, so it's possible your sister let the killer in, knew him. Besides, why would a thief stab her so many times? Once or twice would have done the job." He shook his head. "The crime was too vicious. The killer was angry, out of control, as if he hated her."

"Perhaps he was a thief who despised women," Beret suggested. "Lillie might have reminded him of someone he'd known and hated, his mother perhaps. Maybe his wife. Men are crazy like that sometimes."

"I've heard of theories like that. There are doctors in the East who say such things. It makes sense, I suppose." Mick narrowed his eyes at Beret. "You know something about crime, then."

"Something." Beret picked up her cup and gazed at the coffee. She was used to poor food, but this coffee was so foul that she wondered if she could stomach any more of it.

Mick watched her. She glanced up suddenly and caught him, and Mick reddened, but he pushed forward. "And you know about prostitution."

"Should I not? Wouldn't you be surprised if I were innocent of such knowledge?" She looked directly into Mick's eyes, noticing for the first time that they were green, a shade like unsettled water. Then she had a humorous thought, and she gave a slight smile. "If you are wondering, Sergeant, I have not myself been what the newspapers call a soiled dove. Nor have I worked in any capacity in a house of assignation." Another woman might have been horrified at such an assumption, but Beret found it amusing. It took her mind off her sister for a moment.

"No, I never thought that," Mick said, then grinned, giving the lie to his words. He glanced down at the pie in front of him as if surprised to see it. While Beret had finished her chili, Mick had not touched the pie, and he picked up his fork, carefully cutting off a corner of the cheese that was moldy and shoving it to the edge of his plate. The pie itself was flat, unappetizing, and the crust looked as if it had been cut out of a paper box. He caught Beret looking at it and grinned. "Better than nothing."

"I am sure there are some people who have never tasted pie in their lives, who would find it manna."

Mick looked at Beret curiously, perhaps because that was an odd thing for a lady to say. "I never thought of it."

"No, most people haven't—most people of our class."

Mick gave a slight smile and dipped his head at being included in Beret's "class." It was obvious from the woman's manners and way of speaking that she had breeding. After all, her uncle, the judge, was prosperous and her aunt threw galas that attracted Denver's ton. The Stantons were far superior in social standing to most detective sergeants.

"Now that we've established that I've never been a denizen of the tenderloin, let's talk about the progress of your investigation," Beret said.

Before he answered, Mick sighed and looked out at the street, where a patrolman was threatening a man with his billy. He watched as the miscreant cowered against a building, then slunk off after the officer released him. He turned back to Beret. "Frankly, Miss Osmundsen, as you suggested earlier, there hasn't been much."

"I suspected that. I am well aware that the police department will not spend the time solving the death of a prostitute that it would finding the killer of, say, a prominent businessman."

"You'd be right if this were New York City. Murder's common enough there. But it's not so usual in Denver. Besides, the dead woman is the niece of a judge, who is also a member of the Fire and Police Board. Your uncle has a great deal of influence. He told Chief Smith that he wants us to leave no stone unturned—" Mick stopped, apparently remembering his earlier platitude. "Well, put it any way you like. The chief wants this murder solved double-quick."

"I suspect my aunt would like it brushed under the rug."

"Murder is an ugly business."

"So is a member of the family who takes to the streets." Beret was trying to keep her bitterness in check and was immediately sorry for the remark. Before the sergeant could respond, she said, "If it was not a thief and not one of the other girls, who could have killed my sister?"

"She might have had a mac—a macquereau. That's a—"

"I know what a mac is."

Again, Mick gave her a look of curiosity. "Macquereau" was not a word used by society ladies.

"And have you identified this pimp?"

"No. Miss Hettie didn't know him. He might be new around here. We'll check the gambling halls farther up on Larimer Street. That's where most of them hang out. He is said to be good-looking."

Beret let her face go blank so that no emotion showed on it. "And do you have a description of him?"

"Several. He is tall and blond or he is short and swarthy, but most agree he is dark."

Beret tossed her head back so that the detective wouldn't see how flushed her face was. Then, aware that she was wearing a hat, which was hot and heavy in the steamy air of the restaurant, she unpinned it and took it off, shaking her head and pushing at her hair with her fingers. That her hair was blue-black, thick, and lustrous was obvious, even though it was pulled back into a knot at her neck. Without the hat, she looked less severe. In fact, while clearly not a beauty, she was attractive, nonetheless.

Beret and Lillie had looked nothing alike. Their parents had come from Norway, and Lillie had been pale skinned, her hair so blond it was almost white. She was short and well formed. Beret was a "black Norwegian," dark-skinned with dark eyes and hair, and she was tall and angular.

"She wouldn't have mentioned him to you? I suppose it's not really a thing sisters would talk about . . ." His voice trailed off.

Beret stopped toying with her hair and put her hands into her lap. "My sister and I were estranged, Sergeant. We had not seen each other, nor written, in a year."

"May I ask why?"

"No, you may not."

Mick studied Beret a moment, as if deciding whether to pursue the question. Finally, he said, "It couldn't have been too serious since you've come here to find out about her death."

"You may write that off to guilt. Our parents crossed over some years ago, and I should have looked out for her. I'm to blame for her leaving New York. So for that reason, I am culpable in her death. I owe it to her to find her killer." That was not entirely the truth, but Beret had no intention of taking the detective into her confidence. What had been between Lillie and her was not his business. Besides, Beret was a little afraid of his disdain.

"The police will find her killer."

"You haven't done much of a job of it so far, have you?"

Mick likely was not used to women talking to him in that manner, and he flared. "The department's stretched. I'm the only one assigned to investigate. But I'll find who did it. I promise you."

"I think you promised my sister, too," she said softly. It was a statement, not a question.

Mick looked startled, and Beret continued, "Lillie had that effect on people. They always wanted to do for her—even in death, it seems. Now we'll work together to find him."

"*We?* No, ma'am. *I* will solve this murder." It was clear to Beret the detective sergeant was annoyed with her. Well, that was not her problem. She had no intention of backing off. He would just have to accept it.

A woman sat down at a table near them and ordered coffee and rolls with jam. She stared at Mick until she caught his eye, and then she winked.

"Hello, Elsie," Mick said.

Beret gave a tight-lipped smile and said, "I did not think prostitutes would frequent a restaurant so near City Hall, but maybe the food is that good." She glanced at the sergeant's pie and grimaced. "Or perhaps it's to pay protection money. Are you on the take, Sergeant?"

Mick had cut another bite of the gluelike pastry and was raising it to his mouth. Now he set it down and cocked his head. "You fancy you know about graft—and prostitution, do you?" he asked in a voice that told Beret she had been impertinent.

"I don't fancy. I know."

"How is that, since you say you're not in the business?"

"I work in a mission."

He leaned back with a look of contempt on his face. "I see

now. You're one of those mugwumps who tell the poor out there in their filthy rags that if they'll only pray to God, He'll give them food and decent jobs. Then you go home to your fine dinner, thinking you've done your good deed. Well, let me tell you, lady, the poor are onto you. They despise you."

"Do I look like one of those women?"

He smirked.

Beret sighed. "I will explain to you. Our parents—Lillie's and mine—were wealthy, but when they came to America, they were exactly like the poor you describe. The difference was they were smart—and lucky. Papa became a manufacturer and made a fortune. Mama never forgot the filth they'd lived in, the poverty into which I was born." Mick started to interrupt, but Beret put up her hand. "Oh yes, I remember what it was like in a tenement—the human smells, the dirt that blew through the cracks in the walls, the cold, the rodents, the human refuse. Mama could not go to the market without being accosted." She shivered.

"After Papa became successful, Mama made him pay the women who worked for him a decent wage. And instead of becoming a society lady, she set up a mission, not one of those religious ones, but a place where poor women could get care for themselves and their children. The mission took in women who'd been deserted or beaten by their husbands, and girls who had taken to the streets to survive. None of the women Mama hired was allowed to preach. Mama herself worked there, and I did, too. I am in charge of the clinic now that she's gone. Lillie tried to help, but the filth and the vermin made her sick. So did the people. I couldn't blame her. She didn't remember living in a tenement the way I did. So you see, Detective Sergeant McCauley, I am as familiar with life in a tenderloin as you are. And yes, I recognize that woman as a prostitute, and the one behind you in the green hat and the smart dress, sitting with her pimp, or as you call him, a mac."

Mick turned to look at the woman and said, "That's Sweet Billy Bowen, and the woman is Bricktop. He has a stable of three or four women, but Bricktop's his big earner. She makes five dollars for a quick date and thirty for a stay-over." He paused, perhaps to see if he had shocked Beret. He hadn't, and he continued, "You asked if your sister had a mac. Well, let's ask Elsie. She works at Miss Hettie's." He raised his chin at the woman who'd sat down near them. "Hey, honey, come on over here and meet somebody."

Elsie looked up, and when she saw Beret, she scowled. "Thanks all the same. Looks like she's a Jesus peddler, and I ain't looking for salvation just yet."

"I said come on over," he ordered, and the prostitute stood reluctantly. Carrying her cup and saucer and the plate of rolls, she walked slowly to the table and sat down.

"This here's Miss Osmundsen."

"Pleased to meet you." Elsie's tone told that she wasn't.

"She's Lillie Brown's sister."

Elsie's face softened. "Yeah? Oh well, then, I sure am sorry about her. She was real nice. I told that to Mick, didn't I, Mick?"

"You did."

"You in the business, lady?" Elsie asked.

"I'm from New York," Beret replied, as if that answered the question.

"She came here to find out about Lillie's death," Mick explained.

Elsie broke off part of a roll, which was hard and stale, and looked longingly at the pot of jam she'd left behind. Beret got up and fetched the jam, setting it down in front of Elsie, who nodded her thanks. She spread a dab on the piece of roll, then crunched it between her teeth, crumbs falling onto her jacket. It was an expensive jacket, and despite the age on her face, Elsie was attractive, her hair fashionably arranged, her cheeks touched with only a trace of rouge. Beret could see she was a high-class prostitute, and it gave her a slight bit of satisfaction to know that Lillie had worked in a good house. At least, she hadn't taken to the streets or worked in a crib, having to accept any man with a coin in his pocket.

The two waited for Elsie to finish eating, then Mick leaned forward and asked, "Well?"

"Well what?" Elsie asked innocently, although her face showed she knew what Mick was asking.

"You told me you thought it wasn't suicide," Mick said.

"Well, it wasn't, was it?" She looked at the sergeant coyly. "You never came back to ask me about that."

Beret gave Mick a questioning look, and he said quickly, "I'm asking now."

"I don't think Miss Hettie wants me to talk about it."

"If you'd rather, I can run you in for soliciting. Miss Hettie wouldn't like that, either."

Elsie pouted, but the look was spoiled by the crumbs on her mouth. "Ain't there a reward or something?"

Mick started to answer, but Beret interrupted. "I will pay a hundred dollars to anyone who gives us the information that leads to the arrest of the killer."

Mick scowled. "That'll bring out every tout in town."

"Then I will offer it only to Miss Elsie."

At that, Elsie turned to Beret and studied the woman, taking in her finely tailored suit, the expensive mourning brooch at her throat, the gloves as soft as pudding. High-class prostitutes knew the prices of such things. "That ain't so much for a lady like you. If it was my sister, I'd pay more."

"Don't be greedy, Elsie—" Mick began, but Beret interrupted.

"We are being played, Sergeant. She's wasting our time. I doubt this woman knows anything worth ten cents."

"Oh, I don't, do I? Well, I can tell you Lillie had one or two gents that was crazy mad about her."

"Who?" Mick asked.

"I don't know. I never saw them. But she told me there was one that wanted to marry her. Of course, he was already married, but he was going to leave his wife. He wanted to set her up until he was free, but she wouldn't do it."

"And she didn't tell you who he was?" Beret asked.

Elsie shrugged, and Mick explained, "All the girls like to brag they have somebody on the side wants to marry them."

"Well, some of us do, but I can't say I wouldn't miss the life." Elsie grinned at Beret. "I don't think Lillie made it up. You can ask Miss Hettie."

"What about her mac?" Mick asked.

"Did I say she had one?"

"Didn't she? Most of you girls have somebody on the side."

Elsie thought about that a moment. "You think I could get a drink?"

"Coffee or tea? They don't serve liquor here."

"Well, ain't you swell!"

Mick and Elsie stared at each other in a kind of standoff. Finally, Beret reached over and took Elsie's hand, which she noticed was softer than her own, the nails better manicured. "Elsie, please, I would like to find out who murdered my sister. Wouldn't you like that, too? Wouldn't you feel safer knowing he's not around anymore?"

Elsie sighed, and tears came to her eyes. Beret smiled sympathetically, although she knew that most prostitutes were actresses of a sort and could cry at will.

"I don't know if she had a mac or not. But I know there was one man I saw her with twice. First time I did, I thought she was a mixer." Elsie looked up at Beret to see if she understood, but Beret didn't and turned to Mick for an explanation.

Mick, embarrassed, wouldn't meet her gaze when he replied, "That's a white woman who keeps a Negro man."

Elsie said quickly, "But up close, I could see he wasn't. He was a white man, only dark. You don't have to worry about that, lady."

Beret's nostrils narrowed, and her face took on a look of distaste. She wondered if she could hear this without crying.

"I said he wasn't no colored man," Elsie repeated.

"I heard you," Beret said, then added slowly, "It's just that it shocks me to think my own sister would support a man like that, any man."

"Well, plenty of us does it. I'm not saying she done it, only that twice I saw her with that man outside the House of Dreams. One time, they was having words."

Mick leaned forward, his arms on the table. "About what?"

She dunked the rest of the roll into her coffee, then ate it. "I didn't say I listened in, did I?"

"The hell you didn't," he said.

Elsie pouted a moment, then pointed with her chin at Beret. "Maybe she don't want to hear it."

"I do want to hear it," Beret said.

"He was telling her he don't want her to see that man no more. That's what he said, 'that man.'"

"What man was that?" Mick asked.

"Now how should I know?" Elsie sat back in her chair and plucked the crumbs off her jacket one by one with fingers that were crooked, as if they'd been broken and not set properly. Beret had seen such hands before and wondered if Lillie had been tortured or beaten during her time in the whorehouse. She'd ask Mick about it later.

Elsie caught Beret staring at her hands and put them in her lap.

"Could you identify the man?" Mick asked.

"Naw, Miss Hettie wouldn't like that. She told us we wasn't to talk about Lillie. She'd switch me good if she was to find out I told you. I guess you owe me, Mick."

"Yeah. Next time you get rounded up, I'll make sure you aren't charged."

"I ain't never been picked up yet."

"You will be."

Beret opened her purse and took out a coin and slid it across the table. "We'll consider that the first payment on the hundred dollars."

"Ten dollars. Gee, thanks, lady." Elsie got up then, saying Miss Hettie would be wondering where she'd got to, that with the House of Dreams short a girl, the others had to take up the slack. "Like I said, I sure am sorry about Lillie," she told Beret, who was touched by the woman's sympathy. Then as an afterthought, Elsie asked, "You don't s'pose you could give me her clothes, do you? She had some pretty things, and since a lady such as yourself wouldn't be wearing them, you wouldn't mind if I took 'em, would you?"

"Aw, go on with you," Mick told her.

"It's a shame to let them go to waste," Elsie persisted.

"I'll see if they're still around," Beret told her.

"That'd be swell." Elsie straightened her hat, looked around the restaurant, and smiled at a man, who reddened and looked away. She shrugged and went out.

The two waited until the door closed, then Beret asked, "What do you think of her information?"

Mick leaned back in his chair and shoved aside the pie, which appeared too tasteless even for a policeman. "They lie, of course, all the girls. But I don't think she made it up about the man in front of the parlor house. Why would she? It doesn't mean the man was her mac, of course. Maybe he was just looking for a good time. Miss Hettie said Lillie didn't have a pimp."

"Do you believe Miss Hettie?"

Mick thought about that. "Sometimes."

"So where do we go from here?"

"*We?*"

"I told you I intend to be involved in finding my sister's killer."

Mick put his arms on the table and looked directly at Beret. "I guess I have something to say about that."

"No, Detective, you do not. As you know, my uncle is a member of the police board, and he has told me he wants this murder solved. He approves of my working with you, and if you object, then my uncle—the *judge,*" she added for emphasis, "will speak with the chief of police. I don't suppose you want that, do you?"

When Mick didn't reply, Beret added, "No, I thought not. I am obligated to spend time with my aunt on the weekend, but I shall be at your desk on Monday morning. Shall we say at ten?" She put on her hat, then left a dollar coin on the table and stood.

As she walked to the door, she wondered what her uncle would say when she told him she'd involved herself in the investigation. He'd object, of course, might even order her to stay away from Mick McCauley. But fortunately for Beret, Mick bought her story. By the time he found out any different, it would be too late.

Outside, Beret turned to face Mick. "Thank you, Detective Sergeant," she said, drawing on her gloves. She turned away, because she was going in the opposite direction from City Hall.

"Just a minute, Miss Osmundsen," Mick said, waiting for Beret to turn back to him. She looked at the officer, but Mick only stared at her.

"Yes?" she said.

"There's something you ought to know." Mick took a deep breath. He raised his chin, running his finger around the collar of his shirt, then looked out into the street at a hack driver who was whipping a nag. "Lillie, that is, Miss Osmundsen . . . well . . . you see . . . Dr. Death, that is, the coroner . . ." Mick turned back to Beret and looked her in the eye. "He said she was pregnant, your sister. She was going to have a baby."

Chapter 4

Stunned, Beret left Mick and stumbled down the street in a daze, no longer able to hold in her emotions. Tears streamed down her face, and she twisted her hands together, leaving scratches on their backs. She was as shocked by the detective's parting information as she was about her sister's murder, and wiped her eyes with her gloved hand. Prostitutes knew how to keep from getting pregnant, and they were careful, although no preventive method was perfect. That was why so many desperate women came to the clinic begging for black pills, the reason there were so many doctors specializing in conditions "peculiar to woman," as they put it—abortionists, they were. Beret had buried more than one woman who had tried to rid herself of an unwanted baby by stabbing herself with a knitting needle or eating rhubarb leaves.

The chances were that Lillie's condition was an accident, of course, but Beret couldn't help wondering if it weren't. The pregnancy, the dark-complexioned man. How could she not connect them? Had Lillie gotten pregnant on purpose, one more way to spite Beret? Or maybe there was indeed some gentleman who'd hoped to set her up, as Elsie had said, because he was the baby's father. But how could anyone tell the real identity of a baby's father? Would Lillie try to blackmail a wealthy man into thinking the child was his? A year before, Beret wouldn't have thought it possible, but that was before she'd known about her sister's betrayal. Nothing would have surprised her after that. But still, she thought, a baby! She wiped her damp cheeks again.

Jonas had driven her to the police station, but Beret had dismissed him. She had not known how long she would be there and thought her aunt might have need of the carriage. Now, she hurried up Larimer Street in the twilight, past streetlamps that sent the long shadows of passersby across the sidewalk—businessmen in top hats, sleek women in sealskin cloaks, tramps shivering in their wretched clothes, their hands out. She passed restaurants with smells of rancid grease and fried meat emanating from some, fresh-baked bread and capon simmering in wine from others. The smells mixed with the odor of manure that came from the streets. Office clerks and shopgirls dressed in cheap coats and hats with tawdry bits of feathers and artificial flowers clinging to them scurried out of buildings that were tall for Denver but not so impressive when compared to the skyscrapers in New York. A man jostled her and apologized, but Beret ignored him, not caring whether his touch had been an accident or he was approaching her. Behind her, she heard "What's your hurry, hon," a prostitute's come-on to a john, maybe the very man who had bumped against her. All of that washed over her in a kind of daze.

Beret drew her coat around her. She had planned to walk to her aunt's house, a distance of a little over a mile. But the air was chill, and she was distraught, anxious to return to the comfort of the Stanton house. Sorry that she had let Jonas go, she hurried on down Larimer to the streetcar stop and boarded a car crammed with people, leaving behind a man who had been following in her wake. She hadn't noticed him. He paused a moment, as if to board the car himself, but changed his mind and jogged off.

A gentleman offered Beret his seat, but before she could take it, a large woman with an umbrella and a basket containing potatoes and cabbages plopped herself down and gave Beret a smug smile as she set the basket on her lap and wrapped her arms around it. Beret wanted to protest but saw the woman was dressed in black and white, her ankles swollen, and knew she was a domestic who needed the seat more than Beret did. She rode for a few blocks, but the swaying of the car, the crowd pushing against her, the smells of wet wool combined with sweat and tobacco smoke, nauseated her, and as soon as the car reached Broadway, she got off to walk the remaining half-dozen blocks to her uncle's house.

The cold hit her then. It had been almost spring in New York when she'd left, and she did not consider that Denver was in sight of the mountains, that the cold from the high peaks swept down into the city. So she had not brought a winter coat. But she spent her days among the dregs of humanity at the mission and was used to discomfort. It would not have occurred to Beret to wear furs or even a fashionable warm cloak to the mission. She was used to the drafty building, the floors that were black from the slush and dirt and coal dust that the women tracked in. So she folded her arms around herself to keep out the cold and walked on, grateful for something to distract her from her grief, if only for a moment or two.

As she grew used to the wind, Beret found herself hating Lillie and thinking her sister deserved what she'd gotten, then loving the golden child who had once looked at her with awe and trust. Beret had loved Lillie more than anyone else in the world, more than herself even. But she had hated her sister, too, although even in her despair, she would not have hurt the girl, not physically.

Who could have hated her more than Beret? She shuddered as she thought of the scissors cutting into Lillie's flesh, six, seven, eight thrusts, of the blood spurting out onto Lillie's white breasts, splattering her hands as she tried to protect herself. Lillie's skin was as white as a lily. That was where she had gotten her name. Her parents had wanted to call her Martha Brown Osmundsen, after a friend, but Beret had insisted on another name, had said that with her pale skin and white-blond hair, the infant looked like a lily, and so she had become Lillie Osmundsen, no middle name because Beret said that "Brown" was too ugly to follow "Lillie." But Lillie must not have thought so, because when she'd turned out, she had taken the name Lillie Brown.

Beret walked east to Grant Avenue, then turned south. Night had come on, and the street was dark, lit only by the gaslights whose crystal shades glittered with fire through the leaded-glass windows of the mansions of Millionaires' Row. The street was lined with brick-and-stone castles, their spires and crenellated towers, porches and balconies and cast-iron fences, evidence that their occupants were the newly wealthy of a new city. The houses were not as overblown as those along New York's Fifth Avenue. Nonetheless, they were designed to impress, which they did with their paneling of rare woods, their gilt, their profusion of stained-glass and crystal windows peeking out from behind velvet curtains held stiffly in place by golden cord tiebacks. Beret knew, because on previous trips to visit her relatives, she had been entertained in those houses.

Judge John Stanton's house was less ponderous, less extravagant, more graceful than its neighbors on Grant Avenue, thanks to his wife's good taste, but it was impressive and every bit as expensive—a Palladian-style brick mansion of three stories, fronted by a porch and tall white columns. The house seemed a little at odds with its neighbors, more Southern in style than nouveau riche Denver, more classical. A two-story stable stood beside and a little to the rear of the house, for her uncle was a man who appreciated horseflesh and employed two men to care for his animals—the rodentlike Jonas and an assistant. She looked up, expecting to see the house, and was confused. Deep in thought, she had turned down the wrong street, and it was unfamiliar. So were the houses. Perhaps they had been built since her last trip to Denver. Lost and feeling wretched for causing her aunt to worry, she looked up and down the street, until she spotted a man coming toward her and asked for directions. He explained she had gone blocks out of her way, and now she retraced her steps until, at last, she recognized the Stanton mansion.

Beret stood just a moment to admire it. The house was as fine as the home in which she and her sister had once lived with their parents and in which Beret lived now, alone except for servants, for the judge was as rich as Beret's father, perhaps richer since much of the Osmundsen money had gone to good works.

The two men, who had been as close as their wives, had had much in common. John Stanton was a fatherless boy from Fort Madison, Iowa, who quit school to work as a stableboy. A local banker had taken a liking to the lad and offered him a menial job. The boy worked hard and had been promoted—and promoted again, until not yet in his twenties, he was made assistant cashier at the bank. Too ambitious to stay in the Mississippi River town, John had migrated to Chicago, where he found further financial success. But his sights had been set higher than even Chicago, and so he had joined the Colorado gold rush in 1859, not to prospect for precious metals but to set up a bank on Larimer Street, the most important financial avenue between St. Louis and the West Coast. Using it as a base, he had financed the town's growth, speculating in city blocks and ranchland. It wasn't long before he was one of Denver's first millionaires.

After a time, he tired of the financial world, for he had made as much money as he would ever need. So he turned to politics. He'd had himself appointed judge, and there was talk that he would be named a senator. Beret's aunt had written that it was all but certain that they would be going to Washington soon. Beret was sure that the meetings her aunt had mentioned were toward that end.

Varina had met John, then living in Chicago, when he was on a trip to New York and Henry Osmundsen, a business associate, had invited him home for dinner. Varina Eliason, who was Marta Osmundsen's younger sister, was not so much to look at, but she matched John in both ambition and hard work. John delayed his trip, and the two were married before he left New York. Beret remembered the wedding—Varina's satin dress and a veil that fell from a crown of white roses, the tiny white slippers, because Varina was vain about her small feet, the ring, an elegant circle of yellow diamonds that Varina herself had picked out.

In New York and then in Chicago, Varina had studied the houses and the hostesses, noting what was elegant and tasteful and discarding the ostentatious and the garish, and when the Stantons moved to Denver, she set herself up as one of the city's society leaders. While John built his financial empire, Varina established a fashionable domestic world. And although she had no intention of setting up a mission as her sister, Marta, had done in New York, Varina nonetheless lent her support to the city's fledgling charities. The Stantons had no children of their own, and they adored Beret and Lillie. So it was only natural that when Lillie left New York, she went to Denver to live with her aunt and uncle.

As she climbed the wide steps to the front door of the house, Beret wondered what Lillie had told them about the sisters' estrangement. Surely she would not have told them the truth.

The door opened just as Beret reached it, and the judge himself welcomed his niece, grasping her hands so tightly that he all but squeezed the blood out of them. "Beret. Our dear Beret," he said, then choked and could not speak for a moment. He took a breath and let go of Beret's hands and, affecting a lighter tone, said, "I've arrived only a moment ahead of you. What a worthless old man I am not to have greeted you earlier. Your aunt, I assume, told you it couldn't be helped. This Senate appointment is damn complicated business. Everyone involved must be satisfied." He shook his head, then his face fell. "I can't say as I mind it so much. It must be done, and we tell ourselves we have to go on. Dear Lillie . . ." His voice trailed off, and Beret took his arm and let him escort her into the house.

They did not talk about the murder of Lillie Osmundsen at dinner. "The servants," Varina Stanton muttered when her husband broached the subject. She gave Beret a knowing look. Beret thought the warning unnecessary, because little escaped servants. Still, the three waited until they had retired to the library, which served as the judge's study, before discussing the tragedy.

"Will you join your aunt in a sherry?" the judge asked, taking a crystal decanter from a cabinet built into the wall.

"No, but I will join you in a brandy," Beret said.

Her uncle smiled. "I had forgot you like the stronger stuff."

"I like sherry well enough, but I remember that you have very good brandy."

The judge nodded his approval, and Beret observed that he looked much older than the last time she had seen him, two years before. She wondered if the changes were recent and had been caused by Lillie's death. After all, the Stantons had been responsible in a way for Lillie, just as Beret had been. Her uncle's hair had turned gray, almost silver. There was a sadness about his mouth, and he stooped a little, although he was still an imposing man, a man who looked like a senator. He would be a good one, Beret thought, with affection.

She rose to accept the glass from her uncle, but instead of sitting down again, she went to the fireplace and stared into the fire, at the logs that had burned down, for the fire had been lit in the early evening. Lillie would have stared at the library fire, Beret thought. Lillie had always lit up a room like a bright flame, attracting moths, and now one of them had killed her, extinguishing that light. How could anyone have hated—or loved—her enough to do that?

The wood would have to be replenished if the fire was to continue much longer. Beret was looking at the ashes, as dirty gray as the snow on a New York street, when her uncle said, "I understand you have taken it upon yourself to join the investigation of the murder of your sister."

Beret turned and glanced at her aunt, who shrugged. "I've told him nothing, Beret."

"No, it was Detective Sergeant McCauley. He visited me in my chambers early this evening, saying he had left you only moments before. That explains why I was so late in arriving home. Detective McCauley said you were intruding and asked me to call you off. It seems he believed you had my support." John chuckled.

Beret turned to face her uncle. "And what did you tell him?"

"What did *you* tell him?"

Beret sipped the brandy, which was indeed very good. "I told him that you approved of my joining the investigation, were much in favor of it, in fact. I led him to believe my involvement might even have been your idea."

Varina set down her sherry glass. "Beret, how could you? Your sister's murder is a horrid, ugly thing. Your uncle and I don't want you mixed up in it. That's why we advised you to stay in New York, so you wouldn't have to know about the last months of her life. Dear Lillie's death is a tragedy, but it's best if the whole tawdry business is put behind us. You can't bring her back."

"I want to know why Lillie left here to become . . . a prostitute." Beret could not bring herself to look at her aunt.

"I can't talk about it, Beret." Varina paused a moment. "Think of your uncle's future."

John shook his head as if to wave away the objection. "That's of no consequence here."

"You have worked so hard for it," his wife said.

Beret was appalled that her aunt was more concerned about the judge's ambition than Lillie's murder and that she would not discuss what had caused Lillie to turn out, as the papers put it. She watched Varina wring her hands and thought that Lillie's death had been hard on her aunt. Not only had she lost a beloved niece, but the killing had upset the world she had made for herself and her husband. She didn't deserve the sorrow, nor the notoriety. Perhaps that was why she put social concerns ahead of finding her niece's killer. But that didn't make it right. Beret knew that she herself would sacrifice anything to find out who had murdered Lillie. But perhaps that was to assuage her guilt. Should she honor her relatives' wishes and return to New York, letting the Denver police find Lillie's killer? No. She would not do such a thing. She wanted to chide her aunt, but before she could find the right words, her uncle interrupted her thoughts.

"Our duty is to Lillie, Varina, and if Beret can help find justice for the poor child, I have no objection to it." He drank his brandy in a single swallow and poured more into the glass. "I admit I was surprised and not in the least pleased when Detective Sergeant McCauley told me you had interfered"—he turned to Beret—"and, my dear, I very nearly decided to forbid you to continue. But I know how like a mother you were to Lillie. You knew her better than anyone. And I was sure my opposition would have no effect on you. Besides, I believe you might actually help find your sister's killer."

"How could she do that?" Varina asked.

"Beret is reasoned and smart, and she knows the underworld as few women of our class do."

"Then you don't object?" Beret asked.

The judge shook his head. "Make sure you aid instead of hinder the investigation, but I have complete faith in you." He paused and added, "I only ask that you be aware of your aunt's feelings and do nothing to upset her." He smiled at his wife, who rose.

"Then I shall leave this to the two of you. I am not anxious to hear the particulars of Lillie's death once again. I have a headache. Don't be too long, dear. Beret has had a very tiring day," she told her husband, then embraced her niece, saying she hoped the young woman would rest well. She left the room, and the judge stared at the closed door for a long time.

"This has been very hard on her."

"And on you, too, Uncle."

"Yes." Without asking if she wanted more brandy, the judge refilled Beret's glass. "Sit down."

Beret seated herself on a footstool beside her uncle's chair. "It's my fault, you know. I ordered Lillie out of the house." Beret's voice quivered, and she cleared her throat. She would not allow herself self-pity. She asked in a voice that was barely audible, "Did Lillie tell you about . . . ?"

"Yes. I don't like the man, never did, to be truthful. Lillie blamed him, of course, and said you had wronged her, that he was at fault. She said the two of you had a row over it, that you refused to believe her to be an innocent, and you forced her out of the house. She had no choice but to come to us."

"And Aunt Varina?"

"She knows, too. We heard only Lillie's side of the story, of course, and I have been a judge long enough to know there are always two sides, so I did not believe the entirety of what Lillie said. Perhaps one day you will tell us how you view it. We felt sorry for her, and it was our duty to take her in, although we would have, no matter the situation. You know how we have always felt about the two of you, how we have treated you like daughters in this home."

Beret nodded. Her uncle had always thought of her happiness. He had supported her after her parents died, when she wanted to stay in New York with Lillie and run the mission, instead of moving to Denver. He had even agreed that Beret should raise Lillie. "She had you and Aunt Varina, at any rate, even if I'd turned against her." Beret stopped, because her voice was unsteady. She wished with all her heart that she had not forced Lillie to leave.

The judge leaned forward and gripped Beret's shoulder, until she looked up at him. "You can't blame yourself. Who wouldn't have acted the same in your place?"

"But she was my sister!" Beret almost sobbed.

"This is no time for recriminations. Our duty is to find Lillie's killer."

There was a knock on the library door, and a few seconds later, William entered the room, his arms filled with logs, and busied himself building up the fire. When he was done, he brushed his hands together and asked, "Will there be anything else, sir?"

"No, go to bed," John said, and after the butler left, the judge told Beret, "With all these servants to fetch and carry, I shall die of lethargy. But your aunt likes having them about, so I must put up with them."

Beret had risen from the stool and seated herself in a chair. Her glass was empty, but she didn't want more brandy and set it on the table. "Detective Sergeant McCauley gave me the particulars of the murder. Would he have left out anything?" Beret tried to put her feelings aside to concentrate on the investigation.

"We—he, that is, doesn't know much. You are aware that she was stabbed with her own scissors? The house was empty at the time, except for Lillie and her killer. The detective believes she was murdered by someone in a rage and that he was not a thief, because he failed to take money and other valuables that were in plain sight."

"But he took Lillie's diamond earrings. They haven't been found."

"So they say. But I think it just as likely that the madam or one of the girls pocketed them." He paused, considering something. "You'll excuse me for my indelicacy, Beret, but the coroner believes, after a thorough examination of the body, that she was not raped. At least she didn't suffer that indignity."

Beret did not find that consoling but said anyway, "We can be grateful for that." She looked away and said in a soft voice, "I am told she was pregnant."

The judge swallowed but said nothing.

"Does Aunt know?"

"She knows, but it is best if you don't mention it to her. She has had to face enough as it is."

"Was Lillie tortured?"

The judge shook his head. "Not unless you consider being stabbed eight times by a pair of scissors torture." He put the back of his hand to his forehead for a few moments. "I would not talk about such things with you, but I know your work at the mission prepares you—"

"Nothing prepares me." Indeed, Beret had seen women who had been beaten to death by their husbands, children who had been tortured by parents crazed by liquor or drugs, men who had been slaughtered in rage, but nothing had moved her like the death of her own sister.

"No, of course not."

Beret stared out the window for a moment and was startled to see a shadow pass in front of the glass. "Uncle?"

John looked up. "It's only Jonas. He's begun checking the grounds in the evenings since Lillie's murder. He's under the impression we might be in danger."

"Are you?"

The judge smiled. "Not that I'm aware of, but Jonas feels protecting us is his duty."

"I met him earlier. He seems . . . odd."

"He is that. Jonas is a pet of your aunt's. He was a newsboy.

Varina saw some older boys beating him in the street. They'd stolen his money and broken his leg. She took her horsewhip to them." The judge chuckled. "Your aunt can be a mighty impressive woman when her ire is raised. I believe you take after her in that respect. She got him into her carriage and took him to a hospital, then brought him home and set him up in a room in the carriage house two years ago, not long after your last visit. He's been with us ever since, and there's not a thing he wouldn't do for any of us, especially your aunt. He all but worships her. Sometimes it seems as if he thinks she's his mother. I believe Lillie's death hit him hard, and he makes up for it by patrolling the house and garden to keep us safe."

Beret thought that over. Her aunt might be dedicated to society, but like Beret's mother, Varina was also compassionate. "The other servants liked Lillie, too?"

"As far as I know."

"Then why did she leave? What I don't understand, Uncle, is why she left this house and went to work in a brothel."

The old man looked into the fire, watching as a log snapped, sending up sparks that lit his face. "Don't you?"

Beret turned away and closed her eyes, then gave an involuntary shudder. Despite the fire, she suddenly felt cold. "He's here, then." It was a statement, not a question.

John did not answer.

"A prostitute the detective talked to said she was seen talking to a dark-complexioned man—twice." Beret did not mention that she had talked to the prostitute, too. "But even if he was here, that's no reason for her to leave this house." Beret thought that over and added, "Unless you asked her to."

"No, no, of course not. But I believe she must have left because of him."

Uncle and niece sat lost in thought for a moment. Then Beret asked, "Was there anyone else? Was she seeing someone?"

"A young man. Lillie met him at one of your aunt's soirees, the son of a friend."

"Who?"

"His name is Joseph Summers. His father, a stiff-necked old soul, has mining interests. Joey's a wild sort. I never cared for him, but I didn't say anything to Lillie. I thought he was her business."

"Did she care for him?"

Beret's uncle shrugged. "She saw enough of him. Lillie could be wild, too, you know."

"I suppose so." Had Lillie been wild all along and she hadn't noticed? She was confused. She had learned so many things about her sister that day.

The judge rose then, slowly, as if he were weary. "We can talk about it later, the two of us. It would be best if we didn't discuss this in front of your aunt. She has had a hard enough time of it. Just hearing Lillie's name spoken aloud is enough to send her into tears."

"I'm sorry I've brought this on you."

"You didn't."

"Yes I did."

"It was not your fault, and the sooner you realize that, the better off you'll be."

"Then if not I, who bears the fault?"

The judge went to the fire and hit a log with a poker. It broke apart, the halves settling down into a soft glow. "It was Lillie's."

He left the room, his footsteps echoing as he walked across the marble foyer, but Beret stayed, so intent on watching the fire die that she didn't notice the shadow that passed across the window again. The house was silent, as silent as death, Beret thought, as she closed her eyes only to rest a little, but fell asleep in her chair. When she awoke, the room was dark, the fire dead, and she was covered with a blanket taken from the back of a chair. The idea that someone, even a servant, had stolen into the room while she slept unnerved her.

Chapter 5

Detective Sergeant McCauley sighed audibly the following Monday as Beret walked briskly through the squad room and stopped beside his desk. He stood, and without greeting the woman, he said, "I was hoping your uncle had forbidden you to come here."

"So I understand. But he did not." Beret hoped she sounded more confident than she felt. That morning, when her aunt had asked again what in the world Beret could bring to the search for Lillie's killer, Beret hadn't answered. But now she knew: passion and determination.

"Well, he certainly was surprised to find out he'd given his blessing to your interfering in this investigation."

"I am not interfering. I am participating. And once I explained that to him, he assured me that I had his blessing."

"My bad luck." Mick pointed to the chair beside his desk, and they both sat down.

"What do we have scheduled for today?" Beret asked.

"We?" Mick scoffed. "I was going to talk to Miss Hettie. I'd have left before now, but I got held up. More bad luck. You'll recall Miss Hettie owns the whorehouse where your sister was murdered."

"And this is the first time you've talked to her?" Beret was displeased. Could the authorities really be that slow? Her uncle had assured her this case was a priority. She couldn't help but wonder if the police even bothered to solve the murders of victims who were less important than a judge's niece.

"The second."

"It is early for a brothel to be astir. I can't help but wonder if the madam is up yet."

"She wasn't when I left."

"You may be crude if you want to, Detective, but I think we will get along much better if we are courteous to each other."

"This is a police investigation, not a class in deportment."

Beret would take her lead from the detective. She lifted her head a little. "Quite right. Shall we be on our way?" She stood and started across the room, aware of the smirks directed at the detective sergeant. She wondered how long it would be before he accepted her. Perhaps never.

Outside, Mick told her, "I hope you're used to hoofing it. The department doesn't pay for hacks or even streetcars."

"I am quite used to walking."

He nodded and set off at a fast clip, and when he'd gone half a block, he turned around as if expecting to see Beret lagging behind, but she had kept up the pace. "I can walk as fast as you can, Detective, but doesn't it make sense for us to walk together so that you can tell me of any developments?"

He slowed only slightly. "There aren't any, not since yesterday, at any rate."

"You've already talked with the madam, you said. Why is it necessary to interview her again?"

They had reached a corner, and Mick suddenly took Beret's elbow and propelled her across the street, past hacks and carriages and delivery wagons. Surprised at the courtesy, she nodded her thanks. "The drivers can be treacherous along Larimer Street, but I suppose they're no worse than New York."

"Have you been there?"

Mick nodded but didn't elaborate. "I talked to Miss Hettie only once, the day we found your sister's body. I want to talk to her again, now that she's had time to think about the murder."

"And has she had time to find alibis for herself and her girls?"

"She already had them. What I'm hoping is she'll give us the name of your sister's mac. Miss Hettie hates pimps. I'm thinking if Lillie, that is, Miss Osmundsen, had one, Miss Hettie might be willing to talk about him now. She wouldn't the day your sister was killed. These madams, they don't admit to anything. Why, I bet if you gave her a thousand dollars, she still wouldn't give you the names of your sister's customers." He paused. "But I guess you already know that, you being a mission lady."

Beret ignored the taunt. She was used to such remarks. "Can't you compel her to?"

"To remember something she can't remember? How would I do that?"

"I see your point."

Beret held her tongue then. It was clear the detective wasn't going to confide in her any more than he had. She was grateful he hadn't skipped out on her. They hurried up Larimer Street, past cafés and rooms to let, a millinery, a hardware store, then a block of gambling halls in striking buildings of carved stone and stained glass. Beret paused to glance inside, and Mick told her those were the places the macs hung out—the Arcade, Murphy's Exchange, and two or three others. If Miss Hettie gave them the name of Lillie's macquereau, they would come back and look for him there. Beret shivered to think those were the men her sister had slept with. She studied the few customers visible from the street but saw no one who was swarthy. It was early, however. The men probably didn't gather until later in the day.

They went on, past the Windsor Hotel, an elegant five-story stone castle with cast-iron porte cocheres that would have drawn admiring glances even in New York. Beret had been inside, with her sister, on previous visits to Denver when their uncle had escorted them to the hotel. They had taken in the rotunda with its glass ceiling and marble floor and admired the three staircases, although Lillie, superstitious, had said she would never use the "devil's-head" staircase, which threw a shadow on the wall like the head of Satan. Beret wondered if Lillie had climbed it after all, perhaps to visit some john. She would have to stop thinking of Lillie that way, imagining the men who paid to sleep with her sister.

Instead, Beret concentrated on that afternoon with their uncle. He had ordered champagne and strawberry ices. Lillie had been young then, perhaps twelve, and she had begged Beret to let her taste the champagne. Beret had given in, of course, then watched in astonishment as Lillie drained her glass. The rest of the afternoon, Lillie had been as bubbly as the champagne. If Lillie had gone into the Windsor in the past few months, had she remembered that day when they were so carefree? Beret desperately hoped that Lillie had kept a few good memories of her sister.

Mick turned, and Beret followed him to Holladay Street. "A strange name. Is it purposely misspelled?" she asked.

"Named for Ben Holladay of the Holladay Overland Mail and Express. There's talk the city will change it. Mr. Holladay's friends don't want the most notorious street in the West named for him."

"Change it to what?" Beret asked.

"Market."

When Beret raised an eyebrow, the detective explained, "There is a wholesale market at the other end of the street."

They walked another block, and Mick stopped in front of a sedate brick house whose only adornment was iron cresting on the roof and a shuttered two-story bay window. "This is it, Miss Hettie Hamilton's House of Dreams," Mick said.

Beret was taken aback. The building, which was set back only a few feet from the street, looked like the home of a middle-class merchant. It was neatly kept and hardly ostentatious, with its conservative porch and heavy front door set off by a transom, nothing like the elegant sin palaces she had observed in New York, with their carved-stone trim and crystal windows covered by heavy draperies. "I thought my sister was in one of the better bagnios." The idea of Lillie working in a second-rate house tormented Beret, who knew firsthand how prostitutes spiraled downward from bawdy houses to cribs to the streets. At least Lillie hadn't lived long enough for that indignity.

"This *is* one of the better houses. There's not a one that's better. But don't worry. The outside's deceptive. Wait till you see what's inside. It's much nicer and bigger than it appears. These are all whorehouses along here." Mick waved his arm at the plain buildings around them that Beret had missed.

He started up the steps, but Beret hung back, until he asked, "You're game, aren't you? Or have you changed your mind?" He almost smirked at her.

"Of course I'm game," she replied, and he rang the bell.

After a time, a large colored woman opened the door. "We ain't open, sir . . . oh, it's you, Mr. Mick." She looked past the detective at Beret but said nothing more.

"Is Miss Hettie up?" the detective asked.

"She up. You want talk to her?"

"I do."

"I'll see if she want talk to you." The woman started to close the door, but Mick stuck his foot inside, and he followed her into the house, Beret behind him.

The place was stuffy, sour smelling, and Beret was tempted to find a handkerchief and cover her nose, but that surely would offend Miss Hettie, so she took a few breaths through her mouth, lagging behind Mick as she glanced up the staircase near the door, then peered into the rooms along the corridor. She had helped prostitutes escape from the cribs and brothels in New York and was curious to see how Denver's nests compared to them. There was a front parlor with a piano and easy chairs, a velvet banquette that she assumed was for the girls. Lillie would have sat there stroking her long blond hair.

A Turkish room was next to it, decorated with Arabian rugs and heavy figured draperies, silk fabric on the walls, cushions ornamented with large tassels scattered over the floor, couches and ottomans. The room smelled of tobacco and spilled liquor, and Beret wondered if the windows were ever opened. She hurried to catch up with Mick, passing a dining room where the remnants of a banquet had been left on the table, a chair at its head overturned, and found herself in a large kitchen at the back of the house.

Four women sat around an oilcloth-covered table, eating eggs. Beret recognized Elsie, who gave her a hard stare, and she decided to act as if they had not met. Two others were Elsie's age, women with sleepy eyes and uncombed hair, and they stared at Beret, bored, as they ate. One put out her cigarette in her plate and rose, stretching like a cat and letting her robe fall open to reveal she wore nothing beneath it except for white stockings held up by rosebud garters. She traced a tear in a stocking with her fingertip and said, "Come on, Rose, you said you'd mend my stocking." Her companion dipped a piece of ham into her egg and ate it, then picked up a coffee cup, and together, they went down the hall to the staircase.

"Well, Elsie, ain't you got nothing to do?" asked the fourth woman, who was obviously the madam, Miss Hettie.

Elsie, in no hurry to leave, spread jam on a piece of toast, shoved it into her mouth, and chewed.

"Well, ain't you? And where's your manners anyway, cramming in food that way? What's a gentleman to think if you eat like that?"

As Elsie stood and tightened the sash of her robe, she cocked her head at Mick and said, "Whyu't you come see me later, Mick? Whyu't you?" Without looking at Beret, she left the room, pausing at the door, but the madam flapped her hand to shoo her away.

Miss Hettie had not risen from the table. Clad in an old robe whose lace ruffles had yellowed, she looked a little yellow herself; her face without its layer of powder was sallow. Her hair was a hideous red, almost the color of blood, and the hands that peeked from the yellowed ruffles that adorned the sleeves of the robe were clawlike. Beret noticed that even at that early hour, the madam wore half a dozen rings, diamonds mostly and good ones it appeared. A diamond cross was at her throat. Her earrings were diamonds, too—four-leaf clovers, not stars. Miss Hettie gave Mick a resigned look, and ignored Beret. "Coffee?" she asked him.

"Thanks."

The colored woman glanced at Beret, who nodded, and the

woman brought two cups of coffee in good china cups with saucers. Then she cleared the plates from the table. "You want me to tell them other girls they can wait for their breakfast?" she asked, and Miss Hettie told her yes.

"Might as well sit down," the madam said. "Who's that?" She didn't look at Beret but merely pointed over her shoulder with her thumb. "You didn't bring me fresh fish, did you, Mick? That one ain't so fresh." She gave a hoarse chuckle and cocked her head as if waiting for Beret to react.

"This is Miss Osmundsen. Miss Osmundsen, you are in the presence of Miss Hettie Hamilton, the queen of Denver's demimonde." With a flourish, he indicated Miss Hettie.

Beret felt the introduction insulting to both Miss Hettie and herself and said quickly, "I am Lillie Brown's sister."

Miss Hettie raised herself up and looked directly at Beret for the first time. "You don't say." She scrutinized her—in a way that she must look over the girls who applied for jobs in the house, thought Beret, who did not blanch. "You don't look like her. You look more like a salvation biddy." She seemed to remember herself then and said, "Your sister was a real nice girl. I'm sorry she crossed over."

"Thank you." Beret closed her eyes for a moment. The remark had been kind, even if the madam hadn't meant it. But why should she? Miss Hettie had known Lillie only as a whore, not as the lovely young woman she had been. But which one of them really had known Lillie better?

"You come to shut us down, have you?"

"I am helping Detective Sergeant McCauley find my sister's killer."

Miss Hettie gave a deep laugh, her voice throaty from too many cigarettes. "Oh, you are, are you? I didn't know Denver had lady cops. What do you think about that? *Detective Sergeant McCauley.*"

Mick shrugged. "Her uncle is Judge Stanton."

"Never heard of him."

Beret knew the woman was lying. A madam would know every judge in the city, if not personally, then by reputation.

"Miss Osmundsen would like to hear how you found her sister's body."

Miss Hettie stretched, letting the sleeves of her robe fall away and reveal the veins and heavy cording of her arms. When she saw Beret staring at them, she quickly pulled down the sleeves so that only her hands, gnarled as roots, showed. She took a sip of her coffee and rolled herself a cigarette, licking the paper shut, then waiting for Mick to strike a match and light it for her. She inhaled, drawing the smoke into her lungs, then coughed. "You can't tell her yourself, Mick?"

"I've got a few more questions when you're done."

"All right, then. Like I told Mick, me and the girls were out." She spoke in a monotone, as if she'd been expecting she would be asked again about the murder and had practiced her words. Then she related how she had found Lillie. The story was longer this time—Miss Hettie couldn't help but try to shock Beret by telling her details of the whorehouse operation—but it differed little from the one she'd told Mick the day Lillie's body was found.

Beret didn't interrupt her, but when Miss Hettie was finished, the young woman asked, "You don't know who could have killed her?"

"Well, I'd have told Mick if I did, wouldn't I?"

"Perhaps after thinking about it, you have an idea."

"I don't."

"What about her patrons?" Beret took her first sip of the coffee and found it very good. She knew that food in the best whorehouses was both tasty and nutritious. After all, the girls had to keep up their strength.

"None of them could have done it. We're not open that early in the day."

"Lillie could have let someone in."

"Naw, the ladies know I wouldn't like that. I check out my customers. I don't allow nobody I don't know to come in this place."

"What are the names of Lillie's johns, then?"

"I wouldn't know."

"You said you knew everyone who came here." Beret refrained from sending a look of triumph to the detective.

Miss Hettie cleared her throat and stuck a fork into her egg yolk, letting the yellow run over the plate. "Well, they don't give me their business cards, if that's what you mean. Lady, you don't know nothing about the business."

"I know a great deal about it," Beret retorted, without explaining.

Miss Hettie scraped the yellow to one side. "Well, I didn't keep track of who goes with Lillie."

"Didn't you? How was my sister paid, then? Don't you collect before the customers go upstairs—five dollars for a quick date, thirty for all night?" Beret was glad Mick had told her the prices.

Miss Hettie stared at Beret, then crossed her arms. "I ain't giving any names."

"I told you she wouldn't," Mick interjected.

"Perhaps you can shut her down."

"For what reason?" Miss Hettie flared. "With what I pay you

tin badges, I got protection. Go on, tell her, Mick. Ain't nobody going to shut down the House of Dreams."

Beret let that pass and asked, "Was Joseph Summers one of my sister's regulars?"

Mick, who had been leaning back in his chair as if enjoying the exchange between the two women, sat upright as Miss Hettie's mouth dropped. "Who's he?" she asked, as her face turned bland.

"So he was, then," Beret said, congratulating herself on the reaction.

"How do you know about him?" Mick asked, and Beret could tell the detective was impressed. "Next to Senator Tabor, his father's the richest man in Colorado."

Beret didn't answer. "And what about the older man, the one who wanted to marry my sister?"

Miss Hettie was cagey now. "Mr. Moneybags. Every whore talks about him. I can tell you, lady, if he was real, your sister wouldn't have been working here. Now, are you done with your questions? There's a religious meeting in town. It's a convention of real pious men, and they'll be wanting to get their ashes hauled after all their praying and carrying on. If Jesus knew what those boys did when they visited the House of Dreams, he'd get down off the cross. I got work to do. It ain't easy being short one girl like I am. I got to find me a replacement." She looked Beret up and down, then waved her hand in dismissal.

"There's one more thing, Miss Hettie," Mick said.

The two women stared at Mick, because he no longer seemed amused, and his voice had turned hard. "I want the name of her mac."

"She ain't got one. I told you that."

"Yes she does, and you know who he is."

"I don't."

"You do. And Miss Osmundsen and I will sit here until you tell us."

"You just do that." Miss Hettie stood, but Beret grasped her hand and pulled her back down.

"Detective Sergeant McCauley, I am concerned for the safety of the other girls in this place," Beret said. "I fear the man who killed my sister may return. Could you arrange to station a patrolman at the entrance of the House of Dreams until we find the man responsible? I'm sure Miss Hettie would want that protection for her girls."

Mick grinned at Beret. The smile lit up his whole face, even his eyes, and she couldn't help but smile in return. "Why, that's a first-rate idea, Miss Osmundsen. You don't mind, do you, Miss Hettie? I know you'll want to protect your boarders—and those gentlemen of God, too."

Miss Hettie scowled as she played with her rings, twisting them around her gnarled fingers. "I don't know she had one for sure. I wasn't lying to you, Mick. But I seen her once or twice with one of the gents from the Arcade. He's dark as an Oriental, built like a boxer, not much taller than you." Hettie nodded at Beret.

"His name?" Mick asked.

Hettie looked away and sighed. "I ain't sure of his real name. He goes by Teddy Star."

Beret let out an involuntary, "Oh!," and the other two turned to her.

"Most of the girls have a fancy man. You shouldn't be surprised," Mick said.

Beret closed her eyes for a second to steady herself. Of course she knew the prostitutes had pimps, and she should not have been surprised that Lillie had had one, too, but confronted with that name, she almost lost her composure. The closeness of the house with its sour smells turned her stomach. She nodded and rose slowly, extending her hand to Miss Hettie as if ending a social call. "You have been very kind. I know my sister's death has been a strain on you, too." And then she asked, "May I see my sister's room?"

Miss Hettie glanced at Mick. "I ain't found anybody to replace Lillie, so it ain't been cleaned."

"That's all right," Beret said.

"You sure you want to? It's not something pretty," Mick said.

Beret straightened her back. No, she didn't want to see the room where her sister had died, but she had to. Maybe looking at the place where Lillie had been murdered would help her come to terms with the death. "I'm sure of that, Detective."

The two followed the colored woman down the long upstairs hall, Beret aware of the women watching them from behind half-open doors. "This her room, but I guess you know that, Mr. Mick. I'm Mae. You need anything, you ask. I liked Miss Lillie. She treated me nice, not like some." She glanced over her shoulder at a door that was slammed shut in her face.

She turned to go, but Beret asked suddenly, "Would you show me where my sister kept her clothes? I should like to see them." Mick gave her an odd look, for surely Beret had spotted the clothes hanging in the open wardrobe.

Mae went into the room and pointed at a door. "In there."

"Thank you," Beret said, then slowly opened her bag and took out a five-dollar gold piece and toyed with it. "What can you tell me about the gentlemen who favored Miss Lillie?"

Mae looked at the coin, then glanced out the open door. She lowered her voice. "There's one or two partial to her. That Mr. Joey Summers you mentioned, he one of 'em." She chuckled. "His daddy, I think he the old man that want to set her up. I heard you ask Miss Hettie 'bout that. Didn't want to marry her, though, 'cause he already got himself a wife."

Beret gasped.

"He not such a nice man, not to me, anyways. He treat me like I chicken scratch. But he bring Miss Lillie pretty things—chocolate and silk stockings and such."

Mick had been looking back and forth from Mae to Beret. "And what about her mac? What's he like?"

"Mr. Star?" Mae turned and glanced out the door, because Miss Hettie had called her name. "I got to go. Miss Hettie skin me alive she find me talking to you." Mae snatched the coin and dropped it into her apron pocket and went out of the room, leaving Mick and Beret staring at each other.

"Two generations of Summerses?" Mick said at last. "Doesn't that beat all!" When Beret turned away, he added, "I'm sorry. I forgot for a minute she was your sister."

"Yes, well . . ." Beret turned her back and used the tip of her finger to wipe away a tear. The idea of Lillie sleeping with both father and son disgusted her, and Beret closed her eyes, as if to block out the vision she had of such depravity. Beret began to wonder if she had loved her sister too much to see her faults. She cleared her throat, and asked, businesslike, "This is where you found her?"

The sheets had been removed from the bed, but the mattress was stained with blood. Beret touched it with her fingertip, then examined the finger, but the blood had long since dried.

"She'd been covered up with her robe. That's odd, don't you

think?" Mick asked. "He'd stabbed her like that and then covered her up."

"As if he knew her," Beret said.

Mick considered the remark. "That's what I thought."

"Has the room been straightened?"

"Not so's you'd notice, but it wouldn't surprise me if the girls have gone through it. I don't see any five-dollar gold piece on the dresser."

Beret went to the bureau and opened the drawers. Lillie had never been neat, and the contents—underwear, stockings, gloves—were in disarray. Beret couldn't tell if Lillie had left them that way or if someone had rifled through them. "Did the police take her personal effects?"

"There weren't many, and we offered them to the judge. We pried open her trunk, but the only thing in there besides clothes and jewelry and a few trinkets was an envelope addressed to her at Judge Stanton's house. That's how we found out who she was. The judge was pretty shaken up when we told him. Mrs. Stanton, too. The clothes are here because Mrs. Stanton didn't want them."

"No letters? That's odd. Lillie always saved such things. She was sentimental." Beret went through the bureau again, slowly, but found nothing. On a whim, she turned over the drawers to see if anything had been attached to the underside. She searched the room, the wardrobe, looked into the pockets of Lillie's dresses, and was ready to give up when she reached under the mattress and touched something. As Mick watched, Beret drew out an envelope that was spattered with blood.

He grabbed it. "Let me see that. I'm the detective," he said.

"But I found it," Beret cried. The envelope had belonged to her sister. Beret had the right to it. She reached for the envelope, but Mick held it away from her and opened it, removing a sepia *carte de visite*, a small photograph mounted on cardboard. Mick studied it, then with a look of pity, he handed it to Beret. She clutched the photograph, then dropped it onto the floor as she covered her face with her hands. Mick picked it up, stared at the portrait of a young woman in a sable jacket, her hands tucked into a matching muff, then put it into his pocket.

"The woman, it's you," he said. "She kept a picture of you. Why, do you suppose?"

Beret didn't reply. She couldn't. Instead, she put her hands over her face and wept.

Chapter 6

Beret wiped her face on a handkerchief and mumbled an apology, which Mick shrugged off. Then the two went through the room once again, searching under the mattress, under the carpet, the inside of the wardrobe, the linings of dresses, but found nothing more to interest them. Beret put the dresses over her arm, and as the two started down the hall, she stopped at the door where she had glimpsed Elsie and handed them to the prostitute. "You may have what you like in Lillie's room. I don't want anything," Beret told her.

She and Mick went out and stood on the porch a moment, Beret gulping in the air, which was gray and sooty from coal smoke but still better than the air inside the whorehouse. The visit had overwhelmed her, and she took a moment to compose herself. A man walked past, eyeing Beret, but Mick gave him such a fierce look that he went on his way, muttering over his shoulder, "Too scrawny anyway."

"This has been difficult for you," Mick said. "I'll understand if you want to call it quits for today."

"Will you do so, too?"

"I get paid to do this," he replied. "I'm going to look for your sister's mac."

"Then I'll continue. You can't get rid of me so easily, Detective. I intend to go to the Arcade with you."

"It's not a place for a lady."

"Neither is the House of Dreams."

Mick choked off a retort, then blew out his breath and took Beret's hand. "Miss Osmundsen, you'll forgive me for saying so, but this whole investigation is no place for a lady. Do you think Teddy Star is going to talk about your sister in front of you? Things will go much faster if you'll let me do my job by myself, and I promise to keep you informed. I'll even take you with me if I think you might be of help. After all, we have the same goal. We both want to find your sister's killer, and you're hampering me in doing my job."

"Not so far. You are aware yourself that you knew nothing about Joseph Summers until I brought up his name. And his father." Beret said the last slowly, distastefully, because it was awful to have to say such a thing out loud. "If I find I am an impediment, I will withdraw, but for now, I intend to stick." She thought a moment. "I do not question that you want to find Lillie's murderer, but after all, this is just a case to you, and to-morrow, there will be another one. For me, however, the victim is my *sister*. No, Detective, I will not go home. And because I have my uncle's approval, you may not dismiss me."

"I feared you'd say that."

"There is one more thing I want to ask," Beret said slowly, thinking. "Was there any sign that my sister was a doper?"

Mick pondered the question. "I don't remember any needle

marks, but she was covered with blood, and I wasn't looking. Of course, she could have been on something that didn't need a needle. Why do you ask?"

"I'm not sure. Elsie had marks on her arm. I just thought it was possible . . ." Her voice trailed off.

"Maybe she was a snowbird. Cocaine doesn't leave a mark." Beret thought about that.

"I can't see that it matters much," Mick said.

"Maybe the man she let into the house sold her drugs."

"Could be. But we didn't find any sign of them in her room. I'd say she was clean that way."

He started off down Holladay Street, Beret beside him, as snow began to fall, heavy, wet, late-spring snow that drifted down from the sky. Beret pulled on her gloves, but Mick ignored the weather as he said, "I always despised a man who lived off a woman. I admit I hope the killer is Teddy Star or whatever his real name is. I expect he's scum."

"You don't know him?"

"I never heard of him. So he must be new around here. These leeches show up from time to time, get a girl or two on their string and make trouble. Then they disappear. There's always another to take their place. I wonder how your sister got involved with such a man. Maybe he did give her dope. I wouldn't be surprised." Beret said nothing, and Mick continued, "They're funny, these prostitutes, especially the pretty ones. It's not enough they got men willing to pay them for their company. They need somebody they think loves them, and when they find him, they can't do enough for him. Maybe they never had anybody care about them before."

Beret bit her lip. What Mick had suggested wasn't true. Lillie had never known anything except love.

"There's girls that don't have much choice but to turn out. I guess working in a mission, you know that. They get disgraced, and when their family finds out, they're kicked out. Or maybe they're starving and can't get any other job. Hooking's a lot nicer than going hungry, at least in the beginning. Some of them are widows with children. I don't know the reason your sister ended up in the House of Dreams." He turned to Beret as if he expected her to satisfy his curiosity, but she was silent. She didn't know, either.

"It's not such a bad job when you think about it—good food, nice bed, and the work isn't so hard," Mick said.

"Beatings from drunken sots, disease, drugs, ill-treatment from anyone they encounter, scorn. You wouldn't call that bad?"

Mick didn't reply, because they had retraced their steps and were now in front of the Arcade. "You sure you want to go inside?" he asked.

"I told you before, Detective, I have my reasons for accompanying you."

"You ever been in a gambling hall before—gambling *hell* they call it."

"Indeed I have."

"Not as a patron, I take it." Mick grinned to soften his words.

"To rescue girls. And to raise money to support the mission."

"By gambling?"

"From gamblers. Many of them are kindhearted and are happy to donate to help the needy. I've seen more than one give his entire night's earnings to help some poor unfortunate. I am surprised you don't know that."

"Oh, I know it." Mick looked at her sourly as he opened the door. "Of course I know it. Ladies first."

The Arcade was nicer—and smaller—than the gambling halls

Beret had seen in New York, dank warehouses with dirt floors and overflowing spittoons, whiskey spilled on the counter, drunks passed out on the floor, prostitutes searching their pockets. Instead, the Arcade was like a men's club with a wooden floor and a mahogany bar along one wall. The brass rail in front of it had been polished, and behind the bar, bottles were lined up in neat rows. A bartender, a starched white apron over his white shirt, poured a drink for a man standing in front of him. On the other side of the room under gaslights that hung from the ceiling, men were gathered at gaming tables and around a roulette wheel. There was the clatter of dice, a murmur of voices, as the men placed bets. Although it was early afternoon, the gambling hall was crowded. Many of the men were well dressed, bankers and mining men, merchants, visitors to the big city who had come to see the sights. They stood out from the gamblers and sporting men, who wore string ties and florid vests and did not appear to have much to say.

Beret scanned the room and saw that she was the only woman. The bartender must have been aware of that, too, because he frowned when he saw her. Mick led her to the bar. "Well, Harry, how are you this fine day?" he asked.

"Can't complain, Mick. Yourself?"

"The same. We're looking for someone."

"I thought so. You hoping to find a husband that's skipped out with the rent, are you?"

Beret gave the bartender a dark look, and Mick said quickly, "A fellow that goes by the name of Teddy Star, dark, swarthy. A mac, by all accounts, maybe new to the city. I'm told he hangs out here."

"'Tis a fine place." The bartender raised an eyebrow.

"Now don't be giving me any of your palaver, boyo. It looks

to me like someone I see over there at the faro table is only a lad. You wouldn't want me to report it to the chief that the Arcade caters to youngsters, now, would you?"

"Ah, Mick, your Irish comes out when you want something, does it not? I don't know the gentleman by name, but there is a dark fellow sitting with his back to you. I thought to throw him out the first time he came in, because he looked like a Negro. But he's as white as you and me, and the lady." He bowed to Beret.

"There's a good lad. I'll give you a pass the next time a complaint is made."

"So far, there's been none."

"I can see to that, too." As they turned away from the bar, Mick explained, "We're chums. We grew up together. Our dads were from Ireland and worked the mines together."

"And your Irish comes out when you talk to him?"

"I do what works, talking Irish to an Irishman, street talk to a tout, and proper English to a lady. Have you an objection?"

Beret didn't answer. Instead she stared at the back of the man the bartender had pointed out. Mick started for the table, but Beret stayed where she was, as if she couldn't move, gathering her courage. "Well, have you given up?" Mick asked, and Beret took a few steps, lagging behind the detective.

Mick went to the table and put his hand on the arm of the dark man. "I'd have a word with you," he said, showing his badge.

The man scowled. "And why would that be, Officer?"

"Are you Teddy Star?"

The other men seated at the table stopped playing to watch the detective, glancing from one to the other. Teddy Star threw down his hand. "I am. What's the complaint?"

"No complaint, but I have a few questions."

"Such as?"

"You want to discuss it here or in private?"

Teddy smirked as he told the others, "A misunderstanding. I'm out for now, but I'll be back when I clear this up. He's mistaken, whatever this is."

The men didn't care and returned to the game, while Teddy rose. He was broad, powerful, with black hair and dark skin. But his hands were small, almost a woman's hands. His face was handsome, the nose straight and long, and his eyes were like black diamonds. He moved gracefully, almost like a dancer. "Well, what is it?"

"Over there." Mick pointed to a table.

Teddy started for it, glancing back at Mick. He didn't see Beret, who was half-hidden behind the detective, and when he did, he ignored her. At first, that is. He took a step or two, and then as if the face finally registered, Teddy turned abruptly, and his mouth dropped. "Beret!"

"Yes."

"What are you doing here? What do you want?"

Beret thought for a moment she would faint. She was aware of the man's identity before she entered the Arcade, yet she was stunned to see him. She said in a voice that seemed to slice through him, "Lillie is dead. Or do you pretend not to know that? I've come to find her killer."

"You always did believe in vengeance." He smirked.

"With good reason."

Mick, confused, looked from one to the other. "You know him?" he asked Beret.

"Oh yes. He brought my sister to Denver."

"I did no such thing. You know that, Beret."

"But you're here, and you're her macquereau. Don't deny it."

Beret's face was pale, and the knuckles of her hands, clutching her purse, were white.

"I will deny it! I wouldn't stoop so low."

"No? Then how do you live? You were never much for work. Living off women seems to be the way you've always supported yourself."

The conversation was heated, and the men at the table stopped their game to stare, so Mick took Beret's arm, then turned to Teddy. "You! You come along." The three made their way to a corner and sat down.

The bartender came over with a bottle and three glasses and said, "If you're going to take up a table, Mick, I expect somebody to buy a drink. It's on the house for you and the lady." He lingered a moment, as if hoping to discover what was going on, but Mick waved him away. He offered the bottle to Teddy, who poured the liquor into a glass and drank it down in one gulp. Beret refused, and Mick set the bottle aside.

"He lured your sister to Denver to set her up as a prostitute?" Mick asked Beret. "I believe there's a law against that."

"That's a lie. She followed me."

"Only she got here first," Beret said.

Teddy glared at her. "You know she lived with the judge, not with me. Maybe he's the one who set her up as a whore."

"That is a disgusting thing to say, even for you, Edward. Did you kill her? Couldn't you stand the thought that after what happened she didn't love you after all? Did she discover you were a humbug and a fraud?"

Teddy blanched. He picked up the bottle and poured himself another drink, sloshing the liquor on the table.

Beret watched him, watched him lift the glass to his lips. Then his hand shook, and he spilled it over his shirtfront, wetting his embroidered vest. "You took that sweet child and ruined her. It was you who turned her into a whore." The exchange exhausted her, and she felt drained.

"I didn't. I swear I didn't. It was her idea. I tried to talk her out of it."

Beret leaned forward over the table, oblivious to the fact her coat sleeve was soaked with the spilled whiskey. "No, Edward, you put her there. You ruined her. And then you tried to live off her. You put her to work and took her money."

"And who are you to talk? You were the one who cut her off." Teddy leaned back, as if to get away from Beret. "I wouldn't take what she earned."

"You would. Oh, you would." She turned to Mick. "He is not above living off a woman." At that, she slumped in her chair, as if done with him.

Mick, who had not interfered in the exchange, turned to Teddy. "Did you kill her?"

"God, no!"

Beret's head jerked up, and she started to say something, but Mick put his hand on her arm. "Where were you when she was killed? That was two weeks ago come tomorrow."

"I was in Leadville. There's men there will vouch for me. I'll give you their names. I wouldn't hurt her. I loved her."

Beret stared at Teddy, her face like stone. She had never heard him say that, and the remark pierced her as if it were a knife slicing through a peach. She started to retort, but she could not. She hurt too much. She dug her nails into her palms so she would not cry.

It was Mick's turn now, and he hit the man with a barrage of questions. Teddy admitted that he had arrived in Denver months earlier, had followed Lillie to the city. He swore he wasn't the one who'd set her up at the House of Dreams, but when Mick asked how he supported himself, he said that Lillie had "loaned" him money. He hadn't known she was dead until after her funeral, he said.

"You were heard telling Miss Osmundsen not to see some man. Who was the man?"

"Who told you that?" Teddy asked.

"One of the girls at Miss Hettie's. Who was the john?"

"An old man. She teased me about him, said he wanted to marry her. She wouldn't tell me his name. Maybe she made it up."

After Mick finished his questions, he waved the man away. Teddy stood and stared down at Beret. "Beret, I'm sorry."

She wouldn't look at him, refused even to acknowledge his words.

"Maybe we can talk."

"Talk?" Beret flung the word back at him. "Oh yes, you are very good at talking. But do you think I would believe a word you said?"

"You always were a jealous shrew, my dear."

"Here, don't talk to her like that," Mick told him. Then he added, "Get out of here. Your kind makes me sick."

Teddy shrugged and started for the poker game he'd left, but then he changed his mind and went out onto the street.

Mick studied Beret for a moment, finally touching her arm and asking, "Are you all right, Miss Osmundsen?"

"No, of course I'm not all right. If it weren't for that man, my sister would be alive. He ruined her. She'd be alive if it weren't for him."

"Maybe, but if his story proves to be true, if he really was in Leadville, he didn't murder her. And if that's the case, there's nothing we can charge him with. If we charged every man who ruined a girl, the jails would be full."

"Then you should build larger jails, because whether he stabbed her or not, he's guilty. You are right, Detective, he is scum."

"You knew him, I take it." The remark was obvious, and the detective smiled a little as if to acknowledge that fact.

Beret nodded.

"Did you know him well?"

She thought that over. "You could say that. Quite well, in fact." Beret turned to stare out the door through which Teddy had disappeared. When she looked back at the detective, her face was rigid with pain. "His real name is Edward Staarman. He was my husband."

Chapter 7

Beret did not remember leaving the Arcade or making her way through the crowd as she and Mick crossed the street to the restaurant. She was badly shaken, and all she could think about was the awful confrontation with Teddy. The memories of his betrayal—his and Lillie's—consumed her. It was as if she were living it all over again. Not until she was seated did she come to her senses.

"Would you like tea or something stronger?" Mick asked. Beret focused her eyes, which were the color of the brooding sky outside, on the detective, not quite understanding. "Sherry perhaps?" he asked.

"I would like tea. And brandy."

Mick summoned the waiter and gave the order: tea and two brandies. Then he sat back and watched Beret, waiting.

She looked around the room and recognized the place then. It was Charpiot's Restaurant, "the Delmonico of the West," as it fashioned itself with gold letters over the entrance. Charpiot's had good reason to brag. It was Denver's finest restaurant, and Beret had been there before with her aunt and uncle. Unlike most of the other eating establishments she had seen in Denver with their stuffy and overbearing décor, Charpiot's was simply decorated, plain even, but elegant, very expensive, and well beyond a detective's salary. She wondered why Mick had brought her to such a fine place. Perhaps policemen ate there free, part of the graft that was so common in the cities. Mick did not strike her as an officer on the take, but no matter. She resolved to pay.

Neither of them said anything until after the waiter set down the tea and brandy, placing the cup and the glasses just so, adding a plate with lemon slices, a cream pitcher, a sugar bowl, setting down a polished silver spoon. He bowed a little, glanced at Mick to see if anything more was wanted, and then slipped away.

Mick waited until Beret picked up either her cup or her brandy, but when she continued to sit as still as stone, he said, "Well, Miss Osmundsen—or is it Mrs. Staarman?"

"Osmundsen," Beret said, shutting her eyes for a moment and taking a breath. "I resumed my maiden name when I divorced Edward. I didn't want anything of him remaining in my life. That was last year. What happened today is a shock, although I had suspected Edward had followed my sister here. Still, I never expected to see him again." She lifted the teacup but did not drink.

"So," he said, inviting her to continue.

"So, you want to know what happened, I suppose."

"It might help with the investigation."

"And satisfy your curiosity." She drank a bit of tea, then set down the cup and squeezed lemon into the brew. She couldn't blame him for being nosy. Perhaps he'd savor the story to tell his friends at the station. No, that was not fair, Beret decided. Mick had shown no inclination to gossip. Besides, whatever she could tell him about Teddy might indeed help the investigation. She wondered if she could be objective, then dismissed the concern. She did not care.

Mick sipped his brandy. "Yes, I suppose so. Do you want to talk about it?"

"I never have. Even my aunt and uncle don't know the story, only Lillie's version of it. And what they've figured out themselves, of course."

Mick nodded but didn't speak.

"You'd be the first to hear my side, except for my lawyer and our guardian, Lillie's and mine." She lifted the teacup again, then thought better of it and picked up her brandy glass, inhaled the scent, and tasted it. "I married Edward after my parents died. They'd known him and didn't care for him, actively disliked him, in fact. They'd warned me he was a fortune hunter, a wastrel. Perhaps if they'd been alive, I'd have seen the truth of it, but I was young and hadn't many suitors. Teddy was charming and had an air of sophistication about him. He comforted me after my parents died, let me cry on his shoulder and showed much sympathy, because he hadn't his parents, either, you see, and knew what it was like to be alone. And you saw for yourself, he is a handsome man." Much too handsome for her, Beret thought. Why hadn't she seen that? How often at the mission had she warned women about men who were too charming, too pretty, and yet she had been taken in by those very qualities every bit as much as they.

Beret waited until Mick said, "Go on."

She found herself wondering if the detective understood why she'd been attracted to Teddy. She wanted him to. "Of course, I had the care of Lillie then. She was eleven when our parents died. I was overwhelmed by the loss and the responsibility of looking after her. That was another reason I married. I didn't want to raise her by myself. And I was lonely, too. But mostly, I was in love." She stared into the liquid in the glass, which shimmered in the overhead gaslights. It was still afternoon outside, but the room was darkened by heavy velvet curtains.

"It was a lovely marriage. We went to the theater, the opera, to parties. On my own, I didn't much care for such things, but Edward loved the gay life, and I wanted to please him. I had my work at the mission, too, and he didn't mind that I was gone all day. That meant a great deal to me. Of course, later on, I thought perhaps he had been delighted that I was out of the way." Beret considered that for a moment and wondered how she could have been so trusting, so naïve. How stupid she'd been! Had she been too besotted to see through their charade of a marriage?

"Teddy lived the life of a gentleman. It didn't bother me that he had no work. I had enough money for both of us—the three of us, of course, because with Lillie, we were a threesome. Teddy and I never had children of our own, so in our way, we both became Lillie's parents." Beret smiled at the memory as she picked up the spoon and stirred her tea but left the cup in its saucer.

They had indeed had a lovely time. Beret remembered that first Christmas with Teddy, the three of them hanging the fragile glass ornaments on the tree, then lighting the candles. Teddy had stood by with a bucket of water in case the flames set the tree on fire, while Lillie and Beret opened their presents. There was a grown-up gown of velvet and lace and satin for Lillie, an ermine muff, a gold bracelet, and a pendant in the shape of a flower, covered with diamonds. It had belonged to Lillie and Beret's mother. Beret received a sable jacket and matching muff—the ones she had worn in the *carte de visite*. And she presented her husband with a fur-collared coat and an ebony walking stick with a gold knob.

Lillie hadn't believed in Santa Claus for a long time, of course.

Still, Teddy insisted she hang up her stocking by the fireplace, and after a dinner of roast goose and strawberry tarts, Beret and Lillie went to a midnight service at the cathedral. A groom drove them in a sleigh over snow-packed streets, sleigh bells ringing in the frigid air, the two young women covered with a fur blanket, their hands warm in their new muffs. Teddy said he had eaten too much goose and stayed behind. When the two returned, they heard the sound of bells in the parlor, and Teddy called, "Come quickly, Lillie. You've just missed the old gentleman." And when Lillie and Beret entered the room, Teddy, his face radiant, pointed at Lillie's stocking, bulging now, and a magnificent doll with real hair sitting beneath it.

For a moment, it appeared that Lillie really did believe in Santa again. How Beret had loved her husband for bringing that joy into their lives. Lillie clutched the doll to her breast. Although Lillie was too old for toys, Theodora, as the doll was named, became her favorite possession and remained on a chair in her room as long as she lived in the house. It was there still, Beret recalled. She wondered what had become of the pendant. Lillie must have taken it with her, because it was not among the things she'd left behind in New York. But it had not been found at the House of Dreams, either. Perhaps it had been stolen along with the diamond earrings. Recalling the necklace now, Beret asked Mick, "Was there a diamond pendant in the shape of a daisy found in my sister's room? It was our mother's, and Lillie wore it a great deal. She must have taken it with her to Denver, because it wasn't left behind in New York."

"No, nothing so fine. Her earrings were missing, but nobody said anything about a necklace."

"Perhaps she didn't wear it after she turned out. But it should have been there, in a drawer or else hidden somewhere."

"We searched the room pretty good—twice. You were there the second time. Is it valuable?"

"Rather. But it was the sentimental value that meant the most to us. Father gave it to Mother, and it was her favorite piece of jewelry. That was why I wanted Lillie to have it."

"Maybe she lost it."

"Perhaps." Beret thought about that. Or perhaps someone stole it. Maybe the pendant belonged to some other woman of the streets now, a prostitute who would think of it as a trinket, a paste bauble, not knowing how valuable it was, not caring what it had meant to the Osmundsen family.

"You were saying you had a good marriage, for a time anyway," Mick prompted.

"Oh yes, almost until the end, ten years. You see, I don't think it lasted very long, what happened between them . . ." Beret's voice trailed off. "Our guardian was generous, although not overly so. Father must have been concerned that I would marry Teddy or someone like him, so in his will, he specified that I would have charge of Lillie, but the estate would be administered by my godfather, a banker. Under normal circumstances, I suppose, my part of the estate would have gone to my husband, since by law, I couldn't control it. I was grateful later that Father had made the provisions he did, because that's the only reason Teddy didn't go through the money. He had enormous debts I didn't know about. To save face, I settled them after he left."

Mick finished his brandy and leaned back in his chair, waiting for Beret to continue.

For a moment, she was distracted by a couple who had entered the dining room and was being seated at a far table. The man, wearing a coat with a velvet collar, carried a walking stick with a gold knob that was similar to the one Beret had given Teddy that first Christmas. The woman was fashionably dressed in a gown with a tight bodice and a bustle, and she sat awkwardly, twisting in her chair, her legs to one side, attempting to find a comfortable position. As she removed her gloves, she glanced around the room, caught Mick's eye, and smiled. Mick nodded. Beret glanced at the detective with a questioning look, and he said, "A friend."

"You seem to know a great many people."

"As do you."

Beret wondered if he meant Teddy. She returned to her tea. As soon as she set down her cup, the waiter refilled it, then asked, "Would the lady and gentleman care for something to eat?"

"Soup?" Mick asked her.

Beret shook her head, and Mick told the waiter to bring him another brandy. After the man left, Mick leaned forward and asked, "And what happened?"

The question would have been rude in other circumstances, but Mick was a detective investigating a murder. Beret did not take offense. "I think you can guess." She straightened the fingers of her gloves, which had been lying on the table, then folded the gloves together, not wanting to continue the conversation but knowing she had to. So at last, she sighed and said, "I don't know when it started. Or how, but as I said, I don't think it went on for long, less than a year, maybe only months, perhaps just weeks. Lillie adored Teddy. I suppose she had a crush on him. I never suspected anything, because she had such a busy social life, dozens of suitors. Several had asked Teddy for her hand, but Lillie was having too good a time to get married. Or at least, that's what I thought." She glanced at the woman across the room, who was engaged in conversation.

"It was a Monday, the servants' day off. I'd said I'd be at the mission all day, but I'd come home with a sick headache. That was when I caught them. They were together. In our bed. Can you imagine, Detective? In my very own bed, the one I had slept in ever since I was a girl." Beret shook her head and tried to blink back tears, as she recalled the horror of opening the door and finding the two of them, naked, lying on a spread of cut velvet. Later, she'd told the housekeeper to burn the spread, but there was no way to burn away the memory.

Beret took out a handkerchief then and dabbed at her eyes. "I am so sorry. This is not easy for me. Can you imagine how violated I felt, not only to catch them but to catch them in *my* bed? Perhaps you can't. You deal with the refuse of life, as do I. Such an occurrence must seem unimportant when you compare it with what others we come into contact with have suffered— beatings, rapes, abandonment. But I had not expected such a thing in my perfect marriage. I was shocked, then hurt, then out- raged." She felt the emotions all over again and could not con- tinue.

Mick reached across the table and patted her hand, and Beret was touched by the unexpected intimacy. Beneath the tough exterior of a police officer, he seemed to be a nice man. The waiter set down Mick's glass, and Mick asked Beret, "Would you like more brandy?"

"Yes, I believe I would."

The officer nodded at the waiter and gave the order. Beret put away her handkerchief and smiled a little. "I have turned into a great embarrassment."

"Not at all. I do understand, you know."

"Thank you."

The waiter returned with the brandy, and Beret took a sip. "I behaved badly. I saw that later on, when it was too late. I blamed Lillie when I should have blamed Teddy. I should have known at the time that he had flattered her, seduced her, taken advantage of her. It's the way men do things. How could she have resisted him? I couldn't, you know. After all, I married him!" Beret shook her head at the truth of what she'd said. "You would think after working with so many poor women who'd been abused by their husbands or been forced to sacrifice their honor to their employers that I would have known the man was always at fault. But I'm afraid I reacted like a typical scorned woman. I blamed the other woman—my sister." She almost gulped her brandy.

"And now, do you think she was at fault, too?"

"I don't know." It was a question she had asked herself over and over again in the past few days, ever since she had learned that Lillie had died in a house of prostitution. Had her sister indeed been the temptress? Had she, not Teddy, been the seducer? Beret shook her head to rid herself of the idea, although she was no longer sure.

"You threw them out of the house then." It was a statement, not a question.

Beret nodded. "It was my house." She thought a moment. "It was our house, Lillie's and mine, our parents' house, that is, but neither one of us thought about that. Lillie was so used to deferring to me that she didn't realize she had as much right as I did to stay there."

"But she had money, didn't she?"

"That's the terrible thing I did." Beret glanced down at her hands, too ashamed to look the detective in the eye. "You see, I talked with our guardian. I confided what had happened, told him Lillie was at fault. He's a priggish man, unctuous even, and he was always anxious to please me. I have thought he might even have hoped I'd marry him after Teddy was gone. Perhaps that's why he was so anxious to do my bidding. I told him Lillie should be cut off until she saw the error of her ways and apologized, and that's exactly what he did. He found some reason or other to justify it, a morals clause that was in the will as a matter of course. Lillie didn't know she should protest. Uncle John—Judge Stanton, that is—would have told her what action to take, but I suppose Lillie never discussed it with him. It was abominable of me to have done what I did."

"But understandable," Mick said.

Beret looked at him, surprised again at the sympathetic words coming from a policeman. She sipped at the brandy. "It wasn't quite as bad as you think. I didn't mean for her to be cut off forever. I wanted to teach her a lesson. I thought she'd return, be contrite, beg me for forgiveness."

"Grovel, you mean."

Beret thought that over. Had she been so reprehensible? She nodded. "Yes, I suppose that's it." She looked into her cup at the tea. "I missed her so. I didn't miss Teddy so much, but I missed Lillie. She was the one I'd loved most. I loved her, and I hated her at the same time. Can you understand that?"

The question was rhetorical this time, but nonetheless, the detective answered, "Yes."

"Really?"

Mick shrugged. "So the two of them came to Denver."

"That's the odd thing. Lillie came by herself. Teddy stayed in New York, thinking I'd take him back. He sent me flowers and jewelry. All very expensive." She gave a laugh. "I know, because the bills came to me."

"Did you consider taking him back?"

The question was forward, but Beret saw no reason not to answer it. She had told him everything else. "Not once. My love for him died when I opened that bedroom door. My parents had been wrong about him; he was far worse than Father had imagined. Teddy was greedy and selfish, and he was ugly inside. He took pleasure in my humiliation. Do you know what he did when I discovered him in bed with my sister?" Beret thrust her chin forward, her eyes limpid, a look of utter desolation on her face. "He laughed."

"Miss Osmundsen . . ."

"No. I'll tell you all of it. He told me I was old, dried up, an embarrassment to him with my plain clothes and mugwump life. He said he and his friends laughed at me, that he'd married me only for the money. Of course, he took it all back later on when he realized he had nothing on which to live. But it was too late. I'd seen him for what he was. I had a very good lawyer. Teddy didn't get a penny. Of course, Lillie . . ." Here Beret's voice faltered. "As I said, I arranged for her to be cut off, too, and I suppose I'll go to hell for it."

"Perhaps you've already been there," Mick said so softly that Beret barely heard him.

"No, but Lillie has."

Mick asked if she wanted more brandy, but she declined. They were silent for a long time, until Mick asked, "So they came out here?"

"Lillie did. As I said, Teddy stayed in New York until he realized I wasn't going to take him back. Then he disappeared. I had no idea he'd followed Lillie to Denver. I knew that she was with Aunt and Uncle, of course. My aunt wrote me when Lillie arrived. She knew the two of us had had a falling-out, and she told me we ought to make amends, that we were family and could not let a misunderstanding, no matter how serious, come between us. Family is very important to her, because my aunt and uncle have no one but Lillie and me—that is, me now. But after a while, she stopped mentioning Lillie in her letters, so I supposed she'd figured out what had happened. Or maybe Lillie told her, probably not all of it, but enough so that they knew. They hadn't liked Teddy, either. I'm sure they blamed him."

"But he came here eventually."

"Evidently."

"And do you think that was when she moved into Miss Hettie's?"

Beret shook her head. "I don't know. Of course, Teddy knew where she was. He surely was the dark-complexioned man seen talking to Lillie. And it seems my sister gave Teddy money. He must have made her think she was responsible for my divorcing him. I hate him for that. But whether he introduced her to Miss Hettie, I don't know. I'll have to ask Miss Hettie."

"*We'll* have to ask," Mick corrected her.

"Yes, of course."

"You won't go there by yourself, will you?"

Beret smiled for the first time since they had entered the restaurant. "Not this time of day, Officer McCauley." The tea and brandy had warmed her, and she unbuttoned her jacket.

"Do you think your husband, your *former* husband, killed your sister?"

Beret considered that for a long time. "I've wondered that since the girl from Miss Hettie's told us she'd seen Lillie with Teddy. I never would have thought he was capable of such a thing, although I would like him to be the one. Perhaps he is. It seems obvious, doesn't it?"

"Unless he was in a poker game."

Beret gave Mick a disdainful look. "Do you believe that?"

"I'll check it out."

"Yes, of course." She ran her tongue over her teeth. "He has a temper, but at heart, he's a weak man. I don't think he has"— Beret considered her words carefully—"the *gumption* to kill anybody. And if Lillie was giving him money, why would he murder his meal ticket?"

"Maybe she refused to support him anymore."

Beret nodded. "That could be."

"And maybe he discovered she was pregnant. Dr. Death . . . that is, the coroner, thinks she was four or five months along. Has your husband been here that long?"

"That would have happened after she left New York, since she had been gone a year." Beret thought back. "Teddy was in New York four months ago. I remember that because it was All Saints' Eve, when so much mischief is done. He came by the house, asking me to change my mind. And I saw him in December, on the street near the mission. He was with a woman, a prostitute, it appeared, and he turned a corner thinking I wouldn't see him, I suppose, but I did. I don't know if he was in New York all that time. He could have come to Denver, then gone back East."

"Or maybe someone else was the father of your sister's child."

"The legendary rich man who is going to leave his wife?" Beret almost laughed. She picked up her cup and sipped, but the tea was cold, and she set it down. Immediately, the waiter appeared with a fresh cup and poured hot tea into it. "It seems that if she had been at Miss Hettie's for only three months or so that she was pregnant before she turned out. It happened when she was living with my aunt and uncle. That means it couldn't have been a john, so it must have been Teddy—unless she met someone after she came to Denver, one of the Summers men perhaps." Beret pondered that. "Do *you* think Edward killed Lillie?"

Mick looked down at his hands. "I don't know. It's not un-heard of, a mac murdering a working girl."

Beret winced at the words.

"But what was his motive? There's only one person I can think of with a real motive to want Lillie dead."

"Who?" Beret frowned.

Mick stared at her a long time. "You."

"Me?" Beret's hand holding the teacup shook, and she looked up, startled.

"You've just told me you hated her, that she ruined your marriage."

"But I was in New York at the time. You know that."

"I do, but you could have hired someone. It wouldn't be un-usual with your mission work to come across a man who would be more than happy to kill your sister for a railroad ticket and a few dollars. And as you've said, you have more than a few dollars."

Beret was horrified. "Surely you don't believe that. I wanted to humiliate her, not kill her. I may have wanted things on my terms, but I never hoped she would die."

Mick held his hands in front of him, the fingers pressed to-gether. "Does it make sense? Yes. Do I believe it? No. I think whoever killed your sister knew her. The murder was too vi-cious, too personal. A hired killer would have stabbed her once, maybe twice, but not eight times."

"But you haven't dismissed the idea of my culpability en-tirely."

"No."

"And what can I do to convince you of my innocence?"

"I suppose you could help me find the killer."

Beret smiled a little. "Then you accept my help?"

"I have no choice, do I?"

"No, you don't." Beret stared at Mick until he looked away. "Do you think we should talk to Joseph Summers next?"

"I do, but not until another time. You've had enough for one day." He looked around for the waiter but instead caught the eye of the woman he had nodded to earlier. She and her companion were on their way out of the restaurant, but she stopped when she saw Mick looking at her, and when the man accompanying her paused to greet someone, the woman walked to the table. "Why, hello, Mick. I'd have come to give you my regards earlier, but you were so engaged in conversation, I'd thought you might be interviewing a murder suspect." She laughed at the absurdity of what she'd said and turned to Beret. "He has such a ghastly occupation, don't you agree?"

"Why, I do agree," Beret said, amused.

Mick had stood when the woman approached the table, and now he said, "Caro, may I present Miss Osmundsen of New York. Miss Osmundsen, this is Mrs. Decker."

Caroline stared hard at Beret, and said, "You are Lillie's sister, then. I did not know she had one. I am so sorry. You must forgive my insensitivity at making such a crude joke. Lillie was a lovely girl."

"You knew her?" Beret asked.

"Through Judge and Mrs. Stanton, of course. I called on them after her death. Not many did, I'm afraid. But I always cared for Lillie. She was such fun, so lively. We all adored her."

Beret was touched and liked the woman immediately, thinking her kind to have overlooked the last months of Lillie's life and her grisly death to extend condolences to the Stantons. She was not surprised others, not knowing what to say, had shunned her aunt and was grateful to the woman that she hadn't smirked or exchanged glances with the detective when she realized who Beret was. "Thank you. I know my aunt and uncle were crushed at my sister's death. As was I."

"Are you staying in Denver long?"

"I'm not certain."

"Well, I hope so. We hope to take you up, don't we, Mick? We'll try to occupy your mind with something besides your sorrow." She touched her gloved hand to Beret's shoulder, then turned to Mick. "We've missed you."

He bowed his head slightly to acknowledge her words. "I've been busy."

"Well, I hope you solve this dreadful murder." She nodded at Mick, then turned to Beret and said, "Miss Osmundsen," and joined her companion, leaving behind the scent of perfume. Mrs. Decker whispered something to the man with her, and he turned and waved at Mick.

"Decker." Mick nodded in acknowledgment.

"She's very gracious. I like her," Beret said. "Who are they?"

"Decker is a banker, rather stuffy, with a small fortune of his own. He invests his money—hers, too—and I'm sure he's good at it. Her father's a very successful mining investor." He paused. "His name is Evan Summers. Caro's brother is Joey."

Beret's head shot up, and she looked for the woman, but Caroline was gone.

"Mrs. Decker is Joey Summers's sister," Mick repeated.

A look of disgust came across Beret's face. "She seemed like such a nice woman."

"She is, not at all like her father and brother."

"How do you know her?"

"We grew up together."

"You mean just as you grew up with the bartender at the Arcade?"

Before Mick could answer, the waiter set a check on the table near Mick. He picked it up, but Beret said, "That is my expense, Detective."

"Not at all," Mick said.

"Please. Charpiot's is a very expensive restaurant. I do not mean to insult you, but I know what a detective is paid, and I don't want you to have to eat beans for the next week to make up for your kindness to me."

Mick took out a gold coin and set it on top of the check. "You cannot keep picking up the restaurant checks, Miss Osmundsen. I believe I should clear up a misunderstanding. I do not live on a detective's salary. My father might have been an Irish immigrant, but he was a very successful one. He owns hardware stores in Denver and Leadville. My parents move in the same circle as your aunt and uncle. I can well afford to pick up the tab for tea and brandy at Charpiot's. In fact," he added with a sly smile, "I could even afford to buy you dinner here."

"So, you are wealthy. Then why do you work as a policeman?"

"Why do you work in a mission?"

Beret mulled that over as she rose. "To be of service. I am of that group of people who believe that with wealth comes responsibility." Then something occurred to her. "Your wealth puts you among the smart set of Denver's young people. You must know Joey Summers personally?"

"I do."

Beret took her inquiry one step further. "And my sister, did you know her?"

"I met her." He paused a moment, then taking Beret's elbow,

steered her toward the door. "But I did not recognize her body when I first saw it. She was covered in blood, and to tell you the truth, I didn't know she lived at Miss Hettie's. I didn't know who she was until we went through her trunk and came across your aunt and uncle's names."

Beret thought about that as she pulled on her gloves, straightening them over the backs of her hands. She asked suddenly, "Most men who met Lillie fell in love with her. Were you one of them?"

Mick studied her for a long time, before he said, "No."

"Are you now?"

"Miss Osmundsen, your sister is dead."

Chapter 8

No more snow had fallen while the two were in the restaurant, but the wind had picked up, and Beret shivered as she left the overheated building. The day was ugly. Denver, too, was ugly, she thought, raw and unrefined, too new yet to have much style. Clouds hung over the city, holding down the smoke that came from the coal- and wood-burning stoves and turned the air dingy. The wind blew dried leaves along the streets. A newspaper swirled overhead and swooped down on Beret, attaching itself to her back like an angry bat, and she flailed about trying to remove it, but the paper held fast.

Mick came to her aid, ripped off the newspaper, and crumpled it in his hand. Then as he dropped it into the gutter, he stared hard at someone who was moving quickly in and out of the crowd on the sidewalk, moving low to the ground as if he didn't want to be seen. Beret saw Mick's eyes narrow and followed his gaze as the man disappeared around a corner.

"I've seen him before. Last week, he was outside the restaurant where we met Elsie. I saw him through the window, but I didn't pay any attention to him. I thought he was just a tout.

There are a thousand like him on the street. But it's odd he would be at both places. I don't much like coincidences."

"Perhaps he is following you, Detective," Beret teased.

"It's more likely he's following you. I think I'd better see you home."

"No need, Officer. I know the man."

"You do?"

"After all, you said I knew a great many people, so it shouldn't surprise you." She waited for him to respond, but Mick didn't seem to remember the remark, so she said, "He's a former newsboy who was beaten by a group of bullies."

"From New York? That would be quite a coincidence, indeed. Did he follow you here?"

"Oh no." Beret paused, enjoying Mick's confusion. "He is my aunt's groom. He brought me to the police station."

"And now he's following you? He looks familiar. I've encountered him somewhere."

"He is harmless, Detective. Uncle says the poor man is indebted to my aunt for taking him in. You see, two years ago or thereabouts, she rescued him from the bully boys and took him to a hospital. Then she hired him to work in my uncle's stable. His name is Jonas Silk. Uncle says Jonas feels he let my aunt down by not protecting Lillie, although how he could have prevented her murder, I don't know. I wonder that he knew Lillie had become a prostitute, but I suppose men like that always know. Anyway, he has taken it upon himself to protect Aunt and Uncle and, by extension, me."

Mick mulled that over, thinking. "Jonas Silk. Now I remember him. He's not a very attractive fellow, is he? He looks demented."

Beret chuckled. "Surely, sir, you and I are too experienced to judge a book by its cover." She held out her hand. "Now if you'll excuse me, I am going to take the streetcar home, since any hope I had of riding in my aunt's carriage seems to have been frightened away."

Beret had no intention of boarding the streetcar again, but she feared that if she told Mick of her plans to walk to the Grant Avenue home, the detective, unsure about what Jonas was doing on Larimer Street, would put her into a hack. Or he might even insist that he take her home himself. She did not want that, because of the chance of his encountering her aunt or uncle. She didn't want Mick upsetting them by mentioning they had talked with Teddy. Mick might want to interrogate Jonas, and that would infuriate her aunt. Varina might be angry enough to demand that Beret stay out of the investigation. Besides, Beret had thinking to do, and walking cleared her mind.

She started toward the streetcar stop, just in case the detective was watching, but paid little attention to where she was going and was startled to hear a voice call, "Beret!" She stopped, confused, hoping the detective had not deduced her plans to go on foot. But he would not have called her by her first name, and she knew almost no one else in Denver. Then she realized, disgust building up inside her, that she was in front of the Arcade, and the voice came from just inside. Teddy.

She cringed, and her stomach felt sour, and she hurried on, but Teddy rushed out of the gambling hall and grabbed Beret's arm and held her. "Let go of me," she said, her voice a harsh rasp.

"I have to talk to you."

"There is nothing to say that hasn't been said already." Beret closed her eyes for a moment, recalling the angry words that still taunted her and perhaps always would. She felt the bitterness that had been her constant companion for the past year.

"Please. Let me take you someplace where we can get out of the wind. Would you like tea?"

"I have already had my tea. Let go of me, Edward."

But Teddy wouldn't. "I have something to say to you."

"There is nothing you can say that I care to hear." She looked with loathing at the hand on her arm, but Teddy did not let go. What more could he possibly say? One thing, Beret thought, and told him, "The only thing I want to hear from you is why you murdered my sister."

"I didn't. You know I didn't. I told you that already."

"You've told me a great many things that weren't true."

"I mean it, Beret. I never would have hurt her, although she's not what you think—wasn't what you thought, that is."

Beret yanked her arm away and looked at Teddy fiercely. She had already realized the truth of what he said, but she would not hear those words from him. "How dare you say that! You know as well as I do that Lillie was an innocent child and you ruined her life."

"She wasn't innocent at all. You loved her too much. You didn't see her clearly."

Beret seethed with fury. "Will you tell me then that she seduced you, that she joined a brothel by choice so that she could outfit you in the fashion to which you'd become accustomed by Osmundsen money? You have sunk very low indeed, Edward."

"I never took her money."

"Not at first, of course. I made sure of that. But later on, when what you had gotten from me stopped, didn't you send her to work at Miss Hettie's so that she could pay your gambling debts?"

Teddy started to protest, but Beret put up her hand. "Oh yes,

I know about your gambling. The debt collectors came to me, threatened me, threatened the Osmundsen name, so I paid, paid thousands of dollars. Lillie could not have underwritten your gambling if she had"—Beret considered her words—"slept with every filthy vagrant on Larimer Street. That's what you turned her into, you know—a whore, available to any vag with a little money."

Teddy flinched. "That's not true." He grabbed Beret's arm again and glared at her with such anger that she felt a flicker of fear. She had despised him, had hated him, but she had never been afraid of her husband. In all their quarreling at the time of the divorce, he had never struck her, never raised his hand or even threatened her. Beret wondered what her words had unleashed. If he had killed Lillie, whom he loved, wouldn't he as easily kill her?

Beret was not a timid woman. In her mission work, she had been threatened by drunken fathers, self-righteous husbands, malicious pimps, sometimes even the women themselves, and she had stood her ground. But she faltered now as she looked into Teddy's eyes. She took a step backward and said, "Detective McCauley is contacting the men whose names you gave him, and we shall see if you were in Leadville when Lillie was killed. Neither the detective nor I believe you are innocent."

The anger in Teddy's eyes faded. "I did not kill her, Beret. I swear I didn't. How many times do I have to tell you?"

"And drugs. Did you give her drugs?"

Teddy's eyes widened.

"Yes, I knew you took opiates. It seems you owed the man who sold them to you. He came to me for payment. Did you give drugs to Lillie?"

"Are you saying Lillie was a doper?"

Beret wasn't sure. The housekeeper told her after Lillie left that a maid had discovered a strange substance hidden in Lillie's room, but she had thrown it out. So Beret hadn't known whether it was an opiate or face powder or ordinary flour, for that matter. Many of the women who came to the mission were addicted to drugs. So were some of the members of New York society. When Beret discovered that Teddy experimented with drugs, she could not help but wonder if he had shared them with Lillie. Drugs would explain why her sister had moved into a brothel. Someone— Teddy or maybe Joey Summers—could have provided her with them, and then later on, Lillie could have purchased them from Miss Hettie or one of the other girls, maybe Elsie. Beret hadn't discussed that with the detective sergeant, hadn't wanted him to know she was convinced Lillie was a doper. "I have nothing more to say to you," she told Teddy abruptly.

"But I have so much I want to say to you. I have made a beastly mess of our lives—yours and mine and poor Lillie's. I would give anything if I could take it back."

"Well, you can't, can you? Besides, you have just told me it was Lillie's fault."

"And mine. I will own up to that. I should not have let it happen. I have been unfaithful and cruel, and I have broken your heart."

Beret heard a warmth and sincerity in his voice that had not been there for a long time, but told herself she would not be seduced by it. After all, for the past year, Teddy had been out in the underworld of men who preyed on women for a living. He would have perfected the honeyed words they used to get what they wanted, not that he hadn't known them already. "It was not you who broke my heart. It was Lillie. She was the one I loved. When I found out what you were, I was glad to be rid of you. I could not believe I had married such a scoundrel."

"You loved me once."

"You laughed at me! I caught the two of you together, and you laughed." Beret took a deep breath to control herself. "Please, Teddy, you've already said everything there is to say, and it hasn't worked for you. I don't want to hear any more. No matter what you say, I have no intention of taking you back."

"I don't dare even to hope for that. I'm asking for your forgiveness."

Humility was a virtue Beret did not know her husband possessed, and for a second, she was moved, tempted. Did he mean what he'd said, or was he only being clever? She must be wary. "Forgive you for murdering my sister?"

"No. I told you I didn't kill her. I want you to forgive me for destroying what was between us, not for taking Lillie's innocence, but for taking yours."

Beret shuddered. "I was not so innocent. I knew the way of the world. I just did not believe my husband was no better than the brutes I encountered through the mission. You are worse than they, because they don't know any better. But you, Teddy, you were raised as a man of conscience, a gentleman. You are the guiltier one."

"I won't deny it." He paused as Beret began to shake. "You are cold. I will take you to your uncle's house. You are staying with him, of course. We can talk there."

"Never! They despise you." She cut him off. She would not allow him anywhere near the Stanton house.

"I still love you," he said, his voice almost a whisper. "I loved you once, you know, and I never stopped."

"Not even when you loved Lillie?" Her voice was thick with scorn. She would not let him know how his words tormented her. She had loved him, too, and maybe beneath the hurt and anger, she still did. Would she ever love anyone else as she had Teddy?

He was silent for a moment, rubbing his hand over the gold knob on his walking stick, the one she had given him that first Christmas. Had he loved her then? Beret stared at her former husband, observing for the first time that he had changed. His face, once puffy from good living, was leaner, harder. He had lost weight, but his clothes fit well. Had Lillie paid for them? He was still a handsome man, perhaps even better looking than he had been, less boyish, more mature.

"I lusted for her. I did not love her as I did you," Teddy said.

Beret felt tears form in her eyes, and she rubbed them, complaining about the dirt the wind blew up. No one, not Teddy nor any other man had ever lusted after her. "You are obscene," she said hoarsely. Then she could not stop herself from asking, "How long, Teddy? How long did it go on?" The question had tortured her ever since she had caught them together. It had not been their first time. She knew that. Thinking back, she had realized there were secret smiles between them, touches that were not accidental, excuses that had put them together without her. The thought that the affair might have gone on for years ate at her soul.

Teddy swallowed. "Not long. A few weeks."

She stared at him, then abruptly she turned and started off, not slowing when Teddy called her name. She did not turn around, did not know how long he stood in front of the Arcade looking after her, only knew at some point that he was not behind her.

The anger and distress drove Beret on, and she hurried along the streets. Her heart had begun to heal, a little at any rate, and then she had had to encounter Teddy. She remembered his touch, her hand on his arm, his hand on her cheek. Theirs had been an affectionate marriage, and she wondered if any man would ever touch her the way Teddy had. Those years had been precious, filled with gaiety and caring. She had loved him so much, and surely he had loved her a little. He'd been good to her, kind and courtly. Would she ever allow another man to get that close, knowing as she did now that Teddy had been after her money? She would always wonder if any man who showed an interest cared only about her fortune.

She slowed her steps and took note of where she was. She had left the business district with its crowds of people and conveyances and had come upon a residential area of early Denver mansions, homes that already were being deserted by Denver's upper class for the fashionable Capitol Hill district. Her aunt and uncle had once lived in this neighborhood, until they moved into their Grant Avenue mansion. The homes here were simpler, less pretentious, befitting a first generation just coming into money, just starting to experiment with lavish possessions. The houses were tall, stately, with long Italian windows and iron cresting on their roofs, iron fences outlining the lots, here and there a mansard roof. Families still lived in the houses, but there were discreet ROOMS TO LET placards in some of the windows. On closer inspection, Beret could see signs of neglect—bare wood where the paint had been scoured off by the weather, roofs that needed patching, broken fences, gardens let go.

A SOLICITOR sign hung over the doorway of one of the houses, and a man emerged, staring at Beret as if wondering what she was doing there. Other homes, too, had been turned into office buildings and boardinghouses. Then she recognized the house her aunt and uncle had lived in before they built the Grant Avenue mansion. It was dowdy and needed paint. The stable behind it was now a blacksmith shop. Beret found the change unsettling. She remembered, as a girl, visiting her aunt and uncle and loving their sleek house with its gazebo set in a carefully tended garden, a groom taking her about in a pony cart.

Jonas might have replaced that groom. Beret thought then about the strange man her aunt had hired. Perhaps Mick was right that something was not quite right about him. He was an odd creature, small, bent, with strange eyes that didn't seem to focus. There was something disconcerting about the way he moved around the grounds, silent, peering into windows. Was he really protecting the Stantons—and her—or was it something else, a perverted curiosity, perhaps? At least he stayed outside, or did he? She remembered waking in the night and finding the blanket over her. She'd supposed her aunt or uncle had covered her, but now she realized if they'd discovered her asleep in the library, they'd have awakened her and sent her to bed. Did Jonas have the run of the house? She dismissed the idea. A servant had put the blanket over her, the butler or perhaps one of the maids. The girl would have been too timid to wake Beret. That was it, of course, but Beret still didn't like the idea of Jonas creeping about.

Then she was ashamed of herself. How many of the poor people she'd encountered at the mission, people who had been arrested and jailed, had later gone to work in the homes of her friends, with Beret insisting they were harmless? She herself had hired some of those with the most heinous records. Her housekeeper, Maggie, for instance, had killed her brute of a husband with a butcher knife after she caught him raping their daughter, a girl of five. Maggie had been found guilty, but Beret had promised the judge she would be responsible for her if he let her off with a warning. Beret had argued that giving Maggie a job instead of sending her to prison would turn her into a useful woman—and keep the child, Sabra, from the streets. Maggie had proven an exemplary worker, and Sabra was a charming little girl who was now in grammar school. Lillie had loved the child, Beret thought now, and Teddy had, too. He had not once complained because Beret had brought a convicted murderer and her daughter into their household.

So what right did she have to fear Jonas, who as far as she knew had never been convicted of anything? It was Lillie's murder that had made her suspicious of everyone. Beret put the man out of her mind.

The light outside was dim now. Beret unfastened the tiny watch hanging from her coat and checked the time. It was after five. She did not mind the dark coming on—she was rarely fearful—but her aunt would be worried, and Beret did not want to cause her distress, so she picked up her pace. The decaying neighborhood gave way to terraces, more fashionable than the old houses, more economical, too, because they did not require so many servants. Beret wondered if she ought to leave her parents' house for a smaller place, a flat that would accommodate her and Maggie and Sabra, a cook, perhaps a manservant, for it would be a good idea to have a man in the house. She'd been reluctant to part with the home in which she'd spent most of her life. She'd wanted to keep it for Lillie, but Lillie wouldn't be returning. And now Beret thought it was foolish for her to maintain such a large household.

She watched a man open the front door of one of the apartments and saw a child rush past a woman and cry, "Daddy!" Beret hurried on, thinking she would never again be part of a family. She would never hear a child's cries of greeting, never see a husband come through the door. Her divorce didn't preclude her marrying again, but she would never be sure about any man who courted her. She had married one fortune hunter. She would not marry another.

As she started up the hill, she became aware that a carriage had been moving alongside her, keeping pace with her. Now she recognized it as her aunt's and looked up to see Jonas. "You've been following me," Beret said.

"Mrs. Stanton sent me to fetch you, miss. She worry you out in the dark." He stepped down from his seat and opened the carriage door for Beret.

"You followed me earlier today, long before it got dark."

Jonas said nothing.

"Didn't you?"

"The Stantons don't want nothing to happen to you."

"I think I am quite safe when I am with Detective Sergeant McCauley."

"You shouldn't be out in these dark times. It's not fittin'."

Beret started to get into the carriage, but stopped. "Jonas, has my aunt sent you to spy on me?"

"No, ma'am."

"Then why were you creeping along Larimer Street, peering into windows to see what I was doing?"

A cry escaped Jonas's lips. "I don't want nothing to happen to you, either, like Miss Lillie."

Beret felt sorry for the boy then. "I am not the inmate of a brothel. Nobody is going to hurt me. My sister was killed by a man who wanted her dead. Or maybe a woman." She wondered why she had said that. "It could be a woman," she mused out loud. "I will have to discuss that with Detective Sergeant McCauley." Then she stepped into the carriage, and as Jonas closed the door, Beret added, "There is nothing you could have done to prevent my sister's murder."

"Maybe there was."

Chapter 9

You mustn't mind Jonas, Beret," Varina said at breakfast several days later. Beret and Varina had spent time making social calls on the wives of the judge's political backers, a duty the younger woman found irksome. But she was a guest and must do her aunt's bidding. Besides, she loved her uncle and hoped to see him become a senator. He would do a fine job. Varina had not appeared at dinner the night before because she was feeling ill. Now she sat in her morning gown at the breakfast table in the solarium. The room was festooned with ferns and other plants, and in the morning sun, it seemed like spring. Beret liked that about Denver: one day could be blustery and cold, the next filled with sunshine.

The judge, too, had been away the previous evening, and Beret had dined alone. She had seen Jonas snooping about the house and decided to tell her aunt and uncle. "I have caught him following Detective McCauley and me, too. He makes me uneasy," she'd said. Now she tried to be lighthearted. "Did you send him to protect me, Aunt Varina? It's not necessary. You know I deal with criminals every day. I can take care of myself."

"Of course you can." Varina exchanged a look with her husband. "Jonas just seems to be obsessed with the safety of this family. It doesn't do any harm to be careful."

"He's the most loyal young man I've ever met. There isn't anything he wouldn't do for your aunt," the judge added. "I admit he is a bit odd, but he means no harm. I have had him checked out, and I see no reason not to trust him. If anything, he goes overboard in his possessiveness, and that's not a bad thing if it keeps your aunt safe." He smiled at his wife and patted her hand. She gave him a hint of a smile in return and withdrew her hand to pick up her fork. "You are not unlike your aunt, Beret, in taking in unfortunates. As I recall, your housekeeper has an unsavory history."

Beret couldn't deny that. "Jonas said he might have prevented Lillie's death," she told them.

Her aunt and uncle exchanged a glance. Then Varina sighed. "Yes, he seems to feel if he had been more vigilant, he could have protected her. He broods on it, I think. But how could he have saved Lillie?"

"You've seen Edward?" the judge asked, changing the subject.

Beret had not wanted to discuss her interview with her former husband for fear of upsetting the couple, but now that the judge seemed to know what had gone on, she saw no reason to deny it. "Yes, at some horrible little gambling den. He insists he was in a poker game in Leadville when Lillie was murdered."

"Was he?"

"We'll see. Detective Sergeant McCauley is looking into it."

"I hope seeing him didn't upset you too much," the judge said, and Beret wondered just how much he knew about what had gone on between Teddy and Lillie. Had Mick reported to him?

"It was troubling," she admitted.

"I never liked him. He was not worthy of you—or Lillie, either. I didn't want you to marry him, but I understood you were lonely," Varina said, and Beret realized there was very little her aunt and uncle didn't know. "We mustn't talk about him."

"Yes, you are right," Beret agreed, grateful not to have to dwell on her former husband. She had done too much of that already. She had not slept well for thinking about him, not just his betrayal but the happy times they had spent together. Those memories had upset her even more.

They were silent then, eating. Beret reached into a silver bowl for a muffin and buttered it, taking a bite. She had not eaten much in the days since she'd learned about Lillie's death and discovered she was hungry. Her uncle watched her eat, then said, "Nobody makes muffins like your aunt does. I believe this is her recipe. Cook's results are poorer." He turned to his wife. "Do you remember you made them for Sunday breakfasts when we were young?"

"Why, I do remember," Beret's aunt replied. Then she said, "I almost forgot. I had the most delightful note last evening from Caroline Decker, inquiring if we would come to dinner next week. She said she had met you and found you charming, Beret."

"Detective Sergeant McCauley introduced us at Charpiot's Restaurant."

"Oh, Mr. McCauley! But at least he knows where to take a lady. I'd have been furious if you'd gone to one of those disreputable restaurants near City Hall."

Beret smiled to herself, thinking Jonas had not told her aunt everything.

"He is such a disappointment to his family, working in a police station the way he does. It's not proper for a man of his upbringing. He's a disgrace."

"You mean like me, Aunt. Would your friends say that about me if they knew I worked in a mission?"

To her credit, Varina laughed. "Do forgive me. I am becoming such a snob. After all, we are only first generation ourselves. I took the liberty of replying that we would be pleased to accept the Deckers' invitation. Do I have your approval, Beret?"

"Of course."

"I mean, we are in mourning for Lillie, but I didn't think a small dinner engagement with a few friends would be disrespectful. I would like to use mourning to avoid the calls on all those wives, John, but I know it is necessary for your political ambition. And the women know it, too. So they excuse me."

Or gossip behind her back, Beret thought.

They chatted then, Varina speculating on who might be attending the dinner party and providing information on their pedigrees, their peccadilloes, their family connections, then admitting, "Most of them have no family to speak of. They all arrived yesterday. The best ones have learned to read and write." She turned to her husband, who was hidden behind his newspaper, and raised her voice a little. "Did you hear we are dining with the Deckers on Saturday, John?"

"Fine people," he muttered, still holding the paper in front of him.

"Not so's you'd notice," Varina confided to Beret. "Caroline is a well-bred woman, but her father is a disgrace." She lowered her voice. "A sybarite, and her brother is good for nothing. But they will amuse you."

Beret felt almost lighthearted now, warmed by the sun and the food and her aunt's good humor. The butler came in and replenished their coffee, then retired, and John put down his newspaper. "I've already told Beret about Joey Summers. It's a pity we can't go to the Deckers' without that fool boy being there. Perhaps we can hope he'll be out somewhere raising hell."

"John, such language," his wife said.

"I'm sorry, Varina, but where the Summerses are concerned, I forget myself." He sipped his coffee, then lifted the paper again.

"I'm glad you met Caroline. She could be a good friend to you, Beret. I have been hoping that when we have got Lillie's murder behind us, you will stay on here for a while." And Beret thought that while she might never again have a husband, or children, she had a family, and she was grateful, more than her aunt could imagine.

The judge set aside his paper then and took out his watch. "It's time I head down to the courthouse. I'm going to walk today. Arthur Chalmers and I have decided we must get exercise. He'll be calling any minute." And indeed, just as Beret's uncle pushed his chair back from the table, the doorbell rang. "That'll be Art now."

"Tell him to come in and have a cup of coffee with us," Varina said. "He will be delighted to meet Beret."

The judge nodded and did not get up, waiting until the butler came into the room and announced, "A caller, sir."

"That'll be Chalmers." John leaned around the butler and called, "Come on in and have a cup with us, Art."

"It is not Judge Chalmers, sir. The caller is for Miss Beret."

Beret and her aunt and uncle looked up quickly, but before William could announce him, Mick McCauley strode into the room. The judge rose. "Michael?" he said, holding out his hand.

Mick took it, but he looked at Beret. "I'm sorry to intrude like this, but I thought Miss Osmundsen would want to know, and you, too, Judge Stanton." He realized Varina was in the room and added, "Madam, please forgive me."

Varina nodded curtly. "What is it, Michael?"

Mick studied her for a moment, then seemed to dismiss her and the judge, too, as he turned to Beret. "I am afraid I must tell you that there has been another murder. A prostitute on upper Holladay Street was stabbed to death last night. Eight times. No murder weapon was left behind this time. Her earrings were taken. We know because they were ripped from her ears."

"Oh no!" Varina said, thrusting her napkin against her breast in an almost prayerful manner. "How utterly dreadful. Beret, you must extricate yourself from this business at once. It is much too dangerous. I won't have something happen to you, too."

The judge put his hand on his wife's arm. "Let's not be too hasty. Let the detective sergeant tell us what happened first. Michael." He indicated a chair, and Mick sat down.

The instant the detective was seated, William appeared with a cup and saucer and held them out inquiringly. Mick nodded, and William set down the cup and filled it, placing a napkin and spoon beside it. Mick reached for the sugar bowl, then realizing perhaps that the Stantons served decent coffee, stayed his hand.

"Have you had breakfast?" the judge asked.

"I'm fine."

Judge Stanton turned to his wife. "I don't want to distress you, Varina. You have been through a great deal already, and you don't have to listen to this. We understand if you wish to leave us."

Varina shook her head. "I prefer to stay, if for no other reason than so Beret does not have to hear it by herself."

Beret patted her aunt's hand as if in thanks, although she did not know why having the woman nearby would make the details of a second murder any more palatable. The news stunned her. Could the two murders be connected? She could not imagine that whoever had hated Lillie enough to kill her had hated a second prostitute, as well. The poor girl, Beret thought, wondering if, like Lillie, the dead woman had a family to mourn her. It was more likely that she was alone and would be buried in a pauper's grave.

"Michael," the judge said again.

Mick had gulped his coffee, and now he set down the cup. William came forward to fill it, but Michael waved him away. "I don't know much more than what I just told you, sir. A prostitute's been murdered in much the same way your niece was. A patrolman was dispatched to my door not thirty minutes ago with the news. I'm to go there immediately, but I stopped here to see if Miss Osmundsen might want to accompany me."

"Certainly not!" Varina said.

But Beret was pleased as well as surprised at the invitation. "I want to, Aunt. If Lillie's killer is murdering other women, then I intend to do whatever I can to help apprehend him." She added to forestall her aunt's objection, "I owe it to Lillie."

"Nonsense, Beret. It might have been all right for you to playact detective the past two weeks when we thought Lillie's death was an isolated incident. We understood how you might have felt a responsibility to apprehend her killer. But you would put yourself in danger if there is a madman at loose. Besides, I don't know what help you could give the police anyway."

"Actually, she has been a help," Mick said, and Beret looked at him in surprise, because she thought he'd only been humoring her. In fact, she had been sure he still wanted to be rid of her. Mick glanced at her and shrugged. "You did tell me some things I wouldn't have found out on my own."

"Be that as it may, you must stop this snooping into criminal affairs. John, forbid her from continuing." Varina set down her fragile cup so hard that a tiny chip broke off the bottom and fell into the saucer. William quickly removed them and set down a second cup and saucer, pouring fresh coffee.

"I'm afraid I can't do that," the judge said. "Beret has her mind made up. I could no more stop her from doing what her mind is set upon than I could stop you, my dear."

"Your mother would be horrified," Varina said, as if she were playing her last card.

Beret gave a sad smile, pretending the comment caused her to reconsider, but in fact, in this matter, she was her mother's daughter. Working in the mission had toughened Beret's mother as it had Beret. Both had witnessed the underside of life and felt compelled to do something about it. The young woman knew that in her place, her mother would have made the same decision.

"I'm ready to go," Beret said, not wanting to prolong the confrontation with her aunt. She rose and set aside her napkin.

"We'll take the streetcar," Mick said.

"No," Varina said. "If you must go, then I insist that Jonas drive you. Since you won't take my advice about giving up this venture, Beret, as least save yourself the embarrassment of walking along Holladay Street like a common woman." Beret glanced at Mick as if to say she had not told her relative that she had been tramping Holladay Street not many days earlier.

Varina called the butler and told him to have the carriage readied, and in a few minutes Beret and Mick were riding off toward Holladay Street behind Jonas. If the driver had been startled when Mick gave him the address, he hadn't shown it.

"What more can you tell me?" Beret asked the detective. "Are you quite certain the same man killed both women?"

"Not certain at all, but from what I know so far, that appears likely. The prostitute—her name is Sadie Hops—was alone in her crib, although, as you know, crib girls operate by themselves. There's no madam and often not even a mac to keep track of them. Sadie had been on Holladay Street a long time, five years at least, and was addicted to morphine. She was as pitiful a case as I ever saw—foul, disease-ridden, covered with sores, as profane as a street urchin. The street ages them, the crib girls more than the parlor house women, although in the end, they all suffer. I'd be surprised if Sadie was much older than your sister." Mick shook his head. "She would have had to accept any man with two bits to spend, so she had some pretty tough customers."

Beret knew all of that from her work at the mission. She was pleased that Mick seemed sympathetic, because many of the police officers she encountered in New York not only were immune to the troubles of crib girls but ill-treated them. Some even extracted a tribute—money or favors. "You know her, then?"

"I walked a beat on Holladay Street before I was promoted to detective. I knew plenty of them. She was pretty much like the others."

"So she would not have been suspicious of a man who entered her crib?"

"My guess is she was so doped up she wouldn't have recognized her own mac, that is if she had one, and as I said, she probably didn't. It's doubtful she made enough to support herself, let alone a fancy man."

"She would have been an easy mark, then."

"Indeed. That might be why the killer picked her. He would have gone in as a customer, then stabbed her, and no one would have been the wiser. It was only by chance that her body was discovered this morning. Another girl had promised to loan her a hat and stopped at the crib. Otherwise, Sadie might have been there for two or three days before she was found."

"Until someone noticed the smell." They were driving past the elegant mansions on Capitol Hill, a neighborhood that seemed as far removed from Holladay Street as if it had been on the opposite side of the world. Beret thought of the contrast between the fine homes and the crib where Sadie Hops had been murdered. The poor woman probably had had no idea how Denver's elite lived. Her johns would not have been the millionaires and men-about-town who patronized the houses like Miss Hettie's but instead men as abandoned and depraved as she was.

But perhaps Sadie had started out with someone like Miss Hettie and had spiraled downward as the liquor and the drugs took hold. She would have gone to a smaller, less expensive house, then to one of the nicer cribs and finally to a hovel at the end of Denver's row. Beret couldn't help but wonder if Lillie would have followed the same course if she'd lived. Would her sister have ended her days in one of those foul dens, a used-up woman, a dope fiend, before she was thirty?

Beret shook her head, as if to rid herself of those thoughts. This was not a time for recrimination. There was work to be done. She concentrated on the facts about the two dead women, comparing the circumstances of their murders. "Sadie Hops was stabbed multiple times, like Lillie. And her earrings were stolen. Both were prostitutes. Those are the similarities. Are there others you know about, Detective?"

"Both were young, although most of them are. They don't last long, as you know. I would be interested to see if both had blond hair, whether they were alike in appearance. I remember Sadie was a blonde once, but I hadn't seen her lately."

Beret nodded. "You think, then, that our man, if indeed one man is responsible, is singling out a certain kind of woman?"

"He might be."

"What about the differences?"

"Well, for one thing, your sister worked in a brothel. It would have been harder for the killer to get near her. If he was a thief, I can understand why he stole your sister's earrings. But why Sadie's? They were likely worthless."

"Perhaps he took them for a trophy."

Mick nodded. "Here's another thing. If he's targeting prostitutes, why would he have gone to the trouble of sneaking into Miss Hettie's when he could have gotten to one of the girls on upper Holladay Street?"

"Perhaps he did not think clearly about that the first time, but once he'd embarked on this course, he chose a crib girl for ease of access," Beret said.

"That could be. I think the differences are not so important as the similarities."

"I believe it's clear he hates prostitutes." She realized both of them had accepted the fact that one man was responsible for both murders.

"Seems like it," Mick said.

"Will there be more killings, then?" She leaned forward so that she could look at the detective.

Mick's face twisted, and he would not look her in the eye. "I fear so. I fear your sister's murder was just the first in this madman's career, unless, that is, he's killed elsewhere. Perhaps he's new to Denver."

Like Teddy. Beret wondered if Mick had the same thought.

The detective continued. "But then, we haven't even seen the crib where Sadie was killed. It's altogether possible the crimes were done by two different men. Maybe the second killer read about your sister's murder in the paper and decided to copy it. Such things happen, you know."

"You don't believe that." That was not a question.

"No. I believe a monster has been let loose on Holladay Street. And if we don't catch him, he will kill again."

Chapter 10

The Stanton carriage passed through the residential area and the downtown business district, bustling now with bankers and clerks, messenger boys and shopgirls, the street crowded with hacks and carriages. Beret didn't like Denver any better that morning than she had two weeks earlier. The buildings were small by New York standards, and not very interesting, mostly two- and three-story edifices that appeared to have been thrown up in a hurry and cheaply constructed, as if the builders did not know how long the town would last.

Here and there were churches and one or two cathedrals. Beret wondered if Denver was a religious city. Her aunt and uncle attended services. In fact, Beret had gone with them the past Sunday. And of course, a minister had officiated at Lillie's funeral service. He had called on Beret just the day before to give his condolences. Beret had not wanted to see him for fear he'd talk about hellfire and repentance and dwell on Lillie's sins. But the clergyman had not even mentioned the circumstances of Lillie's last months and had said only that life was precious and it was hard to accept the death of someone so young. He hoped Beret would turn to God for solace. She had thanked him but thought solace would come more readily from finding Lillie's killer.

Now, Jonas turned onto Holladay Street. The morning was still new, it was not yet nine o'clock, and the street had the desolate appearance of a bacchanal that had ended. Bottles were strewn along the sidewalks. Trash cluttered the gutters, along with discarded newspapers. A man's top hat had been blown onto an elm branch and rested there like some wild creature waiting to pounce. The houses were shuttered, and except for a delivery wagon here and there, the street was deserted, the life sucked out of it. Beret marveled at the difference between a tenderloin in the daytime and at night.

She and Mick were quiet as the carriage made its way up the street, each of them looking out at the procession of whorehouses that grew shabbier the farther they went. Jonas slowed the horses, and Beret saw him looking at the cribs, as if searching for a number. Were they numbered? she wondered.

"Up ahead," Mick called, and Jonas brought the carriage to a stop. Two patrolmen stood beside the crib, talking to a handful of women, crib girls themselves or streetwalkers, Beret thought, judging from the carelessness of their appearance. Their hair was frightful, and there were traces of paint on their faces. They were dressed in thin wrappers and shabby coats, their feet in rubber shoes. One girl was barefoot. A whore with a cigarette in her mouth stuck out her lower lip, blowing smoke in front of her face. She observed the carriage languidly, perhaps wondering if the occupant was a john, out for a good time. When Mick alighted, she scowled.

The two officers guarding the door straightened up when they saw Mick, then looked with curiosity as he helped Beret step down. She followed the detective as he greeted the patrolmen.

"We ain't touched nothing, sir," one told Mick, although the man was looking at Beret, appraising her.

"It's a mess in there," the second patrolman said. He was Officer Thrasher, the same young policeman Mick had encountered at Miss Hettie's. "Just like last time, blood, things throwed all over, not a pretty sight. No, sir, not at all. I was the first on the scene, the first officer, that is. I took one look and told Rasmussen over there, you call for Mick McCauley. He's going to want to see this." The officer's voice was loud, as if he were speaking to an audience, and it was clear that he took pleasure in his recitation and in his part in discovering the crime. Then he said to Beret, "You're not going in there, are you, ma'am? It's no sight for a lady."

"You let me see it, and I'm a lady, ain't I?" one of the prostitutes protested, and the officer reddened. "She just looked in the door, sir. I didn't let her go inside," he told the detective.

Mick narrowed his eyes at Beret, as if to ask if she still wanted to view the body. When she showed no inclination to back off, he asked, "Ready?"

"I'll follow you, Detective McCauley." But first she went back to the carriage and dismissed Jonas.

"Mrs. Stanton won't like it if I leave you here, miss. She says to look after you. I'm obliged to do it," the driver said.

"We could be hours, and my aunt might have need of the carriage before I'm finished," Beret told him. "Besides, as you can see, I am with several police officers. I could not be more safe if I were in the Stanton home. I do not want you to wait."

Jonas considered her, then reluctantly picked up the reins and started off. Beret watched him for a moment, then quickly dismissed him from her mind as she turned back to the crib. She did not notice that Jonas drove only a few doors down the block, then turned around and stopped.

Mick had already gone inside with the two patrolmen, and Beret followed, steeling herself before entering the little building. The crib was a shack with a single door that opened directly onto the street, and a window next to it. Sadie would have stood in the doorway to solicit business, or if the prostitute was busy with a john, a customer could peer through the thin curtains on the window, curtains that were torn and gray with dirt.

The crib was made up of two rooms—the front room, fitted with an iron bed and a washstand, an iron stove, and a back room where Sadie would have kept her belongings. From time to time, a prostitute had an accomplice who hid in the back room and stole the customer's money while he was busy with the girl. Occasionally the cribs had closets where a prostitute could hang a man's coat and pants. A door or loose panel in the second room allowed the accomplice, called a panel man, access to the closet. He could go through the clothing for money or other valuables while the john was occupied in front.

Generally, the crib customers were so drunk, they weren't aware that they'd been robbed until later, and when they realized what had happened, they often couldn't remember which crib they'd entered. Some hadn't even planned to go inside, had only walked by out of curiosity, but then the prostitute had grabbed a hat, forcing the man to enter the crib to retrieve it.

Beret had been in such hovels before, rescuing women who were sick or maimed by customers or pimps, but she was never prepared for the desolation, and she held her breath as she stepped into the room and looked about. The walls and ceiling were black with soot and dirt. Newspapers, water-stained now, had been placed over holes in the ceiling as well as the walls, where they were pasted upright, as if Sadie read the articles in her off hours—that is, if she could read. Above the bed was a picture of the Virgin Mary, her face tilted heavenward, her hands together in prayer. The picture was faded, and Beret thought it had been there a long time, probably hung by someone who occupied the crib before Sadie Hops. Risqué drawings of pretty girls, dressed in lingerie or nothing at all, their hands and eyes inviting, were pinned to the walls. They had been torn from the *Police Gazette* or one of the girlie magazines. Beret noticed that someone had blackened the eyes of the woman in one of the pictures.

The rough board floor was filthy, with a path worn from the door to the bed to the rickety table that served as a washstand. A basin half filled with dirty water and a gray rag were on the table. Next to the basin was a pewter spoon in a glass and an empty whiskey bottle, along with dirty pots, broken crockery, and remnants of food. A battered pan holding a congealed mess rested on the tiny stove, which was cold now, the coal bucket beside it empty. A few pieces of ragged clothing hung on nails in the wall. A chamber pot was just under the bed. The place stank of sewer gas and mold and general filth. The only air came from the door, since no one had had the sense to open the window. Beret could not see into the back room but assumed it held a trunk containing any valuables the girl would have had, photographs, perhaps a few mementos of an earlier life, such as postcards or letters or sad little trinkets. Sadie Hops would have kept her stash of liquor in the back room, too, lest a john grab a bottle and help himself.

Mick was standing next to the bed when Beret entered the room, staring down at the corpse, and Beret forced herself to go to his side. The iron bed itself was lopsided and badly chipped. A quilt, the only bright thing in the room, was thrown over the footboard. There was no sheet, just a mattress, grimy and torn. Sadie's body, dressed only in a shift and black stockings, lay on top of it. "My God, Detective, who could have done such an awful thing?" Beret gasped, forcing herself to look at the remains of the prostitute. Her hand over her nose, she stared in horror at the mangled body. Beret hoped that Lillie had not looked like this, had hoped Lillie had died with more dignity. But murder was never dignified. She breathed deeply to keep the breakfast muffins from rising in her throat, and took in the awful stench.

Mick removed a handkerchief from his pocket and handed it to her.

"I thought I was used to the smell," Beret said, putting the small square of fabric over her nose and turning away.

"You get used to the smell of poverty maybe, but not of death. You never get used to it," he told her, and she nodded, understanding.

"Pray God I don't." Beret gave the room a final glance, then forced herself once again to look at the body on the bed. She held her arms to her sides to keep from shaking. "This is inhuman. What fiend could have done it?"

The body and the quilt beneath it were covered in blood. Beret studied the quilt for a moment and was oddly touched by it. The spread was handmade, a delicate design quilted with stitches as exquisite as those used on an opera cape. Had Sadie made the comfort herself? Perhaps she had been a fine needlewoman and had tried to support herself with her sewing, but the life of a seamstress was hard, and she wouldn't have made enough to keep herself. The quilt might have been pieced for her by a mother or grandmother and was a remembrance of another life. Or maybe the quilt had just been discarded by the previous occupant, and Sadie had merely taken it as her own, not knowing whose fingers had made the tiny stitches. Beret frowned at her sentimentality over such a trifle.

The woman's shift was ripped and bloody from where the killer had stabbed her, sinking the knife into her again and again, just as he had Lillie. The woman's chest was brutally slashed and stained with blood and gore. Her face was bloody, too, not from wounds, for it did not appear the killer had taken the knife to her face, but from where the blood that flowed from the wounds on her chest had splashed onto it. Her teeth were missing, but whether the killer had smashed them or she had lost them at some other time, perhaps in a fight or just from general poor hygiene, Beret couldn't tell. If Mick had not told Beret Sadie's age, she would have thought the dead woman was in her forties or fifties. The body looked like that of a dog she had seen in the street once, a dog that had been crushed by a heavy wagon, then run over by other vehicles. Sadie Hops seemed no more a creature who had once lived than a slab of meat in a butcher shop.

Beret removed her glove and touched the woman's forehead with her fingers in a gesture of compassion. She was not aware she had done so until she took away her hand and saw the blood on her fingers. Had her sister looked like this when she was found—bloodied, half naked? As Beret wiped the blood on her hand with the detective's handkerchief, she shook her head at the idea of Lillie's dying like Sadie.

Mick turned to her. "It's a ghastly scene, grisly even for those of us who've seen murder before. Do you want Officer Thrasher to take you outside?" he asked.

"There's whiskey over there if you need it," the officer interjected, pointing to a table. "I'll bet it's strong enough to make a man shed his toenails."

"No. Thank you, Officer." The idea of a drink of Sadie's liquor gagged Beret. "I was just wondering. Is this how you found Lillie?"

The young officer glanced at Beret and said, "You mean Lillie Brown, the soiled dove at Miss Hettie's that got cut?" He all but rubbed his hands together. "Ma'am, a dead whore—"

"Officer!" Mick cut him off. "You will keep your remarks to yourself. Miss Osmundsen is Lillie Brown's sister. I think you can show some respect for the dead."

The officer's eyes grew wide, and his eyes swept Beret from head to foot, wondering perhaps if she were a prostitute, too. He straightened his back when Beret gave him a look of disdain and said, "I didn't know we allowed civilians at a crime scene."

Mick's eyes bored into him. "Miss Osmundsen is an expert in crime, someone who is called a criminologist. Perhaps you've heard of such people. She has already provided us with invaluable information."

"A girl?"

"A lady."

"Yes, sir."

Mick turned to look at the body again, but just then, the coroner known as Dr. Death entered the room, glancing around until his eyes lit on Beret, and he frowned. He started to ask a question, but Mick cut him off.

"This is Miss Osmundsen. She is helping the police department," Mick explained, forestalling any unseemly remarks on the part of the coroner.

If the man was surprised or puzzled by Beret's presence, he didn't show it. "Ma'am," he said, removing his hat, "I'm sorry you have to see such a depraved scene."

Beret nodded to acknowledge the coroner's sympathy and said, "Thank you."

"Miss Osmundsen is a criminologist," Mick informed him.

"I heard about them. Aren't they the people that tell you why the criminal done the crime?" the doctor responded, and when Mick didn't elaborate, added, "Well, I guess it don't matter why, does it? Dead's dead. Let's get to it." He leaned over the body and studied it. "This one's nastier than the other'n. Look how her dress is pushed over to the side, no attempt to cover her up like before. And the wounds are different. She's slashed. The first one, she was punctured. Of course, that could be because he used scissors the first time and a knife on this one." He indicated the knife lying on the floor. "That's what he done it with, must be." Mick let the knife lie, and the three were careful not to step on it.

The doctor took a cloth from his bag and wiped some of the blood off Sadie's chest. "Looks like just about the same number of wounds, eight, wasn't it?" He touched the wounds as he counted them. "And look here, she's got cuts on her hands where she tried to defend herself." He studied Sadie's face. "He must have knocked out her teeth. That's different. You see them around?" He glanced at the floor.

"She didn't have any. I seen her before. She was plug ugly," Officer Thrasher volunteered.

Beret bristled at the remark about the dead woman. After a time, most policemen grew inured to the victims, but it was a pity that an officer just starting out was so insensitive.

The doctor examined the body, cutting away the shift so that Sadie lay naked on the bed. Beret turned away, embarrassed for the dead woman that she was subjected to such impersonal study by the coroner as well as by the police officers, who sent furtive glances at the bed. Sadie had been a prostitute, was used to men staring at her body, but somehow, this curious observation was indecent. Had they looked at Lillie like that, staring as the coroner examined her body? Beret wanted to leave the room as a sign of respect while the coroner did his work, but she forced herself to stay, fearful the men would think she was squeamish.

She *was* squeamish. Her stomach churned as the doctor probed the prostitute's body, and she put Detective McCauley's handkerchief to her face, breathing through her mouth to avoid the smell in the room. Inexplicably her eyes watered, and she dabbed at them with the fingertips of her gloves. She wished someone had stood beside Lillie, crying for her. Did anyone care about the dead woman? Did she have friends among the other whores who stood outside, or was she only a curiosity to them, her death a temporary break from the monotony of their lives?

Dr. Death grunted, scribbled notes on a pad of paper. He took one of Sadie's ears between his fingers and examined the tear where an earring had been ripped out. When he was finished, he drew Mick and Beret aside.

"Was she raped?" Beret asked.

The coroner gave her an odd look. "She was a whore. How could I tell?"

Before Beret could protest, Mick asked, "You think it's the same killer?"

"This murder's worse, and he didn't cover her up like the last time. Remember how her underclothes was pulled over the parlor house girl even though they'd been ripped by the scissors, like he didn't want her to be embarrassed? This time, he just let her lie."

"You think he's getting more vicious?"

The doctor nodded. "I do."

"It's the same killer, then?"

"I don't see how it couldn't be. Tell me, Mick, you been around here, what, ten, twelve years? How many murders like this have you seen? None. Most of the girls that get killed—and there aren't many of them at that—are done in by their pimp or maybe by another girl in a fight. They don't get murdered in their beds. Most street women die from disease or liquor or by their own hand." He blew out his breath, which was as foul as that of a corpse. "Yessir, I think you got a real killer on your hands, a madman."

They had been standing near the door, and although they'd been talking in hushed tones, one of the crib girls outside overheard.

"We got a crazy man slicing up girls," she screamed at another prostitute. "I got to get out of here."

"If word spreads, it could just about close down Holladay Street," the coroner muttered. "If the good ladies of Denver had known that, they might have been behind this." He chuckled, but when neither Mick nor Beret laughed, he cleared his throat and said, "Begging your pardon, ma'am. I'm just saying that the girls along the row are scared as a parlor dog in a street fight when it comes to murder. They'll take off for Leadville or Salida or Kansas City when they hear about Sadie Hops. You know as well as I do, Mick, those girls are superstitious as all get out. A single death is one thing, but two deaths, that means another's coming. Those girls believe everything happens in threes, and they're afraid they'll be the third one. The prostitutes that stay will be as jumpity as bunny rabbits. It wouldn't surprise me if a couple of johns get knifed by scared whores."

"I'll leave the problem of a shortage of prostitutes to someone else," Mick said. "We've got a murder to solve, two murders."

"What other comparisons are there between the murder of the crib girl and . . ." Beret paused and said pointedly, "The murder of my sister, Lillie?"

The coroner jerked up his head at that and stared at Beret

with narrowed eyes. "Your sister? You mean the girl that got killed at Miss Hettie's?"

"Yes. Lillie Brown, that is, Lillie Osmundsen, was my younger sister."

"I'm sorry, ma'am. I didn't know." He thought for a moment. Then he removed his hat and said, "There's one difference. I guess I don't know why, if the killer's aim is to murder common women, he'd go to the trouble of getting into a parlor house where he was likely to get caught, when it's so easy to stab a crib girl."

"Maybe the challenge," Mick said.

"Could be. Or he might have had a reason to kill Lillie, then discovered he liked murdering women and went after another," Beret said, thinking it over. "My sister's death could have unleashed a blood lust." She paused. "You are sure"—she searched for the coroner's name but did not know it—"the same person killed both women?"

"Nothing's sure till Mick catches whoever did this. But I'd say the chances are pretty good the same man done both of them."

Just then, the coroner's wagon arrived, and Mick and Beret went outside while Dr. Death and his assistant wrapped Sadie's body in a sheet and prepared to take it away. A crowd had gathered, mostly prostitutes, here and there a man who Beret thought might have been a pimp or a dope dealer or even an early-morning john. Mick looked over the bystanders and asked, "Anybody see or hear anything last night?" When no one answered, Mick said, "You there, Little Bit, your crib's next door. Didn't you hear Sadie scream?"

"Not me, Mick. I moved on down the street. You ain't been down here for a long time or you'd know."

There were a few snickers at that. Mick ignored them as he searched the crowd. "Pretty Boy," he called to a man who was dressed like a dandy. "Was Sadie on your string?"

The man raised his chin in disdain. "Now, Mick, you know I don't take these girls' money. I'm a gambler, not a mac."

"Since when?" a girl called.

Pretty Boy pointed his walking stick at her as if it were a gun, then told Mick, "You don't think I'd keep someone like Sadie anyway, do you? I got standards."

"You kept her once."

"That's when she had teeth."

"Where were you last night?" Mick asked, taking a step forward.

The man threw up his arms. "At the Arcade. All night. I won a pretty penny off a new fellow."

Beret mulled over the alibi. Was that new fellow Teddy? And if he wasn't, where was Teddy when Sadie was killed? Another poker game? Beret shook her head. She might hate Teddy, but she could not believe he was responsible for Sadie's death. Teddy might have killed Lillie in a fit of rage, but he wasn't so depraved that he would murder a crib girl just for the excitement of it. Of course, anything was possible. Beret wondered if she should tell the detective about her encounter with her former husband outside the Arcade. Why was she protecting him? Was it because, deep inside, she still cared for him? Beret frowned at the thought. No, of course not.

The coroner and his assistant carried Sadie's body outside, and the crowd parted to give them a path to the wagon. The onlookers were silent then, except for the sniveling of some of the prostitutes. "Good-bye, Sadie dear," one called, while another crossed herself. When the wagon started down the street, the crowd broke into knots of people, who watched until the vehicle disappeared. Then they began to drift away.

"That man, Pretty Boy, could he—" Beret began, but Mick shook his head.

"Unlikely. He wouldn't want to get his hands dirty."

"I suppose we must go back inside and search the place now." Beret suddenly felt dirty herself.

"You don't have to do it, Miss Osmundsen. The officers can help."

"You can't get rid of me that easily, Mr. McCauley. A woman might see something a man would miss." She turned and led the way back into the crib. But once inside, she stopped, wishing she did not have to proceed. She wasn't sure about the protocol of examining the room or even if there was one, but that wasn't the reason. She didn't want to go through Sadie's belongings as the police had pawed through Lillie's.

"We might as well start with the bed," Mick said. He went to the mattress, still wet with blood, and leaned down.

Beret stooped down on the other side of the bed until she was at eye level with the detective. "You don't see an earring, do you?" she asked.

"Maybe on the floor." They both looked under the bed, which was covered with dust and rodent droppings. Beret was still clutching the detective's handkerchief, and now she put it over her nose, because the chamber pot was on her side of the bed and had not been emptied. She held her breath as long as she could, then stood and gasped. "I don't see anything."

"Me, neither."

Mick ran his hand over the mattress, feeling for anything that might have been caught in the fabric, but found nothing and wiped the blood from his hands on the ticking. He picked up the knife and laid it carefully on the mattress. They began to examine the room then, looking into the pots, opening the drawer in the washstand. Beret found a *carte de visite* of a little boy, hidden behind the picture of the Virgin Mary, and handed it to the detective. "It could be her brother. Or her son," Mick said. "Or it could have been left there ten years ago."

"Was Sadie Hops her real name?"

"Was Lillie Brown your sister's name?"

"In fact, it was to have been Lillie Brown Osmundsen, only my parents decided against a middle name."

"Sorry."

"No need to be." Beret was not offended as she might have been had another officer made the retort.

Beret went through the clothes on the pegs, felt the pockets and hems for items that might have been secreted there. The two examined the woodwork to see if it had been loosened to provide a hiding place and found four gold coins behind the door frame. "They can go toward her funeral," Mick said. "The girls are good about pitching in, the boys at the station, too, even the gentlemen of the press sometimes. I don't know if you've ever seen a prostitute's funeral, Miss Osmundsen, but it's the one time a street girl can be proud of herself—maybe the only time. The girls'll all turn out for Sadie and sing 'Going Home' and cry as if they've lost their best friend."

"They are really crying for themselves."

"Could be." He studied her a moment. "You really do know these girls, don't you?"

Beret shrugged and thought of her sister. "Not so well as I wish I did."

They finished inspecting the front room. Mick lit the kerosene lamp that had been beside the window and carried it with him into the back room, which was no bigger than a closet. The room was empty, except for a few rags. Beret saw movement, and a rat slid out from under them and disappeared through a hole in the wall. They examined the room quickly, both anxious to be away from it, and found nothing. Then Beret went to the pile of rags, and using Mick's handkerchief, she picked them up one by one, dropping them onto the floor. One seemed heavier than the others and Beret took it into the front room to examine it. The cloth was folded and stitched shut. She broke the thread and discovered some cheap pieces of jewelry—a gilt brooch, a bracelet with a red stone that Beret knew was not a ruby but glass, two gold hairpins, and a child's ring with a sapphire in it. The items were tucked inside a piece of paper folded into an envelope, and on the outside was written, "Mrs. Anson Strunk, Fort Madison, Iowa."

"Do you suppose that's her mother?" Beret asked.

Mick shook his head. "Who knows—her mother, sister, grand-mother?"

"Will you write to her about Sadie?"

"That's the question, isn't it. Wouldn't it be better to let her worry that the worst might have happened to her daughter than to tell her outright that it did? If you were her mother, would you want to know your daughter died a whore, murdered in a crib in the tenderloin?"

"Yes," Beret said, and Mick, realizing what he'd asked, shook his head in a sort of apology.

"I shouldn't have said that," he told her.

"I'm glad I know what happened to my sister. It would be terrible to lose track of her and never know what became of her. The not knowing would be worse. But then"—she gave a wry smile—"I'm a criminologist."

Mick smiled.

"Exactly what is a criminologist, Detective McCauley?"

"An expert in crime. I think you qualify."

"An empty word, then."

"But useful." He tucked the envelope and jewelry into his pocket, then wiped the knife and wrapped it in a rag. "I wonder if Sadie was Mrs. Anson Strunk."

Beret thought that over. "Perhaps you should write to Anson Strunk, then."

He nodded.

"Will you tell him her profession?"

"Not in the first letter. I'll just say she died."

"Then you've done this before, written to families of dead prostitutes."

He nodded. "Nobody else in the department wants to do it. Sometimes it's enough to say the woman's dead. They may suspect the truth and don't want it confirmed. Others—like you—need the details. I wait until they ask. Most of them don't. Most of them don't reply at all. But I still write. They're human beings, after all." He paused, then called to Officer Thrasher and told him to find a piece of wood to nail across the outside door to keep out the vags and the curious.

"Will it work?" Beret asked.

"Not likely. It won't be an hour before some of the girls come in and take Sadie's things. Tattered as they are, her clothes will be worn by somebody, or maybe sold to the ragpicker." He looked around the room. "I believe we're finished."

With a sigh of relief, Beret went outside. The storm of the day before was gone. Holladay Street was bathed in sunlight that already had melted the snow. A spring breeze blew from the west carrying the scent of grass, covering up the manure smell of the street. A white cat, its back arched, walked slowly past Beret, then put its paws against the side of the small building and stretched. As she warmed herself in the sun's rays Beret found it hard to believe that a woman had just been murdered a few feet from where she stood. It was too perfect a day for that. She looked across the street and saw a tulip blooming in a vacant lot. She loved tulips. They meant spring to her. She remembered how Lillie and Teddy had vied with each other to find the first tulips and bring them to her. Once Lillie had spotted a clump of them in the park and picked every one.

"Shall we start for City Hall, Detective? I'd prefer the fresh air to a streetcar, and the distance isn't far," Beret said, pushing the memory of Lillie and the flowers from her mind.

Mick pointed behind her with his chin. "Your driver's waiting."

"What!" Beret whirled around and found herself staring at Jonas, who stood by the carriage a half block away. "I told him to go back to my uncle's house. I won't have him following me," she muttered.

"Like you said before, he's trying to protect you. Don't be too hard on the fellow. I checked on him at the station. Do you want to know who he is? It's not a pretty story."

"I have not heard a pretty story since I arrived in Denver."

"I remembered the case when you told me his name. I'd just started out as a copper. It was before I had the Holladay Street beat, and one of the reasons I wanted it was to keep such things from happening. I was idealistic back then." Mick curled his lip as if to say such feelings had passed, but Beret knew they hadn't.

"His mother was a prostitute, worked out of a crib somewhere around here. Cock-eyed Lizzie, she was called, because one eye was off. She used to keep the boy with her, lock him in the back room when she was entertaining. Sometimes she'd go on a bender and forget about him. Lizzie had a fight with another whore. They were arguing about a john right there in her front room, and the other girl hit her and Lizzie fell against the bed. The boy must have heard it. Lizzie wasn't found for two days, and the poor kid was in the back room all that time, locked in, nothing to eat or drink and maybe knowing his mother was dead. Can you imagine what he must have gone through, a boy like that, not more than five or six? There wasn't anybody to take him in, so he went to an orphanage, and later on, he became a newsboy. He used to hang around City Hall. I hadn't seen him in a long time."

"I wonder if my aunt knows all that about him. My uncle told me only that Aunt Varina had rescued him from some bullies."

"Maybe they thought the story was too sordid to tell you." Mick glanced down at the sidewalk where the snow from the day before was melting and kicked aside a chunk of ice. "But I imagine you know plenty of sordid stories. This one isn't so unusual."

"No, that's the pity of it. I wonder if he thinks of my aunt as a substitute mother. That would explain his devotion to her."

"Could be. You'll hurt Jonas's feelings if we don't let him drive us to City Hall. And you'll hurt mine if you make me walk." Mick chuckled. "Now don't berate him."

"Why, Detective, I believe you have a soft spot."

"That's why I let you come along to Sadie's crib."

"I thought it was because I am a criminologist." For an instant, the sun and the banter made Beret forget Sadie's murder.

She took Mick's arm, and they walked toward the carriage, where she gave Jonas a long look but said nothing. The young man shouldn't be caught between her annoyance and her aunt's anger, for surely her aunt would not have been pleased if Jonas had returned to the house. Now that she knew the boy's background, Beret resolved to be more understanding.

As Mick helped Beret into the carriage, a man approached and said, "I got a tip that your whore killer got another'n, Mick."

"So it seems," Mick told him.

"You want to tell me what it looks like in there?"

"You can imagine the scene for yourself."

"My readers don't want my imagination. They want to know what happened."

"Since when?"

The man ignored the retort as he took note of Beret and lifted his hat. "Miss."

Clearly annoyed, Mick said, "Miss Beret, may I present Eugene Latham. Gene, Miss Beret." The man doffed his hat as Mick added, "Latham is a reporter for the *Denver Tribune*. Crime is his specialty, the more sensational, the better."

Latham looked at Beret curiously, but as Mick divulged nothing about her, he turned back to the detective. "Like I say, I heard another whore was done in, a crib girl this time. Is that right?"

"Sadie Hops," Mick said.

The reporter shook his head. "Didn't know her. Now if it'd been a parlor girl . . ." The smirk on the reporter's face disappeared when he caught Beret looking at him. "Was it the same man?"

"We don't know."

The reporter had taken out a pad of paper and a pencil, and he paused. "Stabbed, I heard, just like Lillie Osmundsen, the judge's niece? You afraid if you say the murders are connected, you'll start a riot? The girls'll stampede out of here like scared deer if they think there's an insane killer on the loose."

"We don't know enough to make any conclusions."

Mick looked at the carriage as if to suggest that Beret get inside, but she stayed where she was, glancing at Jonas, who was transfixed by the conversation. She wished she could take him out of earshot, as she wondered if he had listened to talk like this when his mother died. Perhaps he was remembering conversations he had heard when he was locked in the back room while his mother was working.

"Aw, come on, Mick, give a guy a break. You can trust me. The other boys'll be right behind me, and I want to get into print before they do."

Mick blew out his breath, thinking. "Look, Gene, you tell Thrasher over there I said you could go inside and look around. All's I can tell you is she was stabbed eight times and it happened sometime last night. Her name was Sadie Hops, and I don't know a thing about her, don't even know if that's her real name."

"Now, Mick. You can do better than that. I did you a favor on the parlor house girl that got murdered, made you a household name. My stories got picked up by newspapers all over the country, even New York."

"Why would I care about that?"

Beret looked at the reporter distastefully, for the offensive write-up of Lillie's death, with its clichés and condescending tone, that she had read in New York, must have been a truncated version of one of this man's articles.

Latham continued to badger the detective, but Mick refused to say more, and at last the reporter put away his pencil. He shook hands with Mick and nodded at Beret, saying, "Pleased to meet you." Then as if to satisfy his curiosity about why the woman was there, he asked, "This Sadie some kind of relative of yours, ma'am?"

Beret raised her head a little in a gesture of disdain, a gesture that would have made her aunt proud. "Certainly not."

"Begging your pardon, but it's not every day you see a lady at a murder scene." When Beret didn't respond, he asked outright, "What is it you're here for, if you don't mind my asking, ma'am?"

Beret continued her haughty stare, although the reporter must have been used to such looks, because he did not appear uncomfortable. At last she said, "I do mind, but I will tell you. I am a criminologist."

"A what?"

"An expert in crime," Mick told him.

"You go to school for that?" The reporter smirked.

"Of course. The New York Institute for the Study of the Criminally Insane."

"Doesn't sound like a line of work for a lady."

"She helped solve the Porter-Masters murders. You remember that one, Gene."

"Well, sure," he said, and walked away in the direction of Sadie's crib.

As she got into the carriage, Beret asked, "What were the Porter-Masters murders?"

"Darned if I know. I made it up. What's the New York Institute for the Study of the Criminally Insane?"

"That's made up, too."

Mick took Beret's arm and helped her into the carriage. They were at last a team, Beret thought. Perhaps they would indeed solve Lillie's murder—and the murder of Sadie Hops. She hoped that would be before a third woman was killed.

Chapter 11

Beret ordered Jonas to take the detective to the station. She would bid Detective McCauley good-bye, then go home, get out of her bloodstained clothes, and rid herself of the smell of death. She was anxious to continue with the investigation, but viewing the dead prostitute's body had taken its toll on her. She was tired and heartsick and wanted nothing more than to let the warm water of the bath wash away the taint of Sadie's murder.

She settled back into the seat and looked down at her hands, which still held the detective's handkerchief. It was filthy with blood and gore. "I'll wash this myself and return it to you," she said.

"How do you get blood out of a handkerchief?"

"I have no idea."

He plucked the fabric square from her fingers and threw it into the street. "There, you have better things to worry about."

"Yes." Beret was silent for a while, thinking, and they rode for several blocks. At last, she said, "Detective McCauley, I want to ask you something. Do you think there is a chance the murders could have been committed by a woman? We've been assuming the killer is a man, but is there a possibility the culprit is female?"

Instead of scoffing as he might have done a few days earlier, the detective thought over the question. "It is always a possibility. Some women are as strong as a man, and there are one or two girls on Holladay Street who could best me in a wrestling match. Little Annie must weigh over three hundred pounds, and Iron Betty killed a horse once when she socked it in the head. Of course, that's rare, but yes, it's possible."

"But not probable. Is that what you're saying?"

"I am. If there'd been just one killing, I might have wondered if the killer was a woman. In fact, I did. I never completely dismissed the idea that one of the whores at Miss Hettie's killed your sister. They can get that mad, you know, and anger carries strength. Besides, the first time, the killer used scissors. That's a woman's weapon. And the body was covered up, too."

"In my experience, women operate differently from men," Beret said. "A prostitute might get angry enough to grab a knife—or scissors, as the case may be—and stab another woman in a fit of madness, maybe over a man or a piece of jewelry or some word of insult. She might even plan the murder of a man who's mistreated her. I know of a girl in New York who set fire to her father, a monster who'd forced her to lie not only with himself but with any drunken bum with a dime. And I am familiar with another, an abandoned woman who drowned her children in a bathtub rather than let her husband's new wife take them. But I've never heard of a woman so depraved that she murdered just for the thrill of killing. That's a man's way. Still, perhaps we are too quick to assume the killer is a man."

"As I say, I'd agree with you if there'd been only one murder.

But now there are two, and I believe you are right when you say women don't have the bloodlust that men do." Mick continued, "Now when there's a third—"

"A third." It was more a statement than a question.

Mick looked out the window at the streets that were muddy, now that the sun had melted the snow. The carriage splashed a group of dandies who were too slow to get out of the way, and Beret thought she saw Jonas smile.

"Yes, I'm sure there'll be a third. And the third murder will establish once and for all that our killer is a man. There could be even more than that. If the killer is indeed mad, if it is bloodlust, then he's only begun." Mick thought that over. "Or maybe he's already killed girls elsewhere. He could be new to Denver."

"Teddy?" Beret asked softly.

"You tell me. Is he capable of it?"

"No, I don't think so."

"But you didn't think he was capable of seducing your sister, either."

Beret nodded. "I have been wondering if he gave Lillie drugs."

"Pimps are known to do that. Do you think she was a doper?"

"I don't know. A maid found something in her room in New York, a powder of some kind, but she didn't tell me until after she had thrown it out."

"Was your husband?" Mick asked.

"I know he tried drugs, but to what degree I can't say. I think I need to find out."

"I don't see that it matters so much. Many of the girls try opiates. Your sister didn't die from drugs."

"But I want to know."

"Perhaps we can look into it later," Mick said, dismissing the subject. Suddenly, he put his hand on hers. "This is hard for you. I won't think less of you if you quit. It's all right. I'll keep you apprised of the progress, daily, if you like."

The detective's hand felt warm, and Beret liked the touch. It had been a long time since someone had held her hand, and she'd missed that connection with a man. Nonetheless, she said, "I will not back out now. I don't care what you think of me, Detective McCauley." But she did care.

Mick nodded.

"What do we do next?" Beret asked. "Do we interview Joey Summers?"

Mick looked down at his hand over Beret's. "*I* will interview Joey Summers and maybe his father, too. I told you that."

"Are you sure you don't want me with you?"

"I'll do it alone. Do you really think those two will talk about your sister in front of you? What do you think Joey will say when I ask him if he's been intimate with Lillie? I can talk to him man-to-man, and he'll say more, might even want to brag a little about his conquest. And Mr. Summers, I know him. He'd be furious if I brought you with me." He grinned. "Of course, he'll be furious anyway."

Beret thought that over and decided that the detective was right. "Then I must sit and twiddle my thumbs?"

"No, I would like you to write some letters."

"Letters?" Beret asked scornfully. As if she were some type-writist.

"To police departments. I think we should find out if our killer has been elsewhere. We should write to police chiefs in all the major cities and inquire whether they have had similar murders."

"And you think they would reply to *me*?"

"They'll reply if you sign my name. I'll set you up with names and addresses and writing materials, and you can compose the letters while I'm chasing down Joey Summers."

Beret nodded, although the idea did not appeal to her. She would write a few letters to show she was willing to do her part. But she had other ideas. She would not tell the detective about them just now.

Beret had planned to return to the police station to begin the letters the following morning, but her aunt came down with one of her headaches and begged Beret to stay with her. So Beret had sat in Varina's bedroom, reading to the older woman and filling towels with ice to put on her brow. Caring for her aunt reminded Beret of a time she herself had been ill with the influenza, and Lillie, ten at the time, had come into the bedroom, a white apron over her dress and a white napkin tied around her head and announced, "Hello, madam, I'm Nurse Fish. I'm going to take care of you." Then she'd set a bell and a glass of soda water on the bedside table. "Now drink this up like a good girl," she'd told Beret, handing her the water. When Beret gave her back the empty glass, Lillie had said, "Ring the bell if you need anything, and I will fetch it." She'd left the room, but Beret had known the girl was lurking just outside the door, so after a few minutes, she'd rung the bell, and Lillie had come bounding back. "Yes, madam?" she'd said.

"Nurse Fish, I should like a cup of beef tea."

"I'll talk to Cook," Lillie had replied gravely, putting the back of her hand to Beret's forehead. "And I'll ask her for two pieces of chocolate cake." And so the two had played at patient and nurse until Beret was better.

———

It was longer than she'd hoped before Beret met again with Mick McCauley. He was on his way out of the station when she arrived. "I've made an appointment to see Joey Summers."

Although she knew she could not accompany the detective, she was still disappointed. She did not like being cast aside.

Mick didn't seem sorry and he added, "There's plenty for you to do. The names and addresses of police departments in a dozen cities are on my desk for you. You can write the letters we talked about." Then he softened. "That won't be as interesting for you, but it has to be done. Police work can be tedious, you know."

Beret had not come to Denver to write letters but she agreed it was necessary. So she went to the detective's desk and found the list, along with police department letterheads that Mick had left for her. Ignoring the stares of the officers around her, she settled herself on the chair and opened a bottle of ink, then picked up the pen lying next to it—Mick's pen, she thought, wondering how many police reports he had written with it. She dipped the pen into the ink and began to address an envelope, but the nib was dull, and the ink spattered. She might as well write the letters at home where she had decent writing materials. So she collected the list and stationery and left the room.

"You want me to take you back to Mrs. Stanton's now?" Jonas asked. He had insisted on waiting for her, saying because her aunt was ill, she would not be needing the carriage.

"No," Beret said suddenly. She paused, thinking. Detective McCauley would be furious with her, for going off on her own, but she didn't care. After all, he had excluded her from the interviews with the Summerses. So if he could proceed by himself, so could she. Beret gave Jonas an address on Holladay Street.

Jonas turned around and stared at her. "You know what that is, miss?"

"Of course I do. Do you?" Remembering what the detective had told her about Jonas, Beret regretted her tone. The driver didn't need her scorn. And why wouldn't he know the address? After all, his mother had been a harlot. "I will be perfectly safe, Jonas. I have you to protect me."

"You ain't going to, you know . . ."

At first, Beret didn't understand, and when she did, she laughed. "Join the House of Dreams? Of course not. I merely want to question one of the girls."

"The madam ain't goin' to let you in."

Beret shrugged. "We'll see."

"Mrs. Stanton'll be mad as a turpentined cat."

"Well, don't tell her, then."

When Jonas dipped his chin, Beret didn't know if he agreed with her or was merely underscoring his objection. It didn't matter. Beret would worry about Varina's anger later. Jonas slapped the reins against the horses' backs, and they rode along in silence.

When they arrived at the House of Dreams, Beret sat in the carriage for a moment, gathering her thoughts, wondering if she should send Jonas to fetch Elsie. But she wasn't sure she could trust him and decided to go herself. After all, this was her investigation. She watched as a man went up to Miss Hettie's. The door was opened, then shut, leaving the man outside. He knocked again, but the door remained closed, and he walked away. When the street was deserted, Beret allowed Jonas to help her down from the carriage, then went to the door herself and lifted the heavy knocker. She had not seen who had opened the door a few minutes previous and hoped it was Mae. If Miss Hettie answered, Beret would have to think of some excuse for calling.

But it was indeed Mae, surprise and then consternation on her face. "What you doing back here? Miss Hettie throw you out on your pretty rear end she find you standing here," Mae said, balancing a stack of towels on the door frame.

Beret held out her hand with a gold coin in it. "Tell Miss Elsie I need to speak to her. There is another coin for her. I'll wait in the carriage at the end of the block."

Mae didn't reply, just braced the towels and pocketed the money. Then she shut the door. Beret got back into the carriage and told Jonas to drive down the street. The two sat for more than twenty minutes, and Beret was about to abandon her plan when Elsie emerged from the House of Dreams and sashayed down the street, looking as if she were going for a walk. When she reached the carriage, she glanced back at the whorehouse, then jumped inside.

"You'll get me in trouble if you come around asking for me the way you done," she said, pouting. "I expect you to pay me more than you did last time for all the trouble you put me to."

"That depends on what you tell me," Beret said.

"Well, I already told you everything."

"No, you didn't tell me who supplied my sister with drugs."

Elsie looked away, as if trying to recall something. "I never said she was a doper."

"Well, you are." Beret grabbed the girl's arm and pushed up her sleeve to expose the needle marks.

"Hey, you got no right. That's none of your business," Elsie said. "I ought to go tell Miss Hettie."

"Go ahead. But if you want me to pay you, you'll tell me who was responsible for my sister's drug habit."

Elsie shrugged.

Beret shrugged. "Suit yourself." She reached over to open the carriage door for Elsie.

"Wait a minute. I said I don't know where she got her drugs. Hell, I don't even know if she was a doper. You ask me, I'd say no."

Beret stared at the girl a moment, wondering if that were true. Perhaps she'd been wrong when she suspected her sister of taking drugs—suspected Teddy of plying her with them. After all, she had no proof, and Mick had said nothing about it. But maybe that was to protect Beret's sensibilities. "Where do you get yours?"

"You want to buy some?" Elsie looked sly. "I expect I could get them for you."

"Certainly not. Detective Sergeant McCauley and I will want to interview the person who sells them."

"Oh, Mick," Elsie said fondly, and Beret was surprised at the stab of jealousy. Had the detective and the prostitute been intimate? That was not beyond reason. After all, Mick was a virile young man, and single. At least Beret thought he was single. He had never mentioned a wife. Moreover, he had worked the tenderloin, and many of the policemen assigned to the district sampled the wares. But what Mick McCauley did was none of her affair. She was nothing more to him than the sister of a murder victim. She blushed at her presumption.

"Would she have gotten them from her mac?" Beret asked, keeping her voice calm when she mentioned Teddy. That was a foul charge even for him. But the more she thought about it, the more she blamed him.

"Maybe." Elsie shrugged. "Or maybe she bought them from Chinaman Fong down in Hop Alley off Wazee Street, but I never saw her go there. She never said nothing about him. If she was a user, I bet somebody gave them to her."

"Is Chinaman Fong *your* supplier?" Beret asked.

Elsie looked away and didn't answer. "I got to go. There's hell to pay if Miss Hettie catches me with you. She's got a mean temper, and she'd let loose on me if she found out I was talking to you."

At that, Beret's heart softened, and she wanted to put her arms around the girl, to tell her that she could get out of the life, that she could go someplace where she'd never be mistreated again for stepping out of line. But she knew the girl would scorn her. It was the crib girls and streetwalkers who wanted out, not the well-paid bawds at a place like Miss Hettie's. What could Beret offer that would compare with the excitement and the money Elsie made at the House of Dreams? In five years, if she lived that long, the girl would look for a way out, but not now. Like most parlor house girls, she believed she was there temporarily and would quit when she met a man who would take her away. Or perhaps she dreamed of saving enough money to set herself up in some profitable business, a millinery or flower shop. Beret peered out of the carriage. "I believe it's safe to go." She handed two coins to the prostitute and opened the conveyance door.

Elsie looked around before she stepped out, then she said, "Don't you come around again asking for me. You want to see me, you send Jonas."

Beret was about to ask how Elsie knew Jonas's name, but she held her tongue. It wasn't surprising the girls knew Jonas.

Elsie had not given Beret an address for Chinaman Fong, but Beret assumed Jonas would know it. She watched until Elsie was safely inside the House of Dreams, then told the driver, "I would like you to take me to Hop Alley."

Jonas stared at her. "I ain't doing no such thing."

Beret was tired and annoyed at Jonas's stubbornness. "Then I shall go there by myself."

"You don't know where it's at."

"I will stop men on the street and ask them for directions. Would you prefer that? Or perhaps I should go into the House of Dreams and inquire. I wonder what Mrs. Stanton would say about such a thing."

Jonas stared at her a long time. "You a snowbird?" he asked at last.

"I am not. I do not care to purchase cocaine—or opium or morphine, either. I want to question Chinaman Fong to find out who gave drugs to my sister."

"She wasn't no doper, Miss Lillie wasn't."

"How do you know?" It crossed Beret's mind that if Lillie had taken drugs, Jonas could have been the source for them. He certainly knew his way around the tenderloin. But more likely, it was Teddy. She wanted it to be Teddy.

"I know's all." His little ferret eyes were almost black, and he didn't blink as he stared at Beret. "Miss, you coming here to Miss Hettie's can cause talk, but you go to Hop Alley, asking all your questions, you likely to get killed. That ain't no place for a lady."

Jonas's warning gave Beret pause. He was right. Drug dens were as dangerous as any place in the underworld. She had been inside them in New York, had seen the addicts lying on filthy benches, sucking the bamboo, as it was put, eyes unfocused or closed, smiling at their dreams. The waste of lives had made her sick. The addicts weren't dangerous, but the proprietors were—unctuous men with their greedy eyes, their hands clasped loosely, ready to grab weapons from under their robes. Beret knew of a mission worker who had been stabbed a dozen times when she'd tried to rescue a young girl from such a place. Beret would be safer if Mick were with her. But there was no proof that Lillie had been an addict or that Teddy was her supplier, only Beret's suspicion. Mick had shown little interest in finding out if Lillie had taken drugs. He might even order her not to go to Hop Alley. So finding out the truth was up to her. Beret wished she had the little pistol that she sometimes carried for protection, but she had left it in New York. How could she have known she would need it in Denver?

"I take you home, miss," Jonas pleaded.

"No," Beret said. She sounded resolute, although she was unsure of herself. The decision to talk to the Chinaman was foolish, but she would not turn back. She needed proof that Teddy had given her sister drugs. "The sooner you take me there, the sooner we can return to my aunt's home, and she will never know." She hoped Jonas wouldn't report the stop to Varina. She didn't want to trouble her aunt.

Jonas stared at Beret with his unblinking black eyes for so long that she was afraid he would refuse to drive her to Hop Alley, but at last, he turned on the seat and flipped the reins across the horses' backs. He drove a few blocks, then stopped at an alley. "Fong's the third door, the red one. I take you," Jonas said.

Beret hadn't considered that Jonas would accompany her, and at first, she felt relieved, because she'd begun to think that visiting Hop Alley was not a good idea after all. Jonas knew Denver's underworld better than she did, and he was a scrapper. He'd be good protection. But she didn't trust him. He might tip off the Chinaman with a word or a gesture. For all she knew, Jonas was in the man's employ. "No," she said curtly.

"It's dangerous in there."

Beret shook her head. "I have to do this alone." She opened the door of the carriage and climbed out, telling herself as she started down the alley that she had experience dealing with such men as Fong and that New York's tenderloin was likely to be far worse than Denver's. But she wasn't convinced, and although she held her head high and walked briskly to the red door, she was frightened. Without knocking, she entered the building.

The room was dark, and Beret stood a moment in the doorway letting her eyes adjust to the dim room, which was smoky, sweet with the smell of opium. The walls were lined with bunks, where men and women lay either smoking pipes or caught up in the happiness of dreams. The men she could see were Chinese. White men, except for gamblers and pimps, usually preferred other drugs, Beret knew, and Chinese women rarely smoked opium. She recognized a prostitute she had seen at the café near the police station, and there were two white women, society girls, by the look of them, lying on the bunks with their bamboo pipes, giggling. Smoking opium must be as popular among certain upper-class women in Denver as it was in New York.

A Chinaman closed the door softly behind her, bowed, and asked in his singsongy voice if she wanted an opium pipe.

"I've come to speak to Chinaman Fong," she said in a voice that was stronger than she felt. In fact, she was tempted to return to the carriage and even took a step backward. She had only *suspected* that Lillie had taken drugs, and now Beret wasn't sure at all. Drugs might have played no role at all in Lillie's turning out. But she had to know, and she had to know if Teddy had gotten them for her sister.

The man demurred and gave Beret a sad smile. He was so sorry, he said, Chinaman Fong was busy, too busy to see a pretty lady, but he could sell her an opium pipe, very good price.

Beret took a deep breath then said in a loud voice, "Mr. Fong. I wish to see you."

The man winced and patted her arm. "No, no," he said.

"Then I shall ask louder," Beret told him.

"You wait," he said, and disappeared through the smoke into the back of the room. In a moment, he returned and bowed. "Follow," he said, and Beret made her way down the aisle between the opium addicts until she reached a small room and went inside. The door closed behind her.

Two men sat on stools before a huge wall hanging of embroidered flowers and dragons. Only one of the men was Chinese. He was large and fat, with a stringy ginger-colored mustache that drooped on both sides of his mouth. The white man was small, sickly looking, a doper most likely, and he moved his hands nervously, playing with a cord that he knotted and unknotted. The room was dark, lit only by an oil lamp and the light from a small window encrusted with dirt, and Beret could not see the white man's face. Neither man stood.

"You come to buy opium, morphine?" Fong asked.

Beret shook her head. She had not considered what to say and for a moment was at a loss for words. She glanced nervously at the man behind her.

"Cocaine?"

"No." The men would be curious but have little tolerance for prevaricating. Beret decided to be direct. "I am not here to purchase anything, Mr. Fong," Beret said. "I am after information. I should like to know who purchased drugs for Lillie Brown." She hoped Fong would believe she was aware the drugs came from him and would not deny it, but the moment the words were out of her mouth, Beret knew they were wrong. The man was unlikely to tell her anything.

Fong smiled at Beret and said in respectable English, "I don't know no Lillie Brown."

"That's the whore got killed at Miss Hettie's," the small man told him in a faint voice.

"Quiet, Mr. Sapp." Fong shrugged and said to Beret, "Such sorry business. You with the police, lady?"

Beret was tempted to say she was, to explain she was working with Detective Sergeant McCauley, but she thought now that Fong wouldn't give out the intelligence she wanted if he was aware the law was involved. She knew that about the Chinese. They wanted no trouble. She shook her head. "Miss Brown was a friend." If Beret admitted Lillie was her sister, the man would be similarly inclined to withhold information for fear she would report him.

"Mr. Fong don't sell drugs," Sapp said. He was nervous, twisting the cord around his hand.

Beret scoffed. "Of course he does. Where do those people in the next room get their opium? This is an opium den, and I have it on good authority that the women on the row and their pimps purchase their supplies here. Mr. Fong just offered to sell me something."

"I asked if you wanted," Fong said. "Who says I sell?"

Beret narrowed her eyes. "Please don't play me, sir. The question is not do you deal in drugs but what drugs you sold to Lillie Brown's mac."

"You in the business?" Sapp asked and coughed, sending a yellow glob of sputum to the floor.

Beret thought of saying she was, but the men would know

the prostitutes and madams on Holladay Street, so she only shrugged.

"You will go to the police with your information," Fong said. It was not a question.

"I will if you don't give me the answers." Beret knew that she'd made another mistake. She was in no position to threaten the men. She had never before been this foolish, walking into an opium den by herself. Nobody knew she was there, except for Jonas, and she had ordered him to remain outside. Besides, she wasn't sure she could trust him. She remembered the two white women in the foreroom, but they were in drugged stupors, unlikely to hear her cries. Beret began to perspire from both nervousness and the small airless room. The opium smoke that seeped through the wall made her nauseous. She wanted only to get away safely now.

"She says she'll report you to the police," Sapp repeated.

"No," Beret told them. "I am in no position to go to the police." She thought quickly. "I want to know if a man named Teddy Star supplied Miss Brown with morphine or cocaine. Surely you can tell me that." She smiled a little. "If I went to the police, who would believe me anyway? It would be my word against yours."

"A white woman's word against a Chinaman's?" Fong scoffed.

"What could I tell them anyway? Surely the police are aware of what takes place in Hop Alley."

"A white woman could raise a stink. You could go to the newspapers. Don't matter what's true or not. There was a riot here a few years back, and Mr. Fong don't trust white people. They'd like to shut down Hop Alley. That's what this is about, ain't it?" Sapp told her. "Fong don't want that to happen again." He stretched the cord between his hands. "You get mixed up in that whore's murder, Fong, and you're done for. Ain't nobody going to let you operate then. This white lady's naught but trouble."

Fong smiled and asked, "Are you trouble, lady?"

"No, I am not a reformer," she replied, her voice unsteady. Jonas had been right. Why hadn't she listened to him? Beret had put herself in danger by coming to see the Chinaman. Trouble-makers went into these places and were never seen again. Perhaps she should identify herself as Judge Stanton's niece, but that would make the two men even more wary. They were not going to give her any information about Teddy, and now her concern was getting away safely. "I see you will not give me the intelligence I need. Perhaps I was mistaken in my belief you had sold drugs to Mr. Star. So I shall wish you good day," she said, trying to sound confident.

She took a step backward toward the door, but Sapp had slipped off his stool, and now he slid behind her. He was even smaller than she thought, and he shook as he moved. Beret wondered if she could overpower him. Then she heard him turn the latch. She felt the sweat trickle down her sides. Her head was light from the airless room. She knew she had to keep her wits about her, although her mind seemed numb. She took a deep breath, breathing in the sweet opium-scented air. "It is clear I have been mistaken, and I shall leave now," she told Fong.

"Oh, she'd like to leave," Sapp repeated in a hard voice.

Fong shrugged and smiled again, although his eyes were hard. "You come alone, lady?"

"My carriage is outside."

"I didn't see no carriage when I looked out," Sapp said. "If I's you, I wouldn't take no chances."

"What do you suggest, Mr. Sapp?" Fong asked.

"She can leave, all right, but not through this door." He kicked the door he had just locked.

"There are those who know I am here," Beret told Fong.

"Then where are they?" Fong asked, spreading his hands, his smile exposing rotted teeth.

"She made a mistake, but we don't have to," Sapp said, standing behind Beret. "She's too old for one of the good houses, but Gold-tooth Laura might pay fifty dollars for her."

They were panders, Beret realized. They drugged women and sold them to the brothels. The men would rape her to break her in, then fill her with drugs so that she couldn't get away. Neither Mick nor her uncle would ever think to look for her in a house of assignation. How stupid she had been to venture into this place. She looked for a way to escape, but Sapp blocked the door behind her. He had said something about another door, but she didn't see one. It would be behind the wall hanging, because there were no openings on the side walls, only the window, too small and too high up to allow escape. But even if there were a second door, Fong sat in front of it. And it would be locked, too.

Was this what had happened to Lillie? Beret wondered. Had she been drugged and sold to Miss Hettie? Was that why she had ended up in the House of Dreams? It was possible, of course, but no, Beret thought now. Lillie had turned out for reasons of her own, reasons still unknown to her sister. Lillie had not been a doper. Beret had been too anxious to accuse Teddy of plying her sister with drugs to think things through. She had wanted Teddy to be guilty. She had allowed her hatred of him to cloud her judgment, and now she was threatened with being drugged herself and sold into prostitution. The irony of what was about to happen did not escape her; she had fought against white slavery in New York.

Beret thought again of telling the men who she was, but if they realized she was the judge's niece, they would surely kill her. She was safer if they thought she was nobody, someone who wouldn't be missed. *Safer!* Beret paled at the thought. What the men had in mind was only a slower death.

Beret could not see Sapp behind her, but she knew he had the cord in his hand. Perhaps he would simply strangle her. She took a deep breath, the sound rattling in her throat, as she squeezed her hands into fists to keep herself from panicking. If she grew hysterical, she wouldn't be able to think. She heard the man move to the side and the snap of a cork as it was withdrawn from a bottle, releasing a smell of chloroform. Beret turned to see Sapp pouring liquid on a rag. "No!" she cried, and startling the man, Beret stamped on his foot, crushing the thin bones, and snatched the rag, forcing it against his nose. Sapp was too sickly to fight back. He staggered, let go of the empty bottle, fell against the wall, and slid to the floor.

Beret turned in time to see Fong rise. He was an enormous man, and had not moved when she attacked Sapp, perhaps because he knew there was no way for her to get out of the room. "Very foolish," he said, taking a step toward her. Beret looked around for something to defend herself. She spotted an opium pipe, wood with brass and jade trim, on the table and grabbed it. Fong kept on smiling, knowing the object was too small to inflict damage. "Foolish," he said again, as if enjoying himself. Would he be one of those who would rape her? The thought caused Beret's stomach to knot. She raised her arm to fling the pipe against the man, but instead, she aimed it at the window, throwing so hard that she broke the glass and the pipe sailed into the alley. Then she began to scream.

Fong shook his head at her as if she had been a naughty girl.

"So very foolish," he said, and then he advanced slowly, playing with her as if he were a rat dog and she was his prey. She clutched the rag she had pressed against Sapp's nose but knew the Chinaman would never let her use it on him.

Beret glanced at the door to see if Sapp had left the key in the lock. Even if the people in the next room were high on opium, there were enough of them to give Fong pause, if she could only get through the door. But the key was gone. She would have to go through Sapp's pockets to find it, and that was impossible with Fong advancing on her.

She screamed again, louder, crying for help. The alley outside was noisy. Would anyone even hear her? And who would break into an opium den to save a hysterical woman who might only be coming out of a drug-induced sleep?

Then she saw the silk tapestry move at the same instant she heard the sound of wood splintering. Fong heard it, too, and turned, taking his eyes off Beret long enough for her to grasp Sapp's stool and slam it against Fong's head. The blow was poorly aimed, but it stunned the Chinaman long enough for Jonas to rush through the door and strike Fong in the temple with his fist. He battered the man's face and body, and didn't stop when Fong fell onto the floor and was still. He leaned over the big body and started hitting again, until Beret called him off.

"We mustn't kill him," she said, "although he deserves it, both of them. They are evil."

Jonas, his hands clenched into fists, shook his head, as if to bring himself to his senses. Beret wondered if he would have stopped if she hadn't called him off.

"You saved my life, Jonas," Beret said.

The remark didn't seem to register. "Best get," he said.

"We must call the police."

"No!" When Beret frowned, he added, "They ain't dead. You tell the police, them two deny everything. How you going to explain you being here? What you think Mrs. Stanton say—and that detective?"

"But they are panders. They were about to chloroform me and sell me."

"Or kill you. Maybe you was done for. You go after them, they liable to hurt Mrs. Stanton. I know what I say." Jonas grabbed Beret's arm and pulled her to the back door.

Beret didn't protest. She was too frightened. What if the men came to and attacked them? She had been stupid, stupid. With nothing to back up her charge, she had blamed Teddy for hooking Lillie on drugs and turning her into a prostitute. She had risked her life and Jonas's, and perhaps the safety of her aunt and uncle. Beret hurried after Jonas to the carriage and climbed inside, collapsing against the seat. Jonas slapped the reins against the horses and took off with the speed of a hack driver.

They rode without talking and didn't stop until they reached the Stanton house. As Jonas opened the carriage door for her, Beret asked, "Are you going to tell my aunt about this?"

Jonas stared at her with his strange eyes before he replied, "No, miss. Are you going to tell that detective?"

Beret rubbed her hand over her face, taking in the faint smell of chloroform. "I haven't decided."

Chapter 12

On Sunday evening, Varina invited Beret to go with her and the judge to a gathering in a Capitol Hill mansion, but with not much enthusiasm. "You could do with a diversion after spending your day writing those dreadful letters to police departments, but I must warn you that you would be terribly bored. Ellen Fisk is as sour as spoiled apples, and Mr. Fisk talks incessantly, always about his own importance, which, alas, is the case. We wouldn't subject ourselves to the Fisks except that your uncle does so want to be appointed to the Senate, and Horace Fisk can make that happen."

It was clear that Jonas had kept his word and not told his employer about the ugly episode in Hop Alley, and Beret, of course, had no intention of doing so. "The last few days have been trying, Aunt Varina. I'd rather stay in, if you don't mind."

"Of course I don't. If I had my way, I'd keep you company. I'll make your excuses." Varina sat at her dressing table, attaching a diamond earring to her ear. "I won't tell them what you've been doing, of course. That would shock them." She paused, apparently considering the idea, and gave Beret a sly grin. "I'll just say you are tired from the trip. Of course, I could always tell them you are in mourning, but that would preclude your going to the Deckers' dinner party, and you will enjoy that one. Tonight's gathering is only for politics. Here, Beret, would you fasten my necklace?" Varina had taken out diamonds for the evening—besides the earrings and necklace, she had selected a bracelet of diamonds and sapphires in an intricate design. They looked elegant against her black velvet gown. Beret didn't know if her aunt had chosen black as a sign of respect for Lillie or because it set off her jewelry. She suspected the latter.

"There you are, and don't you look lovely!" Beret said, standing back to admire her aunt.

"Thank you. I dearly love diamonds. But sometimes, I think they make me look old. I am getting old, you know."

"Not so old. We could be sisters," Beret told her, looking at the two of them in the mirror over the dressing table. Her words were a harmless bit of flattery, for Varina did indeed look her age, which was nearly sixty. Her figure was still slender, but her hair had turned a lifeless gray, and there were lines around her eyes and mouth. The black velvet may have set off her diamonds, but it made Varina's skin look colorless.

"Do you really think so?" the older woman asked.

Beret knew that many women who were no longer young were vain and that age was a trial to them. Wealth and station were no solace for women who felt old and rejected. She had seen that with the women at the mission who had been cast aside after years of drudgery. But of course, Varina was not like them. She and her husband were as happily married as any couple Beret knew. John Stanton, as well as Beret, adored her. Perhaps Varina's resistance to growing older had something to do with her childless state. Or her question might be nothing more than

175

trolling for a compliment. "I would not have said it if I didn't mean it, Aunt Varina."

"Would not have said what?" Judge Stanton asked, coming into the room.

"How young your wife looks."

"She does, indeed," he said with a little too much enthusiasm. "She will always be young to me and beautiful, as well, but it pleases me that others see those qualities in her."

Beret found the remark obvious. She had never thought of her uncle as a flatterer. Still, the words pleased her aunt, so who was Beret to find them false?

"Not going with us? Smart girl. I would rather drink sour buttermilk than go to the Fisks', but it can't be helped. Ah, Beret, it is a burden to be ambitious."

"What is life without ambition?" Varina asked, rising, her diamonds sending out rainbows of color in the lights of the bedchamber. Beret wondered which of the two of them was the more ambitious.

She walked with them to the side door, where Jonas waited under the porte cochere with the carriage. "We won't be back until late. Jonas will come for us at one in the morning. We hope to be home not much later, but the party could go on longer. You don't know how these men like to drink and smoke cigars and discuss politics, while the women sit in the parlor and gossip." The judge glanced at his wife, and added, "I mean they like to sit and plan good works."

"Hardly. 'Gossip' is the more likely word," Varina said, then told Beret, "I've already instructed William not to wait up for us, so you may dismiss him whenever you like."

Beret stood outside in the cold, watching her aunt and uncle get into the carriage, then stood on the carriage stop until the vehicle disappeared from sight. She had said she would be lonely without them, but the truth was, she was relieved to have an evening to herself. She had letters of her own to compose, and there were things about Lillie's death she wanted to ponder, in hopes she could see the murder more clearly.

As she went back inside, she instructed William to bring a tray with her dinner to the library, and she went into the room and sat down at the desk. She could write her letters in her room, as she had all day, but the library was cozier, and now that she was alone, she would be in no one's way. The desk was not such a fine one but it was serviceable, with large drawers on the sides and small drawers and pigeonholes above, with a top that rolled up and down for privacy. The roll was closed, and Beret pushed it up, glad that it was not locked. The judge was not a tidy person, which might be the reason he kept the top down. The desk was covered with letters and notes, bills, scraps of paper, pens and penwipes and broken nibs. There was an inkwell, and Beret could see where spilled ink had penetrated the wood of the desktop. A law book lay open, shoved off to one side. Beret searched until she found a pencil, which she sharpened with her uncle's penknife, carefully collecting the shavings and throwing them into the fire, which William had already lighted. Then she took out several sheets of paper and cleared a space for writing. She was careful to note what she had moved so that the items could be returned to their proper place when she was finished. She did not want her uncle to think she had been snooping.

She wrote quickly. Beret was an efficient correspondent, and her prose was devoid of flowery words. She wrote Maggie, her housekeeper, that she would be staying in Denver indefinitely and would telegraph when she was ready to return. She asked the woman to cancel all social engagements. Then she wrote to her assistant at the mission, saying much the same thing, although she inquired after some of the women who were staying there, asking if they had found employment, gone back to husbands, whether they had healed in body if not in spirit. She asked both women to forward any correspondence to her uncle's house.

As Beret finished the second letter, William came into the room with the dinner tray and set it on a small table beside her uncle's chair. "Judge Stanton has his dinner in here when he is working. He prefers to sit in the chair. I hope that will be satisfactory," he said.

As the butler turned to go, Beret said suddenly, "William, I'd like to talk to you for a moment. Will you sit?" The butler looked uncomfortable, and Beret added, "Or stand, whichever you choose."

He remained in place, not looking directly at her. "What can I do for you, madam?"

"I'd like to ask you about my sister."

"A shame what happened to her." William studied the fire.

"Indeed it was. A shame and a shock. But that's not why I want to speak with you. As you know, I am working with Detective Sergeant McCauley in trying to apprehend Miss Lillie's killer. The detective is of the opinion that the same man murdered both Lillie and the prostitute whose body was discovered on Holladay Street. I think that most likely he is right. It is difficult to imagine two different men perpetrating such ghastly crimes. Still, it is in my mind that my sister was murdered by someone who knew her."

William jerked his head around so that he looked directly at Beret. "Someone she knew? Surely not, madam."

Beret shrugged. "It is only conjecture. But it must be considered until we have eliminated everyone with whom she came in contact."

William nodded, and clasped his hands behind his back.

"Who among Lillie's acquaintances disliked her?"

"I couldn't say."

"Of course you could. I am not talking about your employers, of course. I know you would not betray them. And there is nothing to betray," she added quickly. "I mean the others of their social set. I will keep our conversation confidential. You needn't worry that I will tell my aunt we discussed this."

"Thank you, madam." William relaxed a little, although he still looked uncomfortable.

"You could help find her killer," Beret coaxed.

William thought that over. "If she was killed by someone she knew, could it not be a man she met at that . . ." He cleared his throat. "At that house of assignation?"

"That's possible, of course, but unfortunately, we will never know the names of the men she met there." Beret looked down at her hands, not sure whether to confide Lillie's situation to William, but it was likely he knew. Little got past servants. "My sister was with child. It is probable she was in that state before she entered Miss Hettie's House of Dreams. That means the father of her child must be someone she knew, perhaps one of the young men of my aunt's social circle."

If he were shocked by the revelation, William did not show it. After a pause, he said, "I did not like Mr. Summers. He was overbearing and peremptory, although Miss Lillie seemed to care for his company well enough. I myself thought it unseemly. He came here once when Mrs. Stanton was away—he seemed to be aware she was not present. Miss Lillie took him into the parlor and said they were not to be disturbed. I distinctly heard the key turn in the lock. When she emerged fully an hour later, her clothes were mussed."

Although she had come to realize that Lillie had changed, Beret was still shocked to think her sister had been so brazen. To steady herself, she lifted her fork and picked at a vegetable on her plate. The servants generally did not work on Sundays, and Beret was aware that William must have forgone his day off. Cook would have prepared her dinner the night before—cold roast beef, beans, potatoes, bread, a pastry—but Beret was not hungry and wished it were only soup. "Then something improper must have taken place." She tried to hold her voice steady.

"If you say so."

"Did my aunt know?"

"*I* didn't tell her."

"But did she know?"

William went to the fireplace and placed another log on the fire, adjusting it with a poker. "Madam was very angry about something. I heard her tell Miss Lillie, 'He might as well be your father.' She said Miss Lillie had disgraced them. 'Disgrace,' that was the word she used. Your sister left not long after that."

Beret looked up from her tray. "Her father? But surely Joseph Summers was not much older than my sister."

"Not Mr. *Joseph* Summers, Mr. Evan Summers."

"He came *here*?" Beret set her fork on her plate, the vegetable on its tines uneaten, and rose, her back to the butler, while she composed herself. Mae, the maid at Miss Hettie's, had said the elder Mr. Summers had been a customer, but the idea that he had pursued Lillie in the Stanton house unnerved her. Of course, she should have known better. Her work at the mission had taught her otherwise. Still, her own sister engaged in such an unspeakable act with a married man who was old enough to be her father and in this very house was vile. There was so much about Lillie that Beret didn't understand. "He must have seduced her." When William didn't respond, Beret turned. "Is that not so?"

William took a deep breath. "I could not say he was the seducer."

"Oh." Beret rose. She had learned a great deal about Lillie in the past two weeks, but had her sister been that shameless? The images of Lillie as both an innocent and a harlot fought inside Beret.

"I must help in the kitchen," William said.

He turned to go, but Beret touched his arm. She took control of herself and said, "This is not easy for me, William, for either of us. Are you saying that my sister pursued Mr. Evan Summers?" When William refused to answer or even look at her, she added, "Please. If I am to find out who killed her, I must know what happened, even if it distresses me. I will not hold it against you." She seated herself and glanced at the dinner, but she could not eat now.

William considered what Beret had said. "May I sit, madam?"

Beret indicated the chair next to her and pushed her tray aside.

"Miss Lillie . . ." he began, and stopped, looking down at his hands.

"Yes," Beret said when he did not continue.

"The truth is, madam, she was wild, and her standards, well, they were not what Mrs. Stanton would have wished."

"Her standards?"

William looked into the fire. "Madam would be displeased if she knew I—"

"Oh, bosh, William. Mrs. Stanton won't know we talked. I have no intention of telling her. I am trying to find out who killed my sister." Despite what she said, however, Beret hoped William would deny Lillie had been the aggressor.

William turned to her and said fiercely, "She was not a good person, Miss Lillie wasn't. She entertained men on the servants' day off, when Judge and Mrs. Stanton were away. She took gifts from them—jewelry, laces, a fur cape. They are up there still in her room—*your* room. It's no surprise to me she ended up on Holladay Street." Abashed at his outbreak, William stood. "I shouldn't have spoken as I did. Beg pardon, madam."

As the butler rose, Beret told him, "Wait. You are not dismissed. What do you think turned my sister into such a woman?"

"She was always such."

Beret was confused. "Always? What do you mean, *always*?"

"She was like that as a girl. I saw it when you came to visit many years ago, when Mr. and Mrs. Osmundsen were alive, and later, when it was just you and your sister and your husband." He pronounced "your husband" almost with distaste. "Perhaps you did not see how she flirted and pouted to get her way and punished those who wouldn't give it to her. You never saw how she was, you most of all. You were blind to her imperfections."

Beret shook her head. "No, you are wrong, William. My sister was not like that back then. She was as sweet a girl as ever lived."

"Yes, madam," he said, opening the door. "I must be wrong."

"One more thing," Beret said, and William stopped. "Did my husband . . . did Mr. Staarman visit my sister here?"

William looked away. "Do you really want to know, madam?"

"I do."

"Yes, he did."

"On more than one occasion?"

"Yes."

"Did my aunt and uncle know?"

"I couldn't say."

Beret was crushed. She almost could not breathe, and she felt faint and was barely aware that the butler had left her. Teddy had done this. William was wrong about Lillie. She had been a perfect child until Teddy ruined her. Beret was desperate to believe that. Teddy had seduced her in New York, and after Lillie fled, he had pursued her to Denver and forced himself on her. Beret knew from her work at the mission that women who had been raped or seduced sometimes turned wanton—from guilt or shame. Some even ended up as prostitutes, because they had no choice. But Lillie had had a choice. She could have lived with her aunt and uncle, or with Beret, if one of them had only apologized. Kindness and goodness, not deceit, had once been her nature. If that had changed, it was Teddy's fault.

But was it? Could William be right? Beret shook her head as if to rid herself of the possibility that Lillie had been willful and selfish all along. She picked at her dinner, cutting a piece of the roast, but she could not eat. She tried a bite of potato, but it stuck in her throat, and she swallowed several times to get it down. She thrust the tray aside and went to her uncle's liquor cabinet and took the stopper from a decanter of port, pouring a little into a glass and drinking it, relishing the raw taste of the liquor. She was weary and returned to the chair, and in a moment, she dozed off.

She awoke when William knocked on the library door, then entered softly and picked up the tray. When Beret sat up, he asked, "Are you finished, madam?"

"Yes, please don't tell Cook that I wasn't hungry," she said, then added, "You might as well retire, William. I'll sit here only a little longer, then go upstairs." William left, and after a few minutes, Beret thought to thank him for his confidences. She opened the library door, but the lights were dim, and there was no sign of the butler. Except for one or two lights, the house was quiet, and Beret quickly returned to the warmth of the library, turning her back on the dark and silent house.

Chapter 13

Beret felt lethargic and sat down again in her uncle's chair. She did not fall asleep this time but sat in a kind of stupor, considering what she had learned about her sister in the time she had been in Denver.

Lillie had come to the Stanton house as soon as she left New York. She'd lived with her aunt and uncle some nine months. Then she'd abruptly fled to Miss Hettie's. Or had the departure been abrupt? As distasteful as it would be to her aunt, Beret would have to press Varina for information. Beret was sure that her aunt knew more than she had told. She had kept things to herself rather than distress Beret—or perhaps to avoid showing herself in a poor light. Had Varina forced Lillie out when she discovered her niece was pregnant? Had Varina even known Lillie was pregnant? After all, Miss Hettie hadn't known, and Lillie had been as much as five months along when she was murdered.

Then there was the question of the identity of the baby's father. Since Lillie had been pregnant before she entered the House of Dreams, the father couldn't have been a john but instead must have been someone she'd known when she was living in the

Stanton house—Evan Summers, perhaps. He might have been the married man Lillie had talked about, the wealthy gentleman she believed would leave his wife and marry her. Or, as Mick had suggested, was that just a fantasy Lillie had told Elsie, a lie to impress the other girls? Or perhaps young Joe Summers had fathered the child. Lillie could even have been intimate with other men, as William had suggested. It was possible that she couldn't even identify the father.

Or was he Teddy? Beret felt tears come to her eyes as she realized Teddy was most likely the father of her sister's child. It was odd, she thought, that in all their years of marriage, she had never conceived. But her sister had. Could Lillie have been so craven that carrying Teddy's child was an act of revenge against Beret?

Beret found herself faced with too many questions, none of them with answers. She sighed as she sat up and looked around the room. The fire had died out, and she herself had turned down the lamp. She did not want her aunt and uncle to find her sleeping in the library. She should rouse herself and go to bed. But she leaned back in the chair and sat a little longer, and in a moment, she heard a door open into the hall and footsteps come toward the library. William might have decided to linger until she retired. But William moved noiselessly. She would not have heard his footfalls. It was Nellie, then, or another of the Stanton servants returning after a day off. Beret was not concerned.

And then she looked up to see Jonas enter the room. She watched through half-closed eyes as he crept to the fire, but when he saw it was dead, he did not add a log. Instead, he picked up a blanket resting on the back of a chair and started for her, and as he came close, she caught the smell of whiskey. She sat up and said, "Hello, Jonas."

He stopped, startled, as if caught in some wrongdoing. "I

seen you through the window and thought you needed covering up," he said quickly.

"You covered me another night."

Jonas did not answer.

"Sit a moment."

"Not me. I got to fetch the judge."

"It's early yet. I heard the clock strike midnight only minutes ago."

"Then I got to hitch up the horses. Mrs. Stanton don't like it if I'm late."

Beret moved her feet from the footstool and sat up straight, because she felt vulnerable. "Have you told Mrs. Stanton what transpired in Hop Alley?" she asked.

Jonas shook his head. "I ain't telling her. I promised you that. She won't like it if you get sold on Holladay Street."

"You knew they'd do that?"

"Maybe. It turned out all right." Jonas was nervous and blew on his hands. Beret smelled the whiskey again.

"Sit." Beret pushed the footstool a little ways away from her. "I want to talk to you about my sister."

Jonas glanced around the room as if looking for a way out. He rubbed his hands together. "I don't know nothing."

She couldn't ease Jonas into a conversation as she had William, so Beret was direct. "You knew my sister as well as anyone. You drove her about."

"I didn't talk to her none—not much, leastways." Jonas still held out the blanket, which made Beret uneasy.

"Of course you did. You've talked to me. You saved my life. Sit down."

"I'd rather stand."

Beret stood herself then, because she did not care to have

Jonas looking down at her. His standing there with the blanket made her uncomfortable. "I'm told my aunt rescued you from some wicked newsboys. There's nothing you wouldn't do for my aunt, is there?"

Jonas didn't respond but looked at her, suspicious. At last, he said, "I saved you, didn't I?"

Of course, Beret thought, Jonas hadn't cared about her. He was repaying Varina. Perhaps in his strange mind, he felt they were even, he and the Stanton family. A branch knocked against the house, startling her. The wind had come up, and the branch drummed against the roof in a sort of staccato. The room was gloomy, and Beret realized she was alone with this strange man, that no one in the house was likely to hear her if she cried out. But surely there would be no reason for her to summon help. Jonas was odd, but Beret dismissed the idea that he was dangerous.

"You'd be upset if someone hurt Mrs. Stanton—or her reputation—wouldn't you?"

"I wouldn't let nobody chuck her around."

Jonas put down the blanket at last, but then he brushed aside his coat, and Beret saw a wicked-looking knife stuck in his belt. He followed her glance and grinned. "This here's my frog sticker. Nobody's going to chunk me around, neither," he said. His face took on the appearance of an evil imp. Beret went to the fireplace and stirred the ashes. A tiny flame flickered for a moment, then died down. She watched it, her knuckles white in the firelight as she gripped the poker. She told herself Jonas was only a coachman, but there was something not quite right about him. She didn't like being alone in the library with him and wished she had not dismissed William.

"Jonas, I am trying to find out who killed my sister, something that Judge and Mrs. Stanton are as anxious to know as I am. Finding the killer will put this ugly business behind us and let the judge pursue the Senate seat, which is something Mrs. Stanton wants very much." Jonas would be well aware of the judge's ambition. He'd have overheard talk in the carriage.

"She was murdered by a crazy man, her and that other'n," Jonas blurted out. "You know as such. I taken you down there to see where she been done in. The coppers say it was a crazy man. Why you say otherwise?"

"And the police may be right, but I am not sure of it. I have information that while she lived under this roof, my sister acted improperly. What do you know about that? Was she a loose woman?"

Jonas dropped his head to one side, and Beret could see how badly the boy was misshapen. He might have been born that way or else he'd been beaten, perhaps by his mother or her johns, or maybe by boys in the orphanage, who always sensed the weak ones. He would be scarred inside, as well, perhaps worse than on the outside. His mother might have sold him to the perverted men who roamed the tenderloin. Or he could have been used in that manner by the bigger boys. Varina might have been the only person in his life who had shown him kindness. "You do want to help, don't you, Jonas?" She added, "Mrs. Stanton will not know we talked. Was Miss Lillie a good woman?"

He shrugged. "She done things."

Beret waited.

"Sometimes when I taken her in the carriage, she have me to pick up a man."

"Did you tell my aunt?"

"Not when I first come to know how things was. But Mrs.

Stanton found something in the carriage, something that ought'n be there, and she asks me. So I tell her. She say I'm to tell her every time Miss Lillie do something wrong."

"And did you?"

Jonas shook his head. "Not everything. I don't want to hurt Mrs. Stanton none."

"What were the things you didn't tell her?"

"I'm not telling you, neither."

Beret grinned at that, and Jonas looked up and gave her a sly smile. He smiled like a little boy, Beret thought. "How old are you?" she asked.

"Not certain, maybe seventeen, maybe not."

"You must have disliked my sister a great deal."

Jonas looked directly at Beret now, and she saw the freakish scars on his face and thought what a good woman her aunt had been to pick up such an ugly child, a child other society women might find offensive, and take him into her home. In that, she was like her sister, Beret's mother. Marta Osmundsen had been the soul of compassion.

Jonas looked down at the knife and carefully drew it out. He tested the blade against his hand, then looked at Beret, who kept her hand firmly on the poker. "No, ma'am. I liked Miss Lillie fine. She was good to me. Always had a nice word, not like some that looks down on the driver and are all braggy talking. She'd tell me to go get a glass of beer if she was going to stay a while and even give me a nickel to buy it."

Beret made a note to do that the next time Jonas drove her someplace. "Is there anybody you can think of who would want to kill her?" Beret tried to keep her eyes from the knife, but that was impossible since Jonas began to wave it around.

"Nobody that knowed her. Maybe she wasn't a good woman,

but she was as nice a one as I ever met. Like I say, she was killed by a crazy man that cuts up whores. You best believe that." He made stabbing motions at Beret to underscore the point.

"You were good protection for her, as you are for my aunt."

"Nobody ever get to Mrs. Stanton when I'm around." He ran the blade over his knuckles, then pointed it again at Beret. "I cut anybody that hurts her. You remember that, miss."

Beret frowned, not sure what he meant. "I will."

"I got to go now. I don't want to be late."

"Yes, of course. You go on. I won't tell Mrs. Stanton we talked."

"Oh, that's all right. I'll tell her." He gave Beret a crooked smile, although there was no smile in his eyes, and then he said in a voice that made her shudder, "You be careful, miss. You don't want nothing to happen to you like it did Miss Lillie. Maybe you ought to go back home." He gave her a hard-eyed look and slunk away. It was the second time Jonas had warned her.

He was almost like two different boys, one protective, the other threatening, Beret thought, as she returned the poker to its stand.

She went up to her room then and turned the lock on the door. The lock was fragile. Beret herself could have broken it, but she felt safer with the door latched. She considered putting a chair in front of the door, but decided against it. Her aunt would be insulted if she found out.

Beret removed her dress and hung it in the wardrobe. On impulse, she examined Lillie's clothes. There was a fur jacket, and when Beret put her hand into the pocket, she discovered a diamond brooch, a distinctive one whose stones formed a rose. It was expensive. Why would Lillie have left such a fine piece of jewelry behind? Even if she didn't want it, she could have sold it.

Beret returned the brooch to its hiding place until she could figure out what to do with it.

Curious now about the rest of Lillie's things, Beret opened the drawers of the dresser. Nellie had unpacked Beret's bags and put her garments into the top drawers, but Lillie's possessions were in the lower drawers, and Beret went through them carefully, noting the fragile underthings, the lace fichus and scarves, the gloves. She picked up a kid glove, a long white one, and ran her hand over the buttery leather. Then she slipped her hand inside but felt something and withdrew a ring set with a diamond the color of champagne. When had Lillie developed a passion for diamonds? She had never worn much jewelry, only the pendant Beret had given her and their mother's earrings shaped like stars. The other pieces must have been given to her, and she had secreted them so that her aunt wouldn't know.

Beret put on her nightdress and got into bed, but she thought about Jonas and could not sleep. She did not like the idea of his roaming the house when her aunt and uncle were away. After a while, she rose and went to the window and looked out at the stable in the moonlight. The sky was smoky with clouds. In time, she saw Jonas leave the building with the carriage, and much later, she heard the clop-clop of the horses as he returned. She watched as he pulled the carriage under the porte cochere beneath her window, and while she could not see her aunt and uncle, she heard them enter the house, heard the low sounds of their voices as they climbed the stairs. She felt safer knowing they were there—but not entirely safe, she thought.

Chapter 14

The judge was gone by the time Beret entered the breakfast room the following morning, and she found her aunt writing notes. The older woman put aside the pen and paper and said, "It's ever so much nicer sitting here in the sun than in that gloomy library, don't you think?"

Beret remembered that she had left her letters on her uncle's desk and said, "It was cozy writing letters in there last night. I hope you don't mind if I used both the desk and your stationery. I left in such a hurry, I did not bring my own writing paper and did not want to use a letterhead from the police department. I must mail the letters today."

Varina waved her hand. "Of course we don't mind. I gave them to William to post." Beret went to the window and raised her face to the sunlight. A few days before, the lawn had been raked and rid of the detritus of winter, and the earth was fresh and moist. Green shoots had begun to push up in the flower garden, which was Varina's pride. By May, the daisies and heartsease would be budding, the delphinium sending up stalks, and by June, there would be a profusion of flowers, all colors but mostly pink, a dozen hues of it, because it was Varina's favorite color. Beret had seen the garden before, had immersed herself in the perfume of the roses and peonies. She looked closely and thought she saw violets already blooming, but that might have been just crumbs of purple leaves.

The street was serene, peaceful. The trees, tall but not yet full grown, softened Grant Avenue's ponderous houses of brick and stone. There were still traces of snow, drifts of it on the north sides of houses, but the sun had melted most of it, leaving only bits of ice that reflected the light like crystal beads.

"Honestly, Aunt, I don't understand the weather here. One day it snows, and the next, it might be summer. I should have packed for both."

"I think Lillie left enough gowns to allow you to dress for the seasons. They can be fitted to you. I'll have William send for my dressmaker if you like."

Beret did not turn around. "Why is it she did not take her things with her? I was surprised to see them here."

"Who knows how women dress in those places?" Varina replied casually. "She took a few, and I thought she'd send for the rest after she was settled. If you don't want them, then I suppose they can go to the church clothing drive. Some poor woman will think she's a queen."

"They're very nice, and expensive, too. I wonder how Lillie was able to acquire them."

"Your uncle gave her an allowance."

"It must have been a generous one." Beret turned around and smiled at her aunt.

Varina waved her arm. "I loaned her small sums. I said she could repay if she wished when the two of you had worked things out with your solicitor."

"You were very good to her, Aunt." Then Beret said again, "I am surprised she left so much here. Did she leave her jewelry, too?"

"Nothing of value."

William entered then with Beret's breakfast, and she seated herself at the table. While Beret was wondering how to bring up the subject of Lillie's paramours, Varina said, "I am surprised to see you this morning. I thought you'd gone off with Michael in another visit to our underworld. It seems to have taken possession of you. May I hope that you listened to what I said and have given it up?" She raised an eyebrow at Beret. "I suspect you haven't, because Jonas told me you had quizzed him about Lillie."

"A little."

"And what did he say?"

"Not much. Nothing you don't know, that Lillie entertained men."

"I had hoped to keep it from you. I'm sorry you had to find out."

"I wanted to know."

Varina motioned to William to pour more coffee, and then she dismissed him. "You haven't given it up, then."

"I hope to meet with Detective McCauley later today. He is conducting interviews."

Varina clapped her hands. "Surely it can wait until tomorrow. I insist you come with me on an outing today. The Presbyterian Church is having a clothing drive for the poor, and I am in charge. Of course we are happy to take clothing for men and children, but we are especially anxious to outfit the women. It is important that those looking for employment appear well groomed. As you know, too often the burden of supporting the family falls on women, and yet their wages barely put food on the table for one person, let alone a husband and children."

"You are too good, Aunt," Beret said. "You are just like Mother."

"Not that good, I'm afraid. You remember, Beret, your mother and I were born poor ourselves. We knew what it was like to be hungry and ill clothed, so it's little enough I can do. Besides, the work reflects well on your uncle, and I do so want him to get the Senate appointment."

"Is Mrs. Fisk, the woman you dined with last night, one of the women on your committee?"

Varina regarded Beret a moment. "Little gets past you. Is that not so, Beret?"

"I see nothing wrong with benefiting ourselves while we help others." Beret wondered if she really felt that way or was just humoring her aunt.

Varina smiled and stood, saying she had things to do. Jonas would take them to the meeting. Beret finished her breakfast and picked up her coffee cup, opening the door to a small side porch and going outside. The air, colder than it had appeared from the breakfast room, was fresh and clean, and Beret lifted her head to feel the breeze. She leaned against the cold granite of the porch railing as she sipped from the cup and studied the mansions on the street, wondering if the women who presided over them were as concerned as her aunt about Denver's poor or if their only thoughts were of teas and balls and parties. She heard a screeching sound and recognized the call of a peacock, then remembered her uncle telling her that a silver millionaire in the neighborhood had imported peacocks to roam his lawn. One of them must have gone for a stroll, because in a moment, Beret saw the creature walk stiff-legged down the street, his blue head turning from side to side in quick jerks, his bright feathers dragging in the dirt. Beret smiled at the pretentiousness of peacocks roaming the dirt yards of the newly built mansions, whose occupants, her uncle had told her, were only a day away from beans and fatback. A few months before, if they'd seen such a bird, she thought, they would have killed it and skinned it for the supper table.

As if to underscore Denver's questionable sophistication, a carriage the color of the sky drove past, its matching interior gleaming in the sunlight. The driver and coachman were dressed in similar livery, not the subdued uniforms of New York's wealthy, but garish costumes that reminded Beret of Mr. Barnum's museum in New York. She shook her head at the tastelessness of it, and then she laughed, as she realized she liked it. There was something childlike and gay about the nouveau riche culture of Denver, which had existed for less than a generation. In time, the newly rich would copy the style and mannerisms of her aunt, but for now, their lack of sophistication seemed appropriate for a town that was only half built.

The loud uniforms reminded her of the spring that Lillie had been allowed to order her own dress for an Easter party, the first time she had been trusted with such a decision. Lillie had said it would be a surprise, and indeed it was. To Beret's dismay, the dress, cut much too low in front for a girl of fourteen, was yellow and purple. It was more appropriate for a ball than for a religious occasion, Beret had said when Lillie flounced into the room wearing the creation. But Lillie begged to wear it, and Beret gave in, as she always did. After all, Lillie was of an age to begin choosing her own clothes. Beret was aware that the mothers of Lillie's friends were shocked, pointing to Lillie with their fans and whispering to each other, but she couldn't deny that Lillie looked fetching in what they referred to after that as the "Easter egg dress." And Teddy had clapped his hands at the sight and declared Lillie was as delightful as a candy rabbit.

The meeting was not at the church. Only when they arrived at a mansion on Sherman Street just a few blocks from the Stanton house did Beret realize the women on the committee did not expect to sort through and distribute the clothing themselves but instead would oversee the drive—mostly by inviting each other to tea.

Varina introduced Beret around, and the women scrupulously did not mention Lillie but said only that they did not know Varina had such a lovely niece, and wasn't Beret charming? They chatted and gossiped behind their hands, and Beret began to wonder if her aunt had brought her to the meeting just so that the women would not discuss Lillie.

"Your aunt is a little peculiar," Ellen Fisk confided to Beret. "Other churches gather clothing to send to Africa and the Orient, but dear Varina wants us to distribute it in Denver. I know we have our poor, but it's their own fault. If those men would just agree to work, why, their problems would be solved."

"What about the women?" Beret asked. "I daresay some must have been deserted by their husbands and left to feed a brood of little ones. Many women are illiterate and are unfit for employment. What can they do?"

"Well, they should have chosen better husbands to begin with, shouldn't they?" Ellen Fisk said with a little smile.

Beret didn't reply.

"At least they could keep themselves clean," Mrs. Fisk said. "There's no excuse for filth. I wonder about giving them our clothing, since it will be in tatters before the year is out."

Beret had learned long before that arguing with such beliefs only created ill will. Besides, she was mindful that her aunt was cultivating Mrs. Fisk, and she knew that taking issue would only offend her. If this wealthy woman picking the frosting off a piece of cake with her fork and shoving it to the side of her plate had ever been poor herself, she had forgotten. And if she didn't know the causes of poverty, she had no interest in learning them. Beret might tell her that the poor had no running water, that they must carry their water from a public pump blocks away, that they had no rags with which to scrub themselves and no way to make soap. How could she explain the dirt and the vermin, the despair that poverty brought? Arguing would brand her as a missionary or a mugwump and would cause her aunt dismay and maybe thwart her uncle's ambition. And so Beret said, "I'm sure the recipients of your kindness will be grateful."

"Let's hope so."

A butler made the rounds with a tray of small cakes, a maid behind him with cups filled from an ornate silver coffee server. The reason for the gathering, Beret thought, was not so much to talk about the clothing drive—after all, once they had contributed their castoffs, the women had little to do with the project—but to socialize. So she decided to relax and enjoy the chance to get away for a few hours, to put aside thoughts of murder. Beret might spend her days on mission work, but she also enjoyed social gatherings. She and Teddy and Lillie had been part of a young set that gave many parties and entertainments. And Beret had a large circle of women friends with whom she lunched or had tea. What harm, then, to forget unpleasantness and indulge herself for an hour or two?

She looked around the double parlor of the great house and took in the decorations, which were just this side of garishness. The windows were covered with lace curtains and velvet drapes, held in place by thick gold cords. They were topped by valences that had been gathered and pleated into elaborate folds. The furniture, upholstered in red velvet, was rosewood and uncomfortable, and the tables were covered with bright throws on which rested marble statues, a stereopticon, colored glass bowls, and a collection of curiosities. She watched as a woman, her back to Beret, picked up a vase of clear orange and red glass that was twisted and turned into a torturous shape. She set it down, a look of amusement on her face as she turned to the room, then looked guilty as she saw Beret watching her.

"Mrs. Decker!" Beret said. "What a pleasure to see you again."

"Miss Osmundsen." Caroline Decker came forward and took Beret's hands in hers. "I am so glad you can join our little dinner party. I was afraid you might be in mourning—dreadful custom that—and am delighted you have decided to go out in society." She took Beret's arm and led her to a window. A mansion was under construction next door, and Beret saw the huge blocks of cut stone that would compose the walls. Through the glass, she heard the sounds of hammers and saws and was distracted for a moment as she watched two men set a heavy beam in place.

"I hope you will find my dinner more enjoyable than these dreadful charity teas," Caroline whispered, as Beret turned back to her. "In the long run, I suppose we do some good, but if only the effort put into the social events was directed at something of more value." She smiled. "Here I am going on. My mother would be outraged. And you may be, too."

"Not at all. In New York, I run a mission for poor women—women who've been beaten and raped, forced into . . ." She looked around the room and lowered her voice. "Prostitution."

"How interesting. I would like to hear more about it, but I'm afraid Mother is frowning at me and I must go." She leaned forward and whispered, "I have only a little tolerance for teas and must tell you that I am just plain bored."

"I hope that on Saturday, we'll have a chance for a conversation you'll find more stimulating, Mrs. Decker."

"Caro, please, and I shall call you Beret. I hope we'll be great friends." She added as she pulled away, "You must tell me about your name sometime."

As the two young women took leave of each other, Varina touched Beret's arm and whispered, "Mrs. Fisk has asked my advice on a dress she is to wear to a party at the governor's house. I'm afraid I must go with her. Do you mind if Jonas takes you home alone?"

Beret didn't mind at all. In fact, there was time for her to call at the police station yet that day, and she would ask Jonas to take her there. Her aunt would not know in time to object. She said her good-byes, then got into the carriage and told Jonas to drive her to City Hall. He refused to start up. "Mrs. Stanton says take you home."

"Well, I don't want to go home, do I?" she replied sharply, annoyed that Jonas now seemed to be directing her life. She had done as she pleased ever since her parents' deaths, and she felt restricted in Denver, her aunt and uncle attempting to influence whether she could be involved in finding her own sister's killer. The two might have a claim on her actions—after all, she was their guest—but she would not be dictated to by Jonas, as grateful as she was for his earlier assistance.

"Mrs. Stanton won't like it."

"Jonas, take me to City Hall or let me out, and I shall walk."

"You stay out of Miss Lillie's murder. Something happen to you."

"Why do you keep telling me that?"

"There's a madman out there. I heard that detective say there'd be another murder."

Beret sighed. "As I told you, I am not convinced my sister was killed by a madman."

"You will be if there's another'n."

"I've asked you to drive me to City Hall. Will you take me there or disobey?" Beret felt sorry for Jonas, sorry for his wretched life, but she had work to do and would not be controlled by his fear of disobeying her aunt.

"I'm trying to keep you safe, miss."

"Do you think I'd be safer if I got out and walked?"

"No, ma'am." Jonas slapped the reins on the horses' backs, and without another word, he set off. Beret leaned back in the carriage, closing her eyes, wondering if she should tell Mick about the confrontation in Hop Alley. When the carriage stopped and she opened them again, she discovered she was not at City Hall at all but back at the Stanton house. She sighed. Now she would have to wait until morning to see Mick. Jonas had made sure of that.

Beret was relieved to find Mick at his desk in the police station. They had not agreed on a time to meet, or even where they would meet. For all she knew, he would be out the entire day. "You must catch me up. You interviewed the Summers men?" she asked, ignoring the other officers in the room and barely greeting Mick. She sat down on a chair beside the detective's desk and began removing her gloves.

"Both of them—separately."

"And?" Beret leaned forward.

"It was much as you'd expect. I talked with Evan Summers first, at his office. I know him well, and he was glad to see me, although he was surprised when I told him I was there in regard to your sister. At first, I talked about his son and told him that I knew Joey had been keen on Lillie. He allowed as much and said his wife had liked her fine—after all, she was Varina Stanton's niece—but that he never took to her. I asked if he thought Joey could be the father of her child, and he rose up and replied, 'Certainly not.'" Mick smiled a little at the memory. "Then I asked if he might be."

Beret forgot her gloves and leaned forward. "And then what?"

"Then he asked me to leave his office—ordered me to leave, I might say."

"And did you?"

"I took my time. I told him it was known he'd visited Lillie at Miss Hettie's."

"Did he admit it?"

"He said he'd never been so insulted in his life, and if I spread around that vile story, those were his words, 'vile story,' why, he'd horsewhip me. I said it was nothing personal, that I was only doing my job, and he told me that he knew the mayor and the chief of police and if I valued my job, I'd leave."

"Will he follow through?"

Mick leaned back in his chair, unconcerned. "Probably. But my father knows the mayor and the chief of police. And I do, too, for that matter." He mused, "Not that I'd mind getting the sack. Crime in Denver is pretty boring—pickpockets, drunks, fights mostly. We don't get many homicides, and I have to admit I find this case exciting. I wouldn't mind joining a police force in a larger city, but my mother is set on my staying in Denver."

"I must tell you," Beret said, ignoring Mick's last remarks,

"Mr. Summers's interest in my sister isn't just a rumor. As you know, we have Miss Hettie's maid's word on it. And I have discovered that he and Lillie had closeted themselves in the parlor of my uncle's house when both my aunt and uncle were away, and that she was in disarray when she emerged."

Mick grinned. "You just may make a detective, Miss Osmundsen. How did you find that out?"

"One of the servants."

"William, no doubt."

"I promised anonymity."

"What else did you discover?"

Beret told him about her conversations with William and Jonas.

"So, it seems she was involved with half the men in the smart set. I wonder why she turned out instead of marrying one of them. Maybe she liked . . . you know."

Beret said softly, "Sir, you are talking about my sister."

"Oh." Mick looked down at his desk and picked up a pen, rolling it back and forth under the palm of his hand. "Forgive me."

"Did you talk to Joey Summers, too?"

"Yes, at the Fisks'."

Beret had been looking at Mick's hands on the desk and glanced up. "I was invited but did not go."

"I half expected to see you there. Mr. Fisk and my father share investments. Dreary man. I wouldn't have gone, but my father insisted, and as it turned out, it was a chance to talk to Joey as a friend instead of as a copper." He put the pen aside and turned in his chair so that he was facing Beret.

"The poor chap was in love with her. I took him into the library so that we could talk privately. Then I told him I was looking into Lillie's murder, and he began to cry. He said she was going to have his baby, that he'd begged her to marry him, but she wouldn't. She said she was in love with someone else."

"His father."

Mick nodded, thinking. "That's what I said, and he asked what I meant, although I decided to save that bit of information for another time, and changed the subject. I felt sorry for him. He was besotted. I don't think Joey did it."

"Is he hotheaded? Maybe he killed Lillie in a fit of anger."

"It's possible." Mick thought that over, then shook his head. "But like I say, I doubt he is our man."

"What about Summers the elder?"

"That's another thing entirely. He's ruthless. I don't think he'd kill anyone himself, but I wouldn't put it past him to have it done. Perhaps Lillie told him that he was the father, and he felt he had to get rid of her. It's more likely, however, that he'd try to buy her off."

"Or he could have been the married man she expected to marry herself."

"I think we can forget about that. It wouldn't surprise me if Elsie made that up."

"Perhaps." Beret thought a moment, and then she asked whether Mick believed her sister really was killed by a madman.

"It's looking more and more that way."

"I am trying to convince myself it's not so." Beret folded the gloves and put them into her purse. "Perhaps it's just that I want to believe her life had more meaning, that she was important to someone, was killed for a reason. I do not want to think that she was no more than a random victim of some frenzied killer."

Mick nodded as if he understood. The two were quiet for a moment. Then Beret said, "I must confess something to you."

The detective grinned. "Don't tell me you've solved your sister's murder already."

"I'm serious." Beret frowned until the smile left Mick's face. "I was convinced that my former husband provided my sister with drugs. So I went to Hop Alley."

Mick put the pen aside and waited.

"I confronted a man named Chinaman Fong and his associate, a Mr. Sapp. They were not cooperative. I learned nothing."

Putting his hands behind his head, Mick leaned back in his chair. "I'd heard there was a disturbance down there a few days back."

"They . . . ah . . . threatened me." Beret realized that if she gave the particulars, the detective might tell her uncle or, just as bad, refuse to let her continue with the investigation. And it wouldn't be just for her safety. He would question her judgment.

"And?"

"Jonas was there. He was violent. I hope the two men were not too badly injured."

"They'll survive, so they tell me. It wasn't smart of you to do that, you know. But I suppose all's well that ends well, as they say."

"Yes." Beret was relieved he didn't ask questions.

"You know," he said, taking his hands from behind his head and placing them on the desk. "There's talk those two are panders. You could have been sold into white slavery." He chuckled.

Beret gave a slight smile. "Then wasn't I lucky I got away." Oh, very lucky, she told herself. Not like Lillie. Not like Sadie Hops.

Chapter 15

Beret did not sleep well, and she awoke when she heard the door knocker bang, followed by fists pounding against the wood. The door was opened, and a man entered the house, demanding to see her uncle. His voice was loud and a little out of control, as if he had been running. Mick McCauley, Beret thought, and grabbed her wrapper, hurrying out of her room and rushing to the railing to look down into the foyer.

"It's urgent. I must see him right away."

"It is very early, sir. Judge Stanton has not yet stirred."

"Then get him up."

"Detective?" Beret called, coming to the top of the stairs.

Michael stopped pacing and looked up. "Miss Osmundsen. I'm sorry to disturb you. I've come to see your uncle."

"What is it? What's happened?" Beret called. She shuddered as it crossed her mind that Chinaman Fong and his associate might have found out who she was and made accusations. She didn't want to have to tell her aunt and uncle what she'd done. Nor did she want to cause problems for Jonas. She started down the staircase, passing William, who was himself dressed only in nightclothes and a robe. Despite that, the butler did not appear to be in any hurry and walked at his usual stately pace. She wondered whether he would move any faster if the house caught fire. "Wake my uncle," she told him, although it was obvious that was what William intended to do.

Beret was aware she was unsuitably dressed for a caller, but she did not care. She tightened the belt of her wrapper and clutched the robe shut at her neck. "It's very early, Detective, not yet light."

"Most murders take place in the dark."

"Oh." Beret grabbed the banister, taking measured steps, as if she were afraid she would fall. "No, Detective, please, not another murder."

"I didn't mean to wake you. I came to see the judge."

"Is it another murder, then?" Beret had reached the bottom of the stairs and stood with her hand on the newel post, supporting herself. She thought for a moment of the victim's family, wondering if she had a sister who would mourn her as she did Lillie.

A door on the second floor opened, and William emerged, followed by Beret's uncle. The judge looked disheveled and yawned as he came down the stairs. "Well, Michael, what is it that can't wait until daylight? It must be bad news or you wouldn't be here at this hour. Beret, I see you're up. You might as well come along into the library, as this may concern you, too. William, have Cook make us coffee. I expect whatever is wrong, we'll need it."

He led the way into his study and indicated chairs. Beret sat, but Mick paced back and forth. Beret and her uncle waited for him to speak. "Well?" the judge asked at last. "Another murder?"

"Not quite."

Beret was relieved, but she was still apprehensive. The detective would not have awakened them if something dreadful hadn't happened. She thought again of Chinaman Fong. If the man had been badly hurt, she and Jonas might be charged. She dreaded having to explain to Mick about the two men who had threatened to overwhelm her and sell her to a brothel owner. She would be mortified and her aunt shamed. She should not have told Mick that she had been in Hop Alley.

"It was an *attempted* murder. Another crib girl. Blond Bet, she goes by. The man had a knife and tried to stab her with it, but he was killed instead." Mick added unnecessarily, "He's dead."

The judge sighed. "Three killings. A madman, then, but it's over."

"Is the girl all right?" Beret asked, remembering the beastly way Sadie Hops had been cut.

"Oh yes. She was talking to a newspaperman when I left. She seemed to think she was due a reward." Mick sat down on a footstool and put his head in his hands. He hadn't shaved, and his clothes were wrinkled. Beret thought he must have been sleeping when the call came about the attack. Or maybe he'd been up all night.

"Then you think he's the same man who killed that other girl—and my niece?" the judge asked.

"I'm sure of it. The same modus operandi, we call it. All three of the women were blondes, and they were prostitutes. And all of them had jewelry that he wanted. Bet says he posed as a customer, and when she took off her shift"—the detective glanced at Beret in a sort of apology, but she was watching him intently, not interested in niceties—"he ripped a necklace from her throat. Then he pulled out a knife and stabbed her. Got her, too, twice, in fact, although the wounds weren't anything to take notice of. He picked the wrong girl. Bet's a strong one. She grabbed the knife and stabbed him just one time, enough to disable him and let her get away. Poor Bet screamed loud enough to wake the dead, and that brought the girls running out of their cribs, the men, too. But the men ran off. It was the girls who went to help her."

"And they caught him?" Beret asked, feeling relief sweep over her.

Mick shook his head. "A police officer in plainclothes was patrolling the street. He went into the crib, and when the killer attacked him with the knife, the officer shot him."

"Good for him!" the judge said. "When was it?"

"About three this morning. The body's been taken away."

The judge looked around his chair, then stood and went to a cabinet and took out a cigar. Beret and Michael watched as he cut the tip and lighted the end, rolling the cigar around in his mouth. He inhaled deeply and blew out smoke, then set the cigar in an ashtray and turned to Beret. "You'll forgive me for this indulgence, my dear. I think better when I'm smoking." As Judge Stanton sat down again, William brought in a tray with cups, a silver pot and matching cream pitcher and sugar bowl. He poured coffee, then set the cups on saucers and placed them on white napkins on a side table, and Beret thought that even in such circumstances, William could not hurry. He would do things properly, with the best silver and china, the gold and white Old Paris china as fragile as a quail's egg. The butler offered spoons, but only the judge took one, helping himself to sugar and stirring it into his coffee. "Perhaps you'd rather have a brandy, Mick. You look like you've been up all night." The detective shook his head, and the judge raised his cup. "Here's to the police and a job well done. I believe you share in this honor, Mick. Don't you think so, Beret?" he said.

His niece nodded and raised her cup a little. She felt a great weariness leave her. This was why she had come to Denver, to find her sister's killer. It was clear to her that Lillie's murder had been the first in a series of attacks. All three fit a pattern. And now they were over. She closed her eyes in relief. She had wanted Teddy to be the killer, but now she found she was glad he wasn't. She didn't want to believe she had been married to such an evil man.

Nonetheless, Beret found herself sorry she would no longer be working with the detective. She had enjoyed that. It had been exciting and a break from her normal routine and certainly more interesting than attending teas with her aunt. She looked at Mick, who was slouched in his chair, holding his coffee cup but not drinking. Then she saw the bloodstains on his shirt. "You've been down there?"

Mick nodded.

Beret studied Mick's face, and then she knew. She felt an urge to touch him, to put her arms around him or just take his hand. Instead, holding her cup in one hand, she touched his arm with the other and asked softly, "Who was the officer who shot him, Detective?"

Mick looked down at his coffee, at the sheen of oil on the top, and replied, "I was."

"My God, boy, you should have told us," the judge thundered. "I'm proud of you. That is indeed a job well done." He leaned forward and slapped Mick on the knee.

Mick winced, as if he felt he should not be congratulated. Beret set down her cup, but she left her hand where it was. "Oh, Detective, I'm sorry it was you. I know how hard it must be to take a life, even when it is your sworn duty, when you know the person is a foul creature and that killing him saved others. Even though you are a police officer, you have a gentle soul, I believe, and do not take this lightly."

Mick didn't reply, but squeezed her hand.

The judge picked up his cigar, taking several puffs on it before exhaling. "You've never killed a person, Mick? Your generation's not been in a war like mine has. If you had, you'd know killing is necessary. There are times when it can't be helped, and you shouldn't brood about it."

Beret glanced at her uncle. She knew he had fought for the North in the War between the States, but she did not know he had killed anyone. He'd never talked about it.

"The first one's the worst. Still, it doesn't get much easier, if you can believe that," the judge said, "not that I condone killing, of course. But death for a cause, you have no choice."

"I know that." Mick took his hand away from Beret's. "There's something else, sir. It's the reason I came to you now instead of waiting for a decent hour."

Beret stiffened with a sense of dread, wondering what could possibly be worse than what the detective had already told them. She realized suddenly that the detective hadn't named the killer. Was it someone Lillie had known? Was it Teddy after all? She squeezed her hands together between her knees and waited for the detective to go on.

Mick stood up and walked to the fireplace. William had built a fire on last night's ashes, and now a log caught, the flame blazing up. Still, the room was cold, and Beret lifted her cold hands to the warmth as she glanced at her uncle. She was agitated, anxious to know what more Mick would tell them, but the judge sat calmly, patiently, waiting for the detective to continue. Her uncle had been conditioned by years of sitting in a courtroom, she supposed. But eventually, the judge decided he had waited long enough. "Well, what is it, Mick? You can tell us."

Mick turned around quickly then and blurted out, "Jonas! It was Jonas! He's your murderer. He's the one I killed."

"Oh, Detective!" Beret went limp with shock. She dropped

her hands and pressed her elbows into her body to stop the shaking, but it did no good. The idea that Jonas, the boy who had rescued her in Hop Alley, was her sister's killer made her cold all over. He had saved Beret's life, but he had threatened her, too, with a knife very much like the one he had used to murder Sadie Hops. It was as if he were two different men. Had Lillie known that?

"Good God, Jonas murdered Lillie?" the judge asked.

"Oh no!"

The three turned to the doorway where Varina stood, her hand on the frame, supporting herself. None of them had seen her come to the room.

"No, it's not possible!"

The judge jumped up. "My dear, I am so sorry. You should not have heard about it this way. Beret, take your aunt to her room."

But Varina motioned back and forth with her hand. "It is too much of a shock. I can't believe Jonas would do such a thing. He was such a loyal young man." She shook her head as she grasped the door frame, her knuckles white.

"Beret will take you upstairs."

"No, I would know what happened."

Beret and the judge exchanged glances. He had gone to his wife, and now he pried her hand from the door frame and led her to his chair, then poured brandy into a glass and handed it to her. But Varina set down the glass without drinking. When William came to the door, Beret asked him to bring another cup and saucer. "And hurry," she added.

"How long were you standing there?" Judge Stanton asked.

"Only a moment, long enough to hear Mick say that Jonas murdered Lillie and another girl and tried to kill a third. It is horrible, John, horrible. He murdered our dear niece, and I myself brought him into this house. It's my fault." She put her hands over her face and cried, the judge sitting on one arm of the chair, Beret on the other, both comforting her.

"It was not your fault at all. You did a good deed, taking in a poor boy like that," the judge said. "He was a fine and loyal employee. How could you have known he had a black heart?"

William, dressed now, poured coffee into a cup then handed it to Beret, who told her aunt to drink. Varina seemed grateful and took several sips, before her hand began to shake. Beret took away the cup and handed it back to William.

"And it was you who apprehended him, Michael?" Varina asked.

"Yes. I shot him. Jonas is dead," Mick said.

"Jonas?" William broke in. He had been setting the half-filled cup on the tray and spilled the coffee. The butler's face was white, and he had lost a little of his composure.

"Jonas murdered my sister," Beret said, wishing she had thought to ask the butler about the groom when she questioned him. She would talk to him later, when her aunt and uncle weren't around. It seemed as if he knew something.

"Oh, madam, I am sorry." His face was turned to Varina, but his eyes sought Beret's.

Varina roused herself to say, "Don't tell the other servants, William. We don't want to alarm them. The judge will speak to them later." And then she added, "And don't talk to any newspaper people. We do not want this to reflect on Judge Stanton."

"Of course not." William left, closing the door behind him.

The judge asked his wife again if she wanted to go to her room, but she was in control of herself now and insisted that Mick repeat to her what he had told Beret and the judge. So Mick told his story again, and when he was finished, Varina thanked him for bringing them the news at once. Then she all but dismissed him, saying she was sure he had duties to attend to, that the judge would arrange to have Jonas buried. He would be interred in an unmarked grave, and there would be no service, of course.

Beret walked the detective to the door. "It was good of you to think of my aunt and uncle. This will be very hard on them," she told him. "And on you," she added. "I've known others, perhaps more than you have, who've been forced to kill, and I believe this will weigh on you for a long time, perhaps always."

Mick looked away and didn't reply.

"May we talk later?" Beret asked. "There are details I should like to know and loose ends to be tied up. And perhaps the two of us together can figure out why this happened. I think my aunt and uncle care only that it is done with, but I want to know why." She also wanted to see Mick again, she realized. She liked being with him.

Mick leaned against the doorway, weary. It was dawn now. Beret saw that the street was awakening and was aware that it wouldn't be long before everyone in the neighborhood knew that the Stantons' driver had killed two women. Once the servants found out, the news would spread like dead leaves in the spring gusts.

A delivery wagon stopped at a stable not far away. A door closed. Across the street, a servant came out to sweep the walk. Nearby, a man climbed into a carriage, and the sound of it, noisy at first, faded as the vehicle reached the corner. Beret heard the song of a bird. Everything was the same as the morning she had stepped out onto the porch with her coffee, she thought, only for the Stanton household, nothing would ever be the same again. "Go now," she told Mick. "I can wait until you've finished your duties and have slept. I believe you have not been to bed in twenty-four hours. Let me know when you can find time for me."

Mick took Beret's hand and squeezed it. He didn't thank her. He was too tired, but as he started down the steps, he turned and muttered, "I'm sorry."

"Yes, we all are." Beret closed the door and hurried back to her aunt and uncle.

As Beret stepped inside the library, Varina abruptly broke off her conversation with the judge. Beret went to the silver pot and picked it up, offering coffee to her aunt, who declined, and her uncle, who pushed forward his fragile cup, white, with a gold rim, a cup much too dainty for a man. Beret replenished her own coffee, too.

"I wish I had a cup of chocolate," Varina said, and Beret told her that she would go into the kitchen and ask for it. But Varina said no. The servants would be curious enough about the early visitor. She didn't want them quizzing Beret.

The two older people were silent, and it occurred to Beret that she had intruded on a private conversation. She had sat down with her coffee, but now she rose and said she ought to return to her room.

"No, stay," Varina said, and the judge looked at his wife, a question on his face. She told him, "This concerns Beret, too. She is family. The three of us, we're all the family any of us has now."

While Beret waited for Varina to continue, she glanced around the room, at the matching sets of books, bound in leather, the titles stamped in gold on the spines, the cherrywood paneling, the heavy furniture. The room, too dark for daytime, felt musty and cold, dead even, and Beret went to the window and opened

the shutters, letting streaks of light fall onto the red Persian carpet. Then she pushed back the shutters, and the morning light
flooded in. Beret had been in the library only in the evening
and was surprised at how sunny it was during the day. The
stream of light fell fully on her, and she blinked at the harshness,
sitting down on a footstool to keep the glare out of her eyes. She
looked from her aunt to her uncle then, but for a time, neither
one spoke.

Then Varina went to the fireplace and picked up the poker.
But she did not stir the fire, only held the brass rod as she turned
to face Beret. In the morning light, she looked older than she
had the night she'd gone to the Fisks'. Varina had wrinkles
around her eyes and mouth, and the skin beneath her chin sagged.
Her eyes glistened, and she gripped the poker as if she were de-
fending herself. Beret could only imagine the terror and guilt
her aunt felt at having brought Jonas into the house. So Varina's
words surprised her. They were not of disgust or shame or even
compassion. Instead, she said, "We must put this unpleasantness
behind us as quickly as possible." Beret all but gasped. Her aunt
thought Lillie's death was *unpleasantness*? Perhaps that was just an
unfortunate choice of words.

Varina continued. "This comes at an awkward time for us,
Beret. Lillie's death was bad enough, but it will be known now
that Jonas, our own servant, was the fiend who killed her and
the other one. This makes it even harder for your uncle."

"I don't understand," Beret said. She was offended to think
her aunt might be more concerned about her social standing than
the deaths of two women, one of them her own niece.

"The Senate seat," Varina said, waving the poker. Realizing
it was in her hand, she set it down. "No one knew Lillie had
gone into that place until she was murdered. After her death, we

put it about that she was wild and we had only tried to help her—tried valiantly, I might say—since she was our niece, and well, of course, we had a duty. William was a great help with that, spreading the story among servants in other houses. And it took away any blame that attached itself to us, because everybody knows your uncle is a man of honor who would never turn his back on anyone in need. There was gossip, of course. There will always be gossip. But I think few blamed us for having taken a strumpet into our house."

"Strumpet!" Beret said, shocked—and angry, too. "Surely you don't refer to Lillie that way."

"No, of course not," the judge said quickly. He looked uneasy, and his forehead was damp.

Varina wrung her hands. "I'm sorry, Beret. It was a poor choice of words. But surely you see our dilemma. And now Jonas! It is a low blow and entirely unfair to your uncle, who does not deserve a second blot on his character."

Beret was having trouble following the conversation. Varina's niece had been murdered, her coachman revealed as a crazed killer. And her only concern seemed to be her husband's ambition. Beret tried to reconcile herself to her aunt's reasoning. Perhaps the woman was right. What was past was past. John Stanton should not be made to suffer because of the actions of others. Nor should her aunt. Still, Beret was surprised by the lack of compassion for the dead—Lillie, the crib girl Sadie, and even Jonas.

"Varina thinks you can help with this," the judge said. He went to the decanter and poured himself a brandy and drank it down in one gulp. He was unshaven and looked haggard, old.

He turned to his wife to let her explain, and Varina said, "As you know, we've hoped you would stay on with us, at least for a few weeks, Beret. The spring is beautiful in Denver, and we think you might appreciate the rest and the care of your family after what you've been through. And God knows I could use my only niece for solace." She paused, but Beret, edgy now, did not reply, so Varina continued. "People will be curious, and you will receive invitations because of it—and because you are a charming guest, too, of course. They won't ask your uncle or me, but they'll ask you about Jonas, and we thought if you told them how the judge had tried to rehabilitate him, how he had rescued him from the streets and given him employment, it would help our cause."

"Your aunt, too, should be commended for her charity in regard to him," the judge put in.

Varina inclined her head, accepting her husband's words. "And as for Lillie, you could say she was uncontrollable, that you sent her to us to see if we could help her. You could imply that the course she took was all but inevitable, that it was her character, ever since she was a child."

"But that's not so," Beret said.

"Isn't it?" Varina asked. "You see, Beret, Lillie's living here was very difficult for us. We couldn't ask her to leave because she was our niece. But her loose ways reflected on your uncle and unfairly so."

"Varina," the judge interjected, and his wife gave him a pinched-nose look.

"Lillie's nature was not Beret's fault, of course, but she raised her. She threw Lillie out of their home." She was addressing the judge now. "Certainly she would want to make up for her indiscretions by helping you, John."

Beret closed her eyes and turned away. What her aunt had said was unfair. While she had asked Lillie to leave the New York home, Beret had never considered herself to be the cause of her sister's sins. Now Varina was suggesting just that, and Beret was offended.

"Don't do it if it distresses you," the judge told her.

"No, of course not." Varina smiled at her niece. "You have such a sense of honor. We would not want you to compromise it. You have many concerns—for the poor, the helpless, the women caught up in the evils of poverty. Think of the good your uncle could do if he had a voice in Washington. He could help those like Lillie, like Jonas. The cause is greater than what has happened here. You could have a voice in putting your uncle in a position to help others. I believe your mother and father would approve."

Beret found the last remarks disingenuous, and she took her leave. As she started up the stairs, her uncle touched her arm, and Beret stopped. He said in a low voice, "You must forgive your aunt. She has worked hard on this Senate business, and now it's as if her world has fallen apart. She mourns Lillie, but there is nothing she can do about her now. She has only the Senate appointment to look forward to. She deserves it."

"As do you, Uncle." But as she ascended the stairs and considered her uncle's words, Beret knew that the Senate appointment was not her uncle's goal but her aunt's. She shuddered to think that her sister's murder had become a political liability. Perhaps, as Varina had said, Beret had a duty to aid her uncle. After all, the investigation was over. Beret frowned and stopped a moment, grasping the rail. She was not so sure.

Chapter 16

Since Beret had slept little that night, she lay down on her bed to rest for a few moments, and to her surprise, she went to sleep and did not awaken until late in the morning. She rang for the maid, and in a moment, Nellie knocked on the door, then entered.

"Mr. and Mrs. Stanton's gone out. You want your breakfast here or in the morning room, ma'am?"

"Here."

"I'll fetch it to you." Nellie turned to go, then stopped. "Begging your pardon, ma'am, but is it true about Jonas? Did he really kill Miss Lillie, like Judge Stanton says?"

"It appears that way," Beret said. "Are you surprised?"

Nellie twisted her hands in her apron. "I am, and I ain't. He was strange, you know, and he scared me sometimes. He brought me a rock he found once, all pretty with sparkles in it. He said he saw it and saved it for me, and he didn't want nothing for it, like some might. But another time, I saw him creep up on a bird and catch it and wring its neck. Jonas could be real friendly, and other times, it was like there's a black cloud hanging over his head."

"As if he were two different persons?"

Nellie nodded.

"Some men are like that, Nellie. I don't know the reason for it."

"He had no cause to kill Miss Lillie, I say."

"No, there's never a good reason to kill an innocent woman."

"Oh, she wasn't innocent, if that's the word. Not her. And right in this house, too, and him being so much older. It was a scandal." Nellie raised her hands to her face and said quickly, "Oh, ma'am, I'm sorry. I forgot for a minute you was her sister. I didn't mean nothing by what I said, but I could tell you—"

Beret put up her hand to stop the maid. Too many people had already told her about her sister. She did not have to hear it all again. Perhaps she should have quizzed Nellie the other night about Lillie, as she had William and Jonas. After all, the maid would have known more about Lillie than anyone else. Nellie apparently was aware of the liaison between Lillie and Evan Summers. But what did it matter now? Jonas had been caught, and the murders were behind them. Listening to the blots on Lillie's character was painful. Nellie seemed ready and even anxious to talk, but Beret dismissed her.

After breakfasting, Beret dressed and announced to the butler that she was going out. He told her the stable boy would drive her, as the lad was filling in until the judge found a replacement for Jonas.

"He lived above the stable, did he? Jonas, I mean," she asked, an idea forming in the back of her mind. When William replied that the driver's quarters had indeed been there, Beret told him she would find the stable boy herself. "I should like to see what conveyances my uncle has. Perhaps there is one I can drive myself," she said, not revealing her real reason for wanting to visit the stable.

"But, madam, I can—"

"No, never mind, William. I'll see to it. That will be all," and she went out through the kitchen to the large building behind.

Tom, the stable boy, was dressed in Jonas's uniform, which was short and too tight. He looked ill at ease but self-important, and he stood and bowed a little when Beret entered the room. Beret judged him to be about fourteen. "You want me to take you someplace, miss?" he asked, standing at attention.

"Why, I've never been inside the stable. I thought I'd look around."

"Look around?"

"Yes. You don't mind, do you?"

"No, miss."

Beret put her hand on the carriage, then walked slowly to a buggy that she thought she could drive if she had to. She glanced around the cavernous room. On the outside, the structure was a smaller replica of the mansion, made of the same stone and brick, with arched windows. On top was a copper weathervane. In an Eastern city, the copper would have turned a dull green from the moisture in the air, but Colorado was dry, and the copper had only faded to brown.

The stable's elegance was limited to the exterior, and inside, the room was plain, utilitarian. Beret looked at the staircase that hugged one wall. It was narrow and cramped. "Do you sleep up there?"

"Me and Jonas. That is, Jonas did. His room's bigger than mine."

"Did you like Jonas?"

"No reason not to, miss. He taught me how to play cards, and he shared his tips with me when somebody give him one, and he let me drink his whiskey . . ." Tom's eyes grew big, and he added, "You won't tell that, will you, miss? The judge wouldn't like it, and I never drank except at night when me and Jonas was upstairs."

"I won't tell." She started for the stairs. "I think I'll look around up there."

Tom appeared confused. "Upstairs, miss?" He started to protest but must have decided it was not his place to question Beret. So he asked, "You want I should go with you? It's dark up there."

"I'll be fine." She took a kerosene lantern from the wall and lighted it, then started up the steps. Jonas might have hidden trophies of his murderous rampage in his room.

Tom watched her, and then he grinned, relieved. "Oh, I see, you was working with that copper. Jonas told me about that. He said I should watch out for you and not talk to you." The boy thought that over. "I guess I should have watched out for Jonas, seeing as how he was a crazy man." He guffawed, and Beret tried to smile at the sally. "Well, you go on up and see what you can find," he said. "You call me if you want anything. You just call, 'Tom,' and I'll come."

The lantern in one hand, her skirts in the other, because the stairs were filthy with straw and dirt and manure, Beret went up the steps and found herself in a hayloft. The haymow door was open, letting in light, but the rooms beyond it were dark, and she was glad she'd brought the lantern. The first room was small with space only for a cot—Tom's room, she thought. The second was not much bigger, but Beret knew it had been Jonas's. A cot was along one wall, the blanket on it neatly folded, a pillow bare of a pillowslip beside it. Overalls, a second uniform, and two shirts hung on nails on the wall. Newspapers and odds and ends were lined up on a shelf. The room smelled of horses and unwashed bodies, and Beret wished for a handkerchief to put over her nose.

A potbellied stove, its pipe sticking through the exterior wall, was next to a window. The room was cold, and there was little light, but it was a step up from the tenements Beret had visited in New York, and she knew that Jonas had been lucky to be quartered there. Certainly, it would have been better than the crib he had lived in as a boy as well as the quarters he had shared later on with the other newspaper boys. She was surprised at the tidiness of the room. She would have expected the bedcover to be pushed aside on the cot and the clothing heaped on the floor. There was much she did not understand about Jonas.

Beret set the lantern on the cold stove and looked around the room, considering where to start. She went to the shelf and took down the newspapers, wondering if Jonas could read. But of course, he could have read, at least a little. After all, he had been a newsboy. She unfolded the top paper and discovered a story about the murder of Sadie, the crib girl. Beret had not seen it and took it to the window to read it in the daylight.

Last night, just as the revelry on Holladay Street reached its fever pitch, a frail sister was cut down in the bloom of her youth by a fiendish killer. The police believe the same madman who stabbed Lillie Brown, the soiled dove who was later identified as Lillie Osmundsen, the niece of Denver Judge John Stanton, is responsible for the death of Sadie, a crib girl who worked out of a hovel on upper Holladay.

No one witnessed the foul deed. Police say the body was discovered by a member of the sisterhood this morning.

Sadie was lying on the bed of the dwelling that served as both home and place of business, her clothes torn and bloody from where she had been stabbed over and over. Her hands were clasped together in death in an attitude of prayer, as if in her final moments, the wanton woman was asking a power much greater than any she had ever known for forgiveness for her sinful ways and begging for everlasting life.

Why did reporters write such nonsense? It was self-righteous and degrading to that unfortunate girl. Her death had been foul. Why couldn't the reporters leave it alone? The man hadn't seen Sadie's body, because the corpse had been hauled away by the coroner before any of the newshounds arrived. Had someone told him Sadie had posed in prayer as death came on her, or had he just made that up? Probably the latter. Beret remembered that Sadie's arms had been crossed over her body, not in prayer but in defense against the blows. Beret glanced at the rest of the article, which was written in the same overblown prose and filled with more errors, then thrust it aside. She could only wonder at the stories that would run about Jonas—perhaps in newspapers that already were being sold by newsboys—scarring her uncle by association. Perhaps she did have a duty to protect his reputation, and her aunt's, as well.

Beret went through the other copies of the *Rocky Mountain News*. The next one had a front-page story about Lillie's death. Subsequent editions followed the death, but as the killer was not apprehended, each day's follow-up was farther back in the paper than the previous one. Beneath the *News* were copies of the *Denver Tribune,* and the *Republican,* all with stories about the murders. Beret thought that Jonas must have saved all the accounts he could find, perhaps reading them late at night by the light of the kerosene lantern, as he sat on his cot reliving his evil deeds.

Maybe he had read the newspapers to Tom, hinting that he knew more about the killings than the reporters or the police.

The shelf was high, and Beret could not see what else was kept there. She did not want to search it with her hand for fear of touching a rodent. So she found a box in the hayloft and dragged it into the room, climbing on top of it to peer onto the shelf. That must have been where Jonas kept his treasures—two rocks that Beret thought might be ore samples and a silver pen-knife. The knife was an odd thing for a carriage driver to own. There was a deck of cards, greasy and dirty, and a tiny metal implement that Beret recognized as a hold-out, a clip used by gamblers to cheat.

The only other thing on the shelf was a cheese box, and Beret took it down and opened it. Inside were a flint arrowhead and a brass button from a military uniform, a cheap pink hair ribbon, a woman's garter, and a linen handkerchief with an *L* embroidered on it. Beret would compare it with the handkerchiefs Lillie had left behind in the bedroom dresser. There was a penny doll no more than an inch high, without any arms. Beret picked it up and stared at the cheap bisque image, the tiny red mouth. The hair was painted the color of a buttercup, she observed, as she returned the doll to the box.

Lying facedown under Jonas's treasures was a photograph, torn in half. Beret turned over what had been the bottom part of the picture, which showed the lower half of a woman, her legs in striped stockings. Beret picked up the top half of the photograph with the upper portion of the woman's body on it. She was dressed in a wrapper that was parted in the front so that it came perilously close to exposing her breasts. The woman leaned forward, her chin on her hand, her head tilted, her mouth in a seductive smile. But the photograph was chilling, because the face had been slashed with a knife and the eyes scratched out. Beret knew prostitutes sold such pictures and thought the woman might be Sadie or Blond Bet, because she had long blond hair. But she did not resemble Sadie, and Mick had said that Blond Bet was a large woman. The prostitute in the photograph was small. As she returned the two halves of the photograph to the box, Beret wondered if the woman might have been Jonas's mother. There was no inscription, no name on the back.

Setting the box aside, Beret felt along the shelf, but there was nothing else, and she found that disappointing. She had hoped that Jonas would have saved other things. Then it occurred to her that Tom might have gone through Jonas's possessions, could have taken whatever Jonas had of value or anything he found of prurient interest. Jonas might have kept photographs of other prostitutes, and Tom would have stolen them but left behind the mutilated one. If Jonas had taught Tom to play cards and drink whiskey, wouldn't he have taught him other things, as well? The idea frightened Beret a little. She didn't like being alone in the stable with the boy. She would speak with him later, but she would do it outside.

Beret had not found what she was searching for, and looked around the room hoping to discover a hiding place. She took down Jonas's clothes from the nails and went through them, the pockets, the seams, feeling for anything the boy might have hidden there. Then she opened the blanket and examined the pillow but found nothing. She searched the room, much as she had Sadie's crib, looking for places where the woodwork had been pried up but nothing looked suspicious. As she walked across the room, she stubbed her toe and looked down. The floorboards gaped, and she got down on her hands and knees to find one that had been pried up. She had almost given up the search when in the corner of the room farthest from the door, she discovered a short piece of flooring that was unattached and lifted it up.

Underneath was a tobacco sack, and Beret took it out, carefully untying the knot in its yellow string. Then she shook the sack, and two earrings fell into her hand. Beret closed her eyes and took a deep breath. There, she thought, the final proof that Jonas had killed Lillie. That would end her doubts. But as she lifted the jewelry, she knew without looking at them that the earbobs were not Lillie's diamond stars. They were too flimsy. She held them to the light and saw that they were made of cheap metal, fitted with bits of red glass, some of it missing. A strand of coarse blond hair was stuck in a prong holding one of the remaining stones. Sadie had had such hair.

Beret put the earbobs back in the bag and placed it in the cheese box, then searched the hiding place for Lillie's earrings, but they were not there. Tom might have taken them. Perhaps he had realized that Sadie's earrings were only junk and left them behind, to be found by the police—or Beret. But he would have taken the diamonds. Even a stable boy would know about diamonds.

Beret returned the box she had stood on to the hayloft, then tiptoed to the steps and listened. Tom was downstairs, talking to one of the horses. She walked noiselessly back to Jonas's room and gathered the papers and the box and set them on the floor. Then she went into Tom's room and looked around. The cell appeared to have no hiding places. There were no shelves, only the cot and nails on the walls that held the boy's clothes. Beret went to the bed and lifted the mattress, uncovering a stack of photographs tied together with a string. She took out the packet, untied it, and found herself staring at more girlie pictures. These were of different prostitutes posed in various stages of undress. One was of a little girl not yet at puberty. Beret knew that children younger than this one supported themselves and often their families with their bodies. What an evil place the world could be. Beret was suddenly chilled by the cold room and wanted to get out of there.

"What you doing, miss?"

Beret had not heard Tom approach, and she was startled. She looked at the boy a moment, and then she spread the photographs on the cot. She was about to ask Tom where he had gotten such images, but she knew the answer, and instead she asked, "What else did you steal from Jonas?"

"He's dead. He don't care if I have his things. They ain't doing him no good." He reached out a dirty hand, his eyes gleaming as he stared not at Beret but at the images. "Gimme."

"You had no right to them. The police will want them. What else have you taken from Jonas's room?"

"Nothing. I don't steal." He glared at her in such a way that Beret felt uneasy. After all, Tom had been close to Jonas. Jonas might have bragged of the killings, bragged in such a way that Tom was jealous, had made Tom himself consider what it would be like to kill a woman.

It was the second time Beret had been standing in a strange room, frightened, wishing she had waited for Detective McCauley. She raised her chin, hoping Tom would not see that she was uncomfortable. "I would say you stole these. Shall I ask the police to search your room for contraband, or will you tell me where you've hidden it?" She hoped she sounded more confident than she felt.

"Hidden what?"

"Contraband. Stolen articles. I would like you to return my sister's diamond earrings, the ones shaped like stars. Jonas stole them. If you give them to me now, I shall not tell Judge Stanton. But if you won't, then the police will arrest you."

Tom looked around wildly. "I didn't steal no earrings, miss. I took those pictures, but I didn't take nothing else. You look around and see. Lookit here. This is where I keep my things." He pried loose a board from the bottom of the wall, revealing a sugar sack. Tom removed it and handed it to Beret, who emptied it onto the boy's cot. The contents were a collection of odds and ends that might have come from a packrat's nest. There were several marbles, a toy horse with one leg broken, the makings for cigarettes, and two gold coins. He would have taken the coins from Jonas's box, but there was no way Beret could prove it. Underneath were more girlie pictures. "Jonas give me them. They wasn't of no consequence," Tom admitted when Beret picked them up. "There ain't nothing else. I didn't steal no earrings," he repeated.

He might have taken the earrings and sold them, Beret thought, but when would he have done that? He would not have known until a few hours earlier that Jonas was dead. "I should like you to turn out your pockets," she told the boy, who obliged, perhaps because they contained nothing of interest. If Tom had taken the earrings, he could have hidden them anywhere in the stable, and she would have no way of finding them, Beret realized. "All right, Tom," she said. She had been peremptory with the boy, and her voice softened now. "There will be a reward for the earrings. If you find them, I will pay you a hundred dollars, which is far more than they would bring on the street. And I won't tell Judge or Mrs. Stanton. Are we understood?"

Tom's eyes were wide. "A hunnert dollars? If I find them, I'll bring them to you. I sure will, miss."

Beret nodded, and picking up the newspapers and cheese box, she started to leave, but Tom touched her arm. "Miss?"

Beret jumped, chilled by the touch.

"Why do you think Jonas cut up that picture like he done? He showed me the others, but I never seen that one till I went looking."

"I don't know, Tom. Maybe he hated prostitutes because his mother was one."

Tom stared at Beret. "Oh no, miss. Jonas told me she was a nurse. He said she went in a mine at Georgetown to save some men and got killed in a cave-in. They never found her body. She's an angel up in heaven. Jonas told me that, too." He paused. "You think Jonas is up there with her now?"

She shrugged. There was no need to tell Tom that Jonas had made up the story about his mother, probably to elevate himself in the younger boy's eyes. Jonas might even have believed it. Nor would she tell Tom that instead of being in heaven, Jonas was more likely burning in the fires of hell.

Chapter 17

To her disappointment, Beret did not receive word from Mick McCauley to meet with him the following day. So she accompanied her aunt to a luncheon at which a group of young ladies in Greek attire performed a tableau. Still caught up in Jonas's death, Beret paid little attention to the display and later found it difficult to be charming and entertaining. When the discussion turned to how awful it must have been for Judge and Mrs. Stanton to learn that the young man they had engaged to drive their carriage had turned out to be a demented killer, Beret merely nodded, barely able to engage in conversation.

Several women confided to Beret that they had been a little afraid of the strange coachman and had almost refused to ride in the Stanton carriage, and one confessed she had asked dear Varina why she had hired someone so repulsive.

"Aunt Varina has always been aware of the needs of the disadvantaged," Beret replied, wishing her aunt had not subjected them both to the unpleasant afternoon. Was the luncheon really that important to the judge's appointment to the Senate?

"Yes, of course, but to take that fellow into her home. Why, you all could have been murdered in your sleep."

The woman was right, although Beret wouldn't admit that to her. "But we weren't," she replied. "My aunt is the soul of compassion. And my uncle, too," she added, thinking this was the sort of conversation the judge hoped she would engage in. "If those of us who are privileged don't reach out to the poor, who will?"

"Had she any hint?" someone asked.

"No, of course not." Beret paused to gain control of herself and added, "Aunt Varina would have dismissed him if she had, of course."

"Well, it gives us all pause. From now on, I will insist on at least three references for anyone I hire. Will you have cake?" She handed a plate to Beret, as she added, "And then there was that awful murder of your sister. What do you say about that?"

Beret took a slice of cake and picked up her fork, as she replied, "I have always heard Denver was lovely in the spring, and now I can see it for myself. I spied a clump of violets in the garden this morning, so pretty and fresh. My dear aunt suggested I pick them for my room. I love violets, don't you?"

The woman looked disappointed, for she surely wanted to gossip about the murders. Perhaps Beret should inform them that it was their husbands, fathers, and brothers who kept the whorehouses thriving. They were the patrons of the finer brothels—they might even have been Lillie's clients—and they owned the blocks along Holladay Street where the prostitutes plied their trade, making far more money off the business of prostitution than did the girls. But of course, that was never a topic of conversation among ladies. Beret could only wonder what the women would have said about Lillie if she or her aunt hadn't been there.

Varina was right in wanting Beret to accompany her if for no other reason than to keep down the gossip.

Before she left, Beret was invited to two or three other social engagements and knew that she could spend all her idle time in Denver involved in useless entertainments—afternoons and evenings that would be as dull as this one. As long as she was in Denver, she had no excuse to turn them down without giving offense. Before, she might have said she was busy with Detective McCauley, but the murders had been solved. So for her aunt's sake she accepted the social obligations, although she wished she might get the plague or be bitten by a rabid dog before they took place. She hoped she could return to New York soon without offending her aunt and uncle.

Varina was much pleased with Beret's performance, and when they returned home, driven by the stable boy, Tom, Varina announced she had engaged her dressmaker to alter Lillie's dresses for Beret, and the woman, a Mrs. Beaton, would be waiting for them. So even if Detective McCauley had sent for her, Beret could not have met with him that day.

The dressmaker was trying. Beret stripped down to her corset and let her aunt and Mrs. Beaton fit the dresses on her. "You are not as well constructed as your sister, poor girl," the woman said. "She had a fuller figure." Then apparently afraid she had given offense, she added, "You are more statuesque. I always liked a tall figure. It shows off a gown to perfection."

Beret searched for something to still the woman without giving offense. But the dressmaker continued. "A lovely girl. Such a shame." She had mastered the challenge of talking with her mouth full of pins.

"Yes."

"I made this yellow gown for her," the woman hurried on.

"You remember, don't you, Mrs. Stanton? The fabric was costly, but she said she had to have it, and oh, wasn't she a beauty in it?" She stood back and looked at Beret critically. Yellow, Beret knew, was not her color, and the dress, cut low and fulsome in the front, was anything but flattering. "I'll take it in at the bust, perhaps add a little lace there to tone down the color. And the hem must be let out. A bit of trim will cover the crease, and no one will know."

And so it went with Lillie's other dresses, the dressmaker muttering how she would have to alter the gowns, making Beret wish she had refused the clothes. It was bad enough the dresses were unflattering, but she felt uncomfortable in her sister's garments. Finally, Beret tried on one of Lillie's sensible ensembles, a suit of navy blue with simple lines. "Ah, at last, this suits you," Mrs. Beaton said. She pushed and pulled and pinned. "I thought it too plain for your sister, but she looked striking in it." She paused and added quickly, "And you will, too, Miss Osmundsen." As the woman used chalk to draw a line down a seam to show where the jacket should be altered, she turned to Varina. "I made you a suit very nearly like this one. It was from the same material. Do you wear it? It was larger, of course. You hardly have the figure of a young girl." The woman must be a very good dressmaker, Beret thought, or Varina would not have stood for the insult.

"It is too severe," Varina replied.

"Then fetch it to me, and I'll add a lace collar or a bit of trim to soften it."

Varina looked uncomfortable. "I do not care for it much," she said, and appeared relieved when Nellie entered the room and said some problem required her mistress's attention.

The moment Varina was gone, the dressmaker said in a low

voice, "I wonder your dear aunt can show her face. Her coach-man's deeds must be a terrible strain on her. Does she suffer?"

Beret found the question no more appropriate than those asked at the luncheon, and she knew the dressmaker would savor her reply to share with other clients. "I believe everyone suffers when a human life is cut short."

Mrs. Beaton frowned. "Yes, but Mrs. Stanton, how is she taking it?"

"As you might expect," Beret replied.

"Did she know her coachman was a killer?"

"I don't suppose she would have employed him if she had, would she?"

"And the judge, what is his reaction?" the woman asked.

"I haven't inquired."

Mrs. Beaton looked at Beret sharply. "You act as if this man was of no consequence."

"Murder is always of consequence." Beret was tired of the dressmaker's persistence and wished the woman would swallow her mouthful of pins.

The dressmaker sighed, and with a false sense of pity, she said, "Those poor girls. My church helps them. We have found farms to send them to so that they can leave their sinful lives, but they are never grateful. Some sneer at us when we offer them that opportunity. Others run away after a few days and return to Holladay Street." She shook her head, apparently at the ingratitude.

"Many of them come from farms. That is why they turn out," Beret told her.

"Well, Miss Lillie didn't, did she?" the woman said, then asked, "Surely Mrs. Stanton feels responsible for her death, doesn't she?"

Beret, mindful that the dressmaker was sticking pins into the garment she was wearing, took a deep breath and said quietly, "I found violets in the garden this morning. My aunt insisted I pick them for my room. Aren't they pretty?" Beret pointed to a small glass vase shaped like a flower basket. "Violets are the harbinger of spring, don't you think?" She stepped out of the skirt then and laid it on the bed.

Mrs. Beaton removed the pins from her mouth and thrust them into her pincushion. Then she pushed herself off the floor and gathered up her scissors and tape measure and stored them in her workbasket. Beret smiled benignly at the woman. No one would make her gossip about her own family.

Beret was disappointed that Detective Sergeant McCauley had not contacted her again, so the following afternoon, she left the house and walked to City Hall. She was delighted at how much the weather had changed in only a few days. Flowers had begun to emerge. There were daffodils and tiny white flowers like edelweiss, crocuses and violets in the yards she passed. A gardener trimmed bushes in front of a sandstone castle. Two nurses sat on a wall at the side of one of the mansions, gossiping while their tiny charges played in the grass. Beret nodded a greeting, and the two stood and mumbled, "Ma'am."

A groom slouched against a barn, smoking, his eyes sullen as he appraised Beret. He looked away as someone yelled to him from inside. The sun was warm on Beret's shoulders, and by the time she reached the bottom of the hill, she had unbuttoned her jacket. The streets were dry now, although dusty, the air clean, the sun so bright it hurt her eyes. For the first time, Beret found Denver a pretty place, serene, quiet, so different from the bustle of New York.

letter. But when she looked closer, Beret saw that it was part of a police report. The first line was the tail end of a sentence begun on the previous page: "shot him once in the breast, and he fell onto the bed and was still. He had the knife in his hand yet. I asked a crib girl to find another officer, and in ten minutes—" Mick had obviously been interrupted in the middle of a sentence and left his desk. Beret would have liked to read the first part of the report, but she was mindful of the glances from the officers in the room. So she picked up a pencil and idly rolled it back and forth between her gloved fingers, trying to imagine what else the detective had written. She was doing that when Detective McCauley returned.

"Miss Osmundsen," he said, startling her, because she had been deep in thought and had not heard him approach.

"Detective McCauley. I hope this is not an inconvenient time."

He glanced around his desk as if to see whether she had been snooping, then asked, "What can I do for you?" He was formal now, polite but a little distant, as if he were not pleased to see her. He gave the impression that he was busy, and Beret wondered if he'd done that on purpose.

"I had asked when you came to tell us about Jonas whether we could talk again about the murders. Is this not a convenient time?"

He thought a moment. "As good as any, I suppose," he said, "but this is not the place for it. Come." Beret stood, and the detective looked over his desktop again, then reached into his desk for something that he put into his pocket. He led her past the police officer with whom Beret had spoken earlier, saying, "We'll be going now, Jim. Me and the lady's having a bit of a talk."

"Your Irish has come back," Beret observed.

"Only when I'm around other Irishmen. If we try to talk like civilized folks, they think we're putting on airs." He steered her up the steps, and they went outside into the sunshine and found a stone bench. "Does this suit, or do you want to go to Charpiot's?"

Beret sensed the detective was distracted, perhaps pressed for time, and replied that the bench was fine. She would have liked a more private place, where passersby wouldn't intrude, but she seemed to have no choice. "We could talk at a more convenient time—"

"No, no. I don't know when that would be." Mick cut her off. "Except for a few hours' sleep, I've been at the station since I left you. There are reports to be made and interviews. I've been cornered by every newshawk in the city. Have you seen the papers?"

"Only one, and the report was dreadful."

"Don't bother with the others. Each is worse than the one before it. Will it offend you if I smoke?"

Beret did not know he smoked. He had not done so before. She shook her head, and Mick took out a cigarette paper, sprinkled tobacco onto it, licked the paper shut. He lighted the cigarette, then exhaled. "I don't smoke much, but this has been a trying time, and it relaxes me. What a pity you ladies can't indulge."

"And what makes you think we don't?" Beret asked.

Mick laughed suddenly. It was not often that the man had laughed in her presence, and Beret was startled. She liked the warm sound of it. "Forgive me for being brusque. I have been under a great deal of pressure since I saw you last," he said.

"Of course. And I suspect you have little time for conversation, so I shall be as brief as possible. I want to talk about the murders, but first I must make a confession."

"I did not like him much, although he came to my aid in Hop Alley, and that makes me believe he was both good and bad." She thought that over. "Mostly bad, I think. He frightened me at times, but no, I didn't mark him as a killer. Looking back, I can see I missed signs. He followed me, you know, from the first day I arrived. He warned me to watch out for myself, and I thought that was strange. Then one night he came toward me in the library with a blanket in his hands. He claimed he was going to cover me, but I think now he wanted to smother me. It would have been so easy. I don't know why he didn't. He took out a knife he carried and must have sensed I was afraid of him. Perhaps he feared I knew too much."

"So no one was truly suspicious of him."

"That's not quite true. There are any number of my aunt's friends who told me yesterday that *they* did not trust Jonas and were not surprised to find he was a killer."

"Ah, of course. The I-told-you-sos. We frequently see them at the police station. Pity they don't help us *before* a criminal is caught."

Beret laughed. She had put on her jacket before entering the station, and now she unbuttoned it, because the sun made her hot. She took off her gloves, too.

"Do you agree now that Jonas killed both women?" Mick asked. He threw the cigarette butt into the street and seemed to relax.

"It's that very question about which I've come to talk to you. I would like to compare the two murders—that is, the two murders and the *attempted* murder—and see if we can draw that conclusion."

"I think I'd like to know that, too. Denver does not have so many murders, you know. And those we do investigate, well, we find the killer—or don't, as the case may be—and go on to the next crime, without pausing to ask why. I've read of a new science that seeks to find the cause of people's actions. I wish I knew more about it, because, like you, I'm curious about Jonas. Why do *you* think he did it, Miss Osmundsen?" Before Beret could answer, Mick stood. "Would you like to walk down to the river? It isn't much of a river, not very pretty, but it's all we have. It's said about the Platte that it's a mile wide and an inch deep, and a good part of that is mud. As I say, it's not much to look at, but we could talk more privately there."

Beret liked that idea and stood, taking Mick's arm, and the two walked a short distance until they stood at the edge of the South Platte. It was indeed an ordinary river, sluggish, and its banks were covered with sagebrush and thick bushes. Snow still lay on the ground in shady places, and Beret could see animal tracks across it.

Mick stood in front of her, one foot on a broken branch, and leaned forward. "What reservations do you have about the two killings?" he asked.

"There are certain similarities, of course. Both women were prostitutes. Both were blond. And the killer took items of jewelry." Beret reached into her purse. "I found these in Jonas's room in the stable, under a floorboard." She handed Mick the cheap earrings.

"They were Sadie's, I suspect," he said, tossing the earrings in his hand. "We've discovered that killers sometimes take such souvenirs. They fondle them later on to relive their triumphs, for to a man like Jonas, I think, that's what murder is—triumph and power. At least, that's what I've come to believe."

Beret nodded, thinking that over. "The hiding place held only these. My sister's earrings were not there."

Mick looked off to the river as he considered what Beret had told him. "Perhaps Jonas hid them elsewhere. A stable is a big place."

"Yes."

"Or he could have sold them. They were diamonds, after all."

"Perhaps."

"You are not convinced?"

Beret shrugged. "It seems Jonas would have wanted his plunder close to him. As you said, it is not the jewelry's monetary value so much as the souvenir's ability to let him relive the murder. Besides, I do not believe he could have sold the earrings so quickly. They are distinctive, and surely he would know the police were on the lookout for them."

"You may be overanalyzing."

"I may be. We criminologists do this." Her eyes shone at her little joke, and it pleased her that Mick smiled. "But there is one other thing. You told me that whoever killed my sister seemed to care about her, placing her hands over her breast and covering her with her robe. We saw for ourselves that no such gestures were made with Sadie. It's almost as if my sister were killed by someone she knew, while Sadie was a random victim."

"Jonas might have had more time with your sister. And he knew her. Besides, if she was his first killing, he might have felt remorse. He was more jaded the second time."

"I suppose that explains it." Beret picked a weed and stripped its leaves, then twirled the stalk between her fingers.

Mick sat down beside her and took the remnants of the weed out of Beret's hand, throwing it away. He asked what else bothered her.

"The why of it."

"That's always a question, isn't it? You know human nature

as well as I do, rather better, I think, because of your work. But do you want to know what I think?" When Beret replied in the affirmative, Mick continued. "Jonas was a complex young man with an abnormal devotion to your aunt, because she'd saved his life and took him in. I suspect everybody he met before that rejected him, including his mother. He might have seen your sister as a threat to your aunt, someone whose intemperate ways— and because I knew of her socially, I was well aware of them— would cause your aunt grief. He thought he was doing your aunt a service in eliminating her. Or maybe he intended only to talk to her and something she said unleashed his rage." He grinned and added, "I think I am talking like a criminologist."

Beret started to interrupt, but Mick held up his hand. "Let me finish. I think it's more likely that he was in love with her or, if you will, lusted after her, and went to Miss Hettie's for carnal reasons. Your sister might have rejected him, and for him it brought back all the unhappiness of his young life. Jonas was a complicated fellow, because of his mother and because of his looks, and he would have taken offense. Maybe he only wanted to slap your sister, but things got out of hand."

"You do indeed know something about the new science of analyzing actions," Beret said as a compliment.

"I think Jonas might have enjoyed killing. I suspect he hated women, all women except your aunt, because they laughed at him, and this was his way of getting revenge." Mick laughed a little self-consciously. "I could be far from the mark."

Beret considered the words as she looked out at the water. A dog or a muskrat or maybe a large rat was swimming along with the current. She had never swum and thought it might be nice to be carried along in the water's flow like that, although she would prefer a cleaner stream. She considered what Mick had said as she watched the animal fight the current, then reach the shore—it was a dog, and it shook the water off its coat and ran off.

"I think your latter assumption is more likely," Beret said at last. "Lillie did attract men. You know that yourself. And if Lillie could gain the affections of someone like Mr. Summers, then who's to say that Jonas wouldn't have loved her or at least wanted her. He knew what went on in the carriage—and in the house. I interviewed William, and he admitted that when my aunt and uncle were away, Lillie went into the parlor with men and locked the door." Beret bit her lip. "It pains me to have to admit this."

"You're sure one of the men was Mr. Summers?"

"I can't imagine that William would lie. And Nellie the maid all but confirmed it. No, I have no doubt."

Mick turned away and stared across the river toward the mountains, whose peaks were still white with snow. A breeze seemed to sweep down from them. Clouds drifted in front of the sun, and Beret shivered, drawing her jacket close to her. The wind blew dead leaves across her, and when she looked down, she saw a snakeskin and wondered if its owner was nearby. She was cold now, and she wished they had gone for tea, although the weed-choked riverbank seemed somehow more intimate.

The detective turned back to her and studied Beret's face, and then he took her hand and said, "I have something to show you. I was not sure I would do it. In fact, I was not so pleased to see you today, because I knew your presence meant I had to make a decision about it. By rights, it should go in with the other evidence we collected, but I think there is no reason for it now." Mick added, a touch of acid in his voice, "Besides, I suspect it would disappear if a certain party found out we had it."

Mick reached into his pocket and withdrew a book. It was small and cheap, a book of poems, the sort of sentimental trash that young girls read—the sort of poetry Lillie liked. Beret knew at once that it must be her sister's. She reached for it, but Mick held tight to it and did not give it up.

"It's Lillie's," Beret said.

"Yes, I'll grant you that. Elsie gave it to me. She came in with it yesterday and said she thought you might want it. Her price was high—ten dollars. I got her down to six and paid her myself."

"Then I shall reimburse you." Beret thought it odd the detective was withholding the book against the transaction. She would not have paid such a usurious price for the cheap volume, which she would only put into the fire, but she could not allow Mick to be out the money because he had done her what he thought was a kindness. She reached again for the book, but Mick did not give it up.

"It's not the book that matters. It's of little importance, I suspect. But Elsie found something of value inside. She said she likes to read and had borrowed it from Lillie's room the morning your sister was killed—stole it more likely, although she may have intended to return it if she didn't like the poems. She claims she didn't open the book until yesterday and then came straightaway to me with it." He extracted a piece of paper from the book, then handed it to Beret, who took it but didn't look at it. She held out her hand for the paper, and the detective gave it to her.

The paper was cream-colored, heavy, and expensive, like a woman's writing paper. The message inside was written in pencil, and it was undated. Beret studied the handwriting for a mo-

ment, because it was crude and hard to make out, and then she
read the message.

My Dearest Darling Lillie

*Forgive me for not calling on you last night. My wife demanded
my presence, and I thought it best not to aggravate her. So much is
at stake. She is beginning to see reason, and in time, I believe she
will release me. Meanwhile, I have found a house for you—and the
little one. Until I can kiss your sweet lips, I hold you in my heart
and dream of the great happiness that will be ours.*

Your Papa

Beret read the note twice, then set it down on the rock beside her and wrinkled her mouth in distaste. "Well, he's no poet,
that's certain. It's a mawkish note. I would have expected better
from Mr. Summers. Perhaps all old men in love lose their wits.
What do you make of it?"

"It seems your sister was telling the truth when she claimed
a married man was pursuing her—a wealthy one if it was indeed
Evan Summers."

"Do you have any doubt?"

"I hardly think Joey would sign a note 'Your Papa.' And he
has no wife. What do you intend to do with the letter? It's a pity
we're not into blackmail. This would bring a pretty penny. It's
your decision."

"Blackmail?"

"No, the disposal of the letter. Elsie sold it to me, and no one
else but you knows of it. I think if the chief and others were
aware that Mr. Summers wrote it, they could cause a great deal
of mischief. And if it was made public, it could do Evan Sum-

mers considerable harm. That would serve him right, of course, but I wouldn't like to blacken Caro. By rights, it is yours."

Beret thought that over. "I don't know. If Mr. Summers had been the one to ruin Lillie or if we thought he had killed her, then we might be tempted to use the letter to embarrass him. But should we expose a man just because he is unhappily married and was infatuated with my sister?"

"But he was the father of her baby."

Beret stood and took a few steps toward the river so that she was standing on the bank, looking down at the flow, which reminded her of dirty dishwater. "Do we really know that? Did Lillie herself know who fathered her baby? I suspect Mr. Summers was one of several who could have been responsible." Beret picked up the note and ran her fingers along the crease. "It is not easy to talk this way about a sister I loved more than anyone in the world." She stared out at the river, watching as two boys in a boat rowed themselves from one shore to the other. "Are you saying the letter is mine to keep?"

"I am."

Beret placed it inside the book and put the book into her purse. "I think I shall destroy it in time, but not quite yet." She removed some coins and held them out. "And here is your six dollars, unless, of course, the price has gone up."

Mick looked startled and then grinned when he realized Beret was joking. "I'd rather you be in my debt. In fact, I'll extract payment by insisting you go to a music performance at the Tabor Opera House on Sunday."

Beret blushed. She was not used to flirting and was uncertain how to reply.

"Forgive me. I've embarrassed you. That was crude."

"Not at all, Detective McCauley. You have no wife, I assume."

He grinned again and shook his head.

"Then I should be pleased to accept." Very pleased, Beret thought. This was an unexpected turn of events. She liked the detective more than any man she had met since Teddy left, and now she realized she liked him a great deal, indeed. She might stay on at the Stanton house even after the murder was solved, just because of him.

"There is one more thing. Would you call me Mick?"

"Mick."

"And may I call you Beret?"

"I should like that ever so much better than Miss Osmundsen," she said, liking the way he pronounced her first name.

As they parted, she knew the Sunday concert would be the most pleasant event she had attended since arriving in Denver, perhaps since Teddy had left the New York house. She looked forward to it, not just to the music but to being with Mick. The murders were behind them. Of course they were.

Chapter 18

In fact, Beret saw the detective before Sunday, because he was one of the guests Caroline Decker invited to her dinner party. The affair turned out to be more elaborate than Beret had expected, not an intimate supper at all but a gathering of some two dozen of Denver's social elite.

She had brought only a few clothes with her from New York and thought she might wear a suit, but her aunt insisted the dressmaker could ready one of Lillie's frocks in time, and that it would be more presentable. The gown was one of the simpler ones. Even so, the blue silk with its insets of lace and low neckline was much too elaborate for Beret's taste. And she feared that Caroline would recognize it as one of Lillie's. But it couldn't be helped. Beret either had to wear the gown or one of her day dresses, and so she donned the blue silk.

She turned down her aunt's offer of diamonds, however, for she cared little about such adornment. But she did borrow Varina's pearl earrings, which she wore with her own strand of pearls, an anniversary gift from Teddy. After the divorce, Beret had gone through the jewelry Teddy had given her and thought to dis-

pose of it. But then she realized that Teddy had paid for it with
her money—and that she liked the pieces very much. So she
told herself it was as if she had purchased the jewelry herself, and
she kept it. Teddy had had excellent taste and had bought her
presents that complemented her severe style of dress. As she took
out the pearls, she considered wearing one of the diamond
brooches that Lillie had secreted away in a drawer, but she didn't
know where they had come from, and she would not want to
wear something her sister had received from a lover—especially
a lover who might be at Caro's party.

Varina wore black again, with her diamonds, and the judge
was clad in formal attire, and together they looked every bit a
senator and his wife, whatever that meant, Beret thought. She
admired her aunt's poise. A lesser woman would have crumpled
under the shame of a niece who had been murdered in a brothel
and a coachman who had turned out to be a prurient killer. But
Varina possessed an iron will—enough fortitude, if necessary,
for both her and her husband.

The judge himself drove them to the Decker house, which
was a jumble of rusticated sandstone. Beret had passed it earlier
on one of her walks, and not knowing who lived there, she'd
considered it overblown and pretentious with its towers and
porches and too many stained-glass windows. Now, she was not
much more impressed with the interior. The entrance was a
rotundalike room with a massive staircase and a chandelier big
enough for a railroad depot. A stained-glass window depicting
some medieval scene dominated the landing. Oversized chairs,
heavily carved, stood in front of dark linen-fold paneling that
was higher than her uncle's head. The effect was of a baronial
hall, not a gracious home. It was designed to be intimidating, not
welcoming.

Heraldic crests were painted on a frieze near the ceiling, and as she studied them, Beret made out words written next to them. "Shakespeare," Mick McCauley whispered, coming up to her. "Decker fancies himself a bit of a scholar. The complete works of the bard are in the library, although don't look too closely. The pages haven't been cut."

"Why, Detective . . . Mick. What a delightful surprise. I did not know you'd be here."

"I'd have mentioned it if I'd known *you* were coming."

"After you introduced me to Mrs. Decker, she was kind enough to send my aunt an invitation. I met her a second time—at a dreadful tea." Beret smiled as if she'd said something naughty. "She is delightful and told me to call her Caro."

"We're all first names here, at least we younger ones are. I saw Caro and her husband welcome you, but have you met my aunt and uncle?" Without waiting for an answer, Mick steered Beret to a formidable-looking couple and said, "Aunt, Uncle, I have the honor of presenting to you Miss Beret Osmundsen, Judge and Mrs. Stanton's niece from New York City. Beret, Mr. and Mrs. Summers."

Your aunt and uncle, Beret wanted to exclaim, but instead, she bowed her head slightly as she told the couple she was pleased to meet them, hoping the gesture would hide her discomfort. She recovered and said to Mick, "Then you are Caro's cousin. How fortunate you are. I did not know." She turned to the Summerses. "Your daughter has been very kind to a stranger."

"No stranger if you are John and Varina's niece," Mrs. Summers said, giving a tight smile, and Beret felt a little sorry for her. Judging from the note Mick had found in the poetry book, Beret thought Mrs. Summers must have been aware of the liaison between her husband and Lillie, and if she knew the object of her husband's affections, she could hardly be expected to welcome Beret with much warmth. Summers himself stared at Beret so hard that she felt uncomfortable. He was a tall man with powerful shoulders, white hair, and pale blue eyes. Perhaps he'd seen Lillie in that very dress and was aware of its complicated snaps and hooks and buttons.

"Everyone has been so kind," Beret continued, not knowing what else to say. "I believe I am the beneficiary of the affection felt for my aunt and uncle."

Someone greeted the older couple, and they turned away without replying.

"Did she know about Lillie?" Beret whispered to Mick.

He shrugged. "According to the note, it seems likely. You mustn't conclude anything from their manner. They're stiff-necked with everyone." Then he added in a low voice, "Pity you didn't bring the note with you. It would liven up the party."

Despite herself, Beret laughed, and she was happy Mick was there. "Why didn't you tell me the Summerses were your relations?"

"Our mothers are sisters, although Ma doesn't put on airs like my aunt. I keep my family to myself. It doesn't sit well with my fellow officers that my father has money. They assume I was promoted to detective because of my connections."

"And were you?"

Mick looked startled, then laughed. "I'd say it made it harder. I had to prove myself to be one of the boys. That's why I slip into the brogue sometimes, me darlin'. My father's never given up the accent."

"And will I have the pleasure of meeting him?"

"Not tonight."

She turned serious then and asked Mick if it were proper that he had interviewed his own uncle and cousin as suspects in a murder investigation.

"I suppose it's for that very reason I didn't tell you who they were. But who else could talk to them? The chief plays poker with Uncle Evan every week, and my uncle would intimidate the other officers. I think myself to be the only one to stand up to him." He leaned in close and added in a low voice, "You see, I despise the old man as a hypocrite and a philanderer. It'd be no skin off my nose to arrest him."

Beret smiled at the thought of exposing the aging adulterer at the party, and Mick asked, "What are you thinking?"

"That I despise him, too."

"Enough to expose him?"

"No, although it would serve him right, I would not take that course. It would be awkward for my aunt and uncle. Would you?"

Mick shook his head. "It would hurt too many others. Caro, for instance."

At that, Caroline Decker approached them, confiding, "Now that you have been taken up by the most disreputable of our guests—my cousin Michael—I shall rescue you and introduce you to someone more worthy of you. Come." She turned to her cousin. "Although I can understand it, you must avoid the temptation to monopolize her, Mick."

As the two women walked away, Caro confided, "I shouldn't admit it to you—Mick would give me a drubbing—but he inquired whether you were coming, then begged an invitation."

Beret, pleased, felt her cheeks redden but didn't reply. She had liked bantering with Mick and wished Caroline hadn't taken her away. She hoped that he would be seated next to her at dinner. She looked around at the number of guests and said she'd thought this was to have been a small dinner.

Caro patted her hand and admitted she had deceived Beret as well as the Stantons. "I was afraid you wouldn't come, nor your aunt and uncle, and I do love them. They need to get about after the tragedy you all have suffered. Appearances matter, you know, especially in politics. Perhaps I should say even in politics, because some of the most villainous of men are appointed to office. Now who would you like to meet?"

Beret was about to leave the introductions up to Caroline, but then she said, "Your brother. Mick has told me he was a friend of my sister's."

Caro stopped and studied Beret a moment, her smile giving way. "Surely he told you, rather, that Joey was in love with Lillie, that he visited her at that place on Holladay Street," she said frankly. Before Beret could reply, Caro added, "Oh yes, I know all about that. It might even have been Joey who took her there. He does not always exercise the best judgment."

Beret decided to be as honest as Caro. "That's exactly why I want to meet him, because he was an intimate of Lillie's. When she lived with me, she was an innocent girl . . ." Beret's voice trailed off, because she knew what she had said was not true.

"She was no innocent, Beret. Any of us here can tell you that. She was wanton, and she was a schemer. That's not to say I didn't like her. I did. She was funny and fresh in a society that has gotten dull. I was delighted when she came. We all were. But she did not learn her ways from my brother or anyone else in Denver. I wonder you never saw her for what she was." Caro sighed. "But then, who among us clearly sees the ones we love?" She took a step forward. "I ask you to forgive me for being cruel.

Let's speak of it no more. My brother is on the porch if you still want to meet him."

Caro led Beret through French doors to what was more a long narrow balcony than a porch, with a tile floor and a railing of iron tracery. She made the introductions and left Beret alone with Joey.

"I am Lillie's sister," Beret said bluntly.

"I know that. She talked of you."

"And with little affection, I suspect."

"Yes, although she admired you once. But she felt you had been unfair. She told me the circumstances of her leaving, and I have to agree you did not treat her well."

"You know only what Lillie told you."

"Then what do you say?"

"I say it is none of your business." She paused to gain control of her temper. "We have not got off to a good start."

"But a frank one."

Beret appraised the young man. He was stocky but solid, not so tall, but he carried his size well. His blond hair was bleached by the sun, and his face—a very nice-looking face, Beret had to admit—was tan. Since winter was barely over, Beret wondered where he had gotten the sun. Perhaps he was a horseman.

"I have always liked a woman who is frank," Joey said.

Beret tilted her head. "If that is the case, then I ask what your intentions were toward my sister."

Joey turned away and clutched the railing of the balcony, looking down at the stone floor of the driveway a dozen feet below them. "I loved her. I wanted to marry her."

"Then why didn't you?"

Joey stared for a long time before he turned back to Beret. "Because she wouldn't have me."

Beret waited. She had learned at the mission that people often said more following an uncomfortable silence than if they were questioned.

"She turned me down," Joey said at last. "She told me my father wouldn't like it."

"And why is that?"

"How would she know whether my father would approve? She'd only met him once or twice."

Mick had said that Joey didn't know about Lillie and his father. Evan Summers might have hidden his relationship with Lillie while she lived in the Stanton house, but how could the two men not know that the other visited her at the House of Dreams? "I was under the impression that your father was fond of my sister, that they were"—Beret searched for a word—"friends."

"What are you implying?" he asked loudly. "That is despicable. My father is a man of honor." He swallowed down his anger. "It was my sister who was Lillie's friend. Father considered Lillie to be a fortune hunter. He ordered me to stay away from her. How dare you impugn a woman who can't defend herself."

In the darkness, Beret could see Joey's eyes glisten, and he rubbed them with the back of his hand. "Yes, of course," she murmured. Then she said, "There is another thing I would ask, and I would like an honest answer," she said. "Did you take her to Miss Hettie's House of Dreams?"

Joey jerked up his head and stared at Beret. "Good God, no! Why would I do such a thing?"

"Caro thought you might have."

"She always believes the worst of a person."

"In my short acquaintance with her, I have found the opposite to be true, but no matter. You might have taken Lillie to Miss Hettie's because she could no longer stay with my aunt and uncle, due to her pregnancy."

Joey looked forlorn. He took a step backward and leaned against the iron railing, which was low, and Beret feared he might fall.

"Perhaps she would have married you—if you were the father," Beret continued.

"But of course I was. How can you even suggest otherwise— you, her sister?"

"Because you were not the only one who enjoyed Lillie's affections." She felt sorry for Joey, but the words must be said.

Joey raised his arm as if to strike Beret, then thought better of it. "You are talking about your own husband, Miss Osmundsen, the man who seduced her. Yes, I know he followed her here, but she'd have nothing to do with him." Then he added acidly, "I can see why he preferred Lillie to you. Perhaps you should ask *him* why she joined the tarts at Miss Hettie's."

Beret ignored the insult. "Lillie's earnings there supported him."

"It can't be. You've made that up." He swallowed. "You have no right to speak of your sister that way. I can see why she disliked you—and your husband. I met Mr. Staarman once, and had I known at the time how he'd taken advantage of Lillie, I might have killed him. I was that angry."

"And were you ever angry enough to kill Lillie?"

Joey gave her an astonished look, then a harsh laugh as he started past Beret to the door. But Beret grabbed his arm and said, "That is a thing I must know. I promise the answer will remain between us, if for no other reason than my aunt and uncle's sake." She paused, then asked, "Did you murder my sister?" She put her hands against the cold stone wall to steady herself.

"How can you think that?" Joey asked, his voice hoarse with rage. "The police have identified the Stanton coachman as the killer. How can you possibly suggest . . ." Joey shook his head, and suddenly, he rushed from the porch into the room.

Beret let him go, then went to the railing herself and looked down at the roof of the stable below. Slowly, she became aware that someone had come up beside her, although he had made no sound. She turned and found Evan Summers staring at her.

"You are a despicable young woman to treat my son as you have," he said, giving her a look that might have terrified others. Beret did not frighten easily, but she felt uncomfortable and wished Mick were close by.

"Then you heard our conversation."

"Enough of it. You accused my son of murdering your sister."

"I did not," Beret countered. "I asked him if he had done so."

"You put too fine a point on it. You believe he is responsible."

"No more than I believe you are."

Summers's eyes turned even paler, and in the dim light on the balcony, Beret could see the hatred in them. "What are you saying, young woman?"

"That you had a reason to see my sister dead. You were intimate with her, just as your son was." Beret was frightened at her boldness.

"And you have that from my nephew Michael? He has had it in for me ever since I refused to employ him in one of my enterprises." Beret started to reply, but Summers held up his hand. "Oh yes, I know how the two of you have been prowling Holladay Street, talking to whores. It appears you have no more morals than your sister."

Beret might have held her tongue if the man had shown more humanity, but she replied, "Do not lecture me about morals, Mr. Summers. I will not take a scolding from a married man who finds nothing wrong in being intimate with a young girl, getting her with child, and abandoning her in a brothel, with false promises of leaving his wife."

Summers was taken aback. "And do you have proof of these foul accusations?"

"I do indeed. A letter. I have it in my possession."

"Then it is a false one. I do not write letters."

"Lillie hid it. Did you not find it when you went to the House of Dreams and killed her?" There, it was out, Beret thought.

Evan glared at Beret until his eyes were little slits. "It's not enough you accuse my son of murder, but now you accuse me, too? Which one of us would you and Michael prefer to hang, Miss Osmundsen?"

"Whichever one of you is guilty. You deny it, then?"

"I don't answer to you." He took a step forward, backing Beret against the railing.

Beret put her hands on the top rail, realizing how low it was. She braced herself as Evan came forward, fearing his intentions. He was a big man and could push her over onto the stones, claiming it was an accident. She slid to one side, thinking she could maneuver past him into the room, but as if he understood her intent, Summers matched the move. She could cry out, but when she glanced at the door, she realized Summers had closed it, and no one would hear her.

"And now what?" Beret asked at last.

"You should have kept silent. I imagine now you wish you had." He took half a step toward Beret, who glanced behind her, but there was nothing except for the stone driveway. She looked up at Summers, who seemed to be enjoying himself. "People have learned not to cross me, Miss Osmundsen. It is dangerous. That's a lesson I should like to teach to you—and to Michael."

He leaned his head forward, which frightened Beret more than if he had taken another step. She felt her hands begin to sweat against the cold iron. At the mission, she had stood up to men with knives, to drunken louts who threatened to beat her. But she had never come face-to-face with a man who was so controlled, whose face was filled with such hatred, and she was frightened. She had been foolish to confront him by herself. "What do you intend to do here?" she asked, wishing her voice were steadier.

"That is a quandary, is it not? I do not allow anyone to question my character."

"I am well aware of your character. It is not my intention to make public charges, since the police have concluded Jonas killed my sister and the other girl. I wish only to satisfy myself as to the reason for my sister's death."

"And what if I say I don't believe you? After all, you threatened me with blackmail."

"I did no such thing. I was merely trying to get at the truth." She knew now she should have waited until Mick was with her to reveal the letter.

Summers smiled, and Beret was reminded of a panther she had once seen in a cage. "It would be a pity if you fell over the rail while you were trying to get a look at the moon. You wouldn't be a pretty picture, smashed against the stone, your neck broken, not as pretty as your sister lying dead on her bed." He smirked. "I read about that in the newspaper." Summers licked his lower lip. "Poor Caroline would be so distressed. She'd never forgive herself. I wonder if people would think shame drove you to it."

"I do not believe anyone would make such a conclusion with you standing here."

He shrugged, and his lips curled up a little. "No one would know. The room behind me is empty. I would say I tried to stop you. I would be considered a hero," Summers said. He smiled, but his eyes were as cold as winter.

"You would kill me?" Beret asked.

"I wonder what it would be like. But then, I've done so before. That's what you believe, isn't it?"

The two stared at each other, and then suddenly, the door behind them opened, and Caro said, "There you are. We are ready to go into the dining room, Father. I should have known you would be closeted with our most interesting visitor. You and Mick have kept her hostage long enough. It's time she met our other guests. Come along."

Caro stood aside, and after a time, Summers said, "Why, of course, my dear." He held out his arm to Beret and turned to her with his eyes narrowed to slits. "We will continue this, Miss Osmundsen. I shall make sure of it."

Chapter 19

Beret emerged shaken from her encounter with Evan Summers and was anxious to tell Mick about it. But there was no chance to talk, because she sat at the far end of the table from the detective and could barely speak a word to him—or to anyone else that evening. He sent her questioning glances, but she did not respond. Following dinner, as the guests rose, the gentlemen to go into the library for cigars and brandy, the ladies into the drawing room for coffee, Mick whispered, "You've hardly said a word all night. Is something wrong?"

"Very wrong," she replied, adding, "I can't talk now. Later."

"Later" was not to be that night, however, since Varina complained of a headache, and the Stantons left with Beret as soon as etiquette permitted.

Like Mick, the judge observed that Beret had been quiet during the evening. "I hope socializing isn't putting too great a strain on you. Did you enjoy yourself?" he asked, once they were home.

"Yes, of course. I had a fine time, but I think Aunt Varina's headache must be catching," Beret replied. She would have liked to ask him his opinion of Evan and Joey Summers but knew she must talk with Mick first. She did not want to taint the Stantons' relationship with the Summers family for fear her interference would harm her uncle. Summers was that powerful.

Beret pondered whether Evan Summers had been about to kill her. Or was he just trifling with her, letting her know he was not to be threatened? Surely he knew Beret had no real proof he was the killer. Damaging as it was, the note told only that he was in love. If anything, the words he'd written suggested that killing Lillie was far from his mind, Beret thought, as she removed the earrings her aunt had loaned her. She had forgotten to give them back to Varina and would have to return them in the morning.

Beret put on her nightdress and went to the window, staring out at the stable and realizing she was looking at the window of Jonas's room. Everyone else believed Jonas had killed her sister. Why did she resist it? Because she wanted her sister's death to be the work of someone who cared about Lillie—Evan Summers, Joey, or even Teddy. She wanted there to be a reason to Lillie's death, something that made sense, something that was personal. She did not want Lillie to have been merely the victim of a madman.

When Beret awoke, rain was lashing the windows, but the storm was not what had disturbed her. She heard a pounding somewhere in the house and sat up in bed, trying to orient herself. At first, with the noise of the rain hitting the window glass of the cold room, she thought she was in her bed in New York, but then she realized she was in her aunt and uncle's house in Denver. The pounding continued, a knocking. Where were William and Nellie and the other servants? Why hadn't they answered? Then Beret remembered it was Sunday and the Stanton staff had been given the day off so that they could attend church—or that had been her aunt's intention, at any rate.

Her aunt and uncle must have gone to church, too. Well, she was not about to answer the door in her nightdress. Beret lay against her pillow, hoping to go back to sleep. But the knocking did not cease. Then she thought that the insistent caller might be Mick. She did not want to miss him. So she rose and threw on a robe, hurrying down the stairs.

Through a leaded-glass panel on the side of the door, Beret made out the shape of a man in an overcoat, his hat pulled low over his face to keep out the rain. The walking stick in his hand was familiar, and she unlatched the door before she realized that Mick did not carry a stick, that the object belonged to Teddy. But it was too late. The door was open now and Beret's former husband stood on the wet tiles of the porch floor, the collar of his coat pulled up around his neck.

"Hello, Beret." He grinned at her. "I was afraid you'd sleep through the clatter—you did sometimes, you know—and I'd have to go back out into the rain. He shivered. "As you can see, it is as thick as a sheet of iron." Indeed, the rain came down in torrents, splattering against the ground, forming pools of water on the sidewalks. Without waiting to be invited inside, Teddy stepped through the door and removed his hat, flapping it against his leg and spraying water onto the Persian carpet.

The familiar gesture made Beret's heart flutter, and she almost held her arms out to him as she once did when he arrived home in the midst of a storm. Instead, she kept her arms at her sides. She would not let Teddy see how he had affected her. "This is an odd time for a call, Edward. What is the hour?" she asked.

"Early yet, but I wanted to catch you alone." When Beret sent him a scornful look, he continued, "Oh yes, I know that this is the servants' day off, that the Stantons are at church and they rarely come home before mid-afternoon."

"This is when you came to visit my sister, then." She realized her robe was loose, and she clutched it to her throat.

Teddy didn't respond to Beret's remark, but instead, he looked at the folds of her garment and said, "You needn't act so modest. I've seen you with your robe open, seen you with no robe at all, you know. Would that I could see you so now."

"That is an offensive remark." The words tormented her.

"Oh, you wouldn't have thought so at one time. We did enjoy ourselves, didn't we?"

Beret did not reply, for she couldn't deny it. Teddy was right. She gave him a flinty look, however, hoping he did not see that her emotions were in conflict.

"I remember that stare. It would turn a man to stone, but not me. I was always flesh and blood around you. And you, ah, Beret, what a woman you were—you are."

Beret softened as she remembered their times together, how early in their marriage, she could not wait for his embrace. For a tiny moment she wished the past could be forgotten. Then she wondered at herself, that she could be moved by him when she hated him so.

"I have missed you," he said softly. He glanced up the darkened staircase and reached for her hand.

But Beret would not take it. She did not trust herself. "Why have you come here, Edward?"

"To talk to you, of course. To talk to you alone, without your aunt and uncle. Will you invite me into the parlor?"

"No."

"You have turned hard."

"You have turned me hard."

"I suppose I can't blame you. I wish things could be the way they were." He took a step toward her and held out his arms. "I wish you would forgive me and we could go back to what we had."

Beret's good sense reasserted itself, and she pushed temptation away. "In time, perhaps I shall forgive you, but go back, to live as your wife again? No! The divorce is final, Edward. I have no intention of taking you back. I could never trust you. How little you know me to think I could do such a thing. If this is the reason you've come here, you must leave now."

"You are afraid people would laugh at you."

"You should know I care little about peoples' opinions."

"Ah, but you do."

Beret looked at him curiously, aware now that Teddy was playing with her, that his talk of reconciliation had been only a ploy.

Teddy cocked his head and slowly lowered his gaze, taking in her body. "A pity. I think we could make a go of it again, but I can see you are not game."

"Game!" Beret shot back at him. "Game to take back a philandering husband, who caused my sister's death? I do not consider Lillie's murder a game."

"I did not cause it. I told you I had nothing to do with it."

"But you seduced her. Because of you, she came to Denver."

"Surely you have learned enough in your investigation to know that Lillie was as responsible as I for what happened."

Beret had, indeed. Still she said, "You were a father to her. Your action was heinous."

Teddy wiped his face with his coat sleeve, then ran his hand through his hair, which had curled from the dampness. Beret found the familiar gesture too intimate and turned away. "I do not want this conversation again. Please leave, Edward."

"Not before I present you with a proposition."

Beret raised an eyebrow. "Oh yes, I believe you are good at propositions now."

"Still the acid tongue, Beret? How it must wither the malcontents at the mission, but I can withstand your scorn. Who knows better than I what a shrew you can be?" He smiled, not a flirtatious smile as before but a hard one. "Yes, a proposition, because you really do care what people think."

They stood in the wide entrance hall, beside a table, and Beret glanced down to see a note with her name on it. She picked it up, thinking it might have been left by Mick. But the note, written in a garbled hand, was signed by her uncle and told that he and her aunt had gone to church and would lunch afterward with friends. Beret glanced up the staircase, which was dark. In fact, the entire house was dark, and she shivered as she thought of herself alone in that gloomy place with Teddy. "Nothing you can say is of interest to me."

"Perhaps not. But do me the courtesy of hearing me out, and I believe you will not be so sanguine." When Beret did not reply, he continued. "You may not care what society thinks of *you,* but you do care what it thinks of your mission?"

"And what is that to you?"

"Not much. I never cared about the mission, except that it got you away from the house."

Beret gave him a look of disdain.

"The proposition," he said.

"Ah yes. State it, Edward, and then leave."

"You say you don't care what society thinks of you, but you do care what they think of the Marta Osmundsen Mission. New York society, if you must know, believes you are odd, well intended, of course, but strange and a bit of a bore on the subject of raising money for the poor and downtrodden."

"And what is that to you?"

"Oh, I never cared. I rather liked the fact you were a little different. It made you interesting. I didn't even mind that you asked my friends for money to support your little project."

"How gratifying."

"But I wonder now how many of them would be willing to open their doors to you, to underwrite your charity if they knew about Lillie?"

Beret frowned. She didn't understand what Teddy was getting at. "I suppose some people know. I do not believe that would stop them from donating to the mission."

"Ah, but do they know the whole ugly story?"

"About how you seduced Lillie?" Beret was angry and steadied herself by grabbing the table, clutching her uncle's note.

"That part is of no consequence. I'm talking about how Lillie was pregnant, a prostitute, murdered in a brothel. She was a girl from one of New York's wealthiest families, and she ended up dead in a whorehouse."

"I suppose some of that might make the rounds of the gossips. There is nothing I can do about it."

"It's not just the gossips. I'm talking about all of New York. They would read about the scandal in one of the newspapers, in the dirtiest and most sensational of them all, the one the servants prefer behind stairs, the *American*. I'm surprised they haven't found out who the dead whore is. But I could tell them. You see, Beret, all I have to do is approach a reporter friend of mine and tell him about Lillie, how she ran away from a brutal sister who forced her to work in a mission where she learned the ways of a prostitute, how she fled to Denver where she was caught up in society, then abandoned it for life in a bagnio. The public loves stories about a wayward girl caught in the clutches of a mad killer, and this one involves not one but three prostitutes, one of them a New York society girl. And let's not forget that Lillie was pregnant. Oh, what a story it will make. It will be on the front page for a week, and the *Sun* and the *Tribune* and even the *Times* will be forced to pick it up. Everybody will be talking about it. What a delicious scandal. And you know what scandal does to a charity. Why, even your best donors will have their servants close the door in your face." He smiled at her, a smug, vicious smile. "You know what I say is true."

"My donors are loyal."

"All of them?"

Beret dropped the note on the table and turned away. "How could you think such a thing, Teddy? You were my husband. You were my sister's lover. Can you not give her dignity in death? Are you so depraved that you would use her death to destroy what I have worked for all my life?"

"Not so depraved, Beret, only in need of funds."

"And how much would you get for this story?"

"Probably nothing."

Beret looked at him sharply, confused.

"The money would come from *not* selling the story."

"Ah," she said, understanding now, "blackmail."

"Such an ugly word. I think of it as a business proposition."

"How much?"

"Ten thousand. I should ask for twenty, but I am not so greedy. You would be investing in my future. You see, I've turned out to be a pretty good gambler, but I need a stake."

"Ten thousand must be considerably more than what Lillie paid you." Beret stared at him. "Oh yes, I know all about how she gave you money. You were her mac, her pimp, if you like."

"That is disgraceful. I never brought men to her."

"But you took her money. And you placed her at Miss Hettie's House of Dreams."

"The money, I admit, although it was not so much, but I never took Lillie to that place. I was as surprised as you when I learned she was there."

Beret gave him a disbelieving look. "I see your true colors now, Edward, not that I haven't known for a long time what they were."

As the two of them stared at each other, the front door was suddenly flung open, banging against the wall, and the cold air rushed in. Startled, Beret clutched her robe with one hand and reached out the other to Teddy, who took it. When she realized she had only failed to latch the door securely and the wind had blown it open, she sighed and started to put down her hand. But Teddy would not release it. She watched as he raised it to his lips. Then suddenly, he grabbed her in his arms and kissed her. Beret put her hands against his chest and tried to push him away, but he would not let her go, and at last she yielded to him, for what else could she do? He put his cheek against hers and whispered, "Oh, my dearest, couldn't we try again? Don't reduce me to begging for money."

Beret felt the warmth of his arms and closed her eyes for a moment. But it was impossible, and she pushed him away. She took a step backward and placed her hand on the hall table to steady herself. "No, Teddy, not that."

Teddy sighed, and Beret thought that for a moment, he was disappointed. He glanced down at his walking stick, still clutched in one hand, and absently polished its gold knob on his coat. "Then I must go back to my proposition—ten thousand dollars, Beret, and I will be mum as a moth."

Beret could not believe that after kissing her, Teddy still demanded money. She stared at him and did not reply.

"Think of it as coming from Lillie's share of the inheritance. She has done you a favor in dying, Beret. Now her share of the fortune is yours."

"How dare you!" Tears came into Beret's eyes, tears of rage and uncertainty at the way her emotions had bounced back and forth in only seconds. "I never thought you were this depraved, Teddy, but now I know you are no better than the brutes I've encountered who beat their wives nearly to a pulp. You are every vile thing. Get out."

"Don't speak to me like that. I won't have it." Teddy's face was red with anger, and he spat out the words. "You were my wife, Beret. You have no right."

"Thank God, I am no longer your wife, and yes, I have every right. I'm not afraid of you, Teddy. Your words won't hurt me."

"Then this will." Teddy took a step forward and raised his walking stick, while Beret stared at him in surprise as much as horror as she wondered what she had unleashed. But she would not be silent, and with no regard for the consequences, she blurted out, "Is this how it was with Lillie? Were you so angry that she wouldn't give you money that you grabbed the scissors and stabbed her?"

Teddy froze, then slowly turned to look at the uplifted stick and lowered it. "I did not kill Lillie. I have told you over and over," he said softly. "You have no proof of it." He straightened the lapels of his coat and turned, but before he took a step toward the door, he said, "Think about my proposition. Don't cross me, Beret." He went out then, leaving his former wife staring out the open door into the storm.

Chapter 20

Beret returned to her room and dressed, then went downstairs, roaming from one room to another, at last going into the kitchen where she fixed bread and butter and a little fruit for herself. She would have liked to eat in the morning room, but the cold came through the window glass. So instead, she went into the dining room and pulled out a chair. She set down her plate and napkin and silverware and seated herself along the side of the table. Even eating by herself with no one else in the house, she would not be so presumptuous as to take her aunt or uncle's place.

The day was gray and forbidding and she was glad she had the afternoon outing with Mick to look forward to, although she wasn't sure after the confrontation with Teddy that she would be good company. Perhaps she should tell Mick what had transpired. But he would want her to refuse to pay Teddy, and Beret wasn't so sure that was a good idea. After all, Teddy had been right when he'd said her patrons, some of them anyway, might disappear if the scandal were made public.

Beret was restless and as the cook stove had been cold and

she had not wanted to build a fire, she had no coffee to linger over. She returned to the kitchen, and not wanting to make the servants clean up after her, she washed the plate and silver and put them away. Then she wandered around the house. The drawing room was dark and uninviting, and the library with its dead fire was cold. So she went back to her room, intending to read a book. She did not want to think about her sister's murder. She had done too much of that already.

As she picked up a book from her dresser, Beret spotted the pearl earrings she'd borrowed for the Deckers' dinner party and decided to return them to her aunt's room. She walked down the corridor, knocking on the door in case her aunt had stayed behind. There was no answer, so she entered the bedroom, thinking to leave the jewelry on the bedside table. But the top of the table was cluttered with scarves and gloves, a book, a magnifying glass, and various odds and ends, and Beret was afraid the earrings would get lost. She started to return to her own room but then remembered that her aunt kept her jewelry in a casket in the dressing room. Varina had told Beret that she ought to have a safe built into the wall for her diamonds, but she trusted the servants and had not done so.

Varina had half a dozen jewelry caskets lined up on a shelf beside her dressing table, small glass boxes on gilt legs, lined with quilted satin in jewellike tones. Each displayed a piece of jewelry, and Beret thought her aunt must like to admire these adornments as she sat at the dressing table, brushing her hair.

Beret opened a large leather casket fitted with drawers and slots for rings and necklaces, brooches and earrings, and found a space for the pearls. She spotted a ring with a diamond the size of her fingernail, its color like butter, and removed it to admire it. Her aunt's taste in jewelry was as exquisite as her taste in decorating.

She was snooping, Beret realized, and because that was not her nature, she started to close the box, but her eyes settled on the tip of an earring that had caught in one of the casket's drawers, preventing it from closing. She opened the little drawer so that she could place it properly, then gasped, leaning forward to see inside the box. She recognized the earring at once and wanted to slam shut the drawer, close up the jewelry box, flee from the room. But she could not.

Slowly Beret pulled the little drawer out of the box. Resting on its red velvet interior were Lillie's earrings, the earrings that had belonged to their mother, the ones Miss Hettie had described to Mick. She took them out and held them in the palm of one hand, then closed her hand around them, feeling the sharp points of the stones, squeezing until her hand hurt, trying to understand.

They were a copy. That was it. Her aunt had had the pair made exactly like Marta's. Or maybe there had been two pairs. Of course. Just to be sure, Beret took the earrings to Varina's bedside table and picked up the magnifying glass. One of Lillie's earrings had lost a diamond, and Beret had had it replaced with a stone that didn't quite match the others. Varina's earrings would be perfect. Beret held the first earring to the light and was relieved that she did not see an imperfection. She picked up the second and peered at it under the glass. The diamond in one of the leaves was brighter than the rest and there was a nick in the gold beside it. Beret remembered the nick. Lillie had made it when she dropped the earring on a marble floor.

Stunned, Beret sat down on the bed in her aunt and uncle's

great bedroom, which was gloomy even with the lights turned on, and shivered. A fear such as she had never known came over her as she thought of being alone in that dark house where something was terribly wrong. Beret looked at the earbob under the magnifying glass again, hoping she had been mistaken, but both the off-color diamond and the nick were there. The earrings were Lillie's.

Surely, Varina would have known that. She would have put them there herself. How had her aunt acquired them? Beret wondered as she went to the French doors and looked out. She couldn't see the stable. The rain made it difficult to see anything. She heard a noise downstairs and was startled, thinking her aunt and uncle had returned, although she hadn't heard a carriage. Had Teddy come back? Or maybe it was an intruder. More likely, one of the servants had returned.

Beret heard a door close and then footsteps on the staircase. She drew back inside the dressing room, fearful. The house was suddenly a sinister place. She did not care to be in that bedroom, and she especially did not want whoever was out there to be her aunt or uncle.

Then the footsteps entered the room. Varina! Beret thought and felt herself panic.

"Oh, ma'am, you startled me. I didn't know nobody was here," Nellie said.

Beret gave a sigh of relief. "You scared me, Nellie. I'd thought the house was empty. I guess I'm jumpy after everything that's happened. My aunt loaned me her pearl earrings. I was returning them."

"I'll see to them if you'll give them here."

"I already put them away, although I'm not sure they're in the right place. Would you be good enough to check for me?"

She held the hand with the diamond earrings behind her back and watched as Nellie went to the dressing table. "I put them in the large box."

"Oh, that's just for diamonds. The pearls go here. Mrs. Stanton's real particular about where her pretties go." Nellie removed the earrings and placed them inside a casket with a pearl necklace.

"She has beautiful jewelry. I was admiring her diamonds."

"Ain't they fine? She looks like the queen of England all decked out in them. There's nothing nicer, and between me and you, she looks a sight better than Mrs. Summers with her big old pearls the size of onions. Judge Stanton, he give his wife a yellow diamond ring as bright as a canary. That wasn't very long ago. I wouldn't know what it cost, but it must have been a lot, because the judge says she ought to keep it in a bank vault. But Mrs. Stanton, she says how could she wear it if she did that?"

Nellie chattered on, although Beret paid little attention to what she said. She felt more comfortable knowing the girl was in the house, although that did not relieve her of the uncertainty she felt. Nellie paused, and Beret realized she had asked her a question. "What's that?"

"I said do you like diamonds yourself, ma'am?"

Beret shook her head. "I'm not much for adornment."

"Miss Lillie did. She was all the time asking if she could borrow from Mrs. Stanton, asked me to get her a diamond pin that she fancied, but I wouldn't do it." She cocked her head and looked at Beret for a moment, as if deciding whether to go on. "Two of Mrs. Stanton's diamond pieces are gone, that pin and a ring. Mrs. Stanton asked me if I put them in the wrong place. I looked all over, but I couldn't find them."

"Surely she didn't believe you took them."

"Oh no, ma'am. Not me, no. But Miss Lillie? She wasn't so sure about Miss Lillie. I searched her room, but I couldn't find them, so maybe she didn't take them after all. They must have got lost. I told Mrs. Stanton the fastener on the pin didn't work right."

Beret remembered the two pieces she had found hidden, one in Lillie's dress and the other in her glove. She had removed them before the dressmaker came, and wrapped them in a handkerchief that she hid among her stockings. Beret would have to return them to her aunt, now that she knew their rightful owner.

Nellie went back downstairs, and Beret returned to her room, placing the earrings in a tiny pocket in her purse. As she closed the purse, she discovered the book of poems with Evan Summers's note inside and thought her purse was not a very good repository for evidence of a murder. She would have to find a better place. But if she put the items in the bureau, Nellie was likely to come across them. In fact, Beret was surprised that the girl hadn't found the jewelry Lillie had hidden.

Beret would seal them in an envelope with her name on it. That was it. No one would open a sealed envelope. She'd keep them safe until she decided what to do with them—tell her aunt and uncle, or give them to Mick. The note and earrings in hand, she crept down the stairs and went into the library and opened the drawer of the desk where her aunt kept her writing paper. She took out an envelope and slipped the note and earrings inside, then looked about for the sealing wax. The envelope was a perfect fit, she thought, and then stopped and slowly withdrew the note. The note and the envelope matched. Both were made from a heavy, expensive paper. Well, that could be explained. The Stantons and the Summerses frequented the same stationer.

As she pushed the note back into the envelope, Beret read

the words again. And then she blanched. She went into the hall and picked up her uncle's note. The crabbed handwriting on it was identical to that in the message written to Lillie. Both notes were penned by the same hand. Judge Stanton, not Evan Summers, had written the love letter to Lillie. Beret's uncle had been Lillie's lover, the man who had promised to leave his wife for her.

Beret put her arms around herself, for she had begun to shake. "Oh, Uncle, not you," she whispered. Her uncle had been their rock, almost a father to the two sisters. It was Judge Stanton who had supported Beret in continuing the New York mission for women instead of closing it after her mother's death. And while Varina had hoped the two girls would move to Denver where she could supervise them, the judge had agreed with Beret that their home was in New York and that was where they should stay.

But how had such a monstrous thing happened? Had the judge seduced Lillie, or was it the other way around? Had her aunt known? And then Beret thought about the child and was revolted by the idea that the baby could be her uncle's. While Beret was well aware that politicians had dalliances on the side, she knew that the judge's career would be over if it became public knowledge that he was keeping his own *niece*.

"No, no," Beret said aloud, gripping the newel post and sliding down onto the stairs.

"Yes, ma'am, did you call me?" Nellie said, rushing into the hall from the back stairs. She saw Beret on the steps and rushed to her. "Oh, miss, did you fall? Are you hurt?"

Beret shook her head. "I'm all right, Nellie. I twisted my foot is all."

"You want me to get you a basin of water to soak it?"

"I'm fine, just clumsy."

The maid helped Beret to her feet, and so as not to give away her lie, Beret, limping a little, let the girl lead her up the steps to her room.

"You lie down there on the bed, and I'll get a pillow for your foot. That's what the judge does when he has the gout." She rushed out of the room and returned with a satin boudoir pillow, placing it under Beret's heel, then covering her with a throw. Beret was too upset to resist.

"You want some tea. I can fix it in no time. All's I have to do is build up the fire in the cookstove. Cook isn't here, but she won't mind." The girl stood, hands clasped in front of her, anxious to help.

And then Beret remembered something. "You're a dear girl, Nellie. Sit beside me on the bed and keep me company, won't you? This is a big, dark house, and I would feel better if I were not here alone." Beret patted the coverlet.

The maid glanced around, as if what Beret had asked was not proper, then sat down on the edge of the bed, her feet on the floor, ready to spring up.

"How long have you worked for my aunt and uncle?"

"Six years, that is, six years come May. My sister was here before me, but she got married, and she recommended me."

"Do you enjoy it here?" Beret wanted to put the maid at ease.

"Oh yes, ma'am. Mrs. Stanton is real nice, but she's strict. She wouldn't like me sitting on the bed."

"We won't tell her, then. My sister and I used to sit like this and talk. You don't mind, do you? You have a sister, so you know what I mean. It's your day off, and perhaps you have things to do."

"Oh no. I was only going to do my mending. Does your foot still hurt?"

"No, it's fine, thanks to you." Beret leaned back against the pillows. "I was rude when you were talking about my sister the other day, not wanting to hear the things she had done, and I apologize."

Nellie was startled, as if no one had ever apologized to her before. "Oh, don't think nothing of it."

"I believe now that I would like to hear what you were about to tell me."

"What was that?"

"About some of Miss Lillie's doings in the parlor."

Nellie looked away. "I shouldn't have said nothing about that. It's not my place, you being her sister and all. Mrs. Stanton is real strict about gossip."

"We're just having a conversation. That's not gossip, is it?"

Nellie appeared uncertain. "I guess not."

"Thank you, Nellie. You would help me a great deal in accepting Miss Lillie's death if you would tell me about her, that is, about her doings. I need to understand why she went to that awful place."

"That was bad, all right. The servants was surprised." Nellie fidgeted. "Maybe not me and Mr. William. We knew Miss Lillie entertained plenty of men. That's for sure."

"Mr. Joey Summers was one of them?"

Nellie nodded.

"And his father?"

"Yes, ma'am."

"Mr. Staarman?"

Nellie looked away and started to get up, but Beret put out her hand. "It's all right. I know about them." She leaned forward and confided, "It started in New York."

Her eyes wide, Nellie stared at Beret. "I'm sorry, Miss Beret. You're ever so much nicer than your sister."

Beret squeezed the maid's hand. "And Judge Stanton. He was another of Miss Lillie's lovers."

Nellie was startled, and her eyes darted back and forth, not looking at Beret. "How did you know? I never told nobody about that. I started to tell you, but you stopped me, and I'm glad. William would put me out if he knew I told."

"I just know, that's all. You didn't tell me."

"You won't tattle on me, will you?" Nellie begged, looking at Beret now. She took Beret's hands in both of hers. "Mrs. Stanton would let me go without a reference, and where's a girl like me to find another job as good as this one?"

"Of course I won't tell. But I want you to give me the details. William knew, of course."

"Nothing gets past Mr. William. Me and him was the only ones that knew. Cook don't come out of the kitchen, and I kept Louise—that's the other maid—away when Miss Lillie was with the judge."

"That was wise of you."

"It went on for a long time. When Mrs. Stanton left the house, the judge would go in Miss Lillie's room and close the door, and I'd have to make the bed later on. Miss Lillie would tell me she'd taken a nap, but I'm not such a fool."

"When did my aunt find out?"

The maid shook her head. "My mother was sick, and I was out four, five days, and when I come back, Miss Lillie was gone. I asked Mrs. Stanton should I pack up her dresses, but she told me no. Then Jonas said Miss Lillie had gone to that place on Holladay Street. I asked Mr. William about it, but he told me to mind my business and keep my mouth shut."

"And how did my uncle react?"

"He never said a word about Miss Lillie, but he was working

hard to be nice to Mrs. Stanton, gave her that diamond ring and all. I think at first she might have throwed it at him, because I found it on the floor. Mrs. Stanton said she dropped it, but if you drop a diamond ring, you don't leave it there, do you? After a while, she started to wear it."

"So she forgave him?"

"Oh, I couldn't say. They'd have the worst rows you ever heard. Sometimes they were so loud that Mr. William sent Cook and Louise to run errands. But like I say, him and me knew what it was about. Well, ma'am, you couldn't blame Mrs. Stanton, now, could you? She was working so hard to get him in the government, and there he was with Miss Lillie. Ungrateful, he was."

Beret realized her hands were cold, and she rubbed them on the coverlet. "Did my uncle visit my sister at Miss Hettie's?"

Nellie fidgeted, looking down at the coverlet, then tugging at a loose thread. "How would I know that?"

"But you did know. Jonas told you."

The maid looked up as if she'd been caught. "I guess you're pretty smart. Jonas told me, all right."

"And he told your mistress?"

"Oh, I wouldn't know, but I'll tell you one thing. Judge Stanton, he isn't sleeping in the bed with Mrs. Stanton anymore. I can tell he sleeps on the lounge because that's where his pillow and a blanket are when I come to make the bed in the morning, and his side of the bed isn't ever mussed. I expect he'd sleep in another room, except he's afraid the servants would talk." She added quickly, "I never told the others about it, even William."

"I expect he knew."

"Mr. William always knows."

"Did he know my sister was pregnant?"

The maid put her hand to her mouth. "Oh, ma'am, that's a terrible thing." Nellie burst into tears, covering her face with her hands.

Beret squeezed the girl's arm and waited until she had taken control of herself. "And who do you think was the father?"

"Any one of them, I expect."

"Did the men know about the others? Would the judge have known that Lillie entertained other men?" The girl's answer was important to Beret.

Nellie shrugged. "How was I to know? You don't think they'd tell me, do you?"

Beret turned to look out her bedroom window. The rain was still coming down, and the branches of the trees dripped with moisture. The room felt stuffy, moldy, and not just from the dampness, she thought. She reached for the maid's hand and held it a moment. "Now I want you to think carefully and not be afraid to answer me, Nellie." She paused until the girl looked at her. "Do you think my uncle would have left my aunt for Miss Lillie?"

Nellie thought that over for a long time. "He wouldn't have gone to Washington, would he? It would be a scandal." She looked up. "Is that why Jonas killed Miss Lillie?"

"Did Jonas kill her, or was it someone else?"

Nellie's eyes went wide with shock. "You're not saying . . ."

Beret realized she had gone too far. "No, of course not. I'm not saying anything. I was only thinking out loud. I have a hard time accepting Miss Lillie's death, is all. What you said makes sense. Jonas probably stabbed Miss Lillie, thinking he was helping his mistress."

"Then why'd he kill those other'n?"

"That's the question, isn't it? Maybe he liked killing."

Nellie thought that over. "If that's so, do you think he might of killed one of us, I mean me?"

"I can't answer that, but you don't have to worry about it now that he's gone."

"You really think somebody else killed Miss Lillie?"

Beret could see the fear in the girl's eyes, and she said quickly, "No. Detective Sergeant McCauley is certain Jonas is the killer, and he knows more about it than I do."

The two women heard a noise downstairs and turned together toward the door. "My aunt and uncle?" Beret asked.

"I best check," Nellie said. "You won't tell—"

"I won't say a word," Beret assured her. "And thank you, Nellie. You've been a great comfort."

"That's all right, miss." The maid rose and went out, and Beret steeled herself for the hardest confrontation of her life.

Chapter 21

Nellie says you've turned your ankle," Varina said, bustling into Beret's bedroom.

"She makes too much of it," Beret replied, trying to sound casual. "I slipped a little on the stair, and Nellie insisted on my lying down on the bed with a pillow under my foot. I'm perfectly fine now."

"Well, then, come down to the library. I've told Nellie to light the stove and fix a kettle of hot water. Since you don't need it for your foot, your uncle will fix us a toddy. It's a cold and miserable day. You'll feel better by the fire."

For a moment, Beret was tempted to say she would rather rest in bed, but that would only put off what must be done. She placed a shawl around her shoulders, because she was chilled, and not just due to the weather. She slid the envelope into the pocket of her skirt rather than leave it in her room where Nellie might find it, and went downstairs. The library was warm now, bright with the fire the judge had made, and had she not been distressed, Beret would have enjoyed sitting in the cozy room on such an unpleasant day. She watched her uncle mix bourbon and hot water and lemon in a pitcher, sprinkle in a bit of brown sugar, then stir the concoction and pour it into three glasses that were set in silver holders. He handed them around, raised his own, and said, "Here's to better weather." Her aunt and uncle drank, but Beret only sipped her toddy.

"How was church?" Beret asked.

"The choir was lovely," Varina said.

The judge rolled his eyes. "We had a guest preacher. It is my opinion that weak advocates do religion no good. He preached on whether the poor were poor because they were wicked or because they were lazy and refused to work. He concluded both and made no allowance for the man who was born defective."

"Or for the woman who was married to such a man. I hope Jesus was not so devoid of compassion. I spoke with the reverend afterward and found him a nice enough man for a minister," Varina said. "We had thought to ask him to join us for luncheon, but Evan Summers said he'd sooner eat with some degenerate bum. I thought that was quite funny, but when I laughed, Evan looked at me strangely, as if he hadn't intended it as a joke. I am sure Evan has forgotten he was once a member of the lower class."

"They only live to serve him now. And you know, Varina, the man has no sense of humor," the judge said. "He was in a foul mood today. I wonder you could have stood him for even half a minute last night, Beret. You'd think with all his money, he'd enjoy life a little."

"He'd certainly go along with the minister in thinking he is deserving of his wealth, although I do not believe guile and deviousness should be rewarded as they have been with him," Varina said.

The couple chatted about the church service and the luncheon, which they had taken at Tortoni's Restaurant. The judge fixed his wife and himself second toddies, but Beret, who had barely touched hers, declined.

"You are very pensive today. What did you do with yourself while we were away?" Varina asked. She seemed in a good mood, and Beret wondered if she had had wine with her luncheon.

"I did not sleep well," she replied. "For a moment, when I awoke and looked outside, I thought I was in New York. Such weather depresses me."

"It will quickly pass. Have you eaten?" her aunt inquired.

"A little. Teddy came," she said abruptly, sorry at once that she had mentioned him, but she wanted desperately to find a topic of conversation to put off discussing the note and the earrings just a little longer.

"The cad. What did he want?" the judge asked.

"I believe he thinks I will take him back."

"The idea," Varina said. "I hope you sent him on his way."

"I did."

"Good girl," the judge said. "What else did you do?"

Beret considered him for a long time, but there was no point now in postponing the conversation. "I was going to read in my room, but I remembered the pearl earrings I had borrowed last night, so I returned them. I thought to put them in with your diamonds." Beret looked up at her aunt as she said that. "But Nellie told me they went with a pearl necklace."

"She's right. The large casket is for my diamonds. You needn't have bothered. I could have put them away myself." Varina looked unperturbed at her niece's remarks. "I suppose someday I ought to store them in a bank vault, but I keep them here. Your uncle would like to have a safe installed in the house."

"You have lovely diamonds. I saw a beautiful champagne diamond ring."

"Your uncle gave it to me." Varina studied Beret now before she asked, "You went through my jewelry?"

"No, of course not. I merely saw the ring when I opened the lid." Beret paused, not sure what to say. "Nellie said you lost two diamond pieces, a brooch and a ring."

"Yes. Nellie thought the clasp on the one was broken."

"I don't think so, Aunt Varina. I found a diamond brooch in the hem of one of Lillie's dresses and the ring tucked inside her glove. I thought they were my sister's. But if they are yours, I shall return them at once. Lillie must have borrowed them."

Varina exchanged a look with her husband and replied, a touch of acid in her voice, "Or was given them." Her uncle looked away, and Beret pretended not to understand. The judge went to the fire and poked at it, although the fire was burning perfectly well.

Varina smiled at Beret. "Someday all those diamonds will be yours, of course."

"I . . ." Beret didn't know what to say. She had no desire for her aunt's jewels, as she did not wear such elaborate pieces. More to the point, she had not come to the library to discuss her aunt's diamonds. "That's very generous, but—"

"But what? Of course I shall leave them to you. Who else would they go to? I would have left them to both you and Lillie, only . . ." She let the thought linger.

"Yes," Beret replied. She put her hand into her pocket and felt the envelope there. She did not want to accost her aunt and uncle. She was agitated and wanted to get the confrontation over with. So she said suddenly, "I found something in your jewel casket, Aunt Varina."

"Yes." Varina's eyes narrowed, and the judge looked up. The room was suddenly still, except for the fire, which crackled as a log split and fell, sending up a shower of sparks. One landed on the Persian rug, and the judge stepped on it.

The two stared at Beret as she stood and went to the fire, holding out her hands to its warmth, although that warmth did not seem to enter her body. She wished desperately that she had not discovered the earrings, that she had waited until her aunt returned to give the borrowed pearl earbobs to her. Beret had loved her sister, had felt obligated to help find her killer, but now, she was sorry for not leaving the investigation of Lillie's murder up to the police. It was too late, however. She had discovered the earrings, and she had opened the conversation. "I found Lillie's earrings, the ones taken from her room when she was murdered. They were in your jewelry casket."

"What!" the judge thundered, while Varina did not move.

It was out now, and Beret could not take it back. "They are Lillie's."

"They are clearly a copy," the judge said, looking at his wife.

"I thought that, too, at first, but I had had one of the diamonds replaced before I gave them to Lillie, so I am sure these are not a copy. I was hoping you had some explanation," Beret said.

"You are clearly wrong," the judge told her. "What possessed you to snoop among your aunt's things?"

"That is not the point. The point is Lillie's earrings are here in this house. I would like to know how this happened."

"How could you, Beret?" Varina said, wringing her hands. "You are my own flesh and blood. Michael McCauley has turned you into a shrew. You are so caught up in the evil surrounding Lillie that you suspect even us. I would never have allowed you to come here if I'd known you would accuse us. Your mother would be ashamed of you."

No, she would be ashamed of someone else in that room, Beret thought but did not say it. Instead, she told her aunt, "Then I shall leave at once, Aunt. But only after you answer my question. What are Lillie's earrings doing in your dressing room?"

"You're saying Jonas gave the earrings to your aunt after he killed Lillie?" the judge asked.

"That is one possibility. Another is that he put them there himself." Beret almost wished her uncle would seize on the latter explanation.

Instead, he asked, "Or are you suggesting someone else in this house is responsible for Lillie's death?"

"I am saying no such thing, Uncle. I am hoping for a logical explanation."

The judge hit the floor with the poker. "I am greatly disappointed in you, Beret. There is no wrongdoing here. You have no proof. We treated Lillie like a daughter."

"No, you did not!" Beret almost spat the words at her uncle, so angry was she at the falsehood. "Would you have written a letter like this to your daughter?" She removed the envelope from her pocket and took out the note, holding it up. The judge blanched as he recognized it and tried to grab it, but Beret would not give it up.

"What is it?" Varina asked.

"Shall I read it?" Beret asked, her eyes boring into her uncle. The judge looked defiant. "Where did you get that?" Beret didn't answer, only stared at her uncle. He turned, his back to her, and muttered, "It's not necessary."

"What is it?" Varina repeated. She tried to snatch the note

away from Beret, but her niece held it out of her aunt's reach, too.

"Do you want me to tell her?" Beret asked, and when the judge did not reply, Beret said, "I am sorry, Aunt. Will you sit?" Varina slowly lowered herself into a chair and leaned forward. Then Beret said, "This is not easy for me, because I love you both. But Lillie was my sister, and she was ill-used." Beret took a deep breath. "Uncle John had an affair with Lillie. He is the father of her child, or at least he believes he is. He admits it in this note. He intended to set Lillie up in a little house and live with her there."

Varina's face had been placid, curious, but now she was incredulous. "No! That can't be." She looked at Beret instead of at her husband. "How could you make up such charges, Beret? You are a cruel young woman. John, tell her it's not so."

"You didn't know, then?" Beret asked.

"It's all lies."

"No. Here is the note. Read it for yourself."

She handed the paper to Varina, who read it slowly, then looked up, her eyes moist. "Is this indeed yours, John?" she asked.

The judge reached for the note, but Beret intercepted it, afraid her uncle would throw it into the fire.

"John?" Varina asked, but the man turned away from his wife, his shoulders slumped, and suddenly he looked very old.

"You didn't know, then?" Beret asked her aunt.

Varina stared at Beret, bitterness in her eyes, and put her hands over her face and bowed her head. But she didn't cry. She trailed her fingers across her cheeks and then removed her hands. "Of course I knew. I knew your uncle had a dalliance with her but not that there was more. She was a despicable young woman, not at all like you, Beret. I believe she even set her cap for your uncle, flattering him, touching him. I thought it was all inno-cence, but I came to know it was not. She was devoid of all moral fiber. I think you know that yourself now, Beret. Lillie had not one ounce of human decency. She seduced your uncle."

Yes, Beret did know that. Had Lillie been the aggressor, or had it been their uncle? And did it matter? Beret wondered.

"It's true, just as she seduced *your* husband," Varina contin-ued. "She bragged to me that she had enticed Teddy, had made him fall in love with her, just to spite you. She must have hated the women in our family to have betrayed us in such a manner."

Beret trembled. "But why?"

Varina shook her head. "It was Lillie's character."

The judge put his hand on his wife's shoulder, and she winced. "Please don't touch me," she said, her voice hard.

"I didn't know what to do," he pleaded. "I didn't want to throw away everything we'd worked for, Varina, but there was the baby—"

"Don't," his wife said. "Don't shame me in front of Beret."

"I will make it up to you. I've already tried. I gave you the ring—"

"You think I can be bought?" Varina was indignant.

"No, of course not." John sat down on a footstool and put his head in his hands. "You should not have brought this up, Beret. You should have kept your discovery to yourself."

"The sin is not mine. I merely exposed it." But oh, Beret thought, she wished she hadn't discovered it. She closed her hand around the earrings, feeling the diamonds press into her flesh, and said, "We have got off the subject of the earrings. I would like to know how they came to be in this house."

John and Varina exchanged a long look, and he said, "I would like to speak to my wife alone."

"No, I won't allow it," Beret told him.

"*You* won't *allow* it!" The judge stood then, fire in his voice. "*You* won't allow me to speak to my wife in *my* house! Who do you think you are, young woman? Does it not occur to you that you are alone in this house with us? You threaten to expose me, to destroy everything your aunt and I have worked for now that we are on the threshold of our goal. You are the one who should be threatened." Grasping the poker in his fist, he shook it at Beret as he rose and took a step toward her. "You will not stand in my way any more than your sister did. Be very careful, Beret, or you will end up like her. She deserved it." The old man was enraged, his face red, as he raised the poker.

Beret took a step backward as her uncle advanced. "You can't mean that?" she said. Then she remembered his telling Mick and her that sometimes killing couldn't be helped, that death in a cause was justified. The blood drained from her face.

"Oh, I can." He took another step toward her.

"John," Varina said, reaching out a hand, although she did not stop him.

Beret stepped backward. She would not turn away from the judge. She had been unwise to confront her aunt and uncle in that silent house, but it had never occurred to her that she might be in danger. Now her uncle would smash the poker into her head and claim she had fallen down the stairs.

"You killed Lillie, then?" Beret took a step back, then another, until she was at the door to the library. "Do you deny it?"

The judge looked to his wife and sighed.

Beret glanced at her aunt, who stared, motionless, as if she could not interfere in what was happening. She did nothing to stop her husband. If the judge had killed Lillie, whom he loved, he would not hesitate to take Beret's life. As soon as she was through the door, she would slam it and then run to her room and lock herself in. But then what would she do? She would have to figure it out then, maybe crawl out the window. Perhaps Nellie would come to her aid. Beret took a final step and reached for the door as the judge raised the poker higher, ready to strike. Then Beret felt a hand on her shoulder. She turned suddenly and found herself facing Mick. He pushed her behind him.

"I'll take that, Judge Stanton," Mick said evenly.

The judge was startled. He continued to move forward, but he loosened his grip on the poker, and it fell to the floor. He stared at the poker as if he didn't recognize it. He looked at his hand, then at Beret, and he crumpled onto a chair.

"What are you doing here?" Beret whispered to Mick.

"We had an engagement, remember? When no one answered my knock, I let myself in. I heard you arguing and decided to listen."

"Then you heard."

"Enough." Mick turned away from Beret and approached the judge. "It appears you murdered your niece, then took her earrings and put them in with your wife's jewels. Is that not right, Judge Stanton?"

The judge looked up, not at Mick but at his wife, staring at her for a long time. He was silent a moment, as if considering the detective's words. At last, he said, "I'm sorry, Varina. Forgive me." He slowly turned to Mick. "I put the earrings into my wife's jewelry box. You are right. I am the one who killed Lillie."

Chapter 22

Varina sat stonelike in the chair in the library. She had not risen when Mick came into the room nor when he led Judge Stanton away but had only watched, mute, as she and her husband exchanged long looks, and then he was taken out of the room. The judge had not been placed in handcuffs. At least Mick had shown him that courtesy. Varina raised her hand in a useless gesture at the two men, who had already turned their backs and were leaving the room. Then she let her hand fall into her lap.

Beret, her arms wrapped around herself, for her blood had seemed to stop its coursing through her body, accompanied Mick and her uncle to the door. "I am sorry, Uncle John," she began, but the judge held up his hand, and she was silent, knowing anything she could say was meaningless.

"I will stop to see you later," Mick whispered as he led the judge down the steps. "Under the circumstances . . . you understand, of course, that the concert is off."

"Of course."

"Perhaps another time."

Beret nodded. "I would like that."

The men climbed into Mick's buggy. Beret, who had followed them outside, saw a bouquet of tulips lying near the door. Mick must have brought them for her and dropped them when he heard loud voices in the house. It was hardly appropriate for him to present them to her now. She watched from the sidewalk as Mick picked up the reins, and flicked them on the horse's back, then followed the buggy with her eyes until it disappeared. Returning to the house, she retrieved the bouquet and took it inside, setting it on the hall table.

Beret returned to the library, where her aunt appeared not to have moved, although the fire had been replenished. William must have done it. He would have returned, or perhaps he had been in the house all the time. Did he know what had occurred in that room? But of course he did. As Nellie had said, William knew everything. Beret sat down on the footstool next to her aunt and took the older woman's cold hand in her own warmer ones. Her aunt did not look up. "I'm sorry I came here," Beret said at last.

"Yes, I was afraid it would mean trouble. You never could let well enough alone. But I'm sorrier yet that your sister came. I should not have allowed it."

"What else could you have done?"

Varina shook her head. "You threw her out. I had no other choice."

"The fault is mine."

Varina didn't respond but gave a nod.

"I have had to accept that Lillie was not what I thought."

Her aunt looked up at Beret then. "I have told you she was never as you thought."

"Is that my fault, too? Did I pamper her too much? I never held her responsible for what she did. I always thought 'poor motherless girl.'"

"She was always willful. I knew it the first time I saw her when she was not yet a year old. It was her lack of character. But you did not help her, Beret." When Beret started to interrupt, Varina held up her hand. "I don't blame you."

"You are forgiving."

Varina shook her head but said nothing, so Beret changed the subject. "May I fetch you something—a glass of sherry, tea? Nellie is here. She will fix it. A little tea would do us both good."

"Yes," Varina said without enthusiasm.

Relieved to have something to do if only for a moment, Beret rose and went into the kitchen. Nellie was there and Beret wondered where she had been when Mick arrested the judge, perhaps listening at that very kitchen door.

"Is it true?" Nellie asked.

"Is what true, Nellie?"

The servant looked around, anxious, and then she lowered her voice. "Mr. William said Judge Stanton had only gone out with Mr. McCauley, but I heard what happened. I was listening." She looked away, abashed. "I didn't mean to, but you was all talking loud. I would have had to plug my ears not to hear what Judge Stanton said."

"Then you know as well as I do what transpired." Beret thought a moment. "Did William hear it, too?"

"I don't know. You see—" She stopped abruptly as the butler entered the kitchen and spoke her name.

"Hello, William," Beret said quickly. "I have just asked Nellie if she would be kind enough to make tea for Mrs. Stanton. She was telling me it would not take long, because she had already built a fire to heat water. I would like her to bring it to us in the library, when it's finished."

"Very good," William replied.

"And Nellie, I know it is your day off, but if you would be kind enough, I need your help in my room. I shall be leaving soon."

Nellie stared at Beret, a question on her face, but it was William who replied, "Of course, madam."

Without another look at Nellie, Beret left the kitchen and returned to the library.

Varina had lifted her feet onto the footstool and was leaning back with her eyes closed, and for a moment, Beret thought her aunt was sleeping. She picked up a throw, the very blanket Jonas had put over her, and started to cover her aunt, but Varina said, "I don't want that."

"You are awake, then. William will bring your tea. Nellie is making it. I've asked her to help me pack after she is finished in the kitchen. She can make arrangements for the train, or perhaps William will do it for me."

"You're leaving me?" Varina sat up and opened her eyes.

"I—"

"You'd leave me here alone to face this?" Varina asked.

"I thought that was what you wanted. You said—"

"That was before your uncle's arrest. It is a horrid thing that's happened. What would people think if you, too, deserted me before it is all sorted out? I cannot face this alone," Varina pleaded. "You do want to do this for me, don't you?"

"Of course," Beret replied, hoping her reluctance did not show. The truth was she had been relieved at the idea of returning to New York. She did not want any more of the sordid business. She would be glad to get away from it, although she would be sorry to leave Mick, because she had enjoyed his company. She had even hoped that the outing they had planned for today might lead to a closer association, but that was impossible now that he had taken her uncle away. Beret held herself responsible for the judge's arrest, so she had no choice but to stay if her aunt wished it. She was all her aunt had.

"You have come this far with your investigation, I would expect you to stay on to exonerate your uncle," Varina said.

Beret stared at her aunt, wondering if the woman were in shock. Or perhaps she had heard incorrectly.

"You have a duty to clear him," Varina said.

"But you heard him. He confessed. And he admitted he put the earrings into your jewel casket. We knew they were taken by whoever killed my sister."

"He is my husband. I have lived with him for nearly twenty-five years. Don't you think I'd know if he was capable of murder?"

"But the note—"

"It is a schoolboy note telling of a crush on a girl. It is not a note confessing a murder. You know yourself that what was between them was nothing more than an infatuation."

Beret looked at her aunt incredulously. Did the woman believe what she was saying? Had her mind tricked her into thinking that her husband had had nothing more than a dalliance with Lillie? "He said he was the father of Lillie's baby, a baby we know was conceived while Lillie lived in this house."

Varina dismissed the idea with a wave of her hand. "Who can say whose child it was? There were other men in Lillie's life. Why, your uncle and I have never had a child, and the fault could well be your uncle's—an illness he had when he was a young man."

Beret was dumbfounded at her aunt's departure from common sense. "But why would he confess?"

"We know—the police know—that Jonas murdered Lillie. You must find out why John thought it necessary to protect Jonas. That is what the confession is about, of course."

Beret raised her hands, palms upward, in a show of helplessness. "He confessed to save Jonas?"

"Now you understand."

"But why? We know Jonas murdered the crib girl and attacked another."

"I'm sure you will find it out, Beret. Now we must dress. I have a dinner engagement this evening. I'll send William to say Judge Stanton was unexpectedly called away and that he will be unable to attend, but that you will come in his place. I'm afraid all this jockeying for the Senate seat is getting rather tiresome for you, but it must be done."

Beret thought her aunt had taken leave of her senses. She cringed at the idea of accepting the social engagement.

Nellie knocked on the door then, carrying the tea tray and setting it on a table next to Varina. She poured the tea into the cups, adding cream and a lump of sugar to Varina's cup, then handing it to her. Beret picked up her own cup and rose, kissing her aunt on the forehead and saying, "If you'll excuse me, I want to lie down a moment, Aunt Varina. Nellie, would you come with me, please."

"Yes, have a rest," Varina replied. "It will be a tiring evening tonight."

Nellie left the tea tray on the table and followed Beret upstairs. "I'm sorry you're leaving, ma'am. It's a shame Mrs. Stanton will be by herself with her husband in the jail and all. I don't know how she'll manage, poor lady."

"But I'm not leaving after all," Beret told her.

"Then you don't need any help packing." Nellie looked confused.

"I would like to talk to you."

They had reached Beret's room, and Nellie stopped in the doorway. "I don't know, ma'am. Mr. William won't like it."

"You do not work for Mr. William. You work for my aunt. Besides," she added sympathetically, "you heard Mr. William say you should help me after tea was fixed."

"Yes, ma'am," Nellie said.

"I have decided to stay on to be of some use to my aunt, Nellie," Beret said, her voice rising, for she thought William might be listening. "Unfortunately, I had begun to pack my things myself, and now I'll need your help unpacking them."

The two women went into the bedroom, and Beret closed the door. She sat down on the bed, and indicated the chair to Nellie, who chose to stand. "You have been my aunt's maid for several years," Beret began. "I should like to ask you about her health."

"Oh, she's strong as a mule."

"I mean the health of her mind."

Nellie frowned.

"Has her mind been a little unsettled? After all, she has been under a great strain. Is she acting . . . differently?"

Nellie thought that over. "She hasn't been happy, if that's what you mean. She don't eat much, and I see her in the parlor just staring out the window. But after what's happened, well, that makes sense to me."

Beret was getting nowhere, so she asked, "Does Mrs. Stanton have trouble accepting the truth? What I mean is, when something bad happens, does she pretend otherwise?"

"Oh, you mean like with Miss Lillie. As far as I could tell, she pretended she liked Miss Lillie, that she missed her after she left, although I know that wasn't so. I mean how could she?"

Beret was frustrated now, so she decided to be blunt. "Have you seen signs that your mistress has lost her mind?"

Nellie smiled. "Oh no, ma'am. She's just as good as she's always been. Forgetful sometimes after she takes her medicine. You'd have to ask William about them."

"What medicine is that?"

Before the maid could answer, there was a soft knock at the door, and William said, "Nellie, if you are finished, you should see to your mistress."

The girl turned quickly, grateful to have a reason to leave. Beret, however, thought that the butler had overstepped. It was he and not Varina who had summoned Nellie. She wondered if William did not trust her, and then she realized she did not trust him. There was something about him that bothered her. She flicked her fingers toward the door and said, "Go on, Nellie. We are finished with our conversation." And before the girl could reply, she added, "Please don't tell William about it."

"No, ma'am," Nellie said, relieved.

The dinner party was the strangest event that she had ever attended, Beret decided the following day. The guests surely knew that Judge Stanton had been arrested, but they said not a word, while Varina chatted merrily about the heavy load the judge was carrying and how she worried about his health. One or two of the guests approached Beret with vague inquiries about her uncle, but Beret pretended not to understand, so the topic of conversation that was on all their minds was never spoken—until she and her aunt had taken their leave, Beret thought. Then the tongues would have wagged.

As she rose that morning, still thinking about the evening before, Beret nearly laughed at her aunt's remark on the way home, "I thought that went well." The engagement had gone anything but well, but there had been no need to tell Varina how absurd the party was. It was enough that Varina had been pleased with her performance.

But that was last night. Beret had to consider what she would do now. Mick had not returned, as he'd promised, and as her uncle had not come home, he must have been incarcerated.

Beret dressed, thinking she would breakfast before her aunt awakened. She would decide how to proceed and be out of the house before Varina came downstairs. But when she went into the breakfast room, Beret found Varina sitting over coffee, a newspaper beside her plate. Beret had forgotten about the Denver newspapers. After all the space they had given to the Holladay Street murders, they would be frenzied over the judge's arrest, and she was right. Reading upside down, she made out the headline PROMINENT JURIST ARRESTED IN HARLOT MURDER. And beneath it in smaller type, "Judge Stanton Had Been Considered for the Senate Seat." She glanced at her aunt, who looked haggard, her skin gray. She had been through too much. "Damn the newspapers," Beret said in an unseemly burst of anger.

"They will recant, but you must act quickly, dear. I've asked William to have the carriage readied. I will take you to the police station to see Detective McCauley. You must explain to him that your uncle did not really confess, that he was not in his right mind."

"Joking?"

"Of course."

"Are you going with me, then?" Beret asked. She did not want her aunt exposed to the squad room, to the stares and snickers and rough treatment. The reporters would discover who her aunt was and ask their rude questions.

"Oh no. I will ask the new coachman to drive me about as Jonas used to do. We'd roam the city for an hour or more, sometimes the better part of the day, just the two of us, even in poor weather. He was such a fine lad. He never complained, because he knew it pleased me to drive about."

"Jonas?" Beret asked.

"Of course, Jonas. You remember him."

The two women said no more, and after Beret finished her breakfast, she and her aunt donned black, for they were in mourning of a sort, and rode down Larimer Street in the Stanton carriage. Beret was let off at City Hall.

Although it was early yet, the squad room was crowded with newspapermen, because the judge's arrest had created a frenzy. Beret had heard the newsboys in front of City Hall hawking papers, yelling out the judge's name in their high, shrill voices. As she alighted from the carriage, Beret had scanned the headlines, which were as brazen as the one she'd seen in the newspaper on her aunt's breakfast table: PROSTITUTE'S KILLER PROMINENT JUDGE, SENATE CANDIDATE JAILED FOR KILLING SOILED DOVE, and simply THE MIGHTY ARE FALLEN. JUDGE STANTON MURDERER. The cacophony of boys' voices grated on Beret's ears, but her aunt, she observed, seemed oblivious to the commotion.

Now as Beret stood in the doorway of the squad room viewing the newsmen milling around, she was glad that her aunt had gone off. Beret herself was unnerved by the men as she glanced toward Mick's desk, hoping to spot the detective. He was not there. She searched the room, and as Beret did so, Eugene Latham, the reporter she had met on Holladay Street, near Sadie Hops's crib, approached her.

"Miss Osmundsen," he said, sneering.

Beret gave him a frosty look.

"Criminologist, was that it?" He blocked her way into the room.

"Please let me pass," Beret said.

"Please let me pass," he mimicked. "I know who you are. You're Lillie Brown's sister. There's no New York Institute for the Study of the Criminally Insane. And no Porter-Masters murders. I checked."

"How clever of you."

"Don't take that tone with me, lady. Who do you think you are? You got a sister that's a dead whore and an uncle that killed her. You can't turn up your nose at me."

The other reporters heard the confrontation, and they grew quiet, staring at Beret, waiting for her to reply. Beret was furious. She had been in police stations before. She should have been prepared for the pack of newsmen, should have known they would be lying in wait. For a moment, she felt light-headed and a little sick to her stomach. But she drew herself up and stared at the reporter. "Let me pass, sir," she said, her voice steady, even if the rest of her was not.

"That right?" a second reporter asked, taking a pencil from behind his ear and jotting down something on a pad of paper. "You really related to Judge Stanton?" The others drew closer.

"You think he's guilty?" another yelled.

"Of course he's guilty. He confessed, didn't he?" someone said, then asked Beret, "How'd you know it was him?" A reporter demanded, "Were you scared? Did you think he'd kill

you, too?" The others began yelling at Beret with so many questions that she covered her ears.

The men crowded about Beret, and she felt overwhelmed.
She was reminded of a bunch of rats fighting over a piece of
meat—and she was that flesh. A reporter grabbed her and asked,
"Why do you think he did it, lady?"

Beret turned her head slowly, letting her eyes rest on the
hand a moment. Then she raised her head and stared at the man
so long that he removed his hand and took a step backward. But
another immediately took his place and asked, "Your name
Brown, or is it Stanton?"

"It's Staarman," Latham said. "She's married to that gambler
at the Arcade, Teddy Star, the one that thinks he's so swell." He
sent her a triumphant look, but Beret did not deign to glance at
him. "Snooty one, isn't she?" he asked. He stepped forward then,
coming so close to Beret that she could smell the sweat on his
clothes, and his breath, which was like stale whiskey.

Another reporter put his hand on Beret's back, and asked,
"That right, you're Mrs. Star?"

Beret flinched, and for a few seconds, she closed her eyes.
Then she opened them and searched the room again, but Mick
was not to be seen. Instead, she spied a policeman in uniform
sitting at a desk nearby, and she asked in a loud voice, "Officer,
would you ask these men to unhand me?"

The officer looked up and surveyed the crowd of half a dozen
reporters. Then he stood and said, "Okay, boys, you've had your
fun. Mind your manners now. Let the lady go."

Several of the reporters stepped back, but two still blocked
Beret's way, and the officer said again, "You let her go, I said. You
want a knock on the noggin with my billy?" He put his hand on
the club attached to his waist, and the men stepped away.

"Thank you, Officer," Beret said. She pushed through the reporters into the room, but as Mick still was not at his desk, Beret wasn't sure where to go. She knew the newsmen were watching her, so she would not let herself lose face by turning and walking out of the building. Besides, once outside, she would be fair game. No one there would protect her from the reporters. So she headed toward Mick's desk, determined to remain until the reporters gave up. Just as she reached the desk, she spotted Mick in the doorway talking to a man she knew was William Smith, the chief of police. He had nodded to her on Beret's earlier visits to the station. The chief stared at her until Mick turned, recognized her, and motioned her forward.

"This is Miss Osmundsen, Judge Stanton's niece," he said, although it was obvious the chief remembered her.

He invited her into his office and offered her a chair, then dismissed Mick, but Beret said she would prefer that the detective stay.

Chief Smith shrugged, and Mick closed the door, then leaned against it. "Your uncle has hired a solicitor who claims Detective McCauley arrested Judge Stanton without cause," the chief began. He stopped and waited for Beret to respond, but she did not. "He says our detective here was so anxious for promotion that he made up a story about the judge confessing. This lawyer says it's a pack of lies and that he can prove it." Chief Smith glanced up at Mick, who said nothing, either. "He brought a sworn statement from Judge Mitchell Strong in which he claims he was playing billiards with Judge Stanton the afternoon Lillie Brown was murdered."

"He can't back it up," Mick interjected. "I checked. Judge Strong lives alone with only a manservant who comes and goes, and he wasn't around that day. So nobody saw your uncle at Judge Strong's house."

"Nevertheless, it's a pretty good alibi," Chief Smith said.

"It is no alibi at all," Beret said. "My uncle murdered my sister. He confessed it to me. In fact, he was so angry that I feared he would strike me. I did not know that Detective McCauley was listening in the foyer. Only his intervention saved me from harm."

The chief raised his eyes at Mick. "I didn't know about that. Mick said you were in the room, but I thought you might change your mind about what you heard when you found out you might be asked to testify to it in court."

"You think I would not testify to the truth of what I heard?" Beret was incensed. "I am willing to do whatever is necessary to convict the man who killed my sister, even if that man is my uncle."

"*If?*" the chief asked.

"If," Beret replied.

"But you said you heard the confession."

"Yes."

"Mick?" Chief Smith was confused.

Mick studied Beret a moment. "Miss Osmundsen was convinced Jonas, the coachman, did not kill her sister, even though the evidence pointed that way, and it appears she was right. Are you saying now that despite what happened in the library yesterday, you don't believe your uncle is guilty?"

Beret thought about her aunt then, about how the woman had begged her to deflect suspicion from her uncle, and she hesitated.

"Beret?" Mick asked, and the chief raised an eyebrow at the familiarity.

"My aunt says he is not guilty," she replied at last. "She believes he is covering up for Jonas."

"Then why would he confess?" Mick asked.

"I don't know. People do not always tell the truth when they confess. My aunt seems to believe that. She is not herself. She seems not to grasp what is going on, the seriousness of it."

Mick exchanged glances with the chief.

Beret looked from one to the other. "What are you not telling me?"

The chief nodded at Mick, who said, "Opium. The Stanton butler, William, frequents Hop Alley, and Jonas did before him. They may have bought it for your aunt."

"Opium?" Beret asked, frowning.

"A drug made from poppies—" the chief started to explain.

Beret waved away the words. "I know perfectly well what opium is. I . . ." She decided not to mention her confrontation in Hop Alley.

"Ladies in Denver, even those of the highest social levels, have been known to visit the opium dens. I'm not saying Mrs. Stanton is guilty of that." The chief's voice trailed off as if waiting for Beret to interrupt again.

"But my aunt? Surely not." Beret felt it necessary to defend Varina, although she had begun to wonder if drugs might explain Varina's failure to grasp reality.

"Well, we are not investigating her. You had only asked . . ." Mick said lamely.

Beret pulled herself together. "Is there any evidence, any at all, that my uncle did not murder my sister?"

"None," Mick and Chief Smith answered together.

"Surely you don't suspect him in the death of Sadie and the attack on the other girl."

"No, Jonas did those, although we don't know why. We were trying to put it together just now," Mick said.

The two men looked at Beret, as if she could shed light on

Jonas's actions. "I believe Jonas must have known my uncle killed Lillie. Perhaps he drove him there, and being of a devious and unsound nature, he was inspired, if you will, to do a similar deed. He must have liked killing. There are men like that, you know." She looked up at the chief. "Of course you know. You are a policeman. The act unleashed something in him, and he would have gone on killing if Detective McCauley had not stopped him."

"That's pretty much what we thought," Chief Smith told her. He stood, and Beret rose, too. "I'm thinking you might not have to testify, Miss Osmundsen. Your uncle's guilt is so obvious that he might plead guilty if we would agree to spare his life. How would you feel about that?"

In all that had happened in the past day, Beret had not thought that her uncle might be hanged for killing Lillie. The idea sickened her. "I am against murder, whether by the hand of a fiend or that of the state," she said.

The chief nodded, then looked down at the papers on his desk by way of dismissal, and Beret left with Mick.

"You believe, then, that the judge murdered your sister, and Jonas was responsible for the other two attacks?" Mick asked, a little uncertain.

Beret took a long time to answer. "Yes." Her voice was tentative.

Mick stopped and looked at Beret, "You're not sure."

Beret was hesitant. "Yes, I'm sure," she said, then added, "Unless Jonas was responsible for all three attacks and my uncle is covering up for him in my sister's death. But if that is the case, I can't imagine why." Then she added, "I intend to find out."

Chapter 23

The rain had stopped overnight, but the day was oppressive, damp from all the moisture. The sky was overcast and dark, and Beret felt it weigh on her like a wet cloak as she walked to the trolley stop. Mick had offered to see her home, but it was clear that he was preoccupied. She'd assumed he was busy with details of her uncle's confession, but then a newsman made a remark about the Arcade, and Beret realized Mick had made plans to go off with his fellows later to celebrate the arrest of one of Denver's most prominent citizens. Mick would be a celebrity as long as the story of the Holladay Street murders was news, and that could be a very long time. Beret would not be asked to join the officers and reporters, of course, and she did not want to interfere with Mick's plans by allowing him to escort her home. She had no claim on the detective. They were only acquaintances thrown together by the circumstances of her sister's death, and now that that murder was solved, there was no reason for them to see each other. She was grateful to him not only for his help in solving Lillie's murder but in protecting her from her uncle. That made her obligated to him, not the other way around.

That idea depressed her even more. After a year alone, she had met a man who had intrigued her, had treated her as an intelligent woman, had made her laugh. And she thought he had liked her. But any hope she might have had that their relationship would go further was dashed. She could marry a second time, of course. There were always men who would marry a divorcée if her fortune were big enough, but Beret would rather live the life of a spinster than wed one of them. And that was the life she envisioned for herself now. Mick had been a pleasant acquaintance, but that was all.

If her uncle accepted some sort of plea agreement, there would be no trial, and this might be the last time she would be with the detective, Beret thought, as Mick took her hand and bowed a little over it. "You have my gratitude. My sister's murder would not have been solved without your fine work," she said.

"And yours," he replied.

"I am staying on for a time to help my aunt. I hope I shall see you again."

"It would be my pleasure," he said, although he did not suggest a meeting. The aborted concert date seemed to have been forgotten.

Beret took her leave, pausing in the doorway and glancing back at Mick, but he was already in conversation with one of the officers. There would be other cases for him to solve, and he would remember Lillie Osmundsen mainly because her killer had been an oddity—not a pimp or a vagrant but a man of high social standing. He certainly would not remember the case because of the dead woman's sister. Mick McCauley had meant more to Beret than she wanted to admit, but it was foolish to think there was anything between them besides their mutual wish to bring a murderer to justice.

Outside, Beret tried to hail a hack, but seeing none, she walked up Larimer Street to the trolley stop. She felt sticky in the dampness and hoped it would not rain again, for she had not thought to bring an umbrella. The wind blew trash into her path, dirt and cigar butts and orange peels, and Beret dodged a sheet of newspaper that flew past her and wrapped itself around a streetlight. She pulled the veil of her hat over her eyes, but that did little to keep out the dirt that swirled around the sidewalk. There was the smell of spices from a tamale cart mixed with the stench of offal in the streets. People hurried past her to get out of the wind. A man's hat blew off, and street urchins raced to catch it, demanding a penny for its return. A young dandy cursed a wagon that turned in front of him, splashing dirty water from the rain the day before. A bootblack knocked his box against her and failed to beg pardon. Beret paid them all little attention and hurried on, thinking this was an odd city, with snow one day, followed by flowers and blue skies the next, then rain and chill weather on the third.

She reached the streetcar stop just as a trolley started up, which meant that she had to wait for the next one. Drops of water were falling now. She turned up the collar of her jacket, but the dampness of it lay against her neck like some dead thing, and she backed up under the awning of a store whose window displayed men's collars and shirts. A newsboy held up a paper and shouted out headlines, and Beret realized they were about her uncle: "Extry, extry. Denver judge murders own niece," the boy yelled.

Would she never get away from the scandal? The story would be picked up as far away as New York now, and some enterprising reporter would undoubtedly discover that Lillie was an Osmundsen. Beret remembered Teddy's demand that she pay him not to tell the papers in the city. Poor Teddy, she thought with satisfaction. The newspapers already had the story. He could no longer threaten her with selling it. Another of his schemes had come to naught.

The streetcar came at last, but it was crowded, and no man was gentleman enough to offer Beret a seat. She was crushed by shoppers carrying parcels tied with string, by workmen in dirty clothes clutching lunches that smelled of sour pickles and brined meat. A man next to her spat tobacco onto Beret's skirt. She gasped, but the man only glanced at the fouled garment and aimed in another direction.

The rain had begun in earnest by the time Beret reached her stop, and she hurried along the street, wishing she had bought one of the newspapers with its garish headlines, not to read but to protect herself from the weather, but she had not had that foresight. By the time Beret reached the Stanton house, her hat was drenched, in danger of losing its shape, and she herself was wet throughout, her skirt soiled with dirt and tobacco juice.

The foyer was deserted, and Beret wondered if the sound of rain had kept William from hearing her enter. She found a bell and rang it, then examined her hat, thinking Nellie might be able to steam it back into shape. Her skirt would have to be brushed before it dried. Nellie could take care of that, too. But before anything, Beret wanted the maid to draw her a hot bath. She rang again, and in a moment, William emerged from the butler's pantry, taking his time, Beret thought, annoyed. Then she reminded herself that he was her aunt's employee, not hers.

He stood before her and said, "Yes, madam?"

"Would you ask Nellie to come to my room, please. I should like a bath, and my clothes need attention. You can see for yourself that they are drenched from the rain. I could not find a hack and had to take the streetcar home." He seemed unsympathetic, and Beret understood. Servants could not afford hacks. Nor could they arrive home and demand hot baths. She should have been more discreet. "I shall live, but I smell like a cook's bad day, and I believe you, too, would appreciate my being more presentable," she said in a lame attempt at levity.

William stared at her and did not reply, and Beret wondered if he ever found anything amusing. She had never seen him smile.

"So would you please send Nellie to my room," Beret continued, starting for the stairs.

"That is not possible, madam."

Beret frowned. "And why is that?"

"Nellie is not here."

"Surely she was not sent on an errand on such a foul day."

"No, madam."

William's lack of forthrightness was annoying, and Beret demanded, "When will she return?"

"She won't."

"What do you mean, she won't?"

"Nellie is no longer with us, madam."

Beret stared at the butler, not understanding at first. "You mean she quit?"

"You could say so."

"Quit or was let go?"

William shrugged.

Beret was angry now and demanded, "I asked you did Nellie quit, or was she relieved of her position?"

"I couldn't say."

"Was it your idea or Mrs. Stanton's?"

"You will have to ask her, madam. Is there anything else?"

"Yes, there is. I assume my aunt is not here. When will she return?"

"She went with the stable boy for a drive. You yourself left with them. Perhaps she told *you* when she would return."

Beret stared at the butler for a long time, thinking he was impertinent and she didn't like him. She wondered if he would be more forthcoming later but suspected he would not, so she decided to get the confrontation over drugs behind her. "Do you supply my aunt with opium?" she asked.

William's eyes went wide with surprise, and Beret congratulated herself at getting at least that small reaction from him. "No."

"Morphine, cocaine?"

"Certainly not."

"Then you yourself must use it."

"You are wrong to accuse me. I have never used opium." There was a look of defiance—and perhaps hurt—on William's face.

"But you have been seen in Hop Alley. The police have observed you there. You cannot deny it."

William did not reply at first, thinking. Then he said, "And so have you?"

Beret bristled to realize that he was aware of her confrontation with Chinaman Fong. "We are not discussing me. Have you been buying drugs for my aunt?"

"No, madam." He stared hard at Beret before muttering, "I obtained opium for Miss Lillie. Your sister."

"You what?" Beret was incensed and paused to calm herself. She said, "You gave my sister opiates? How could you? I am disgusted with you, William. That is an offense for which you could be discharged."

"Begging your pardon, madam, but I don't work for you."

Beret ignored the impertinence. "Did my sister take the drugs with her?"

"No, miss. I believe Mrs. Stanton confiscated them."

"And threw them out?"

"Of course." He paused. "Did you want to acquire something? Perhaps that was why you were in Hop Alley."

Beret glared at the butler. Then fearing she would say something she would regret and perhaps cause further anguish for her aunt, she turned and rushed up the stairs to her room, and once inside, she locked the door.

She removed her clothing and brushed the skirt as best she could, but the tobacco stains were still there. She threw the garment on the bed and went into her bathroom and turned on the taps. When the tub was full, Beret climbed into it and sat in the steamy water, wondering whether, as her aunt had claimed, the judge had admitted to Lillie's murder to protect Jonas. But there was no reason for that. The events of the past weeks had only affected Varina's mind. She had escaped them by denying reality.

Perhaps after the whole sordid business was resolved, Beret would take her aunt on a tour of Europe. She could live with Beret in the house in New York. She could even help at the mission. There were just the two of them, and they must care for each other.

The bathwater had grown cold, and Beret stood and dried herself, then went into her bedroom and donned a day dress. She did not know what to do with herself. Her aunt had asked her to find the real killer, but Judge Stanton was the real killer. There was nothing further for Beret to investigate. Her refusal to continue looking into the murder would anger Varina, who might ask Beret to leave. But that would be all right. Beret had no reason to stay on, and she was anxious to return to New York now. Varina would come to her senses later, and the two would eliminate any disharmony between them.

Beret went to the window and saw William striding down the street, an umbrella protecting him from the rain. She had been unfair to him, rude even. The disruptions in the Stanton house had interfered with his routine, and she had made things worse with her meddling. She didn't want to, but she would have to make amends with the butler if the household were to run smoothly.

She brushed the skirt again and laid it on the bed, and as she did so, she thought about Nellie, sure that the girl had not quit. She was curious. Perhaps Nellie had left something behind that would explain her disappearance. Beret glanced out of the window, but William was nowhere to be seen. And she would have heard the carriage if her aunt had returned. Cook was in the kitchen, and there was no sign of the second maid.

The servants' quarters were upstairs. Beret had never been there, but she knew well enough where the help slept. She unlocked her bedroom door and opened it noiselessly, peering down the hall, which was dark. Only one light had been turned on, and it was near her aunt and uncle's bedroom. Beret listened but heard nothing, so she eased the door shut and walked quickly to the stairway leading to the servants' quarters.

The stairs were not carpeted, of course, and try as she might to be quiet, she could hear her shoes on the steps. Well, what of it? Beret thought. She was not only her aunt's guest but her heiress. She had every right to go into a maid's room. She reached the third floor and looked around, not sure which room was Nellie's. It would be a small one, of course. William would have the best room, and Cook the next best. She wondered if Nellie slept with the other maid but remembered the girl saying once that working in the Stanton house was the first time she had ever had a bed to herself.

Beret thought about the outside of the house and decided William would have the room with two windows looking out over the stables, the one above Beret's own room. But just to be sure, she opened the door to that bedroom and looked in. A man's coat hung over the back of a chair. Beret closed the door and went to the next room, where she found a uniform on a hook. Cook's room. The third room was empty. It might have been Nellie's, but there was dust on the floor, and judging from the musty smell, Beret thought no one had been in that room for a long time.

The room next to it was small with a white enamel bed covered by a spread that must have seen its first use in one of the rooms downstairs, then been consigned to the servants' quarters when it began to show wear or was discarded in a redecorating. The room was clean but bare of any personal items. No clothes hung on the hooks. Nor were there books or letters or the kind of knickknacks that servant girls collected. Nothing was in the wastebasket. The room had been emptied out, and not long before, because it was clean and did not smell shut up.

Beret went inside, closing the door behind her, and much as she had examined the prostitute Sadie's quarters, she then examined this room, for surely this had been where Nellie slept. She pulled back the spread and saw that the sheets and pillowcase had been removed. She checked under the mattress and in the drawers, the underside of the bureau, but there was nothing. Well, what had she expected? Did she really think Nellie would have left some clue for her? And a clue to what? The murders had been solved. The girl had been dismissed. She had simply packed her things and cleared out. There was nothing in the room that suggested anything else.

As she turned to leave, Beret heard footsteps in the hallway, and she froze. Then a door was unlatched. Beret tiptoed to the door of Nellie's room and stooped down so that she could peer through the keyhole. A door at the far end of the hallway was open. The room was one that was deep under the eaves and must belong to the second maid. Beret opened Nellie's door just enough so that she could see into the room and part of a figure dressed in a maid's uniform. The girl's back was turned, so Beret slipped into the hall toward the stairs, but at the last moment, she turned, and pretending she had just come to the third floor, she walked to the hired girl's room, making enough noise so as not to startle the maid.

The girl heard her and turned, surprise on her face when she recognized Beret, for she must have thought the footsteps belonged to William or to the cook. "Oh," she breathed. "Miss. What are you doing up here? Is something wrong?"

"I heard you on the back stairs and thought I would ask you if you could clean my skirt for me. It was spoiled on the streetcar."

"I . . ." She looked around, flustered. "If it's all right with Mr. William, I could try."

"Thank you. I was going to ask Nellie to do it, but I was disappointed to learn she is no longer here."

"Yes, ma'am."

"I liked her. I did not know she was thinking of leaving."

The maid nodded.

"You are surprised, too?"

"I didn't say nothing, but yeah, I guess so."

"Did she find a better position?"

The maid shrugged, uncomfortable.

"Then she was let go?" Beret asked. When the girl didn't reply, Beret continued, "She must have done something terribly wrong to be dismissed without notice."

"I dunno, miss. She was a worker." She leaned close to Beret and whispered, "I think she got the sack."

"I can't imagine why. I hope I didn't cause it."

"Oh no, ma'am. She liked you. She told me. She says you was different from your sister—begging pardon, ma'am."

"That's all right—Louise, is it?"

The girl nodded.

"I should like to help her, Louise. Can you tell me where she is?"

"Over on the west side someplace. I don't know the address. You could ask Mr. William. He'd know."

"Yes, of course." The girl couldn't—or wouldn't—reveal anything, and it was clear she was nervous, afraid perhaps that in talking to Beret, she, too, could get fired.

"If that's all, ma'am, I got to get back to the kitchen. I only come up to change my shoes. They're new, and they pinch my feet." Beret dismissed her, and Louise hurried down the stairs.

Disappointed that she had learned nothing, Beret started to follow her, and then she glanced at William's door and wondered what might be in his room. There was nothing left in Nellie's quarters. Perhaps the girl had left something behind, and William had taken it. Beret tiptoed to the stairs to make sure Louise was gone, then walked quickly to the butler's room and opened the door. She went first to the window and drew aside the curtain a little to make sure William was not coming back, but the street and yard were empty. The window, she noticed, looked directly into Jonas's room in the carriage house. It struck her that William could have seen anything Jonas did there.

She looked around, not certain what she was doing in the room. She almost laughed, because she had no idea what she was after. The top of the bureau was bare, and she went through the drawers quickly, thinking she might find something of Nellie's, or even opium, but there was nothing but clothing, neatly arranged. She put her hand under the mattress and pulled out a magazine, a girlie magazine. Well, the butler had that in common with Jonas, Beret thought, and suddenly she was ashamed of herself for prying. She had no right to be there. William had done nothing to merit her suspicion. Beret returned the magazine to its hiding place and backed out of the room. Before she could close the door, however, she heard footsteps, and when Beret turned, William was standing in the hallway.

"Madam," he said. His voice was as flat and unemotional as always, although he had every right to be angry with her.

"Hello, William," she said, her voice as calm as she could make it. After all, she had confronted bullies, drunks, men with knives, although it had not been because she had sneaked into their quarters.

"May I help you with something?"

"Yes, I am looking for Nellie's room," she said. "Clearly this is not it. I felt a draft and was checking to make sure a window was not left open."

"I always close the window."

"I can see that."

"That is Nellie's room." He pointed to a door. "Is there something you need there?"

"I was hoping to find her address. She was very good to me, and I wanted to send her a gift as a way of thanking her."

"She did not leave her address."

"Even in her room?"

"No."

"Then no one knows where she went?"

"No. I believe Louise told you that. Do you want to check her room—again?"

Beret colored. "That won't be necessary. Thank you, William," she said, walking past him toward the stairs.

"Madam."

Beret stopped. "Yes."

"Mrs. Stanton believes the third floor is the servants' sanctuary. She would not be pleased you were here."

Nor would you, Beret thought, but she said, "And will you tell her?"

"Do you wish me to?"

Beret did not reply. She hurried down the stairs, thinking again that she did not like the butler much.

Chapter 24

Beret returned to her room, not at all pleased with her performance. She had made a fool of herself. She had found nothing to interest her, and she had aroused William's dislike and suspicion, although it was clear to her he already disliked and was suspicious of her. Well, she was suspicious of him, too. There was something about his actions that wasn't right. Beret wondered if he would tell Varina she had been snooping.

She closed the door of her room, thinking to lock it, but that would be hypocritical after the way she had snooped upstairs. She had not slept well the night before and was tired. The soiled skirt was on the bed where she had thrown it, and she picked it up and started for the wardrobe. Beret would have to take it to the kitchen later in hopes she could remove the stains herself.

She opened the wardrobe and looked for a place to hang the skirt. The wardrobe was filled with clothes, Lillie's clothes, of course, although right in the center was the suit that the dressmaker had altered for her. It hung where she couldn't miss seeing it. Nellie would have put it there before she left. The dressmaker had said the suit was too plain for Lillie, but Beret had liked it best of all of her sister's clothes, much better than the ball gowns. Her aunt had mentioned a meeting with the solicitor, and the outfit would be suitable. It also would be appropriate for the train—in case Varina asked her to leave. She remembered her aunt had a suit of the same material, and would have to inquire whether Varina planned to wear it that day, so that the two would not be dressed alike.

The idea amused Beret, two women dressed like twins. That would give the ladies of Varina's circle something else to gossip about.

Beret decided to try on the ensemble to see if it had been altered properly. She removed her dress and stepped into the skirt, buttoning it. Then she put on the jacket and went to the long mirror that rested in the corner of the room to admire herself. But the fit was off. The skirt was too short, the jacket too large. Beret frowned, wondering how the dressmaker could have been so sloppy. The suit would have to go back, and Beret removed the garments, laying them on the bed.

She donned her day dress and returned to the discarded suit, then she realized the mistake. This was not her suit at all but Varina's. Nellie must have hung it in Beret's wardrobe by mistake. The dressmaker would not have returned an outfit that was crumpled—and dirty, Beret realized, as she lifted the jacket. The piece was badly stained. She held the garment close to her face to examine the damage. The stains were dark against the dark fabric, which was why Beret had not spotted them at first. She studied the skirt and found it, too, had been fouled. She felt her heart race as a thought occurred to her, and she went back to the wardrobe. Hanging on the hook where the suit had been was a white shirtwaist covered with blotches that stood out against the starched white cotton—deep red stains, almost brown. It was as if Varina had been sprayed with something.

Beret held the blouse close, then wet her finger and rubbed it on the stain. She examined her finger and shivered, hurrying into the bathroom where she ran the taps until the sink was full, and dipped the shirtwaist into the water, watching as the water turned red—bright red, red the color of blood. No, Beret told herself, staring at what were now pink smudges on the blouse. It was a mistake. She sat on the edge of the tub and put her forehead down on the cool porcelain of the sink. "No," she said out loud. "Aunt Varina, you couldn't have."

"Oh yes I could," a voice said from the bedroom. Startled, Beret looked up and found herself facing Varina. With the taps running, Beret had not heard her aunt enter the bedroom.

The shirtwaist still in her hand, dripping bloody water onto the tile floor, Beret went to the bathroom door. "What is this blood?"

Varina didn't answer.

"Is it Lillie's?"

Beret's aunt cocked her head.

"You stabbed Lillie?"

At that, Varina gave a harsh laugh. "You didn't think your poor besotted uncle did it, did you?" Her eyes glittered in her gray face.

"Your own niece? How could you?"

Dressed in black, as if she had just returned from a solemn social event, Varina stood in the middle of the room, staring at Beret. "She was indeed my niece. How could *she*?"

"You killed her?" Beret had not fully processed the idea.

"Oh, I didn't intend to. I only wanted to talk to her. But you know how insolent Lillie could be. She laughed at me." Varina's back stiffened, and she repeated, "After all she had done, after she betrayed me, she laughed at *me*. You know how she was."

Beret knew. She knew now. But nothing Lillie could have done justified her murder. "What happened?" Beret asked, thrusting aside the dripping blouse and wiping her hands on her skirt.

Varina studied her niece for a long time. "I suppose I can trust you," she said, as she leaned against one of the bedposts. "I went to that foul place to ask her to release your uncle. He fancied himself in love with her. At his age! He was willing to give up everything we'd worked for to be with her. He was convinced the child was his, although I'd told him a hundred times she had been with other men. Jonas had told me about them. But your uncle didn't care. He didn't care that another might have fathered the baby. He was that crazy to have a child. It was enough that the baby was Lillie's. He would have thrown me over for her! How could I compete with Lillie? Look at me, Beret. I'm old and wrinkled. I would have been alone and shunned, and all because of her."

"She was selfish," Beret said, trying to sound sympathetic.

Varina ran her hand against the post. "Jonas had found out Lillie was alone at that place, and he drove me there. He parked the carriage in an alley so that no one would see us, and I went to the back door—me, in that degraded place. Lillie opened it, expecting your uncle or some other degenerate, I suppose. She was surprised to see me, oh my, yes. But it didn't seem to bother her. 'Hello, Aunt Varina. Nice of you to call. Won't you come in? I'll fix tea.' That was what she said to me, just as if it were natural for me to call at a whorehouse." Varina spat out the last word. "Perhaps it was. It was I who sent her there, you know, after I found out about the business between her and your uncle. It was fitting. She was already a harlot. I sent Jonas to speak to Hettie Hamilton. She didn't know Jonas worked for me, but she figured Lillie was from a society family, so she demanded five hundred dollars."

"You paid her to take in Lillie?"

"Oh, I knew I didn't have to pay, but I did. I wanted Lillie gone that much. And she was amused at the whole idea of being a prostitute. Amused! I didn't even have to insist on it. She told me, 'At least it's an honest life, Aunt. We're all fallen women one way or another. You included.' Oh, you didn't know her, Beret, although you do now. She was a degenerate. A fallen woman is worse than any man."

"You thought Uncle John wouldn't visit her in such a place?" Beret asked.

"I was wrong about that, wasn't I? Jonas told me what was going on. Your uncle had the impertinence to ask Jonas to drive him there."

"He was loyal to you, Jonas."

"Oh yes. More than to your uncle."

"So the two of you went to see Lillie?"

"No, Jonas stayed outside. I went in alone. Lillie took me to her room. I offered her money to give up John, jewels. She didn't care about him. I knew that. Women like Lillie play games, you know. They make men fall in love with them, and then they throw them over."

"I have seen it," Beret said.

"She turned me down. So I told her I'd have her arrested for stealing my diamonds. I knew she'd taken them. She said if I did, she would tell the newspapers your uncle had given them to her. And then she laughed. She said, 'It was so easy to make him fall in love with me. I was tired of him, but now I think I'll keep him on my string. Poor old dried-up Aunt Varina.'"

"That was cruel."

Varina nodded. "I had never been so angry. She wouldn't stop laughing at me. I picked up the scissors. I didn't intend to hurt her, but I had to stop her from laughing. You understand, don't you, Beret? She must have laughed at you, too. She told me how she and Teddy laughed at you." Varina searched Beret's face for some sign of sympathy.

But Beret's face was rigid now. "And so you stabbed her," she said in a monotone—a statement, not a question.

"You understand, don't you, Beret? You would have done the same thing, wouldn't you?"

"And then you took the earbobs."

"I saw them sitting on the bureau, but I forgot about them until I got to the carriage. I sent Jonas back for them. I had to. I couldn't leave my own sister's jewelry for some *whore* to wear. You wouldn't have wanted that."

"I would not have wanted you to kill my sister," Beret said by way of reply.

"They were Marta's, and they are yours now."

Beret could not believe her aunt could speak so casually about jewelry after admitting what she'd done. "I don't want them," she said. Then she had a sudden thought. "If you killed Lillie, why did Uncle John admit to it?"

"Why, to protect me, of course, because it was all his fault. He knew that. I'd gone there to protect him, you see. He knew the minute you showed him the earrings what I'd done, but he couldn't allow me to take the blame. You must know that. He is honorable that way. But he was foolish. He should have said Jonas put the earrings into my jewelry box. That would have been so much easier. He thought he could trust you, I suppose. How would he know that detective was lurking behind the door? Now you must convince the police it was Jonas, after all, that your uncle confessed only to protect him." She all but smiled at Beret.

Beret ignored the suggestion. "I don't understand why Jonas attacked the other two prostitutes."

"That was his idea, and I told him it was brilliant. We agreed that if another prostitute or two was murdered, people would think a madman was on the loose. I knew he would take care of things for me. He was such a loyal boy."

"You would've let him kill two women?"

"They were only whores. I'm sorry Jonas is dead, but it worked out perfectly, don't you see? You shouldn't have any trouble making the police believe Jonas was guilty of Lillie's death, too. You'll find a way to explain it to them."

"But he wasn't guilty, Aunt Varina."

"A small point. The thing now is to clear your uncle before all this scandal robs him of the Senate appointment."

Speechless, Beret stared at her aunt. The woman thought after everything that had happened, Judge Stanton would become a senator.

"No, Aunt. You must go to the police and tell them the truth."

"What?" Varina jerked up her head and stared at Beret.

Beret nodded.

"Why would I do that?"

"Because it's the only thing that will save Uncle John."

"I thought you understood. I thought when I explained what had happened, you would help me. We are flesh and blood."

"So was Lillie, and you murdered her."

Varina looked incredulous. "You won't help me?"

"No. I will accompany you to the police station, and if you refuse, I shall go there myself."

"Who would believe you? It is your word against mine."

"Detective McCauley will believe me, and I think Chief Smith will, too."

"You are as heartless as your sister, Beret. I should have known I couldn't trust you. I will make sure you tell no one."

"You would stab me, too? There are no scissors in this room."

Varina stared dumbly at her niece, and then she said, "No, but I have this." Varina fumbled in the pocket of her jacket, then withdrew a small gun and pointed it at Beret. It was a woman's pistol that contained only one shot, but Beret knew if the gun was aimed properly, it would be deadly. "I always carry this when I go out. Jonas gave it to me."

Beret stood very still and thought about how she could reason with her aunt. "The servants will hear the shot. And how would you explain my death to the police?"

"William will take care of everything. He is loyal to me. And don't bother to cry out. The servants are in the kitchen. They won't hear you."

"What about the suit? Look there, on the bed." Varina looked away, and at that instant, Beret leaped forward, knocking the older woman down. Beret reached for the gun, but Varina held on to it, as the two women rolled across the floor. Beret felt the gun against her head and was still.

"I am sorry, Beret. You were my favorite. I thought if I explained, you would understand, that you would help me. But you give me no choice," Varina said.

Desperate for some words to stop her aunt, Beret closed her eyes, and at that instant, a voice said, "Madam." She felt the gun ease as her aunt turned to the voice, and Beret reached up and yanked the gun from her aunt's hand. She rolled away from the older woman and stood, not knowing whether to point the weapon at Varina or at William.

"Take it from her, William," Varina hissed.

William looked at the old woman, then at Beret, who realized then that the butler might be the greater threat. If she shot Varina, William could overpower her, but without William, she had a better chance with her aunt. Beret pointed the gun at the butler.

William stared at it, disdain on his face. And then he said, "You may put down the weapon, Miss Osmundsen. We have heard the confession, Louise and I, and can back you up. Louise has already gone to summon the police." He turned to Varina and helped her stand. "I am sorry, madam." Then he looked again at Beret. "And I am sorry we put you in danger. I allowed this to go too far."

"You knew about my aunt?"

"We suspected after the judge was arrested, but we had no proof. Then this morning, Nellie found the garments hidden away in Madam's dressing room. She brought them to me, and I knew the blood on them was Miss Lillie's. I sent Nellie away for fear Mrs. Stanton would harm her if she found out Nellie had discovered where the clothing was hidden. It was I who placed the soiled garments in your wardrobe where you would be sure to see them. I believed you would know the right thing to do. I had assumed you would take them to the police and had not thought you would confront Mrs. Stanton. Fortunately, I saw her go into this room and took the liberty of listening at the door." He said, as if explaining a breach of etiquette, "It was not closed, you know."

The three of them stood like that, not speaking, until they heard heavy footsteps on the stairs. "That will be the police," he said, glancing over his shoulder. He turned to go, then stopped and looked at Beret. "Will that be all, madam?"

Beret closed her eyes and nodded. "That is all."

Chapter 25

Varina Stanton did not go to jail for the murder of her niece Lillie Osmundsen. Judge John Stanton, Varina's husband, was a powerful man with many friends in the judiciary, and he arranged for his wife to be found insane and incarcerated in a sanitarium for the rest of her life.

The judge did not stay on in the Grant Avenue house. He moved into his club and put the house with a sales agent. Beret offered to help him make the adjustment, but he said it was not necessary, that William would do it. Judge Stanton offered Beret his wife's jewels, but she wanted nothing and suggested her uncle sell the pieces and donate the proceeds to charity. There was no further mention of a Senate appointment.

Beret sought out her former husband, Edward Staarman, to bid him good-bye. She wished him well, and they parted amicably. Neither brought up the subject of a reconciliation. Later, Teddy married a California widow who had inherited a good-sized estate. Beret never saw him again.

She called at the police station for a final meeting with Detective Sergeant Michael McCauley but was told the detective had been sent to Leadville to bring back an escaped prisoner and would not return for several days. Beret was downhearted by the news, because she had wanted to see Mick one more time.

So just a week after her aunt was arrested, Beret left Denver. She felt uncomfortable and unneeded in the Stanton house, as William had taken complete charge, and there was no further reason for her to remain. She returned to New York, although not by herself. Nellie, the maid, would be out of a job as soon as the Stanton house was sold. So the girl accompanied Beret, who gave her employment at the Marta Osmundsen Mission. Nellie was both tough and compassionate and became a great favorite among the women and children who sought help there.

Beret returned to her duties. With time, she came to accept her sister's death and the sordid events that surrounded it, although she never could bring herself to forgive her aunt for murdering Lillie. From time to time, she remembered Detective Sergeant Michael McCauley and wondered what might have been between them if things had been different.

Epilogue

Mick McCauley sat at his desk in the police station for the last time, looking around the room where he had worked for so many years. He straightened the chair beside him where the snouts and boosters, the bummers and touts once sat and swept off the top of the desk with his arm. Only the pen and ink bottle, a sheet of paper and an envelope remained.

"You going to miss it?" Officer Thrasher buttoned the coat of his uniform. The buttons were polished, but the coat was a little worse for wear now, and so was the policeman. It hadn't taken long.

Yes, he would miss it, Mick thought. He would remember the harlots and macs, the pickpockets and panel men who had made the job interesting, even the newshawks who had turned him into a celebrity after the Lillie Osmundsen murder six months before. "Maybe. Would you?" Mick asked.

"I'm too bare-ass poor to afford memories," the officer replied, picking up his hat and heading toward the door. "You coming, or you going to sit around moping?"

The boys were waiting for him at the Arcade. Mick's cousin Caro had thrown a grand party for him the night before, attended by a large portion of Denver's upper crust. His uncle, Evan Summers, had declined to *attend, but Judge Stanton, who was going out in society a little now, was there. Tonight would be a bruiser, and what with everybody wanting to buy him a drink, Mick wondered if he'd be sober enough to catch the train in the morning.*

There was just one more thing to be done, and he had delayed it, put it off because he did not want to give time for a reply. Mick smiled a little to himself as he opened the bottle of ink and dipped in the pen. It would be a short note, nothing fancy. He wrote, Dear Miss Osmundsen. *But Beret had told him to call her by her first name, and Mick liked that. He crumpled the paper and pulled out another sheet. It was foolscap, the paper the reporters used, but she didn't seem the type to demand proper writing paper. He dipped the pen into the ink again and started over.*

Dear Beret,

I've quit the police force in Denver and am going to New York, where I've been hired on as a detective. I'm leaving on tomorrow's train and should arrive on Thursday. I look forward to resuming our friendship.

Mick

Mick read the letter and grinned. It was short and to the point. She wouldn't like anything flowery. He folded the paper and slid it into an envelope, which was already addressed and stamped. Then, making sure that Officer Thrasher was gone, Mick went to a cabinet and searched through files until he found the one for the Osmundsen murder. He flipped through the notes and papers and reports to the carte de visite *of a woman in a sable jacket, her hands in a matching muff, that he and Beret had found under the mattress in Lillie's room at Miss Hettie Hamilton's. He removed the picture of Beret and put it into his pocket.*

He wondered if Friday would be too soon to call on her.

340

Acknowledgments

Some fifty years ago, when I wrote my first nonfiction book about the American West, prostitution was the province of male historians. They emphasized the glitter and naughtiness of the parlor house girls and their affluent clientele, whose cold and haughty wives drove them to the dens of iniquity. The brothels were monuments to ostentation in which good taste played little part. There were grand pianos, rich woodwork, and lavish draperies and furniture, along with mirrored walls and ceilings that showed off the parlor girls to advantage. The women were beautiful and elegant, and many had turned to the sporting life because it was exciting. Or so the historians wrote.

Only after I began researching did I realize how multilayered prostitution in the early West really was. While there were indeed a few exclusive brothels where jewel-bedecked inmates were feted at champagne suppers, far more common were the women at the other end of the spectrum, the "crib girls." An 1886 newspaper account of a suicide, which I quoted in *Cherry Creek Gothic,* my history of Victorian architecture in Denver, describes in Dickensian manner the hovel of one such prostitute:

The walls and ceiling were absolutely black with smoke and dirt, excepting where old, stained newspapers had been pasted on them—on the ceiling, to exclude rain and melting snow, and on the walls, to cover up spots from which the plastering had fallen. The floor was rickety and filthy. Around the walls were disposed innumerable unwashed and battered tin cooking utensils, shelves, for the most part laden with dust, old clothing, which emitted a powerful effluvium, hung from nails here and there; or tumble down chairs, a table of very rheumatic tendency, on which were broken cups, plates and remnants of food, were [sic] scattered all over its surface. An empty whiskey bottle and pewter spoon or two. In one corner and taking up half the space of the den was the bedstead strongly suggestive of a bountiful crop of vermin, and on that flimsy bed lay the corpse of the suicide, clad in dirty ratted apparel, and with as horrid a look on her begrimed, pallid features as the surroundings presented. No one of her neighbors in wretchedness had had the sense to open either of the two little windows in the room to admit pure air, hence the atmosphere was sickeningly impure and almost asphyxiating. "My God!" exclaimed Coroner McHatton, used as he is to similar scenes and smells in his official capacity, "Isn't this awful?"

With the rise of women historians, the depiction of the West's sporting women changed. Feminist writers emphasized the depravity and degradation of prostitutes, their addiction to drugs and alcohol, the squalor of their lives, their victimization, and the beastly conditions that led to suicide. Often the women started out in high-class houses, then spiraled downward. Some turned to prostitution after they were thrown out by their families be-

Acknowledgments

cause of indiscretions, while others were enticed by white slavers. And then there were women so poor they turned to prostitution as the only alternative to starvation.

The truth is both of these extremes existed, as did a middle ground. In Butte, Montana, some of the prostitutes were widows of miners, and they worked out of cribs during the day, when the kids were in school. In Breckenridge, Colorado, the prostitutes were part of the fabric of the town. The madam, Mae Nicholson, riding on her horse Gold and Silver, led the July Fourth parade. When I lived in Breckenridge in the 1960s, our neighbor was one of Mae's former girls, a wiry, white-haired woman who fished early in the morning and left her catch on our doorstep for breakfast.

Like that generous neighbor, western prostitutes have always seemed to me to be real women, not stereotypes. So I've tried to depict them as such in *Fallen Women*. The novel is not so much about prostitution as it is a story of family relationships, primarily between sisters, but set against a background of nineteenth-century vice.

In researching the manuscript, I consulted a number of books on prostitution, from Nell Kimball's *Nell Kimball: Her Life as an American Madam* to David Graham Phillips's *Susan Lenox: Her Fall and Rise* to Max Miller's *Holladay Street*. The outstanding book on Colorado prostitution and early western law enforcement and the one I consulted most, however, was Clark Secrest's *Hell's Belles*. I'm greatly indebted to Clark, an old college buddy, not only for this extraordinary body of research but for reading my manuscript for errors. Among his corrections: police call boxes were not in use in Denver in 1885, and the "ladies" in Colorado were not referred to as "hookers" until the twentieth century.

Acknowledgments

My dear friends at Browne & Miller Literary Associates, Danielle Egan-Miller and Joanna MacKenzie, are not just agents but editors who sent me back to the drawing board again and again, until they were satisfied with the manuscript. It's my good fortune that Browne & Miller took me on years ago and has shepherded every one of my novels to publication. At St. Martin's Press, my superb editor, Jennifer Enderlin, with Sara Goodman, were helpful at every stage of the editing and printing process. My friends Arnie Grossman and Wick Downing supported me as only other writers can. And then there is my family—Bob, Dana, Kendal, Lloyd, and Forrest—whose love is infinite. And so is my love for them.

The activity picked up as she left the residential area, however. Beret found herself being careful of the carriages and wagons that rushed by, careless of pedestrians. A man astride a horse nearly knocked her down and did not have the courtesy to apologize or even to look back. Another doffed his hat impudently and Beret ignored him. Perhaps Denver was not so different from New York after all. Still, she enjoyed the walk, the chance to get out of the house and away from the stuffy drawing rooms of her aunt's friends, and she was almost sorry to reach her destination. But she had come with a purpose, and would not delay it. She went into the building and down the stairs to the police department.

Detective McCauley was not at his desk, and Beret wondered if she should have sent him a note, asking for an appointment. The reason she hadn't was if he had ignored it, she'd have been in a quandary about her next move. She looked around the room but didn't see the detective, so she inquired of an officer who was stationed near the door.

"Mick? A bit of a hero, our Mick is today, ma'am. P'raps you know he killed the man what's been troubling the whores . . . begging your pardon. I didn't mean to suggest that's a subject you'd be knowing about, a lady like you. I expect you're one of his society friends. You wait over there at his desk if you want to. He's talking to Chief Smith now. Shouldn't be more than a minute. The chief don't talk much, you know, but us boys has got to listen." He guffawed.

Beret thanked the officer and made her way across the room to Mick's station and sat down on a hard chair. The desk was tidy, pencils lined up next to the pen with the dull nib, an open bottle of ink beside it. Government forms were stacked to one side, and in the center was what appeared to be the page of a letter. But when she looked closer, Beret saw that it was part of a police report. The first line was the tail end of a sentence begun on the previous page: "shot him once in the breast, and he fell onto the bed and was still. He had the knife in his hand yet. I asked a crib girl to find another officer, and in ten minutes—" Mick had obviously been interrupted in the middle of a sentence and left his desk. Beret would have liked to read the first part of the report, but she was mindful of the glances from the officers in the room. So she picked up a pencil and idly rolled it back and forth between her gloved fingers, trying to imagine what else the detective had written. She was doing that when Detective McCauley returned.

"Miss Osmundsen," he said, startling her, because she had been deep in thought and had not heard him approach.

"Detective McCauley. I hope this is not an inconvenient time."

He glanced around his desk as if to see whether she had been snooping, then asked, "What can I do for you?" He was formal now, polite but a little distant, as if he were not pleased to see her. He gave the impression that he was busy, and Beret wondered if he'd done that on purpose.

"I had asked when you came to tell us about Jonas whether we could talk again about the murders. Is this not a convenient time?"

He thought a moment. "As good as any, I suppose," he said, "but this is not the place for it. Come." Beret stood, and the detective looked over his desktop again, then reached into his desk for something that he put into his pocket. He led her past the police officer with whom Beret had spoken earlier, saying, "We'll be going now, Jim. Me and the lady's having a bit of a talk."

"Your Irish has come back," Beret observed.

"Only when I'm around other Irishmen. If we try to talk like civilized folks, they think we're putting on airs." He steered her up the steps, and they went outside into the sunshine and found a stone bench. "Does this suit, or do you want to go to Charpiot's?"

Beret sensed the detective was distracted, perhaps pressed for time, and replied that the bench was fine. She would have liked a more private place, where passersby wouldn't intrude, but she seemed to have no choice. "We could talk at a more convenient time—"

"No, no. I don't know when that would be." Mick cut her off. "Except for a few hours' sleep, I've been at the station since I left you. There are reports to be made and interviews. I've been cornered by every newshawk in the city. Have you seen the papers?"

"Only one, and the report was dreadful."

"Don't bother with the others. Each is worse than the one before it. Will it offend you if I smoke?"

Beret did not know he smoked. He had not done so before. She shook her head, and Mick took out a cigarette paper, sprinkled tobacco onto it, licked the paper shut. He lighted the cigarette, then exhaled. "I don't smoke much, but this has been a trying time, and it relaxes me. What a pity you ladies can't indulge."

"And what makes you think we don't?" Beret asked.

Mick laughed suddenly. It was not often that the man had laughed in her presence, and Beret was startled. She liked the warm sound of it. "Forgive me for being brusque. I have been under a great deal of pressure since I saw you last," he said.

"Of course. And I suspect you have little time for conversation, so I shall be as brief as possible. I want to talk about the murders, but first I must make a confession."

Mick gave her a curious look. "Not another visit to Hop Alley, I hope."

Beret smiled a little and shook her head. "I did not tell you that I saw my husband, that is, my former husband, Mr. Staarman, a second time. I encountered him in front of the Arcade. I had the sense he might have been lying in wait for me. In any case, he was quick to accost me." She related the gist of her conversation with Teddy, then said, "I suppose it doesn't matter now that we know Jonas and not Teddy murdered my sister. But I do not want you to think I deliberately withheld information from you."

"Why did you?" Mick asked.

"I'm not certain."

"You must still care about him. Perhaps with your sister out of the way, you'll take him back."

The remark was impertinent and Beret thought to rebuke him, but then for a moment, she wondered if he might be right. She had been lonely, and Teddy had once made her happy. There was a fine line between love and hate, she realized. But she replied, "No, I don't think so."

They had not gotten off to a good start, and Beret thought she should not have come. It was obvious to her the detective was pressed for time and in no mood to humor her. But she was there, and this might be her only chance to talk to him. He would take on other investigations and have no need to interview her, and it was unlikely their paths would cross socially. So she smiled at him and asked, "Did you think all along that it was Jonas?"

Mick shook his head. "I wish I could tell you so. I thought Jonas an odd fellow, but I was as surprised as anyone when I looked into his face after I shot him and saw who he was. Did *you* suspect him?"